THE MATCHMAKER

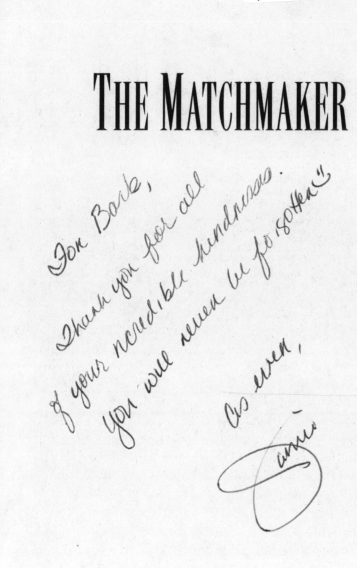

For Bob,
Thank you for all
of your incredible kindness.
You will never be forgotten.

As ever,

THE MATCHMAKER

JAMIE DENTON

KENSINGTON PUBLISHING CORP.
http://www.kensingtonbooks.com

*This book can only be dedicated to a very
special group of individuals, for without them,
it never would've been possible . . .*

*Eric Fackler, Michael Fetterolf,
William McGrail, James Ham, Wayne Christopherson,
Donna Spadero and Razvan Gramatovici.*

Thank you for allowing the dream to continue.

Chapter 1

THE DEAD ALWAYS had a story to tell. Luckily for the departed, Parker Hennessy knew how to listen, and he welcomed with great pride the responsibility of his extraordinary gift.

He sat quietly in the tapestried Queen Anne armchair, with an expensive black leather portfolio—a Christmas gift from his beloved Susan—open on his lap. He took extreme care in the appearance he conveyed for the benefit of his living clients. The somber, compassionate professional epitomized. The dark patterned tie, respectfully subdued, matched his severe yet elegant navy suit. His shirt, crisp and white. His shoes, rich mahogany wingtips, polished to a high sheen. Hair, expertly groomed, with a subtle sprinkling of gray applied to his temples. Nails, neatly trimmed. Parker Hennessy—*the* consummate professional. *Always.*

Counselor. Confessor. Caring and trusted confidant. All portrayed with nothing less than absolute perfection. He made certain of that, too, and he *never* faltered, regardless of the role he assumed.

He waited until the bereaved widow dabbed her eyes with a tissue from one of the many boxes he kept within easy reach, then quickly dipped his gaze to reacquaint himself with her name. Madelyn. Her name was Madelyn Strom.

Sometimes the names became a jumble in his mind, like white plastic balls bouncing frantically inside a Plexiglas container pumped with air, waiting for the chance to escape and be noticed. *B-9. I-25.*

So many names. So, so many. Some he'd forgotten. Others remained forever etched in his memory. A few burned there, too and, if he allowed himself, he could still breathe in the acrid smoke scented with the stench of their burning flesh.

"Given the circumstances of your husband's passing, you'll want a closed casket," Parker suggested. He kept his voice soft, his tone evenly modulated to convey the appropriate level of respect. The living demanded consolation in their time of bereavement, and he never failed to deliver.

Dead was dead in his business—at least insofar as his living clients believed. What mattered to him was that Walter Strom had died an unhappy man. Why else would a fifty-three-year-old man have been compelled to chug down an entire bottle of prescription tranquilizers with a fifth of vodka?

The widow looked at Parker and nodded, her pale hazel eyes rimmed in red and banked in misery. He tried to imagine her sorrow—and couldn't.

He tried to imagine her husband's misery—and seethed.

Madelyn Strom lowered her gaze suddenly. Not, he knew, because he revealed an inappropriate emotion. He never did. He had a rare, exquisite gift. He was too good now to make a novice's mistake.

Had guilt caused her to look away? Perhaps, he mused, surreptitiously sliding the box of tissues over the gleaming surface of the low oval table closer toward the distraught woman. Perhaps she'd been the one responsible for her husband taking his own life. A highly likely scenario, in his experience. Experience that extended Parker Hennessy's boundaries, but gained from the lives of many.

So, so many. G-56.

Madelyn drew in an unsteady breath. Parker waited for the payoff for his supreme patience, and wasn't disappointed.

"Walter was unfaithful," she said on a strained whisper. "And I never knew."

Madelyn's confession hardly surprised him. The dead always had a story to tell. All he had to do was wait for the truth to be revealed to him. His living clients trusted him. Counselor. Confessor. Caring friend. They trusted him with their grief—and their dirty little secrets.

An hour later, he finally showed the widow to the door. Her hand trembled as she shook his.

"Are you sure there's no one I can call to drive you home?" he asked her.

"No, thank you, Mr. Hennessy. I . . ." she hesitated. Her grip tightened and her eyes teared up again. "I . . . I'll be fine."

He doubted it, but he didn't care, either. In the time he'd spent with her, he'd learned all he needed to know about Walter Strom.

Poor, poor Walter. A gentle, soft-spoken man with a weakness for pumpkin pie, foreign films—and young, pretty brunettes with large breasts who charged him by the hour for their services.

He settled his left hand over Madelyn's in the gesture of comfort expected of him. After promising that Hennessy's Mortuary would ensure that her husband's final event would be one of dignity and respect, he waited for her to descend the steps leading from the veranda before silently closing the wide front door.

The barest hint of a smile touched his lips in anticipation of the task ahead. He left the public area of the funeral home and took the stairs down to the lower level where his small staff readied the body of Francine Meeks, an eighty-nine-year-old former high school chemistry teacher whose career highlight was marked by flunking a certain NASA big shot out of her eleventh-grade chem class during the seventies. Parker stopped to inspect the makeup artist's work. Satisfied the mourners attending the service tomorrow afternoon would be pleased, he offered Opal Jones a brief nod of approval, then quietly walked into his office and closed the door.

The public memorial of Walter Strom's short, tragic life would be dignified and respectful, as promised. None of the mourners would ever learn from him or his staff that the tears that will be shed by the Strom widow during the upcoming service, to take place in three days, will be because her husband had been infected with HIV, courtesy of a prostitute he frequented. Oh, yes, the Strom interment would be one of beauty and grace, but much less meaningful than the private celebration only he was qualified to perform—that was his duty to perform.

Walter Strom needed him. Required his guidance. His expertise. His skill in uniting him with his true mate, the perfect woman worthy enough to remain by his side for eternity.

Parker's blood hummed with excitement, but he tamped down the anticipation. There was work to be done before he allowed himself to begin the search for Walter's special lady. He must service the living first. Retrieving the body from the morgue, arranging delivery of the very expensive casket selected by the widow, undoubtedly in an attempt to assuage her guilt for driving her husband into the arms of prostitutes throughout their marriage. There were calls to the florist, the printer, and the writing of the obituary. Afterward, he would give his full attention to answering his calling, his unique gift. Only then could he provide his very special services to his rightful and deserving client.

Yes, he mused, the dead always did have a story to tell. As their keeper, he was duty bound to ensure they were given the happy ending they'd been deprived of yet deserved.

And Parker Hennessy *never* failed to deliver.

Greer Lomax closed the heavy volume of municipal codes and blew out a frustrated stream of breath. After wasting her lunch break pouring over the lexicon, she hadn't come up with a violation for anything more than garden-variety vandalism. Not a single act of legislation could she find that specifically declared tombstone-tipping illegal, giving her zilch by way of criminal charges to take to the district attorney.

She rubbed at her temple with the tip of her index finger, which did nothing to alleviate the slow, steady throb, caused from lack of sleep. The ruckus created by the angry mob of blue-haired widows who'd stormed the Magnolia County Sheriff's Department office this morning, loudly demanding swift and brutal justice for the disgrace to their husbands' graves, had only increased the pounding in her head.

Two aspirin, and enough strong coffee to seriously threaten the lining of her stomach, hadn't provided so much as a modicum of relief. Experience dictated she wouldn't be rid of the pain unless she crawled into bed for a few hours of uninterrupted sleep. Being the only officer currently on duty, however, that was one luxury that would have to wait.

She had bigger problems than a headache to worry about, like a bunch of crazy old bats threatening to stake out the local cemeteries themselves and take matters into their own arthritic hands. Greer let out another sigh and stood to return the code book to the bookcase across the room. She should've done a better job humoring the old gals instead of taking the honest, direct approach by telling them the best she could do was to issue a few vandalism citations, provided the kids responsible were even caught.

"Just another day in paradise," she muttered, then snagged her blue and white Magnolia Mavericks mug from the ancient, heavy metal desk and took off down the corridor toward the break room for more coffee. Chances were the vandalism was nothing more than another prank by some of the frat boys from Seaside College. All she had to do was lean a little heavy on the right pigeon and she just might save herself a bored-out-of-her-skull stakeout of Shady Knolls Cemetery.

She stopped suddenly and frowned. What the hell was the matter with her? She should be grateful that high stress was no longer a daily supplement on the job. Instead, here she was bemoaning a quiet night of tepid coffee and patrolling the bone yards within the county's jurisdiction. If the only challenge she faced entailed tracking down rambunctious frat brats with too much time on their hands, or keeping a bloodthirsty group of geriatric vigilante-wannabes in line, she should be thankful. After close to six years of being up to her ass in body bags, she'd better conduct a reality check and welcome an innocuous investigation of a few tipped headstones and quit whining about the lack of excitement.

You can't have it both ways, Lomax.

Damn straight. She continued down the corridor and entered the break room, where Blythe Norton, one of the day-shift dispatchers and the wife of Kyle Norton, another of Magnolia County's deputies, attempted to relax. A difficult-enough feat in the hard plastic chairs surrounding the laminated wood-grain table, but near impossible, Greer imagined, for a woman in her ninth month of pregnancy.

Greer nodded a greeting to Blythe as the other woman sipped a fragrant tea from a delicate china cup. She'd pulled another of the chairs in front of her and topped it with a plush, burgundy velvet pillow. Leaning back, she sat with her swollen feet propped on the pillow.

A grin tipped Blythe's wide mouth. "I thought for sure I was going to have to call for backup," she teased Greer as she balanced the tea cup on her well-rounded tummy.

Greer managed a small smile that felt more like a smirk. "The day I can't handle a bunch of fired-up little old ladies is the day I hand in my badge."

For good this time, she silently added.

A sharp pang of regret took her by surprise. She should've known taking another job in law enforcement was a mistake, but she'd been caught off guard and had suffered a moment of weakness.

When Sheriff Travis Willows had come begging with a job offer in his hands, she should've locked and bolted the door. He'd promised her the deputy position would be a temporary one and, like a fool, she'd fallen for the line he'd fed her. She was supposed to help out only until he could find enough warm bodies to fill the sudden vacancies caused after losing three deputies to higher-paying jobs elsewhere. If it'd been anyone else but Travis, she wouldn't have hesitated to give him a roadmap straight to Hell to see if ice water was being served there on tap. But Travis had been a longtime friend of the family. Saying no to him would've been like saying no to her dad—if Buddy Lomax had been alive.

Against her better judgment, she'd taken the job. Not a month in uniform, the political climate changed and severe budget cuts followed, hitting the department hard. Eighteen months later, she was still pulling four to six shifts per week, along with the occasional double when necessary.

Temporary position, my ass.

Blythe's tired smile widened. "After that panty-raid episode during Hester Simpkin's funeral two weeks ago, can't say I blame the old girls for being upset."

In the past few weeks Shady Knolls Cemetery had become the prime target of every high school and college prankster in the county. Two weeks ago a panty raid of the Delta Sigma Kai Sorority by liquored-up frat boys had resulted in the decoration of several of the cemetery's trees. No one had noticed the colorful scraps of satin and lace dangling from the highest branches of a weeping willow near the gravesite where Hester Simpkins was being laid to rest—until a stiff breeze had blown in from the Atlantic, sending a rainbow of panties raining down upon the mourners, most of whom were elderly.

Greer rinsed her mug, then poured herself a refill. She managed an answering chuckle as she walked to the table and sat opposite Blythe. "They won't be happy this time unless the 'evil miscreants' are hanged at the intersection of Main and Chestnut."

Evil, she silently scoffed. As if these people had any idea of the evil that really existed in the world. As if they even knew the meaning of the word.

Her stomach grumbled and she frowned. She peered into the pink bakery box in the center of the table, hoping for a chocolate-covered anything. Chocolate with anything but jimmies. They reminded her of ants.

Blythe blew on her tea before taking another sip. "Look at the bright side," she said, resting her hand protectively over her protruding tummy. "With the kids tipping headstones, the local bovine have been temporarily spared the humiliation."

Greer nodded in agreement as she plucked a Long John donut coated with maple icing from the box. "Better expect a call from the DA's office," she said before taking a bite. "I overheard Betty Riddle issuing orders to the troupes as they were leaving."

"Oh, that reminds me." Blythe set her cup on the laminated table. "I have a message for you from Travis. He's tied up in another meeting with the county's budget committee and needs you to be on-site for an exhumation at two-thirty."

Greer nearly choked on her Long John. "Me?" she blurted. "Why me?"

"Because you're the only one available. Kyle's testifying today on a DUI that went to trial, Grant's still on medical leave and—"

"Where's Orson?" Greer demanded. Tate Orson might be fresh from the Academy, but she didn't give a rat's ass who was on hand for an exhumation. Anyone but her.

Blythe shook her head. "He's off duty until the weekend."

Greer chucked the half-eaten donut in the garbage can, her appetite vanished. So much for lunch. "Call him in anyway."

"No can do. He's vacationing at his granddad's cabin up at the lake. No electricity, no phone and no reception on his cell."

"Vacation? He's been with the department less than six months," she complained. She'd been on the job she hadn't even wanted a helluva lot longer, and had yet to take so much as a sick day. Something was wrong with this picture.

Blythe let out a weary sigh. "Travis warned me you'd probably pitch a bitch."

"Yeah, well, he was right about that much," Greer snapped irritably. "I don't do autopsies. Not anymore."

Blythe's auburn eyebrows drew together in confusion. "I thought you only had to be on-site while they open the grave and provide escort for the transport of the body to the coroner's office?"

A deep chill settled in the pit of Greer's belly. She was going to be sick.

"You have to be present for more than just the opening," she explained, barely managing to suppress a shudder. "Call Travis back and tell him to find someone else."

She stood, her chair scraping loudly against the gray- and blue-speckled asphalt tiles. She had to get out of here. Air. That's what she needed. Fresh air, to hopefully rid her memory of the stench of decaying flesh.

"Greer, wait—"

The chair nearly fell over, but Greer caught it without taking her eyes off Blythe. "Better yet," she said, "I'll call him myself."

And tell him I quit.

No way in hell could she subject herself to an autopsy. If being on-site for an exhumation was the only requirement, she'd find a way to get through it—somehow. It was the thought of what came after the dig that had her throat already starting to close up in cold, stark fear.

"You know he can't leave the meeting," Blythe reminded her. "He needs to squeeze as much as he can from the budget committee."

Damn you, Willows.

If Travis managed to wrangle additional funding for the department, he could hire more deputies, which would, thankfully, number her days in uniform. Wasn't that her goal? To hang it all up—for good?

She wrapped her fingers around the back of the chair and squeezed until her knuckles ached. "Can't the dig be postponed?" she asked, not caring that she sounded desperate. She *was* desperate.

Travis didn't have a clue what an assignment like this could do to her. The setback it could cause. No one did.

She hadn't suffered a panic attack in almost a month, not even after last night's nightmare. The thought alone of walking into that autopsy room was enough to make her crave the sweet, numbing effects of an oval pink pill. A handful of them, in fact.

Courtesy of national press coverage, Greer's history as a special agent with the Federal Bureau of Investigation was no secret. Two years ago her photo, positioned beside that of an old mug shot of Alan Henry Vicar, had graced the front page of every major newspaper in the country. From her hospital bed she'd watched television news reporters recount the grisly murders of nineteen young women at the hands of The Preacher, as the press had dubbed Vicar, because he'd dressed up like a priest to hunt his victims.

To make matters worse, she'd been subjected to dozens of sound bite–fueled interviews conducted with top psychiatric professionals. The bastards had made one outrageous assumption after another about her ability to function normally after surviving such heinous brutality, until it made her physically ill. Oprah, Dr. Phil and even Jerry Springer had jumped on the media express, dedicating entire shows to survivors of violent crime and posttraumatic stress disorders—all of which her star-struck mother had taped, of course.

She'd spent three weeks in the hospital recovering from the wounds the notorious serial killer she'd profiled had inflicted upon her. If being alive meant she had to cope with a pain-in-the-ass case of PTSD, then she considered herself damn lucky. Members of Alcoholics Anonymous weren't the only ones to chant the mantra "one day at a time." For weeks afterward, one hour at a time had been the code she'd adopted. For every second of those sixty-minute stretches, she never once forgot exactly how fortunate she was to be alive. She didn't care how unreasonable she sounded, there was no way she could witness an autopsy and not suffer for it later, or risk her panic attacks becoming public knowledge.

Blythe's expression filled with sympathy. "The judge had been reluctant to approve the order to exhume Lowell Archer's body as it is. The DA's office has only a short window to have the body exhumed, collect evidence and bring the case before the grand jury. It can't be postponed. I'm sorry, Greer, but you're it."

Greer closed her eyes and tried to relax her death grip on the back of the chair. She could do this. One goddamn *second* at a time, if necessary.

Couldn't she?

Not no, but hell no.

She pulled in a slow, unsteady breath. Okay, maybe she was overreacting. All she had to do was stay calm, keep her mind clear and planted firmly in the present. It'd take a miracle to pull off, but she just might make it through the afternoon without losing the half of the maple Long John she'd just eaten.

Who was she trying to kid here? Asking the Almighty to whisper next Saturday's winning Power Ball numbers in her ear would be more of a sure bet.

She was screwed. Officially and royally screwed.

She opened her eyes and looked at Blythe. "I really don't have a choice, do I?"

"We all have choices," Blythe answered. "Some are just tougher than others."

No shit.

She'd made enough tough choices to last her a lifetime. When she'd allowed herself to become a sadistic killer's target, for one. Regrets were plentiful, too, but regardless of what her decision had ultimately cost her, she couldn't help the satisfaction she felt late at night, alone in her bed when she couldn't sleep, of having been the one to drive a crowbar through Vicar's skull.

She attempted another deep breath, more steady this time, and let it out evenly. She wasn't coming face-to-face with a serial killer. All the assignment required of her was to be at the dig, provide escort, then stand by while a corpse six months in the ground was transferred from casket to slab. The minute the coroner, Manny Cantrell, picked up his scalpel, she was out of there.

Resolving herself to the unpleasant task ahead took a concentrated effort. "I thought Archer kicked from a heart attack?" she asked Blythe. The insurance broker had been only in his late-fifties, but he'd been overweight, smoked three packs of Kools a day and had been married to a woman half his age.

"He did," Blythe confirmed. "But his daughters are accusing Reba Archer of poisoning Lowell. I guess they've convinced the DA their accusation has merit."

Greer pulled the chair back around and sat, intent on ignoring the sharp, metallic taste in her mouth. "So, with Archer's death supposedly from natural causes, no autopsy was performed. I take it this is about money?"

"Isn't it always?" A hint of cynicism underscored Blythe's tone. "If his daughters can prove their evil stepmother killed Daddy off to inherit, then the estate reverts to them."

Greer's brows winged upward. "He was worth that much?"

"From what I've heard"—Blythe lowered her voice—"Archer was worth a lot more than people in this town think. The squabble is over a piece of prime real estate on the Outer Banks that had belonged to his first wife. When she died, the property went to him. It should've gone to their daughters. But because he died intestate, legally everything belongs to Reba."

Greer leaned back in the chair and folded her arms. "How convenient for her," she said with equal cynicism. "The man was an insurance broker. You'd think he'd be smart enough to leave a will."

"You would think," Blythe agreed. "Anyway, the probate proceedings have been stayed. If the DA can't prove Reba offed the old man, I guess Magnolia will have itself another rich widow in the social registry."

A rich, *young* widow, Greer thought, since Reba Haskell Archer couldn't be more than twenty-six or twenty-seven, and a good seven to ten years younger than Archer's two daughters.

The problem with becoming a deputy in her hometown was that she'd known most of the residents her entire life. She'd gone to school with two of the four Haskell boys and hadn't liked them much. "No 'count white trash," as her mother often whispered whenever the Haskell name was mentioned. The family always had spelled trouble, a reputation that age had done little to dispel. Whether a fair judgment or not, if Lowell Archer's surviving children suspected their father's young wife of poisoning him, Greer's money was on the Archer girls.

"Do you have a copy of the order?" Greer asked, not because she was anxious to head out to Upland Hills Memorial Park, but because the drive would take her a good fifty minutes or more.

"On Travis's desk."

Blythe started to lower her feet, but Greer motioned for her to stay put. "I'll get it."

The intercom beeped, followed by the gravelly voice of Addy Ricker, the department's secretary, filtering over the loudspeaker. "Greer? You in there with Blythe?"

Addy had been with the Sheriff's Department when Greer was in grade school, and had outlived two husbands and a son. The woman had to be close to retirement by now, although Greer couldn't imagine the department ever finding anyone to replace Addy.

"Yes, ma'am," she shouted so Addy could hear her. Have something for me, please, she prayed. Anything. A naked jaywalker, a bicycle theft at the elementary school, *anything* to save me from attending the Archer exhumation.

"It's your mama," Addy said. "Line three."

Greer groaned. Blythe coughed, no doubt to hide what sounded suspiciously like a snicker.

Shooting her friend a narrowed-eyed glance, Greer walked to the counter and picked up the receiver. "Not today, Addy. Please. Can you take a message? Tell her I'm out and will call her later." Like next week.

"Greer Garson Lomax," Addy scolded. "That's no way to treat your mama. Lyin'. It just ain't right."

Greer tipped her head back, pinched the bridge of her nose and counted to ten. Who needed a conscience when they had Addy around?

"It's just a tiny one," Greer pleaded. "I'm on my way out now."

"She says it's important."

To June Lomax Fulton, the televised broadcast of *Mrs. Miniver* or *A Streetcar Named Desire* classified as important. "Tell her whatever crisis has her panties in a wad will have to wait until after I go dig up a body, okay?"

Before Addy could scold her further, Greer hung up the extension. She might not be able to avoid attending the exhumation of Lowell Archer, but there wasn't a chance in hell she'd subject herself to her mother *and* an autopsy on the same afternoon. That much of a masochist she wasn't.

Chapter 2

SPECIAL AGENT ASH KELLER muttered a curse, as dark and ominous as the swirling, gunmetal-gray thunderheads darkening the Minneapolis skyline, when the boarding attendant announced yet another flight delay. At least he *thought* he was in Minneapolis. Just one more airport terminal out of hundreds that all looked alike. He'd been on the road so long he could barely keep track any longer.

With his leather garment bag and laptop case parked beside him, he settled back against the ivory-toned vinyl chair to wait out the severe thunderstorm that had been hammering the Twin Cities for the past two hours. The delay did little to improve his already-dismal mood and the storm showed no sign of clearing anytime soon. Dead time always made him edgy, gave him too much time to think, as if the inactivity was a license for his mind to wander into places better left alone.

Through the line of plate glass windows of the terminal, the occasional jolt of jagged light streaked across the horizon like a strobe light of bad flashbacks, one flickering into the next until they melded together into a blazing ball of fire burning a hole in his gut. He scrubbed his hand down his face, wondering again if the job hadn't finally gotten to him.

Maybe the time had come for him to seriously consider getting out before he started making mistakes.

And do what? Retire to Florida and swallow a bullet after six months because he couldn't cut it as a civilian?

Like father, like son.

Like hell.

Ash hailed from a long, distinguished line of law enforcement, seven generations' worth, all of whom had sworn to protect and serve since Ian Keller stepped off the boat at New York Harbor nearly two centuries ago. Bucking the long-standing family tradition had never crossed Ash's mind. It was in his blood, a part of his genetic makeup. Hell, he'd practically been born a cop.

He hadn't even minded coming up under his father's shadow. When he'd followed the old man's footsteps right into the FBI Academy, he'd known being the legendary Abbott Keller's son meant he'd have to work harder and smarter than his fellow trainees. As a result, he'd graduated at the top of his class and was given his choice of plum assignments. But rather than accept one of the handful of cushy posts offered, he put in for a position with the Bureau's Investigative Support Unit.

From the beginning, Ash followed the rules. He refused to take shortcuts and volunteered for the worst assignments offered to avoid so much as a hint of nepotism. Every step of his slow-but-steady climb up the ranks in the Unit he'd earned on his own.

In the end, the joke had been on Ash. The shadow of his superagent father had become nothing more than a dark, heavy cloud, forever seeded with the stigma of being the spawn of a top deep-cover agent who'd fallen from grace—hard.

The familiar, bitter taste of resentment filled Ash's mouth, followed by the sharp, raking need for a cigarette, the nicotine patch on his arm as ineffective as a Band-Aid. He wasn't

about to undergo the hassle of the various checkpoints just
to slip outside for a smoke. Yet, with a four-hour flight
ahead of him, and who knew how long before the storm
cleared, the temptation was damn hard to resist.

Everyone had a weakness. Human nature practically demanded it, and as much as he'd like to believe himself infal-
lible, he was no exception. Good Irish whiskey, the drag of
a cigarette first thing in the morning, and a certain leggy
blonde with big blue eyes and a smile so goddamn sexy just
thinking about her made his dick hard.

Fuck, he missed her.

He leaned forward, rested his elbows on his knees and
stared at the subdued pattern of the industrial carpet between his feet. He'd had a bitch of a week, and today
wasn't looking any better. With nothing to distract him, the
past had caught up with him and he was too tired to outrun it.

He could use a goddamn cigarette. And a drink. He didn't
give a rip that it *was* the middle of the afternoon, or that he
was officially on the government's clock.

A flash of brilliant light lit up the blackened sky, followed
by a thunderous crack and boom. Wind and rain pelted the
grounded aircraft parked outside the Jetway, and beat
against the plate glass windows. Greer Lomax had hit him
like that, he thought. Like a bolt of lightening, which had
jolted him in ways he'd never expected. God knows he'd
tried to put their relationship behind him, especially since
she'd made it patently clear she never wanted to see him
again.

She'd disappeared from his life when she'd gone running
back to that little Southern town where she'd grown up, yet
she continually occupied his thoughts. The woman had gotten under his skin in a bad way, and it pissed him off that
even after two years there were times when he still wanted
her so badly he ached. Like now.

Screw the rules, he thought irritably. He stood suddenly, grabbed his gear and left the crowded waiting area filled with weary and impatient travelers, in search of the nearest cocktail lounge. What the hell had following the rules gotten him anyway? A reputation as a hard-ass, a train wreck of a marriage that had predictably ended in divorce, two daughters, ages ten and thirteen, whom he hadn't seen in over a month, and dreams haunted by a woman who'd rather eat ground glass than be anywhere near him.

On his better days, he didn't blame Greer, not after he'd been responsible for putting her in the hands of a monster. On his bad days, he cursed himself, and her, for being a weakness he couldn't afford.

He stopped at a newsstand for a paper, then weaved his way through the crowd to the lounge. After a quick survey of the patrons, he claimed a vacant booth at the back of the bar. A tired-looking waitress with a bad bleach job glanced in his direction.

"Coffee. Black," he told her.

Ooh, big, bad rebel, aren't you, pal?

Maybe the job *was* finally getting to him, he thought again as he slid into the booth. After fifteen years in profiling, he'd seen some of the best agents crack under the constant pressure. Some made it back, some didn't. Some went to Florida and swallowed a bullet.

When lives were on the line, the stakes were high. He accepted that—hell, he thrived on it. But how much longer could he continue to crawl inside the heads of sociopaths, psychopaths and other types of the worst scum mankind had to offer and not lose his own mind? Would he know when he'd finally seen too much, or would he end up blowing off the back of his head because he no longer possessed the ability to turn off the cries of the innocents he hadn't been able to save?

He did his best, but sometimes even his best wasn't good enough.

He waited until the waitress delivered his coffee before opening the paper. Too much death and mutilation and too many families broken apart and shattered. He'd seen the worst of the worst. The bold headline of the Minneapolis *StarTribune* announcing the capture of a serial murderer who'd been terrorizing the neighboring state of North Dakota for months served as his own testament.

Ash had felt the deep, dark chill of bloodlust rushing through his veins once before, and it sickened him to think he had the capacity to be as cold and calculating as the sociopaths he profiled. He'd recognized the feeling again when the unknown subject he'd assisted the Special Task Force in tracking down had surrendered peacefully. Not even the fact that he wasn't alone—that every single one of the law enforcement personnel he'd accompanied on the predawn raid was hoping for an excuse for a clean kill— gave him comfort.

Two days ago, they'd finally gotten a break in the case when a trio of fourteen-year-old girls were waiting near the mall entrance for the mother of one of the girls to pick them up at a specified time. The girls were approached by a man driving a white, late-model Dodge Ram pickup, asking if they'd seen his dog, a German Shorthaired Pointer he'd claimed had somehow escaped from the Vari-Kennel in the bed of the pickup while he'd been in the auto-parts store across the parking lot.

Thank God the mother had arrived on time, scaring off the guy. She'd also been paying attention to reports strategically released to the public, and had immediately called the police from her cell phone. After questioning the girls, confirming the description and obtaining a partial license plate number, shortly before dawn Ash accompanied the locals to a modest farmhouse located forty miles outside of the Bismarck city limits.

He read the reporter's watered-down account of the story, then folded the newspaper and set it on the seat beside him. Ash knew from years of experience they'd be hard-pressed to find a single member of the community who suspected Jacob Wilson of being a brutal sociopath. They'd be filled with shocked disbelief that the mild-mannered farmer who lived down the dirt road from them, who was considered friendly by his neighbors and who attended church services faithfully, could be responsible for the torture and mutilation deaths of two dozen known victims, all of them adolescent girls under the age of sixteen.

Ash had perfected the art of shutting out the horrors of the job in order to concentrate on the facts and provide local jurisdictions with the tools necessary to bring the bastards down, but he didn't know of a single agent in ISU who wasn't affected when an investigation involved kids. He might have garnered the well-earned reputation of having a heart of steel, but he suspected the Wilson case would haunt him for many years to come.

Some cases hit closer to home than others. Some too close.

For as much as he'd fought and argued with Greer to stay, he suddenly realized she might have been right in walking away. Her leaving had torn him up, not only because she'd thrown away a brilliant career, but also because she'd been willing to walk away from *him*. She'd checked out of the hospital, packed her bags and never looked back. She'd said she loved him, but in the end, it hadn't been enough for her to forgive him for handing her over to a killer.

The cell phone vibrated in his pocket. He flipped it open and instantly recognized the number. For an instant, he considered ignoring the damn thing.

He didn't. "Keller."

"Where the hell are you?" Quentin Constantine barked by way of greeting. "You're supposed to be back in DC."

"Grounded in Minneapolis," Ash said to his superior, unfazed by Con's customary brusque manner. "Mother Nature's on the rag."

Con swore some more, then pulled a one-eighty. "How bad was it?" he asked, referring to the Wilson investigation.

"Bad," Ash told him.

"You all right?" As head of the ISU, Quentin "Con" Constantine made Ash look like a marshmallow in comparison when it came to nominations for Prick of the Year. But Con genuinely cared about the men and women who served under him and had earned, rather than demanded, their respect. He expected perfection, and every last ISU agent made damn sure they gave the top cop nothing short of 150 percent on every investigation they handled.

Ash gave two hundred.

"I will be," Ash replied. "You know how it is."

"Yeah," Con said, an understanding in his voice born from his own experiences. "I do."

Ash drained the last of his coffee. "We done with the touchy-feely bullshit yet?"

"How do you feel about Detroit?"

Ash held back a curse. He'd been out so long he could hardly remember what his apartment looked like. "Not a bad place when the Pistons are in town."

Con made a sound that somewhat resembled a brief chuckle. "The locals will fill you in when you get there," he said, his tone brusque once again. "I've sent you the files, so download when you check in to the hotel."

"What are we looking at this time?"

"An unknown subject who's gone from slicing up hookers to coeds."

Which meant no one bothered to pay attention until a

couple of pretty little college girls had shown up butchered. Slice and dice a crack whore, no one gave a damn. Clues were missed. Evidence destroyed or, worse, never collected. In other words, he'd be walking into a shit storm of nervous politicians and a public on the verge of panic. The usual.

No, he thought, as the weariness slipped away. Not the usual. His job.

He slid out of the booth. As Con filled him in on the details, he fished a five out of his pocket and dropped it on the table. "Ask Faith to run everything we have so far through the system and call me on my cell." Faith Pettit, one of ISU's analysts, was the best. If a pattern or a link existed in the evidence that could lead them to the killer, Faith would find it.

With his gear in his free hand, he left the lounge, his mind already zeroing in on what awaited him in Michigan. Through the windows of the terminal, the storm continued to rage.

"I'm driving to Detroit." He took off down the Gold concourse toward the transportation deck. "I'll call when I arrive," he said, then ended the call.

He faced a solid eight-hour drive, but if he managed to outrun the slow-moving storm, he stood a shot at making it in less. The sooner he arrived, the better, because in his line of work, every second counted.

Upland Hills Memorial Park, located forty miles west of the city limits, resembled a park more than a final resting place. At least that was Greer's opinion as she drove through the wrought iron gates and followed the winding blacktop roadway toward the mausoleum at the top of the hill.

Rather than swing sets and sand boxes, or slides to ignite a child's imagination with rocketships to the moon or fairy castles and a prince determined to rescue his princess, the sloping grassy knolls were littered with granite monuments.

There were no scoreboards or baseball diamonds lit by stadium lights and filled with proud parents shouting encouragement to Little Leaguers, only markers honoring the deceased and Greek Revival statuary to watch over them.

She parked her cruiser near the mausoleum. Since she'd bolted from the station to avoid speaking to her mother, she'd arrived a good thirty minutes early and had time to kill until the cemetery manager and crew arrived to rip into the ground and remove Lowell Archer from his grave.

Standing before the imposing structure, she wondered briefly if she'd come early by design or an accident of fate. Design, she decided, then climbed the concrete steps. She no longer believed in fate.

The heavily carved oak double doors stood open, as they always did during daylight hours, and Greer walked purposefully through the doorway. The cavernous marble corridors were empty and silent except for the creak of leather from her gun belt and shoes as she passed the familiar wall of tombs.

At the end of the corridor, she turned left and walked to the end near the stained glass window with the scene of St. Patrick and the snakes. The irony of the location of the small, private alcove never failed to make her smile. She removed her sunglasses as she turned right to pass under the arched marble doorway with the Lomax name carved in bold block letters above and inlaid with gold foil.

Nothing but the best for the great Buddy Lomax, she thought, with only marginal cynicism today. For that, she blamed her mother, June Reed Lomax Fulton, otherwise known as Mama June by her nearest and dearest.

With her hand pressed against the smooth marble face of the tomb where her father had been interred twenty-five years before, Greer whispered, "Hey, Daddy. It's been a while."

Too long, she thought, tracing her fingers over the carved letters in the monument honoring Buddy. The last time she'd come here had been on one of her rare trips home after joining the Bureau. She had made one attempt to visit Buddy once she'd returned to Magnolia for good, but she hadn't made it past the front gates. Like a Catholic avoiding the confessional, guilt ate at her for not honoring her daddy, but she made it a point to steer clear of anything connected with death.

For that, she blamed The Preacher.

Luckily for her, Magnolia County was pretty damn dull, so even her extended sojourn donning a badge hadn't forced her to face death again. Oh, she did have to deal with the occasional dead body, but those instances usually involved the elderly folks in the county who'd passed peacefully in their sleep. She merely had to be on-site to wait for the coroner to arrive, and by the time the body was rolled out, she made sure she was a safe distance away, usually parked in her cruiser, preparing the Incident Report.

She'd been only nine years old at the time of Buddy's death, and oblivious to the hushed whispers and surreptitious finger-pointing by the residents of the quiet, sleepy town where both her parents had been born and raised. During their college years, June Reed had successfully landed North Carolina State's star quarterback and that year's first-round NFL draft pick—football legend Buddy Lomax. Until the day he'd dropped dead from a massive coronary, her father had realized fifteen stellar seasons with the New Orleans Saints. Buddy believed in playing hard—a philosophy not necessarily restricted to the gridiron.

Greer's innocence had received a rude awakening a few weeks after Buddy dropped dead while in Miami for a game. Hattie, their housekeeper, had sent her to the town drugstore to pick up another prescription of sleeping pills for Mama June, who hadn't left her room since Buddy's funeral.

While waiting for the pharmacist to refill the prescription, Greer had been flipping through one of the teen magazines her mother forbade her to read, when she'd overheard a pair of women in the feminine-needs aisle gossiping with Mrs. Milner, the nice lady from the drugstore who let her read the magazines without having to buy them. The women, obviously unaware of her presence, had said Buddy had spent all his football money on gambling, cars and women, and then had the bad taste to up and die in a hotel room with a woman of questionable morals. Mrs. Milner had even made rude assumptions about what her mother was going to do now that the family had been shamed and left destitute.

She'd been too young at the time to fully comprehend the meaning of all that the three women had said that day, but wise enough to know it wasn't good. With her mother spaced out on Valium and Hattie refusing to discuss the subject, she'd questioned Vivien Lee, her older sister by three years. Vivi told her the unvarnished truth—they were dead broke and their daddy had died while doing a hooker.

Greer didn't like to think about the tumultuous year that followed, how the bank had foreclosed on their stately home in the wealthy section of town or how most of their belongings had been auctioned off to cover the debts Buddy had run up while playing hard. Thankfully her dad's antique car collection had brought in a good deal of cash, but after all Buddy's debts were paid, they'd been able to afford only a shabby, two-bedroom apartment on the poor side of town.

About the only good thing she could recall about that time was the lack of money meant she and Vivi wouldn't be shipped back to that exclusive girl's school in Massachusetts. Her father had insisted his daughters attend St. Margaret's Academy, but Greer hated the place with a passion. She'd been overjoyed by the prospect of joining her best friend, Selma Reyser, in public school.

The changes in their lives had been an adjustment, but the real shock came the day after the one-year anniversary of Buddy's unfortunate demise. Her mother had announced she would be marrying Davis Fulton, the bank manager who'd foreclosed on their house.

Vivi swore she hated Davis and blamed him for every misfortune that had befallen them the previous year. Greer blamed her womanizing father and had liked Davis despite Vivi's claim the soft-spoken bank manager was nothing more than no 'count white trash trying to better himself by marrying their mother. From the beginning, Davis was nice to Greer. He'd certainly paid her more attention than her own father ever had, but what she really appreciated was the fact that her new stepfather came home each night at precisely six-fifteen. Unlike Buddy, Davis never provided an ounce of grist for the Magnolia gossip mill.

After a brief honeymoon in Atlantic City, Davis moved them from the shabby apartment into a spacious older home in a better part of town. Her mother and Davis still lived there, and while Greer loved the old house, she did all she could to avoid it, too. Something else she blamed on her mother.

It had taken Vivi a couple of years before she eventually, but grudgingly, accepted Davis. Greer's life became easier once she was no longer caught in the middle of Vivi and Davis's feuds. Her mother eventually resumed her former place in Magnolia's society food chain, although she had slipped down a few links. June pretended not to notice and threw herself into charity work with the Junior League with a vengeance. Though it took the membership committee several months to officially reinstate Mrs. Davis Fulton to their roster, she never missed a single meeting or an opportunity to volunteer her services to the Daughters of the War of Northern Aggression. Even the exclusive Ladies of Polite Southern Society miraculously accepted her back into their elite fold—after Davis gifted the club with a sizeable donation for the annual garden festival it hosted.

For the next seven years, Greer did her best to ignore the gossip about how Magnolia's own Southern belle had been forced to marry beneath herself by snatching up the first meal ticket willing to take on a widow with two children. But June Reed Lomax Fulton hadn't had a choice, bless her heart, they'd said. She'd done what she had to do to feed and clothe her children. Of course, she wouldn't have been forced into such dire circumstances if her late husband, God rest his soul, they'd add, hadn't been a skirt-chasing gambler who'd lost all their money and shamed the family when he'd died while banging a twenty-dollar prostitute.

Greer couldn't wait to get as far from Magnolia, North Carolina, as possible.

By the time she'd left for college, her sister had already dropped out during her junior year, and married and divorced a man too much like their father and was already on the hunt for her next husband. Unlike her sister—who had dutifully followed in her mother's footsteps by pledging to the same sorority and landing a husband cut of the same disreputable cloth as Buddy Lomax—Greer had lived in a dorm, worked hard to keep her name on the dean's list and had planned to land herself a job on Wall Street. She'd dreamed of one day being able to afford to start up her own investment firm, anywhere but in Magnolia.

At least she'd achieved one of her goals, she thought, propping her shoulder against the marble column of the doorway into the alcove. She'd stayed away for a number of years, but rather than heading for Wall Street, her plans had changed—all because she'd walked into the wrong room.

In her last year of college, she'd been on the verge of successfully obtaining her business degree in banking and finance when her plans for the future had been irrevocably altered. During Career Week, when the Fortune 500s and Corporate America competed for graduates—seducing them with hiring bonuses, 401k plans and promises of fast track career advancement, she'd been completely captivated by the FBI rep's speech and suddenly something inside her awakened that she hadn't even realized existed. She'd been overcome by a strong sense of justice, combined with a compelling need to be a part of the bigger picture, a place where she could make a real difference in the world.

She hadn't planned on becoming an FBI agent, or becoming a profiler in the Investigative Support Unit. But she must've made an impression during her interview with the rep, because her application to the FBI's training academy had miraculously been accepted on her first try. The classes she'd attended there, given by the ISU instructors, made an even bigger impression on her, and she'd taken the steps necessary to ensure she'd be given a shot at becoming a member of the FBI's elite team of profilers.

Her mother had been mortified by Greer's decision to become a mere government employee. Her stepfather had outlined a detailed budget based on a rookie agent's salary, complete with pie charts to show her where to safely invest twenty percent of her annual income, then started a portfolio for her with five thousand shares of Intel stock as a graduation present. Vivien Lee hadn't so much as balked so long as Greer promised to be home in time to serve as a bridesmaid in Wedding Number Two.

Her job now might be dull as dirt, but she really didn't mind—too much. Rounding up rowdy rednecks on a Saturday night or popping local teens for busting curfew was a hell of a lot less stressful than defusing ticking human time bombs before they killed again. And again . . . and again . . . and again.

She bit the inside of her lip. After six years riding a highly stressful emotional roller coaster, she welcomed dull. After traveling to more cities across the country than she could name to assist local jurisdictions and the task forces they established to capture serials, she preferred boring. Despite her preference for dull and boring, with little effort she easily recalled each of the scumbags she'd profiled, down to the precise details of the various crime scenes and body dumps. She'd attended more autopsies than Manny Cantrell, Magnolia County's medical examiner, had probably performed in his entire career. She'd provided expert testimony in countless trials, and had manipulated more hungry reporters than the public relations people for JLo, Madonna and Garth Brooks combined.

She couldn't state she'd *loved* her job, no one in her previous line of work could, but she'd been damn good at it. With each killing spree she'd helped bring to an end, she'd always experienced a swell of relief. Occasionally she did suffer a twinge of regret for flushing her career, and the life she'd built for herself, down the can. She had brief moments when she missed the thrill of the chase, the satisfaction of a job well done. But pigs would sprout wings and compete with the bald eagle for a perch atop a blue spruce before she'd ever crawl back inside the dark, twisted mind of a killer.

"He was one of the best. A real legend."

Startled by the sound of a man's voice, Greer looked over her shoulder. She hadn't heard Monroe Younger approach and wondered if maybe she was going soft. "So I'm told," she answered as she pushed off the marble column. "I take it you came looking for me because they want to get started?"

Monroe stood with a dirty blue ball cap clutched in hands Greer imagined, deeply calloused from operating the backhoe to dig the graves of the citizenry of Magnolia County.

"Yes'm," he said, lowering his gaze. "We're ready."

Ready? An odd term, she thought. She'd never be ready when it came to digging up a rotting corpse. Still, she nodded, said a silent good-bye to her father and followed Monroe through the maze of tombs.

There were days when she hated the boredom and monotony of her job as a deputy sheriff. She wished today was one of them.

Chapter 3

THE AUTOPSY ROOM at the county coroner's office did a good job of masquerading as a hospital operating room, but Greer wasn't the least bit fooled by the innocuous surroundings. She knew exactly where she was—at the entrance of Hell—and she had the churning stomach to prove it.

Trying not to think about the past, but doing a lousy job of it, she smoothed a glob of mentholated rub over her upper lip. The Vicks usually kept the stench to a minimum, but for her, the vapor rub served only as a reminder of the vast ugliness she'd witnessed for too many years with the Bureau. Memories were a bitch. Some worse than others. All too often she lost the battle and the dark walls of her past closed in on her before she could stop them. They squeezed the breath from her lungs, strangled her and sent her over the edge into an insane vortex of panic, leaving her with little control. She hated that feeling, and concentrated now on maintaining even, controlled breaths.

She offered the blue plastic jar to Pamela Reynolds, the county's assistant district attorney, while Manny Cantrell and the assistant he'd introduced only as Dale, prepared for the opening of the casket housing Lowell Archer's body. "This might help," she said to Pamela.

"Thanks," the ADA replied, her brown eyes avoiding what had once been an expensive rosewood coffin with gold-plated hardware, already showing signs of rot from being beneath the moist, dark earth. "I hate these things." She poked her finger into the jar of Vicks. "Do you ever get used to them?"

"Never." Greer then offered the jar to Seth Hughes, the attorney representing Archer's widow.

Hughes shook his head. "No, thanks. I'll be fine."

Sure you will, tough guy.

She didn't know what the lawyer thought he was trying to prove, but she'd come across his type on countless occasions. No doubt figured he was tougher than a couple of women. Apparently he'd never attended a postmortem, let alone an exhumation. She predicted he'd be making a mad dash for the closest receptacle to puke his brains out, or she'd be helping Dale scoop the arrogant jackass off the floor the minute he caught a whiff of six months' worth of rotting and decayed flesh. The embalming fluid helped to a small degree, but nothing could completely eradicate the stench of death.

"Suit yourself," she said with a shrug, then cast a quick glance at Pamela.

Pamela smirked.

Greer screwed the top back on the jar. Concentrating on the mundane sometimes offered a reprieve and kept the memories from closing in on her. She'd pay the price later, of that she was certain, but that was fine by her so long as it meant she wouldn't lose it in public. Panic attacks were a pain in the ass, but she had no choice but to hold herself together, or risk revealing her little secret . . . that she was nothing more than a fucked-up, emotional head case.

"Let's get this show on the road." Manny's booming voice filled the tiled room. His assistant jumped to attention and immediately opened the coffin's latch.

Greer suspected the kid was an intern. The tall, reed-thin blond fellow gave his status away the second he turned as green as the ghastly colored ceramic tiles covering the walls and floor.

Manny nodded to Dale. Together they raised the lid of the casket.

Greer maintained a safe distance. *Breathe,* she reminded herself. *Slow, even breaths. Hold it all inside until you're safe. Flipping out now is* not *an option.*

She prayed she'd pull off the scam. Opportunity to freak and deal with a full-blown panic attack could come once she was in the privacy of her own home.

"Oh, my God!" Dale quickly turned away. He went from green to pasty white in less than 2.2 seconds.

Greer immediately tensed.

Manny looked down into Archer's coffin. "Well now," he said, "just who might you be?" He glanced at Greer, a wide smile canting his mouth. "You better come over here an' take a gander, Miz Lomax."

Hughes didn't take so much as a peek inside the coffin before his gag reflex kicked into gear. "Excuse me," he managed in a thin, pathetic voice, before bolting across the room to upchuck in the sink.

Dumb ass, Greer thought.

"What is it?" Pamela asked Manny. Her voice sounded only slightly brittle.

Greer didn't share Pamela's morbid curiosity. She could easily walk out of the room now and never care what had Manny so amused. She'd lay odds she wouldn't find anything funny about the situation, either. Hell, she was lucky to be breathing somewhat normally, given the circumstances.

Manny inclined his bald, shiny-as-an-eight ball head in the direction of the open coffin. "Old Lowell's got himself a guest."

"Jesus, Manny," Greer snapped irritably and frowned at the six-foot-five coroner. "Don't go there. We can live without the blow-by-blow of whatever creepy crawlies are keeping company with Archer's body."

Manny's smile faded. "I'm serious, Greer." he said, his voice suddenly turning as somber as his expression. "You'd really better take a look. I'll bet even you haven't seen anything like this before."

"I doubt that," she muttered, remaining where she stood. According to the parade of shrinks she'd seen, she'd witnessed far too much. She didn't consider herself in a position to argue with their assessment, either. Frankly, she *had* seen too much, more than Manny ever would—so long as he remained employed in the quiet, peaceful county.

Pamela's curiosity apparently overruled her caution. She stepped around Greer and slowly approached the casket. "Oh, good grief," she exclaimed, her eyes widening in stunned disbelief. "Who the hell is that?"

Greer still didn't want to look. She flexed her hands at her sides, her short, trimmed fingernails digging into her palms with each hold and release.

"What?" Reba's attorney demanded, his voice hollow, courtesy of the echo effect from having his head inside the cavernous metal sink. "What? What is it?"

The ADA stood with her gaze transfixed on the contents resting amid the coffin's water-stained, ivory satin interior. "A body."

Pamela's voice conveyed a combination of revulsion and shock that nudged Greer's better judgment. Reluctantly, she moved to Manny's side and gasped, as stunned by what she saw as the others. Eventually she swore. "Like I need this shit," she complained, unable to tear her gaze away. She swore again, vividly, causing Manny's eyebrows to wing skyward.

Hughes rinsed his mouth, then straightened. "Good one,

Sherlock," he said sarcastically. "You figure that one out all by yourself, Reynolds?"

"There are two bodies here, you smug bastard," Pamela fired at him.

"That's impossible," Hughes scoffed.

Pamela taunted Hughes with a smug expression of her own. "Care to see for yourself?"

Hughes obviously reconsidered and took a step backward. "I'll take your word for it," he said in a more civil tone, suddenly showing great interest in the floor tiles.

"You'll both have to step outside," Greer told the attorneys, her attention on the corpse nestled against Archer's body.

"What are you thinking?" Manny asked her.

"The decomposition of the female makes it difficult to discern her age," she told him, "but from the style of her gray hair and that matronly dress, I'd estimate her age to be somewhere in the late-forty to early-fifty range."

Manny looked closer. "This body's been embalmed," he said quietly, and to no one in particular.

"Excuse me, Deputy," Reba's lawyer blurted, as if he suddenly remembered his purpose for being there. "Counsel has a right to be present."

Greer faced Hughes. "Not anymore, you don't," she told him in an authoritative tone that had him visibly bristling. "Out. Now."

"I'll file a contempt motion," he threatened.

"Try it," she snapped at him. "I'll have your ass in my jail on obstruction charges before your secretary can transcribe your chicken-shit motion."

"Piss off, Lomax," Hughes argued. "There's no evidence a crime has been committed."

"Then explain that woman's body with Archer inside what was a closed and buried coffin." Pamela interjected.

Manny turned his imposing body to face Hughes. "You'd

better leave," he said, the threat evident in his voice. Built like an offensive lineman with skin the color of rich, dark chocolate, Manny was a huge, hulking man. He was always gentle as a lamb—until someone stepped over what he considered to be the line.

Hughes turned an even deeper shade of green. Whether from Manny's unspoken threat or the reminder of their unexpected discovery, Greer didn't much care. She had her own problems. Like a murder investigation she wanted no part of, for one.

"I thought so," Pamela said haughtily.

Under normal circumstances, Greer would've enjoyed seeing Pamela put the arrogant jerk in his place, but there was nothing normal about standing in an autopsy room with an open casket containing an extra dead body.

"I'm sorry, Manny," Greer said, "but I need to preserve the scene until the state crime lab can collect evidence."

"Not a problem. I won't mind being home in time for the missus's meatloaf." He pulled off the latex gloves from his big, beefy hands and tossed them in a metal bin marked HAZARDOUS WASTE.

Dale, still pale and a safe distance away, hastily followed suit, anxious to separate himself from the scene. Greer didn't blame the kid. She'd sell her soul, if she had one left, to do the same.

"It'll be hours before the state boys get here, Greer," said Manny. "You're more than welcome to join us for dinner. Lattie's meatloaf is the best in three counties."

"Maybe next time," she said, and turned her attention to the two attorneys still glowering at one another in a silent standoff. "Manny's office will advise you when the postmortem on Archer will be performed. More than likely, that will be tomorrow morning." She looked to Manny, who nodded in confirmation. "This area will be treated as a crime scene until further notice."

Dammit, she didn't do dead bodies. Willows would owe her big time, and she'd make certain the sheriff paid her asking price—by accepting her resignation.

She didn't need, didn't want anything to do with a hardcore criminal investigation. Unfortunately, only the Sheriff's Department had jurisdiction. With no homicide division, and no detectives to pass the buck to, the investigation belonged to her as first officer on the scene.

Archer and his unidentified companion were now her responsibility. Whether she liked it or not.

By the time Ash reached Detroit, checked into his hotel and downloaded the files Con and Faith had e-mailed to him, it was half-past nine. He still hadn't reviewed the case file, but had made contact with Jerry Clark, the head of the Detroit Police Department's Special Task Force. A meeting with Clark and two of the lead investigators on the case was scheduled for seven the next morning.

Ash showered, ordered a bowl of soup and a pot of strong, black coffee from room service, then settled down to study the file after turning on the television to the local NBC affiliate, hoping to catch the eleven o'clock newscast. He wanted to see what the public had been told, if anything, about the UNSUB. The task force had dubbed him The Red Light Slasher, but the press was usually more creative in coming up with headline-worthy monikers for homicidal maniacs and sociopaths. Ash simply referred to them as UNSUB, unknown subject, until he had a name.

Now that he'd been called in to assist, they'd eventually determine a solid identity to pin on the Detroit UNSUB. With any luck, the killer's name would be printed on a toe tag in the not-too-distant future. He sure as shit hoped they could save the law-abiding taxpayer base the expense of supporting the son of a bitch for the duration of a life sentence without the possibility of parole, all because the state of Michigan and the death penalty were not synonymous. If the UNSUB was unfortunately captured alive, some glory-seeking, self-proclaimed hot shot defense attorney would crawl out of the woodwork, drag out the trial and file one appeal after another to have the sentence reduced.

A damn pity, he thought, as he got up from the desk, when a terminal case of lead poisoning was so much more satisfying. Setting the empty dishware on the room service tray, he carried it to the door and set it in the corridor. He hadn't always been such a hypocrite, saving lives one minute, then praying for an UNSUB's death the next. In fact, he'd never given the death penalty a whole lot of thought one way or another. It existed and he hadn't been for or against it. It simply was, until a hot, humid night two years ago during the monsoon season in Phoenix changed his attitude forever. And not necessarily for the better.

He shook off the path of his thoughts before they had a chance to lock him into a place better left alone and poured himself another cup of coffee, debating instead the wisdom of checking out the contents of the minibar. A shot or two of whiskey added to his coffee sounded like a mighty fine idea to him, but he had a case to familiarize himself with and keeping a clear head was more important than quieting the demons becoming louder in their haunting. How clear his head would be after nine hours on the road, most of which had been spent in the storm he hadn't been able to outrun, he wasn't about to hedge any bets. Still, he had a job to do, and the job always came first.

He carried the thermal carafe with him to the king-sized bed where he'd left his laptop and set the stainless container on the nightstand along with his refilled coffee mug. After settling against the mound of pillows he'd propped against the headboard, he lit a cigarette and took a deep drag before he opened the file containing digital photographs of the first known crime scene.

As was his habit, he studied them before reading a single written word on the investigation. He preferred to draw his own conclusions than be unconsciously influenced by police reports, autopsy reports and, if they were extremely fortunate, a witness statement.

After examining several photographs, he made notes on the legal pad at his side. These weren't shots of a crime scene, he decided, but instead were of a *dump site* where the killer had discarded the partial remains of a woman's body. He enlarged one of the photographs and stared hard at the image of the nude torso of a rail-thin black woman. The fact that she'd been dismembered didn't faze him, and he enlarged the image yet again. The cuts were clean at the joints, as if she'd been butchered like a whole frying chicken.

He made more notes on the legal pad, then opened the photos of the subsequent kills. Each was an exact replica of the first, with one vital exception—a woman's handbag had been arranged to shield the vic's pubis from view.

"Twisted fuck." Ash spat. He rose from the bed and carried the laptop to the desk where he hooked up the portable photo printer. Once the prints were complete, he then connected the accompanying inkjet printer and started running the documentation files supplied to ISU by the task force.

Taking the prints with him, he spread them on the bed and began jotting down the list of questions buzzing around in his head.

The killer had changed his MO from the first kill. Why? To make some sort of statement? Again, why?

He studied the photos from the second known scene and compared them to the first. Why use a handbag to shield the sexual organs? If the UNSUB was offended by the women's sex, then why leave the sexual organs intact at all? What significance did the handbag carry for the UNSUB?

The printer stopped and he got up to add more paper. He

circled the bed, stubbed out his cigarette, then stood with his arms crossed and feet braced apart, studying the photographs once again.

So what connected the vics? he mused. The largest percentage of serials were white males, eighteen- to thirty-five years of age, but these vics were all black women. To him, that meant the UNSUB was more than likely an African American male, since serials tended to hunt within their own ethnic group.

From his conversation with Con, he knew the first three vics were prostitutes, while the latter two were college coeds from Wayne State University. Why the change? Prostitutes were easy prey. Unless, he thought, a potential vic had managed to escape. Risk of capture often caused an UNSUB to seek fresh hunting grounds. A living, breathing witness created one helluva liability.

The UNSUB's use of dump sites made perfect sense to Ash. Dismemberment took time and required privacy. The UNSUB chose his prey, went to the actual crime scene to live out his sick fantasy, sliced up the vic, then dumped the torso and staged the scene. So where the hell were the rest of the body parts?

The printer stopped again, but Ash remained transfixed on the photographs, unanswered questions running and rerunning through his mind on a continuous loop. Possible answers surfaced, but he systematically discarded most of them based solely on gut instinct. He picked up a shot of the first vic discovered and zeroed in on the way she'd been treated after death. His gut told him the mutilation occurred post-mortem. The cuts were too clean. A bound vic, even one who'd been mildly sedated, would manage some struggle against such excruciating pain.

"Precise," he murmured. "Too precise." There wasn't a shred of evidence that he could see of tearing, or of a jagged edge from the blade of a power saw, like Dahmer had used to chop up his victims. The UNSUB knew exactly what he was doing. He was experienced.

Butcher? Perhaps, Ash thought.

A cold chill suddenly crept up his spine as the ramifications of what his instincts were telling him hit full force. He knew. God help him, he knew.

Without studying any more documents, the fate of the missing body parts was suddenly crystal clear, making him damn relieved that the meal he'd ordered from room service contained nothing carnivorous—just a bowl of potato-cheese soup and a chunk of crusty French bread.

With dear Walter's funeral scheduled for tomorrow afternoon, Parker had no choice but to work faster than he liked. He preferred to take his time in making his selection of the perfect mate, but the cemetery of Walter's interment had recently implemented the use of burial vaults. He couldn't present Walter with his perfect mate if he was sealed inside a vault with an eight-hundred-pound concrete lid. Because his client's memorial would not entail an open casket, he'd been presented with a golden opportunity that enabled him to complete Walter's destiny. He'd made a promise before he'd left Hennessy's Mortuary late this afternoon, and he *always* kept his word to his clients.

From behind the wheel of a rented Chevy Malibu parked below the thick, drooping branches of a willow tree, Parker maintained his vigil over the parking lot and entrance of Jo-Jo's BBQ Pit thirty miles west of Raleigh. The midsummer air was warm and thick with humidity, typical for inland North Carolina, and he lightly dabbed a pristine white handkerchief along his brow.

In the dimming dusk of the evening, a pair of headlights streaked across his windshield. Instantly alert, Parker followed the vehicle's progress and waited anxiously for the occupant to leave the car.

Anticipation whipped through him, exciting him. He touched himself through his twill trousers. How he loved his work.

As he'd hoped, a woman emerged from the vehicle. Young. Curvy. A brunette with big tits.

His breathing quickened and his dick hardened beneath his palm while he observed the sashay of her full hips beneath a short, tight black skirt as she made her way to the entrance. She'd arrived.

The loud *thwack* startled him. A sharp, stinging burn lashed his back and he winced against the pain searing his skin.

He released himself and closed his eyes. "Leave me alone," he said, appalled by his own begging whimper. "Leave me alone."

He was Parker Hennessy now. He was not subject to the evil of others.

Parker Hennessy . . . Hennessy . . . Hennessy . . .

He must ignore the hateful taunts chasing through his mind. There was work to be done. His promise to Walter to keep. He would not fail.

Refusing to listen to the high-pitched screeching reverberating through him, he clamped his hands over his ears. Rocking back and forth, he whispered in a rush of sound, "La-la-la-la-la-la-la." The litany grew louder, then louder still. He rocked and chanted until all he heard was the sound of his own terrified voice.

Minutes later, he lowered his hands. A choir of sparrows serenaded him from the high branches of the willow, intermingling with the whirr of speeding traffic from the interstate.

He was Parker Hennessy now. Safe from the evil of others.

With his confidence restored, he left the rental car and crossed the parking lot to the entrance of the restaurant. In a place like Jo-Jo's there were no hostesses, only a bevy of waitresses carrying trays laden with slabs of Jo-Jo's famous slow-cooked beef or pork ribs—generously slathered with sticky, sweet sauce. The tables were covered only by thin, disposable red-and-white checkerboard paper cloths. No elegant tapers or even drippy candles. Nor was champagne available here—only cold beer, along with stacks of cheap paper napkins and mammoth food portions.

She sat facing the entrance at a table in the center of the dining room. Not a timid woman, he surmised, or at least one who didn't mind being appreciated by the opposite sex—based on the short, sexy skirt she wore and the low-cut, bright-yellow top clinging to her perfect tits.

Oh, yes, she'd be absolutely perfect.

She looked up as he approached and held his gaze with vibrant sea green eyes beneath dusky lashes generously coated with mascara. A mixture of relief and approval played across her lightly sun-kissed face.

"Please tell me you're Melanie Engle," he said to her in a lightly flirtatious tone.

A becoming smile tilted her wide mouth. "And you must be Walter Strom."

Chapter 4

THE WINDOWLESS OFFICES of the National Center for the Analysis of Violent Crime, located in Virginia on Marine Corps Base Quantico, were housed sixty feet below ground. Ten times deeper than the dead, as Con occasionally reminded the ISU agents. The lack of sunlight didn't bother Ash. For him, it served as a symbol of the justice he'd promised would belong to the victims, the ones he hadn't been able to save in particular.

As he walked down the corridor toward his own office, he paid only passing attention to the various blowups of grisly crime scenes, victim autopsies and other related investigative photographs. They were tacked to the walls with poster putty or propped against desks, chairs, cardboard boxes stuffed with closed cases or any other available surface. Not that the vics didn't matter to him, but they were more a fact of his life, an integral part of the career path he'd chosen to walk.

On this Friday morning at precisely seven thirty, he entered his office and was greeted by three mountainous stacks of files, neatly arranged on the edge of his desk by Diane Littman, one of the two administrative clerks he shared with the dozen agents under his supervision. A majority of the files required his review for the purpose of consultation, for his so-called expert opinion on the personality type of the UNSUB. Some he handled personally, others he assigned to less-senior agents for either consult or actual on-site assistance if he deemed Bureau intervention necessary. He had no criteria, no standing checklist. His decisions were based solely on his gut reaction, the assignments delegated based on the level of the agent's experience. All too often he ended up handling the worst of the worst himself, like the mess he'd wrapped up in Detroit two weeks ago.

Unfortunately, before Theodore Buford McNitty, aka The Red Light Slasher, had been stopped, the bastard had claimed two additional victims, one on the very night Ash had arrived in Detroit. Consciously he knew nothing he could've done would have spared the seventh victim's life, but that didn't alleviate the guilt from stacking up against him like bricks on the wrong side of the justice scale. Maybe if he'd arrived in town sooner. Maybe if the case information had been provided to him twenty-four hours earlier. Then, just maybe, he would have been able to save at least one of the two girls who'd been murdered on his watch.

His profile had been dead on, however, as McNitty had indeed worked in a butcher shop as Ash had suspected. Only McNitty Meats hadn't been located in the seedier part of town where he'd initially suggested the task force focus their attention. A delay that had resulted in two final victims, and for that Ash blamed himself for overlooking the obvious.

Like any predator, serials hunted where the feeding grounds were plentiful. What could be more abundant than his own goddamn neighborhood? The vics weren't being plucked from the run-down section of town or even the Wayne State campus. They were taken right out of their own exclusive neighborhood, all within a five-mile radius of McNitty's butcher shop.

No one had been more surprised than Ash when the location of McNitty's enterprise became clear. The break in the case came when the housekeeper of a prominent local physician had called the police after finding what appeared to be a section of a woman's finger inside two pounds of ground sausage purchased from McNitty's store. The partial fingerprint obtained had matched that of the fifth victim.

At least McNitty wouldn't be standing trial. Instead, the bastard had been carted off to the morgue, zipped up in a body bag and sporting a toe tag, courtesy of the task force's lead investigator. A damn satisfactory end to a particularly gruesome case, in Ash's opinion. An opinion, he admitted as he hung his navy suit jacket on the peg behind the door, becoming more and more jaded every day.

He slung his freshly packed garment bag onto the tan vinyl armchair in front of his desk. In the two weeks since Detroit, he'd gone to Seattle, followed by Oklahoma City and then home. He'd been back only four days and now he was scheduled to take an afternoon flight to Idaho Falls, Idaho.

He carried a stack of the pressboard folders on his desk over to the metal folding table along the far wall in his office. After turning the switch for the swing-arm lamp clamped to the edge, he opened the first file and spread the 8x10 glossies out to study.

With his hands braced on the table, he leaned forward and examined each of the photographs. Random sites, he quickly determined, actual scenes of the crime where the kills took place. An unorganized killer. A boiling pot of anger no longer able to contain his emotions, as indicated by the increasing level of damage to each subsequent kill. A younger man unable to appreciate the value of patience.

Before he could guesstimate a list of possible causes for the UNSUB's escalation of violence, a light rap against the doorjamb drew his attention away from the photos. He glanced over his shoulder as Faith Pettit, one of his closest friends as well as being a top analyst in the Unit, entered his office. Her pink-tinted lips were set in a grim line. Because he'd known her a good ten years or more, he easily spotted the tension in her shoulders.

Despite their friendship, Faith reported directly to him. She was what he referred to as a paper agent—one with minimal field experience, more of a think tank agent and a vital cog in the bigger machine. Nearly every agent in the Unit called upon her because of her uncanny ability to find patterns where none were obvious. She'd earned herself a stellar reputation for being able to locate the proverbial needle in any size haystack.

"What's up?" he asked Faith. Half the time she was his right arm—the other half, his conscience. Before he and Greer split, they often socialized with Faith and her husband, Andrew, an agent turned lawyer now employed by Homeland Security.

"You need to see this." She slid a reddish-blonde hank of wavy, chin-length hair behind her ear, revealing a small emerald stud that matched the intense color of her concern-filled eyes. "It was entered in VICAP's database last week, but went to the Missing Persons Unit."

Curious, he straightened and took the crime analysis report from her. He scanned the face page of the document filed by an agent in their Charlotte, North Carolina, field office. The name of the investigating officer caught his attention and his heart squeezed painfully in his chest, then thumped madly, the sound a deafening, hollow echo in his ears.

Greer. *His* Greer was listed as the officer in charge of a homicide investigation. Impossible.

He looked at Faith. "When did she become a cop?"

No way. Not Greer.

Faith shrugged her thin shoulders. "I was just as surprised as you. The last time I spoke with her she'd just bought herself a run-down Victorian and was planning to convert it into a bed and breakfast, of all things."

What a blatant waste of talent, he thought. A damn shame, too. Greer had been one of the best profilers in the Bureau with a sixth sense to rival his own. With a career on the rise, the only place for her to go had been up—until she'd thrown it all away.

Because of him.

Guilt slammed into him, hard.

"If she'd wanted to return to law enforcement," he said irritably, "Con would've welcomed her back to the Unit no problem. A cop?" A deputy sheriff in some backwater, hick town, he thought, jamming his fingers through his hair. "I don't believe this shit. She should've told me."

"What do you expect? She hasn't exactly kept any of us on speed dial."

That bit of truth hit him like a mule kick to his ass end. He didn't give a damn. Given their history, didn't he have a right to know what the hell she was up to? So what if they hadn't spoken since she'd left? She shouldn't have kept something so important from him. Dammit, she was . . . what?

Not sharing his bed any longer, that's what.

Not dulling his razor because she'd used it to shave her legs.

Not around to give him hell when he forgot to turn off the coffeemaker.

Not calling him in the middle of the night when she was out of town, tired, frustrated and feeling beaten down by a case. Not calling when she was filled with exhilaration because she'd nailed another UNSUB.

Anger and resentment sliced through him like a knife, tearing open old wounds. After two years without her in his life, he had his doubts those wounds would ever fully heal.

As ever, when the subject was Greer, concern managed to elbow past his disappointment. A murder investigation, one she'd been compelled to contact the Bureau for because of the missing person status, had to be playing hell with her. Every demon she'd been trying to exorcise probably resurrected. He'd witnessed the fallout of posttraumatic stress. After what she'd suffered at the hands of The Preacher, Greer's name on a violent-crime analysis report as the investigating officer put his protective instincts on elevated status.

Faith tucked her hands in the pockets of her dark olive slacks and leaned against the edge of his desk. "When the Carolina crime lab ran the victim's prints," she said, inclining her head to the report still clutched in Ash's hand, "they came back as a missing person. Greer followed procedure by contacting the Charlotte field office. It was turned over to the MP Unit, but when Special Agent Striker saw her name on the report, he thought you should know about Greer's involvement."

Made sense to him, he thought with a brief nod of acknowledgement to Faith. From day one his relationship with Greer had been one of the Bureau's worst-kept secrets.

He rubbed at the knot of tension building in his neck and shifted his attention back to the report. The Crime-Classification section asked if the investigating officer believed the offender had killed before. The box UNABLE TO DETERMINE had been checked, but the distinction did little to ease his rapidly growing concern for Greer's emotional well-being. Striker wouldn't have broken protocol by sending him the crime analysis report if he hadn't suspected the incident was more involved than it appeared on the surface.

He slowly walked to his desk and read further. The victim had been discovered due to an exhumation on an unrelated matter. Basically, the discovery of the body had been a fluke. Exactly, he thought. Who would think to look inside a buried coffin for a missing person?

"The perfect murder," he murmured, even though no such thing existed. His gut reaction redlined, shifting his instincts into overdrive.

He looked at Faith, a deep sense of foreboding seeping into his bones, chilling him. "Whatever Greer found is only the beginning."

Faith let out a sigh. "That was my initial reaction, too," she agreed. "Except the report didn't support my hunch."

He never ignored his instincts. Just because Greer was involved, he wasn't about to start now, either.

"Pull together everything you can find on her investigation," he ordered Faith. "Check for similars in the area, too, while you're at it."

"I already did."

"And?" That sinking feeling in the pit of his stomach expanded.

"An unusually high rate of missing persons from the coastal region, all of them women. Ages range from mid-teens to late-seventies."

"How many?"

"I only went as far back as the last twenty-four months. There are thirty-two women still on the MP list. Some could be runaways," Faith said, "but for such a sparsely populated area of the country, the high rate could very well mean something else."

"Like some*one* else."

"We don't know that for certain."

Ash picked up the phone to dial Diane's extension. "The hell we don't."

"At first glance, this report doesn't even meet ISU's criteria for a serial offender," Faith reasoned.

His gut said otherwise.

The perky administrative clerk answered on the first ring. "Mornin', boss."

Even at such an early hour of the morning, Diane's voice was as chipper as ever. Usually her bright personality made him smile. Not today.

"Find Agents Burke and Hornbeck and tell them to pack," he instructed. "Then cancel my flight to Idaho Falls and book it for Burke and Hornbeck instead."

"Ash?" Faith's strawberry blonde eyebrows pulled into a frown. "What do you think you're doing?"

Following my instincts.

"Call me on my cell if you run into any problems," he told Diane, then hung up the phone.

"You're going to North Carolina, aren't you?"

He didn't miss the accusation in Faith's tone. "What do you think?" he answered, his mind zeroing in on Greer and whatever she might already be facing. Not only professionally but personally. He'd witnessed the nightmares during the weeks she'd been hospitalized, the stark fear that had clouded her vivid blue eyes, scaring him half to death. He had no choice now but to step in and assume jurisdiction, if only to protect Greer from the past.

"Ash, don't do it. For you to even consider involving ISU in an investigation, there has to be no less than three murder victims, various crime scenes or at the very least three different body dumps and a noticeable cooling-off period between the crimes."

He hauled an empty Bankers Box from under his desk and packed it with files to take with him. "Have you seen my laptop?"

Faith folded her arms. "No."

He found the black leather case nestled beside the bookcase crammed with books, reams of computer printouts and old case files.

"You can't seriously believe this is a good idea."

He wasn't that stupid. The odds weren't exactly in his favor and he knew it. He understood he could be making one more in an already long list of mistakes where Greer was concerned. When she realized what she was up against, she'd need him, and that's all that mattered to him now. Hell, she's all that had ever really mattered.

"A good idea?" He laughed, the sound caustic, bordering on bitter. "Not by a long shot. But I have to go to her." He set his laptop next to the box of files.

Faith's glare turned frigid. "Dammit, Ash. Would you stop and think for a minute exactly what you're about to do?"

"I have."

"No, you haven't. There's been no official request to assist," she argued. "Only one incident has been reported and not only is there no evidence the case is even a serial, there isn't a shred of proof a crime has been committed across state lines. You have no authority to assume jurisdiction."

"Then find me the evidence," he told her.

"Would you think of Greer for a minute? Do you even care what your showing up could do to her?"

Greer was all he ever thought about. All he cared about.

He came out from behind his desk. "She's the reason I'm going," he said, reaching behind the door for his jacket.

Faith let out a stream of breath full of frustration. She shoved his office door closed. "That's a load of bull," she challenged him. "This is about nothing but your goddamn ego."

His patience took a sharp nosedive. "You're out of line," he said, his voice as glacial as the look in his friend's eyes.

Faith planted her hands on her hips. "Ask me if I care. This is about you still holding yourself responsible for what went down in Phoenix."

"Unless you care to turn in your credentials, Agent Pettit," he said, his voice tight with anger, "I suggest you mind your own fucking business."

Faith glared right back at him. Just the way Greer used to do whenever he'd pulled rank on her.

"Don't bully me," she spat out, her tone low and heated. "I'm telling you this as your friend, not your goddamn flunky, so you can just shove the hard-ass routine. It doesn't fly with me."

He didn't have to listen to this shit, and made a move to step around her before his temper shot through the roof. She stepped with him, blocking his path.

"You can't fix what happened to Greer in Phoenix," she continued. "As tragic as it was, it's over. You're both alive. Move on, Ash. Greer has, in case you haven't noticed."

Oh, he'd noticed all right, and he sure as hell didn't like Faith reminding him of the fact. He'd been the one left in the dust while Greer packed her things and moved out, never once looking back to see the damage she'd left behind.

In the beginning he'd attempted to contact her, but she'd never returned his calls. Eventually she'd changed her number. His e-mails to her went unanswered, then eventually bounced. She'd changed her e-mail address, too. He'd been tempted to use Bureau resources to keep tabs on her. Not exactly one of his proudest, or most ethical, moments, but he'd come to his senses before stooping to the level of stalker.

He shrugged into his jacket. "Just e-mail me whatever you find," he told Faith, purposely changing the subject. "I should be in Magnolia in a few hours."

"What am I supposed to tell Con when he asks where you've gone?"

That I'm out of my freaking mind.

"Nothing." He slung the strap of his garment bag over

his shoulder. After tucking the box of files under his arm, he snagged his laptop case. "I'll handle Con."

Later, he thought. Once he was buried ass deep in whatever shit storm his gut told him was heading straight for Greer.

Faith moved to the door, her hand stilling on the knob. "I hope you know what you're doing."

So did he, but he wasn't holding his breath. When it came to his borderline obsession with Greer, he didn't have so much as a clue to what he was doing. And that, he thought as he left his office, wasn't exactly headline news.

Chapter 5

THERE HAD BEEN a time, not all that long ago, when a murder investigation would've been Greer's sole focus. She would've been chasing down leads, examining evidence, viewing crime scenes, attending victim autopsies and using every skill she'd honed to develop a profile of the UNSUB. That she would take time out to prepare a shrimp-and-spinach quiche for a lunch date with her sister would've been inconceivable.

Maybe she wasn't as screwed up as she thought.

She cleaned the last of the shrimp and felt a moment of gratitude that the person she'd been no longer existed. Upon the discovery of the body buried with Lowell Archer, she'd teetered dangerously close to slipping back into the same old destructive patterns but, thankfully, had come to her senses and distanced herself from the Trina Stewart homicide investigation as much as possible, leaving much of it to Travis despite his objections.

And it was driving her nuts.

She wasn't used to maintaining distance from a case, but she couldn't allow herself to become obsessed. No more working around the clock for her, or becoming so involved in an investigation that her health suffered.

Constantly reminding herself there was more to life than

work helped somewhat. When that failed, she allowed herself a brief moment to recall the hard lesson that had almost killed her—literally. She didn't like thinking about her close brush with death, because it was too easy for her to throw herself a pity party. Unfortunately she'd been feeling melancholy ever since she'd schlepped out of bed at three in the morning after a few restless hours of dreams filled with disjointed, frightening images.

The brief reprieve she'd been granted from the terrors in the dark had been revoked without warning. She didn't need her therapist to point out that her bad dreams had been triggered by the discovery inside Archer's casket. What she did need, however, was a night of uninterrupted, dreamless sleep. Her only solace stemmed from not having suffered a single panic attack, which usually accompanied the nightmares that continued to haunt her.

She rinsed the cleaned shrimp, then set the stainless colander on the six-foot-long, granite-topped island in the center of the only completely remodeled room in the house. She attempted to concentrate on cutting the shrimp into bite-sized pieces, but the mundane task gave her mind an opportunity to wander, right back to the Stewart investigation.

"Progress, my ass," she complained, then let out a weighty sigh. Apparently more of the old Greer existed than she cared to admit.

After two weeks she had more questions than she had answers. She couldn't let them go, either, as the questions constantly nagged at her.

She wanted to know exactly how the embalmed body of a fifty-two-year-old woman ended up in an occupied coffin. She'd interviewed Archer's pallbearers and Jerome Jackson, the funeral director of the Magnolia Funeral Home who'd handled the Archer interment. Not one of them recalled anything unusual.

Before the lab rats had arrived, she'd examined the casket herself, but had found no abnormalities. Not for a second did she consider it a coincidence that Stewart's son reported his mother missing around the time of Archer's funeral. Yet, as far as she'd been able to determine, no connection between Stewart and Archer existed—at least while they'd both had a pulse.

The doorbell sputtered in a mocking semblance of melodic chimes. Grateful for the distraction, she dried her damp hands as she glanced at the clock over the stove. No way could that be Vivi. Her sister wouldn't dream of arriving a second earlier than the agreed-upon time. Why, anything else would be considered ill-mannered and rude.

"Heaven forbid," she said, resurrecting the Southern drawl she'd shed in college.

She glanced out the bay window of the nook as she passed. A smile curved her lips when she spied Selma's shiny red Dodge pickup truck rather than her sister's BMW, a parting gift from Vivi's second ex-husband. Or was it her third?

In the narrow hallway, she stepped over Eula, the Bulldog she'd reluctantly adopted. When Eula's previous owner had passed, the dog had been destined for the canine gas chamber. Greer hadn't been able to leave Eula on the animal shelter's answer to death row. She'd taken the contrary animal home in hopes of finding her a suitable home, but Eula remained Greer's roommate. And as cantankerous, opinionated and lazy as ever.

The dog lay on her back, spread-eagled and snoring, her chubby pink belly exposed. The dog didn't so much as twitch a whisker or open a droopy eye at the second sputtering ring of the door chimes.

"I'm trading you in for a Doberman first chance I get," Greer threatened.

Eula kept snoring.

Greer entered the foyer, rich with the scent of freshly var-

nished oak of the balustrade of the grandiose staircase leading to the second level of her beloved, if mostly ramshackle,
Queen Anne Victorian. She peered through the new double-
paned glass of the side panel to be sure it was indeed Selma,
then opened the door.

"Why didn't you use the key?" Greer asked her oldest
friend and the handiest carpenter to ever swing a hammer.
Selma stood on the partially refurbished veranda, dressed to
make an impression in a short, creamy-white skirt and an
electric-blue silk, scoop-necked tank that showed off her
statuesque frame perfectly.

"I take no chances." Selma strode into the foyer and
handed Greer a sleek leather portfolio. "After the time I
walked in on the Clearys doing the nasty on their dining
room table," she said, kicking off a pair of black spike-
heeled pumps, "I learned a valuable lesson. *Always* ring the
bell first."

Greer's eyebrows winged skyward. "Gerald Cleary has to
be, what? Seventy-nine? Eighty?"

"Viagra," Selma said with a husky laugh, scooping up
her shoes. "The stuff of geriatric wet dreams."

Greer snickered as she led Selma to the kitchen. She didn't
bother to remind her friend there wasn't a snowball's
chance in hell of her being caught doing the nasty anytime
soon—and not because they hadn't finished the renovations
on the formal dining room, either. She kept quiet, knowing
if she said a word, she'd end up enduring one of Selma's
well-meaning lectures on the pathetic status of her sexual
habits—or lack thereof. Not that she was in any position to
even consider having sex. Yet one more piece of her puzzled
past she carefully avoided thinking about—*ever*.

"Is this what I think it is?" Greer asked hopefully, opening the portfolio. She pulled out two poster-sized sketches
and set them side by side on the round, antiqued white
dinette table.

An image flashed through her mind, so vivid and real her entire universe tilted upside-down, then shifted sideways. She grabbed hold of the back of the nearest chair and held on tight to the top rail, her grip so hard her knuckles turned white.

"Two options for revisions to the attic space," Selma said.

Greer heard the dull thud of Selma's pumps hitting the floor, but her mind had already started to slip into the past, trapping her. Instead of the cozy table in the freshly painted nook, she saw a square metal table covered with large glossy photographs. Bodies of women. Too many women, each sliced from throat to pubis, their bluish-tinted flesh open, revealing empty cavities. She tried to count the bodies, but they kept multiplying.

"The designer was able to include the built-in storage cabinets you wanted." Selma's voice drifted farther away, hollow and tinny, until the husky undertones became nothing more than unintelligible, distorted sounds.

The photographs faded and Greer was held down by thin, dampened leather bindings she felt cutting into the tender flesh of her wrists and ankles. The stench of rotted flesh assailed her nostrils as she stared helplessly into the cold black eyes of death.

Selma nudged Greer with her shoulder. "Hey!" she said in a sharp tone. "Where are you?"

Greer swayed. "Sorry," she murmured and blinked several times as the images slowly faded. "My mind's been wandering all day." An understatement.

"No kidding." Selma's gaze grew intent with concern. "Jesus, Greer, what just happened? You're so pale all of a sudden. Are you sure you're all right?"

Loosening her death grip on the chair, Greer rolled her shoulders. She drew in much-needed oxygen in an attempt to recapture her composure. "It's nothing. I'm fine." A weak grin was the best she could offer by way of confirmation. "I skipped breakfast, is all."

Selma didn't look convinced.

Greer widened her grin. "Stop worrying and tell me again about the designs."

The skepticism remained in Selma's golden-brown eyes. "I had said if you want the additional storage space in the attic," Selma repeated, "then you'll have to decide between one larger guestroom with a private bath, or two smaller guestrooms with a shared bath in between."

Greer nodded, but avoided looking at the sketches again by returning to the island to finish the quiche. She hadn't experienced a flashback since she'd moved into the house. Nightmares, yes, those she battled on an almost-nightly basis, but the unexpected reappearance of flashbacks made her nervous. God forbid she become trapped in her own mind while on duty—with a loaded gun at her side. The possibilities of what could happen chilled her.

The renovations to the one hundred fifty-year-old Victorian she'd purchased for a song not long after returning to Magnolia had served as her emotional balm—until now. Whenever the past crowded her, or the nightmares were too vivid and realistic, she turned to the old house for solace. Rather than drowning in a container of Ben & Jerry's or a fifth of vodka, she'd remove varnish, strip wallpaper or tackle any number of the ongoing projects on the eight-bed-room monstrosity she called home.

The Bureau's shrink had suggested she immerse herself in some sort of creative project, or find a useful, distracting hobby that would give her a sense of purpose again. Knitting would've been a lot less expensive, but the old, abandoned house had been just what she'd thought she needed at the time. Renovating a thirty-eight-hundred-square-foot Victorian promised a couple decades' worth of distraction.

When she was a little girl every day on her way to and from school, she'd passed the old house and had slowly fallen in love with its unique character and quaint charm. She'd always dreamed of owning it, and so was thrilled when she got a chance to purchase the dilapidated Victorian. Its location in the center of town fueled her insane idea of converting it into a bed and breakfast. The plan had been so completely illogical, yet it had made perfect sense to Greer. Making a life-altering decision when she obviously hadn't been in her right mind might not have been the smartest move she'd ever made, but she possessed enough self-awareness to recognize the emotional significance of her choice. The once-grand old place wasn't all she needed to restore.

As usual, her mother hadn't understood and had been scandalized by her plans. Her stepfather took his usual pragmatic approach and helped arrange the financing for the renovations. Her sister, Vivien Lee, had been too self-absorbed in the drama of another divorce to pay more than cursory attention. About the only person not convinced she'd gone crazy had been Selma, even if her friend's motives were questionable since Selma had much to gain from Greer's momentarily lapse of reason.

"Let me sleep on it for a couple of days," Greer said, referring to the revised design plans. A definite figure of speech, since she hadn't slept more than twelve hours in the past four days. Maybe sleep deprivation had spurred the waking nightmare. She could only hope.

"Just don't think too long." Selma shot her a meaningful glance as she tucked the sketches back inside the leather portfolio. "Or you'll end up changing your mind—again."

Selma did have a point, Greer thought, as she set green onions on the cutting board. She hadn't always had such trouble making decisions, or sticking to a plan of action.

Lately, the more time she spent weighing the consequences of her available options, the more confused she became until finally, she put off making any decision whatsoever.

She paused with the knife midair. "We'd probably be finished by now if I wasn't always altering the designs."

Selma helped herself to a Diet Coke from the fridge. "Ages ago," she said, pulling out a stool on the other side of the island.

Greer frowned. "Has it been that bad?" she asked worriedly.

"I'm teasing," Selma told her. "What is with you today?"

Greer shrugged and chopped up the green onions. "Must be hormones."

She whipped up the eggs, sprinkled in a few spices, then added the shrimp, spinach and green onions before stirring in the feta cheese. "Stay for lunch?" she asked, pouring the mixture into a deep-dish pie shell. She crumbled more feta over the top, then set the quiche in the oven to bake. "Vivi should be here in a few minutes."

"Only if you promise I won't have to break bread with the Dragon Lady."

A smile tugged Greer's lips. "Don't worry. Mama June refuses to step foot in this place until . . . How did she put it?"

"The dump burns to the ground?"

"No," she said, and laughed as she reached into the built-in hutch for her good dishware. "'Until the old girl is properly suited to receive guests.'"

Selma rolled her eyes as she slipped off the stool and took the luncheon plates from Greer. "Guess that means you'll be spared for years the way you keep changing things." She walked to the table, then added with a sly grin, "Sounds Freudian to me."

"Gee, you think?" Greer shot back. She did love her mother, but it was no secret they rarely shared the same opinion—on any subject. Greer's career, her choice in real estate, her marital status and her adoption of Eula, to name but a few.

"Davis stops by fairly regularly and keeps Mama apprised of the progress."

"Of course he does," Selma said, her voice dripping with sarcasm. "You do realize he's her spy."

Selma's attitude was nothing more than a deep-seated defense mechanism when it came to dealing with Mama June and her blue-blooded cronies. Her mother and her so-called friends were nothing more than snobs, plain and simple. Her mother had disapproved of her friendship with a girl of "questionable lineage," but Selma's illegitimacy never made a difference to Greer, or to Davis, who often counseled Selma on her own financial concerns. The blue bloods' unfavorable opinion of Selma had taken an even deeper nosedive when she'd dropped out of college, returned to town to sling a tool belt around her hips and took over her late mother's construction business.

"You gonna tell me what's up with the girl clothes today?" Greer went to the fridge for the ingredients for salad dressing. "Or do I have to guess?"

Selma's wide mouth eased into a smile as she climbed back on the stool. "A meeting with the designer hottie, remember?"

"Ah . . ." For months Selma had been lusting after the designer Greer had hired. No wonder she never protested whenever Greer decided to alter the renovation plans. "Any luck this time?"

Selma wrinkled her nose. "I swear, the man has to be gay. The girls are chafed from brushing up against him all morning."

Greer laughed. "You are such a slut," she teased.

"A damn pitiful one, let me tell you," Selma complained.

"This gawd-awful uncomfortable push-up bra was a fifty-dollar waste of time. He didn't so much as peek, drool or lust once over my magnificent cleavage." She took a drink of her soda. "And I gave that idiot more than enough opportunity, bending over his drawing table. Do you realize the kind of strain that puts on a girl's back when she's used to wearing construction boots all day long?"

"Maybe he's not into tall, smart-ass brunettes."

Selma drummed her fingers on the counter. "Naaah. He's gay," she said, then narrowed her gaze. "Maybe he prefers half-pint, stubborn, opinionated blondes. Next time, you go and we'll see if he hits on you."

"Sure, Sel. Like that'll tell you if he's batting for the other side."

"Or catching."

"No thanks." Greer lowered her eyes. She wasn't interested in any man, even if he was a hottie. Living like a nun was wiser. The last thing she needed were more complications in her life, especially emotionally messy ones. One of these days she might even get around to tying up a few loose ends she'd left dangling because she hadn't been able to cope with another emotional minefield. Maybe.

Someday she'd deal with her past. Just not today.

She looked over at Selma. "Why don't you just ask him out and get it over with?"

"Why, Miss Greer, how could you suggest such a thing?" Selma feigned a look of pure innocence and batted her long, sooty lashes. "A Southern lady would never dream of making such a bold move."

Laughter bubbled up inside Greer. "Oh, that's rich. And suspiciously hypocritical, coming from you." Selma lacked the shy and coy genes. She was, however, overly compensated with a triple dose of bold and brazen.

"That must be Vivi," Greer said as a car pulled into the drive.

Selma glanced out the window and gasped. "Guess who's coming to dinner?"

"Mama? No." She did not want to deal with her mother. Not today when her emotions were already scraped raw.

"Uh-huh. And she's nagging poor Vivi about something, by the looks of it." Selma shuddered and slid off the stool. "Put me down for a rain check on that lunch."

"Selma, stay. Please," Greer pleaded.

"The woman hates me," she argued.

"Mama doesn't hate you."

"Strong disapproval, then. One rejection per day is my limit."

"If you leave me here alone with her, I swear I'll never make another alteration to the designs. It'll be bye-bye Hot Design Man."

"Like that would ever happen," Selma scoffed and went to retrieve her shoes.

Greer's cell phone rang at the same time the doorbell gave a pathetic sputter. "It won't be that bad." Greer crossed the kitchen for her cell. "It'll be worth it just to hear about Vivi's new man-hunting method. She's resorted to on-line dating in search of her next marital casualty."

Selma shook her head. "God help Victim Number Four. I hope he has a better lawyer than the previous three."

Greer plucked the cell from the charging unit. "Hello?"

"Greer, it's Blythe."

"Hold on a sec." Greer covered the receiver with the pad of her thumb and shot Selma one last pleading glance. "I'm begging, Sel."

Her friend let out a long, weary sigh. "Okay, you win. But it'll cost you—big time. I don't care how fabulous the new designs are going to be for the renovations of the formal sitting room, you're rejecting them."

"Promise," she said and let loose with a sigh of her own, one filled with relief. She'd much rather run interference for

Selma than be subjected to Mama June's disapproval herself.

"I'll set another place," Selma said as Greer left the kitchen to answer the front door.

"Sorry, bout that, Blythe," she said after lifting the cell phone to her ear.

"No problem," the dispatcher said in a rush. "I'm really sorry to be botherin' you on your day off, but there's a situation and Travis needs you out at the cemetery in Cornwall Cove pronto."

She opened the door and waved her mother and sister inside. "Vandals?" she asked, but from the urgency in Blythe's voice, she doubted she'd be getting off that easy.

"No. An open grave," Blythe said. "And a DB."

Greer's skin went from cold to clammy in a single, thundering heartbeat. Her legs started to tremble and she reached for the balustrade for support. "Tell me."

"Caucasian, Female. Early- to midtwenties. The ME is on-site." Blythe paused for a moment. "Greer?"

"Yeah?" The hesitancy in Blythe's voice had Greer's stomach churning with dread.

"Travis said to tell you the body's been embalmed."

Chapter 6

THIRTY MINUTES LATER, Greer pulled her Ford Escape into the dusty gravel lot outside the cemetery at St. Andrew's parish in the picturesque small town of Cornwall Cove, located on the northwestern edge of the county line. She dreaded whatever awaited her on the other side of the wrought iron fence surrounding the graveyard, and almost would have preferred sticking around at home to see what had prompted her mother's unexpected arrival with Vivi. But Travis would never have instructed Blythe to call her in on the first day off she'd had in the past ten if the body found at Cornwall Cove and the Stewart homicide investigation weren't somehow connected.

So much for her passing the buck.

She parked to the right of the pair of police cruisers. To her left, near the open gate, she saw two vehicles she didn't recognize. The groundskeeper, she thought, from the looks of the battered, oxidized silver Chevy pickup. The nondescript dark blue Chrysler sedan next to the truck more than likely belonged to an official from the Cornwall Cove town council, on-site making ridiculous and impossible demands on an overworked, understaffed Sheriff's Department still operating without a budget.

She opened the center console and snagged the badge

clipped to the end of a black lanyard and slipped it over her head before exiting the vehicle. In the distance, she spied the coroner's transport, parked on the grounds amid the rows of granite and marble headstones. Reality sucked. Her reality, in particular.

She stopped with her hand on the door of her Escape. What was she doing walking headfirst into another nightmare? She should climb back inside her four-by-four and drive away while she still had the chance. Her mother and sister hadn't been too pleased with her for running out the minute they'd arrived. Making amends and kissing her mother's society ass was suddenly preferable to inspecting a crime scene.

Once Greer had assured her miffed mother she'd stop by her place later, she'd gone directly to her closet for the shoulder holster she hadn't worn since leaving the Bureau, as if it was the most natural act in her world. She'd half-expected the leather to feel confining, restrictive or, at the very least, uncomfortable. But after the first few minutes, she barely noticed the holster or the weight of the weapon tucked securely inside. She'd thrown on a lightweight lemon linen blazer over the pink and white-checked sleeveless shirt she'd been wearing with her faded jeans, thanked Selma for offering to lock up once the quiche finished baking, and left.

Knowing she had no other choice, she slammed the door to her SUV and walked hesitantly through the gated archway. The scent of freshly mown grass assailed her as she cut across the grounds to where Travis and Manny Cantrell waited for her by the gravesite. Damp grass clippings clung to her white sneakers, staining the edges green, and she swore. Damp grass made it difficult to locate trace evidence, which had more than likely been washed away by the automatic sprinklers during the predawn hours.

Tate Orson, the department's rookie deputy, waved to

her as she approached. She hadn't even noticed him leaning, arms crossed, against a marble monument a good twenty feet or more from where Travis and Manny were crouched next to the body of a young woman. Without seeing her face, Greer quickly confirmed Travis's estimate of the girl's age. She based her assessment on the updated style of the short, brightly patterned summer dress; the long length and shine of her heavily streaked hair; the sleek perfection of her tanned, bare legs; and the long fingernails, painted in bold neon shades in an airbrushed design.

She shifted her gaze to safer territory and caught sight of a tall man in the distance with short-cropped hair, brown or black, she couldn't quite determine. His shoulders were broad and he wore a well-fitted dark navy suit, totally unsuitable for the rising heat and high humidity of a midsummer Southern day. He took notes as he spoke to a shorter, heavyset guy wearing dingy denim coveralls and a desert camouflage ball cap. A pain-in-the-ass reporter, hungry for a story, no doubt.

"What's he doing here?" she asked Tate, inclining her head in the general direction of the reporter.

"Interviewing the groundskeeper who made the 911 call," the rookie answered. "I was first on the scene."

Greer nodded, but her mind was drawn back to the *New York Times* wannabe. He could conduct all the interviews he wanted, but not a single word would make it to print until she was prepared to release a public statement. The department didn't need a panic on their hands. Besides, she'd never been above using the press to her advantage on a case and she wasn't about to have information released before she knew exactly what she was dealing with, even if she did have a pretty good idea.

The reporter flipped his small notebook closed and tucked it into the inside pocket of his jacket. Greer frowned. Something about the way the guy moved, in a relaxed, almost careless or bored manner as he continued to speak to the groundskeeper, sparked a familiar chord she couldn't quite place. Despite his casual stance, she had the distinct impression he was completely aware of everything around him, including her arrival.

He turned his head in her direction and her stomach muscles tightened. Dark sunglasses shielded his eyes, but she had little doubt he was scrutinizing her just the same.

A chill passed over her skin and she trembled despite the stifling humidity. "Don't let him leave until I speak with him," she instructed Tate.

Suddenly uncomfortable, she turned away and carefully approached the gaping hole in the ground. Wood planks were placed inside the grave, shoring up the interior dirt walls, preventing them from caving. Whoever did the digging knew *precisely* what he was doing.

Since avoiding the body lying next to the grave was out of the question, she slowly circled the opening, looking for any clue left behind or the tiniest bit of trace evidence. She glanced at the marker, indicating the final resting place of Thomas Gartner, age twenty-six, beloved son who'd passed away close to six weeks ago.

When she reached Travis and Manny, she forced herself to crouch beside the ME, next to the body. "Any guess about cause of death?"

The coroner pulled out a pair of rubber gloves from his pocket and handed them to her. "I'll know more when I get her on my table, but she's been embalmed."

That certainly explained the girl's unnatural, waxy complexion. "Same as Stewart?" Greer asked him.

"Not quite." Manny lifted the woman's hair from her neck and pressed his gloved finger below an incision near the carotid artery. "Typical instrument insertion point for embalming," he explained. "This little lady received the full service package, too."

He gently pried open the victim's mouth. Bright red lipstick uncharacteristic for such a young girl, stained the tip of Manny's glove. Greer ground her teeth and struggled to maintain an even flow of breath as the image of bloody fingerprints flashed in her mind.

Lipstick, she reminded herself. It's only lipstick. She witnessed the transference but that didn't stop the flashback from flickering like a strobe light in her mind.

Travis groaned as he hefted his bulky frame to stand. "I'm getting too old for this crap," he complained, his voice gruff and raspy from too many cheap cigars.

"Laying off the blueberry muffins wouldn't hurt, either," Greer said to him and flashed him a cheesy grin, grateful for the timely distraction.

He gave her a dirty look, then mopped the sweat from his forehead with the handkerchief he'd pulled out from the pocket of his uniform. Travis Willows wasn't exactly heavy-set, but the fiftysomething sheriff had developed a noticeable middle-aged paunch in recent years.

Manny coughed to hide a smirk. Tate chuckled.

"Take a closer look at this," Manny said to Greer. He pulled up the vic's top lip to reveal a thin wire with a hooked barb on one end. The wire had been inserted into the upper gum line. "See the swelling?" he asked, indicating the upper lip.

Greer nodded, her mind filling with questions from the implication of Manny's find. The Stewart woman had also been embalmed, but the UNSUB hadn't gone to the same lengths as he had with the most recent vic. Was he changing his MO? And if so, why?

The hair on the back of her neck stood on end. "The damage isn't postmortem."

"I'm afraid not." Manny repeated the process with the victim's lower lip. He revealed another wire in the vic's lower gum line as well as more swelling. "If she'd already been embalmed, there'd have been no blood left in the body, so no swelling would've occurred."

Travis walked up behind her to look over her shoulder, his bulk shielding her from the blazing sun overhead. "Jesus," he whispered. "You mean to tell me this poor girl was alive when the sick bastard did this to her?"

Greer's stomach rolled and she blindly gripped Manny's beefy forearm to keep from tumbling headfirst into the open grave. She worked to maintain her breathing, but felt as if her airway was slowly being constricted.

Not now, she prayed. *Please.*

She tried to stand, but her knees were suddenly weak. She teetered on the balls of her feet, but Travis's hand on her elbow helped steady her as she slowly stood.

"The vic was prepared for burial while she was still breathing," she told Travis. "That wasn't the case with the Stewart woman." She yanked off the rubber gloves and stared down at the lifeless, waxlike face of the pretty young girl whose life had been snuffed to fulfill the twisted fantasy of a sociopath with no regard for human life.

Manny rose to his feet and pulled off his own gloves. "I'll need to do an autopsy to be sure, but that's my initial opinion as well."

"Christ almighty," Travis said, mopping his forehead again. "What kind of sick son of a bitch does something like this?"

Still unable to look away from the girl, Greer shook her head. "I don't know," she lied. God help her, she did know. She knew exactly the kind of person capable of such an inhuman act.

An organized killer.

"What do you mean, *'you don't know?'*" Travis demanded, his voice surprisingly sharp. "You have to know. You've been trained to know."

Methodical. Attention to detail. An older man. Thirty to

forty, possibly older. Someone with a working knowledge of mortuary science.

"No." She looked at Travis. She understood the deep scowl, felt the same anger now lighting in his eyes, just as she'd always done when faced with such horrible brutality. But what Travis would never understand was that he was one of the lucky ones. He'd never been subjected to the ugliness she'd seen on a day-to-day basis. He didn't know what something like this could do to her. "Not anymore I don't."

She wouldn't, couldn't let him pull her back into a world from which she'd narrowly escaped with her life. Travis was asking too much of her if he thought she was going to handle what she knew, clear down to her toes, was a serial. He was asking so much more than she had left to give.

His frown turned even more fierce, and she swore she detected a brief flash of panic in his gaze. "You're running the investigation, Lomax," he said, his voice as hard as the steely glint of his eyes.

Manny laid a hand on the sheriff's shoulder. "Take it easy, Travis."

He shrugged off Manny's grasp. "No. She's got the experience to stop this bastard before he kills again."

And for every victim she couldn't save, she'd suffer. No way could she subject herself to that kind of pain and expect to survive a second time. The power to rid the world of monsters, even one at a time, did not belong to her. It never had. A lesson she'd learned the hardest way imaginable before she finally got it through her thick ego. She would not risk another person's life just to prove she was right.

"Goddammit, Travis," she snapped. "I don't want it."

"How many more women have to die because you no longer have the guts?"

Manny stepped between them. "Okay, that's enough."

She shouldered past Manny and faced Travis. "Don't you

dare lay this on me," she argued heatedly. "I quit profiling, in case you've forgotten."

"This is your investigation." His frustration with her caused his voice to rise. "End of discussion."

She glared at her boss and longtime family friend. "What part of *no* didn't you understand? I don't want it."

"That's just too goddamn bad. It's your investigation, Deputy. Now, do your job."

Her temper soared to the point where her entire body shook with the force of her rising anger. "That sounds suspiciously like an order, Sheriff Willows," she said, her voice as cold and hard as Travis's.

"It was."

"Forget it. I quit." She turned to walk away, but Tate Olson blocked her path.

"Her name was Joanna Webb," he said, his voice soft and hesitant.

Greer frowned. "Excuse me?"

"Joanna Webb," Tate said again. "I think she's about twenty. I'd heard she moved to New Bern to go to beauty school."

"How do you know her?" she automatically asked.

Travis came up beside her. "Tate?" he prompted when the rookie remained silent.

Tate let out a sigh. "She dated my kid brother back in high school."

"Where's your brother now?" she asked him.

Irritation flashed in Tate's blue eyes as he pulled off his hat. "On a cattle ranch up near Bozeman, Montana," he said, shoving his hand through his wavy blond hair. "He's been there since he went off to college two years ago. He'll be starting his junior year at UM in the fall."

"I'm sorry, Tate," she apologized. "I had to ask."

He nodded his understanding, but it was clear he didn't appreciate her line of questioning.

"A local girl," Travis said. "One of our own. Still willing to walk away?"

"The crime lab will be here any minute now," Manny said to her before she could answer Travis. "If you want to take a look around before they show up, you'd better do it now."

She didn't want to look around. She didn't want the investigation. Period. But dammit, now she realized she couldn't walk away, either, not when she knew she had the skills, however rusty, to end the UNSUB's murders. She only hoped she survived the aftermath.

She turned and glared at Travis. "I'm going to hate you for this," she told him.

Travis responded with a relieved sigh. "You'll get over it."

"Just forget being invited to Mama June's annual Christmas open house."

Travis winked at her and she tossed him a narrow-eyed hiss before walking back to the open grave and Manny. "Get rid of that reporter," she said irritably to Travis. "Make sure he knows he's not to print a word until he hears from me."

Travis's smug expression faded into one of confusion. "What reporter?"

She pointed to where she'd last seen the *NYT* wannabe. "That . . ."

"Hello, Greer."

The husky undertone of *that* voice slammed into her with all the subtlety of a runaway freight train. ". . . reporter," she finished weakly as she turned around and faced her past.

The air between them sizzled. She looked into the breathtakingly handsome face of the one man from whom she had no secrets.

The high-pitched ringing in her ears deafened her. The

ground beneath her feet shifted. This simply could not be happening. Why did that damn loose end she'd left dangling for so long now have to become a noose tied around her neck? Why today?

Ash.

Her every dream, her every regret rolled into one painful reality staring her in the face. Those delicious dark brown eyes once filled with affection were now colder than the granite headstone behind him. She expected, no, deserved, nothing less.

"What the hell are *you* doing here?" she blurted rudely. The suit. She should've known. Standard FBI blue, she thought, remembering her own closet, once filled with the same dull rainbow of subdued hues.

"The report you filed with VICAP. It was brought to my attention."

"Faith." Who else? Faith worked closely with Ash, and had been the only person she'd kept in contact with at the Bureau for a short time after she'd left. Of course Faith would've passed the report on to him. She was Ash's eyes, ears, nose and throat, for crying out loud.

Ash nodded. There was an underlying arrogance to the slight curve of his mouth that set her teeth on edge one second, then made her as nervous as a whore trapped in a confessional with a judgmental priest the next.

"And you thought you'd just come on down and take over my investigation, is that it?"

Travis cleared his throat. "I thought you—"

She glared at her boss, warning him to shut up. True, she wanted no part of the investigation, and now having Ash breathing down her neck wasn't something she was anywhere close to being able to handle, either.

Thankfully, Travis wasn't a stupid man. "Never mind," he said, then clamped his teeth around a half-smoked, unlit cigar.

A glinting flash of light caught her eye when Ash moved his hands to tuck them into the front pockets of his trousers. Probably just the sun reflecting off his watch, she thought. Anything else was unthinkable.

"You know how the system works, Greer," he said with a slight shrug of his shoulders.

"You're right. I do. And this case doesn't come close to meeting the criteria for ISU's involvement. I don't recall a section in the manual about steamrolling an investigation, either. You're not wanted here, Ash." She didn't want him anywhere near her. "Go home."

He leaned toward her and she breathed in his scent. Flashbacks of a different kind peppered her. A private celebration. Candlelight. Champagne. Making love until dawn. His hands, his mouth. Never getting enough of each other.

"You develop a sudden understanding of the word?" he asked in a low voice with enough of a hint of controlled anger to push her past the edge of reason.

"Go to hell, Ash," she snapped angrily. "You know exactly—"

"Excuse me," Travis interrupted, "but is there something going on I should know about?"

Ash straightened and looked at Travis. "I'm here to assist."

"Assist with what?" Greer railed. "We haven't made a determination that we're even looking at a repeat offender." The similarities of the crimes were no coincidence, and they all knew it. She was grasping, and they knew that, too.

Ash let out an impatient sigh. "You're in over your head, Greer."

"The hell I am." She was sick and tired of everyone around her trying to tell her what was best for her. Her mother, her sister, her stepfather, her boss, even her best friend. And now Ash? As if he still had the right to interfere in her life? She didn't think so. Okay, fine. So maybe she was a fucked-up emotional mess. That didn't mean she was incapable of making her own decisions or trusting her own judgment.

Most of the time.

"You know exactly what you could be facing." His tone turned as calm as a lake in summer, and irritating as hell. "Are you really ready to deal with it?"

Of course she wasn't, but . . .

"That doesn't give you the right to take over my investigation."

"I have the authority to claim jurisdiction and you know it."

Travis stepped up and nudged Greer aside. "Now you wait just a goddamn minute—"

"You want it? Take it. Just leave me the hell alone." She looked up at her boss. "You heard him, Travis. This matter is no longer our concern. We can all go home and sleep easy now that Supercop is on the case."

She had a feeling she'd never sleep again now that Ash had showed up in Magnolia. She didn't want to think about why he'd come, but she wasn't stupid enough to believe the report she'd filed with VICAP was the only reason for his sudden appearance.

Travis yanked the unlit cigar from his mouth. "Just what the hell is going on here?" he demanded.

"Ask him," she said and folded her arms over her chest. "He's the one in charge now."

Travis gave her one of those impatient looks, the kind he used to nail her and Selma with when they were teenagers after they'd gotten into mischief. "I'm asking *you*, Deputy."

She felt cornered. Trapped. The air grew thick with tension, so thick her next breath took more energy than she had left.

Oh, God. Please. Please, not now.

"I'm not doing this." She peeled off her linen blazer,

shrugged out of her shoulder holster and shoved it at Travis. The lanyard holding her badge was next. "I quit."

She faced Ash while she still had the ability to draw breath. "Stay away from me," she said, then did what she did best. She ran.

"Greer, wait," Ash called after her.

She kept moving, struggling for breath, somehow managing to put one foot in front of the other. Until the ground swelled beneath her, then fell. She fell with it, desperately gasping for air.

She hit the warm, moist earth with a hard thud. Her forehead landed on the surface of something harder than grass and the world around her shifted to a murky gray. She tried to breathe, but the more she tried, the more her lungs were deprived of oxygen. She felt the vibration of pounding footsteps rushing toward her, but she couldn't move, couldn't escape. Travis's bellowed shout penetrated the sharp, tinny ringing in her ears, but she couldn't make out the words.

Seconds before blessed nothingness claimed her, she witnessed the stark fear in her husband's beautiful dark brown eyes as he scooped her into his arms. And for the first time in a very long time, she wasn't afraid.

Chapter 7

"WHAT DO YOU MEAN you're admitting me?" Greer hated hospitals. No way would she remain a single second longer than absolutely necessary. If that long. She detested the smells, the sounds, the poking and prodding, and she especially despised the resurfacing memories of the last time she'd been in an emergency room.

Claire Endicott let out an exaggerated sigh. "You have a concussion," she reminded Greer. "Humor me."

Greer attempted to sit. Big mistake, she realized too late. Surrendering to the horrendous pounding inside her skull, she eased back down on the bed. "I thought you said it was mild and nothing to be too concerned about?"

"Be that as it may, you were unconscious. Let's not take any chances, okay?" Claire set the chart on the bed and gave her a stern look. "With no one to keep an eye on you, you're staying, so stop arguing." A half-grin tipped the doctor's mouth. "I hear the food's not half bad."

Greer blew out a frustrated breath. "So says the health nut," she groused.

Claire's smile widened. "Doctor's orders."

"I'm getting a new doctor."

"You won't. We're friends, remember?"

"Wanna bet?"

A nurse Greer didn't recognize came around the curtain and handed Claire a sheaf of papers. "You're not exactly behaving like my favorite patient at the moment," Claire said to Greer.

"Yeah, well, you're not exactly acting like my favorite doctor, either."

"Sounds like a match made in heaven," the nurse said with a chuckle, then disappeared again.

Hardly, Greer thought, as Claire read the report the nurse had brought her. Heaven was the way Ash had held her close as she'd drifted in and out of consciousness during the drive to the hospital. Held her as if she still mattered to him, as if she hadn't torn both of their lives to shreds when she'd left everything behind because she'd been afraid.

Fear, she decided, was relative. Like any normal human being, the level of her fears varied by degree, ranging from concern to sheer terror.

The difficulty she had lately in making decisions had her moderately concerned. A symptom she understandably related to being preoccupied with the renovations on the house, family, her job and trying to make and stick to a solid plan for a future that didn't involve any form of law enforcement whatsoever.

Her nightmares spooked her, but her coping skills were showing improvement in that area. In her opinion, a cold sweat and a few moments of disorientation were preferable any night of the week to a full-blown anxiety attack.

Today's flashback scared the crap out of her, though. All she could do was hope the episode had been nothing more than an isolated incident, and not the warning shot she feared.

Many things frightened her these days, and that irritated her because there'd been a time when she had little to fear, least of all her own freaking shadow. But nothing sent the cold chill of fright sliding down her spine like the realization she'd had today when Ash had taken care of her. Not since The Preacher had stood above her with a scalpel in his hand had she felt safe. How was it that she'd felt so completely unafraid in the arms of the last person in the world she should trust to actually keep her that way?

The answer evaded her.

So what's new?

Claire set aside the report and checked Greer's pulse. "So, you going to tell me about the beefcake pacing the lobby like an expectant father?"

Greer's pulse picked up speed.

Claire's eyebrows shot up. "That good, huh?"

"You have an unfair advantage," Greer complained.

"Just one of the perks."

Greer wasn't prepared to answer questions about Ash, so she decided to keep quiet. Besides, what could she say that wouldn't create more curiosity? He wasn't her *ex* because neither of them had ever filed for divorce.

Estranged? Perhaps. Except, she didn't like the implication. In her mind, she associated estranged with marital problems, which didn't necessarily apply to them, at least in the classic, marriage-in-crisis sense.

She hadn't left because she'd stopped loving Ash. Essentially, she'd run away in a desperate attempt to forget all that had happened to her, to rediscover a sense of peace, something she'd never accomplish if every time she looked at Ash she'd be reminded of the most terrifying event in her life.

No, the problem had been hers and hers alone. One she'd somehow have to find the courage to face whether she was ready to or not.

The pastel-striped curtain moved suddenly, the guides scraping in their track. Ash. She should've known he'd make an appearance sooner rather than later. On all counts.

He circled the bed to her side, his expression framed in

concern. He had that ragged-around-the-edges look she'd seen before, and a fresh round of guilt started gnawing at her insides.

"How is she?" He posed the inquiry to Claire, but kept his gaze on Greer.

Greer looked away in time to see Claire peer at Ash over the rims of her square, metallic-turquoise glasses. "And who are you?"

"Her husband."

"Really?" Claire's burnished-red eyebrows hiked up again. "Greer never mentioned she was married."

Greer winced. Not from the pounding pain in her skull, but from the flash of hurt in her husband's beautiful brown eyes.

So much for keeping her marriage under wraps, she thought, as Claire and Ash exchanged introductions. Upon returning to Magnolia, she'd gone on the hunt for a physician to deal with the everyday, run-of-the-mill type of medical issues, and had specifically selected Claire Endicott because she'd been new to the area. She'd wanted someone unaware of her history, had wanted anonymity. To a degree that's exactly what she'd gotten—until the doctor–patient relationship evolved into friendship. Still, there were parts of her life Greer preferred to keep to herself. Like the state of her marriage for one, a subject she refused to think about, let alone discuss.

Claire smiled at Ash. "Physically, she'll be fine," she told him. "Her concussion is mild, but we're keeping her overnight just—"

"Like hell you are," Greer interrupted. She attempted, more successfully this time, to sit. "I don't need, or want, a baby-sitter."

"For the next twenty-four hours you do."

"Claire—"

"Stop being so damn stubborn. You have a concussion,

Greer. If you should become dizzy, you could fall. Maybe even lose consciousness again. That knot on the side of your head didn't happen because you blacked out, but because you hit something on the way down. Someone needs to be able to call 911, and I don't think Eula's going to be the one to do it."

Ash frowned. "Eula?"

"My dog."

Ash looked genuinely surprised. "You have a dog?"

Greer shrugged.

He turned his attention back to Claire. "If she really wants to go home, I'll stay with her."

"I don't think so," Greer said. Ash? Stay at her place? Was he nuts? She thought she was the only one in the room legally declared certifiable. Apparently there was room for two on the insanity express.

The move cost her dearly, but Greer slid off the hospital bed. "No." She reached for the closest object to steady herself as the room started to swim—which just happened to be Ash. "Thanks anyway," she told him, "but I can take care of myself."

He caught her before she landed flat on her face again. "I can see that," he said, helping her into the hard yellow plastic chair next to the bed. "Let Dr. Endicott admit you. It's only for one night."

"When hell freezes over." She'd had her fill of hospitals, thank you very much, and Ash of all people knew exactly how much. She should have Travis arrest him for even bringing her to one in the first place.

Claire let out a long-suffering sigh. "You're determined to go home?"

"Damn straight I am."

"Then either someone stays with you tonight, or you're checking in. Your choice."

"What is this? A conspiracy?"

"There's nothing wrong with your imagination," Claire said dryly. "Or your lousy attitude."

Greer glared at her friend. "I have a headache," she answered defensively. She saw only one way out of her current no-win situation. Lie.

"All right, you win," she fibbed. "This time."

"Good. But if you end up back here in the next twenty-four hours, your ass is mine, Lomax. Got it?"

Greer nodded, then rubbed her throbbing temple. "Got it. Just let me the hell out of here."

"I'll send a nurse back to help you dress." Claire looked at Ash. "If you'll come with me, I'll go over the discharge and after-care instructions. And don't let her buffalo you into thinking she'll be okay on her own."

"Don't worry, Doc," he said, following Claire. "I think I can still handle my wife."

That's what *he* thought, but Greer wisely kept her mouth shut for a change. There wasn't even a snowball's chance of survival in summer that Ash Keller would step so much as a foot in her house. She knew her limits and a night alone with Ash wasn't one of them.

"You call this a remodel?" Ash asked as he followed Greer down the hallway into the kitchen of the money pit she had the gall to refer to as a home. Everywhere he looked, some type of construction was ongoing in and around the aging Victorian.

She opened the refrigerator, pulled out a couple of cans of Diet Coke and handed him one. "The Bureau shrink suggested immersing myself in some sort of project could be helpful." She popped the top on the silvery can. "Guess I went a little overboard."

Setting his soda on the distressed white table in the nook, he shrugged out of his jacket and draped it over the back of a matching chair. "A little?"

She shrugged. "I needed something to keep me busy."

"Mission accomplished," he said dryly. He returned to the island, slid out one of the bar stools and sat. Other than to give him directions and thank him for having her car brought home for her by the deputy he'd met at the cemetery, she'd been silent on the drive to her place. They had a lot to say to each other, but he honestly didn't have an inkling of where to begin. Their marriage? The investigation? How much he wanted to kiss her and tell her how much he'd missed her?

Perched on the stool on the opposite side of the island with a wary expression, she appeared just as fragile as the last time he'd seen her. He figured after everything she'd been hit with today—the realization she quite possibly had a serial offender in Magnolia, his showing up unannounced and a trip to the hospital—it was understandable.

"Why are you really here, Ash? What is it you want?"

He wanted her back in his life, but decided to table that discussion for the time being. "I came because I'm convinced you have a serial right here in Magnolia."

She nodded slowly, then sipped her soda. "And you just thought you'd do us all a favor and swoop in to save the day, is that it?" Her expression turned skeptical. "Go sell your bullshit story somewhere else, 'cause I ain't buyin' it. You had no way of knowing from the single incident report I filed with VICAP that we have a serial on the loose."

"After what you saw today you still feel that way?"

"No, I don't. But unless you've gone psychic on me, you couldn't possibly have known about the Webb girl." She set her soda on the granite countertop, folded her arms and gave him a level stare. "So, you either have evidence that I know nothing about, or you're here for another reason. To ask me for a divorce, maybe?"

Her matter-of-fact tone unnerved him, and that made him edgy. He frowned. "Why would I want a divorce?"

She gave a careless shrug. "Maybe you met someone else. It's not like I've been what you'd call the perfect wife the past couple of years."

No, she hadn't, but she was still everything he'd never been able to forget. Oh, sure, there were changes, and not all of them what he'd call an improvement. She was too thin, much thinner than he ever remembered seeing her. She'd weighed next to nothing in his arms when he'd pulled the knight-in-shining-armor gig and carted her off to the hospital, and he guesstimated she'd dropped more weight than she could afford to lose.

She'd changed her hair, too, or rather ignored it completely. The once short, sassy style now hung limply around her face, reaching an inch or two beyond her shoulders. Dark circles underscored her eyes, and not from the bump on the head she'd suffered, either. The bluish stains beneath her big blue eyes marked the only real color in a drawn, pale face—a clear indicator she was still having trouble sleeping.

She looked like hell, and it worried him.

"No, but you're still *my* wife," he said with meaning.

"Don't you think that's a stretch? We haven't experienced what most people would call a real marriage in a long time."

He stood and circled the island. Irritation along with a trace of fear flashed in her eyes as he closed the distance separating them. "That's always been your problem, sweetheart. You think too much."

She turned to face him, but whatever she'd been about to say never made it past her lips as he closed in on her. Bracing his hands on the counter behind her, he trapped her within his arms. Damn, but she smelled good. Like warm sunshine and . . . freshly cut grass?

She frowned. "I do have a headache, you know," she sassed.

"If I hadn't witnessed that nosedive you took myself, I might think you're avoiding me."

"I'm trying to."

Perhaps, but at least she was talking to him. That was more than they'd managed in too damn long. The fact that she hadn't yet attempted to throw his ass out gave him a sliver of hope that perhaps he stood a chance of eventually convincing her to come back to him.

He brought his hand to her cheek, unashamed at how his fingers trembled as he drew them lightly over her satiny-soft skin. "God, I've missed you," he whispered.

She looked up at him, her eyes filled with a longing to equal his own. That was all the invitation he needed.

He dipped his head, his mouth brushing across hers in a light, feathery kiss. He expected a protest, but instead her lips were soft, welcoming. Pressing his advantage, he deepened the kiss before she thought to change her mind.

Her hands landed on his chest and he half-expected her to push him away. Instead, she curled her fingers into his shirt and hauled him close. He didn't hesitate to pull her into his arms and hold on tight when she slid off the stool, wreathed her arms around his neck and pressed her too-thin body against him.

Emotion flooded him. He'd spent too many long nights thinking about her, dreaming about her, cursing her for leaving him. To finally have her in his arms, tasting her, was nothing short of heaven.

She dug her hands into his hair and swept her tongue across his. Blood pounded hotly through his veins, threatening to burn through the thin threads of his restraint. She was in no physical condition to make love but, God help him, that's exactly what he wanted from her. He wanted her hot and naked, wanted her legs wrapped tightly around his waist, welcoming him inside her slick, wet sheath. He wanted to hear his name on her lips as she came, needed to feel her body clench around his, milking him until he had nothing left to give her. He wanted her raw and wild, begging him for more until neither one of them had the strength to do more than breathe.

He slid his hands to her bottom and lifted her. She moaned in his mouth, the sound as sweet and intoxicating as the feel of her denim-covered legs wrapping around his waist. Shoving the barstool aside with his foot, he set her on the countertop and nudged her bottom forward. His dick throbbed painfully within the confines of his trousers and he nearly came out of his skin when she rocked her hips, rubbing herself against his erection.

Smoothing his hands from her bottom, he slid them over the deep indentation of her waist. She was too thin, he thought again, sweeping his hands upward along her rib cage. Dangerously thin.

Although it nearly killed him, he ended the kiss and pulled her arms from around his neck. He took a step backward, hoping the distance would cool his blazing libido.

Greer stared at him in confusion. Her passion-glazed eyes nearly had him ignoring his good intentions. He dragged his hand through his hair. "When was the last time you ate a decent meal?"

Her honey-blonde eyebrows slanted downward. "What?"

He took a good long look at her. Her collarbone appeared more prominent, so did her cheekbones, for that matter, creating a deep hollow in her cheeks. "How much weight have you lost, Greer?"

With a trembling hand, she reached up and twisted the length of her hair into a loose knot. "Don't worry about it. I can take care of myself."

"Bullshit. If that were the case, then you wouldn't feel like nothing more than skin and bones. Christ, Greer, you're so thin you could put an anorexic to shame. What gives?"

She narrowed those gorgeous blue eyes. "None of your

goddamn business." She slid off the counter and bent to pick up the stool he'd knocked over.

"You look like you haven't slept in a month," he said, taking the stool from her and sliding it back to the island.

"I'm fine."

Yeah, then why the hell wouldn't she look at him when she said it? Because she'd never been able to lie to him, and that apparently hadn't changed.

He snagged her wrist and pulled her to him. "The hell you are."

"Leave it alone. Leave *me* alone."

He ignored the warning in her voice. "What are you doing to yourself?"

She tugged her wrist free of his hold. "Surviving," she fired at him vehemently. "No thanks to you." Regret instantly filled her expression. "Ash. I'm sorry. I didn't mean—"

He scrubbed his hand down his face. "Yes, you did," he told her. Whatever hope he'd been harboring about convincing Greer to come back to him evaporated in that instant. And it was high time he pulled his head out of his ass and accepted the fact that his wife would never be able to forget that he'd been the one to put her in the hands of a monster.

Chapter 8

"PARKER? IS EVERYTHING all right?"

At the sound of his wife's soft, tentative voice, Parker pressed the MUTE button on the remote control, quieting the evening news broadcast. For the past ninety minutes he'd heard nothing mentioned about the discovery of a body found today at Cornwall Cove Cemetery. Not so much as a whisper of Tommy Gartner's failed union on any of the local channels.

Turning to look over his shoulder at Susan, he offered her a reassuring smile. She stood in the doorway between the den and kitchen with a wicker laundry basket clutched in her hands, her soft hazel eyes filled with worry. For him.

His Susan. His beloved. Parker Hennessy's perfect mate—and his, too.

"Of course it is," he said while patting the space next to him on the Italian leather loveseat. "Why do you ask?"

She walked into the room, the silky fabric of her long, floral skirt swirling around her slender legs as she moved toward him. After angling the basket filled with freshly laundered towels onto the seat of the nearby rocking chair, she sat beside him. "You hardly touched your dinner." A tentative smile curved her smooth, thin lips. "When you barely eat more than a single piece of my lemon-grilled chicken, I worry." A slight frown creased her brow. "Are you sure you're feeling well?"

Parker took her small hand in his, laced his fingers with her thin, delicate ones and gave her a tender squeeze. Funny, but he truly cared for this woman. He didn't know if he was capable of such an obscure emotion as love, but whatever he felt for her ran deep into his soul. Warmed him, deep inside, each time he gazed into her gentle eyes, sat beside her during Sunday services at the Presbyterian church they attended weekly, or when he watched her from the kitchen window as she tended to her flower or vegetable gardens.

"I'm sorry you went to so much trouble," he said with sincerity. He brought their joined hands to his lips and brushed his mouth over the back of her hand. "I should have called to let you know I'd stopped for a quick bite this afternoon while I was out." He smiled. "Forgive me?"

She accepted the lie so easily, just as he knew she would. She never doubted him, and rarely questioned him unless it was out of concern for his well-being. Susan believed in him, was devoted only to him and lovingly catered to his every need. At least the ones she was capable of fulfilling. For that she'd earned his respect. In his own way, he remained equally devoted to her. He understood his own emotional limitations, and he'd learned to compensate for them.

Color stained the translucent skin of her cheeks and his smile deepened. She had a sweet face, her features individually striking. Sharp hazel eyes, perfectly almond shaped, but set a little too close together. When she toyed with her needlework, a pair of gold-toned bifocals perched on the end of her straight little nose, she almost appeared cross-eyed. Not that it mattered. He hadn't chosen her for her beauty, but rather for her loyalty to Parker. To him.

"There's nothing to forgive." Her frown returned and she looked at him curiously. "I worry you're working too hard again."

Perhaps he would visit her room tonight. Make up for his inconsideration for all the trouble she went to just to please him. He attempted to recall the last time he'd joined with her and drew a blank. Lately his calling required more of his internal energies, leaving him spent in a way that fulfilled him on a plane much higher than mere base desire. He supposed he could liken the sensation to an orgasm, he mused, as he toyed with her fingers still entwined with his. Several orgasms, in fact. To the point he had precious little left to give.

Yes, perhaps he would indeed visit her room. Last night's near discovery left him feeling restless and unfulfilled. Susan would serve him well and satisfy his needs. Tonight.

"Are you sure everything is okay, Parker? You seem more distracted than usual the past few weeks."

So in tune to him, to his moods, his needs, always ready to fulfill his desires. She gave freely of what she knew how to give . . . herself.

"The last time you worked such long hours, you almost made yourself sick from exhaustion."

She looked at him as if she had the power to read the darkness in his soul, to unveil the truth and reveal the secrets of his calling. A lesser man would be concerned, too intimidated by her quiet strength, by her intensity, to ever consider binding himself to her.

But that was the point of his existence, wasn't it? To show how far he stood above the rest, how much more powerful in his gift in knowing precisely how to care for his very special clientele? Never again would he qualify as one of the lesser, now that his emergence was near completion. The process had been slow and painstaking, but he took constant care and made sure he thoroughly enjoyed every sweet, successful union that brought him closer to his own total purification.

"You worry too much," he told her, wanting to ease her mind.

"I can't remember the last time we spent a quiet evening together."

He detected a note of desperation in her voice and let go of her hand. How dare she nag him.

"Nonsense," he said sharply.

What was wrong with her? It wasn't like her to make demands or expect an explanation of his whereabouts. Her quiet acceptance of him marked the beauty of their togetherness, made her his perfect soul mate.

She folded her hands meekly in her lap. "You were out for so long in this dreadful heat today," she said, looking away suddenly to stare at the mute images flickering on the television screen. "I worry."

He'd had no choice, his living clients had required his attention, but he'd been compelled to satisfy his curiosity and had driven out to Cornwall Cove. He'd parked over a mile away and hiked the remaining distance to the cemetery. For most of the afternoon he'd remained out of sight while observing the authorities as they desecrated the sacred ground of the union he'd failed to complete.

He'd never once been even close to being discovered, until last night when he'd been forced so unexpectedly to abandon the union. He'd been seen, he was sure of it. By whom he didn't know, but he would learn the intruder's identity. How many muscle cars with a leaky exhaust pipe could there possibly be in a town the size of Cornwall Cove?

The union remained incomplete and it saddened him when he thought of how he'd disappointed Tommy Gartner. A certain level of risk was always involved when he was called to extend his very special services beyond the needs of his own clientele, but he accepted those risks as his duty. But Tommy had died so young, so tragically alone. Of course, he'd been called to serve. Only he hadn't. Life had failed Tommy and now so had he.

He manufactured a tired smile to appease his wife. "My sweet, sweet, Susan. Always looking out for me."

She shifted her attention back to him, her smile tentative and shy once more. "Taking care of you makes me happy, Parker."

Pleased by her answer, he leaned toward her and placed a chaste kiss on her warm lips. So warm. Inviting.

Alive.

Unexpected desire stirred his blood. "What do you say we have some of that cobbler you have cooling in the kitchen and make it an early night?" he whispered against her ear.

He drew his mouth over the warm, soft flesh of her throat until she trembled beneath his touch. If he touched her breasts, her nipples would be hard little evidences of her desire for him. If he exposed himself to her now, she would take him into her mouth. If he commanded her to open her legs for him, she would, because only his desire mattered to her.

But tonight needed to be special. Tonight he needed to bestow his unique power upon her, if only to remind her how very fortunate she was that he cared for her.

"I'd like that," she whispered as she slid her arms around his neck.

Suddenly ravenous with burning need, he kissed her hungrily. She belonged to him. Heart. Body. Soul. She was *his* perfect, devoted mate. Her sole ambition, the only purpose to her pathetic existence, was to please him. And tonight she would in ways that would shock her. She would know his superior power, and would thank him for it when he was finished with her.

* * *

Greer pulled on a pair of comfortable cotton shorts, then searched the top drawer of her dresser for her favorite gauzy, loose-fitting tank top. Her fingers brushed against the small, chintz-covered jewel case she kept hidden there. She found the top and slipped it over her head, then tempted fate by reaching back inside the dresser for the jewelry box.

Carrying it with her to the four-poster bed, she sat and carefully opened the case. She'd never been a jewelry-hound like her sister, who kept the gems she'd collected from three husbands, and counting, in a built-in safe in her bedroom, but she had managed to accumulate a few pieces of minor consequence that were important to her. Only she wasn't interested in the small gold hoop earrings, the pearl-and-diamond studs and matching pendant, or any of the other items she'd purchased for herself or received as gifts over the years.

She plucked the delicate bridal set from between the faded red velvet cushion. The half-karat princess diamond still sparkled when she held it under the light of the lamp on the night table. She'd opted for a full sleeved ring guard rather than a traditional matching wedding band. The alternating rows of tanzanite marquis and channel-set diamonds gleamed as brilliantly as when Ash had first slipped it on her finger, the day she'd married him before a justice of the peace at a courthouse in Pueblo, Colorado.

At the cemetery today when she'd had a lightening-quick glimpse of Ash's hands, the blazing sun had reflected off the simple gold band he still wore—not his watch. Irony obviously had a wicked sense of humor, but she wasn't laughing. She hadn't been able to remove the heavy weight from her finger fast enough the day she'd left him. She didn't think she'd even been out the driveway when she'd yanked the bridal set from her finger and tossed it into her purse.

It wasn't that she didn't love Ash. God help her, she doubted she'd ever stop loving the man. Hadn't the way she'd responded when they'd kissed this afternoon proven as much? He'd been everything to her, but that didn't mean she could be anywhere near him without losing her tenuous grip on her minimal sanity. Loving him was one thing. Living with him quite another, especially when each time she'd looked at him she'd been reminded of what Vicar had done to her, of the nightmare she'd endured and managed, by some miracle, to survive.

Against her better judgment, she slipped the ring on her finger, surprised by how loosely it fit her now. The diamond solitaire caught the reflection of the light. Glinted. Like steel. Like the steel blade of a scalpel.

She shuddered, shaken by the realistic image that flashed through her mind. Her heart started to race, pounding hard enough for her to feel each heavy, rapid beat.

She slid the ring from her finger, dropped it inside the jewel case and snapped the lid closed. After returning the case to the back of the bureau drawer, she hurried into the bathroom and headed straight for the medicine chest. Her hands shook uncontrollably, making opening the mirrored cabinet door a challenge. She knocked half the bottles off the shelf and they clattered loudly into the sink. Frantically, she rummaged through the prescription bottles in search of chemical salvation.

"Greer? What's going on?"

She jumped at the sound of Ash's voice. Her heart rate accelerated. "I'll be fine," she snapped. "Just as soon as I find my goddamn pills." She'd apologize for biting his head off once she was back in control.

She located the bottle of Xanax and flicked off the non-childproof cap with her thumb. Because her hands were shaking, she spilled half the contents of the plastic amber container into her palm.

He stepped into the bathroom with her. "What the hell do you think you're doing?"

"Leave me alone. Please."

His hand locked around her wrist, holding her tight. "Answer me."

"My heart's racing," she said, the words as rushed as the blood roaring in her ears. "I need to calm down before I lose it."

"With a handful of pills?" he demanded harshly.

"You think I'm suicidal?" His implication felt like a slap in the face.

"To tell you the truth," he said as he released her, "I don't know what to think anymore."

That made two of them.

She returned all but one of the pink, oval-shaped pills to the bottle. He snagged the glass she kept next to the bathroom sink, filled it with water and handed it to her.

"Regardless of how fucked up I am, I haven't ever tried to take my own life," she told him, then walked out of the bathroom on unsteady legs.

She made it as far as the overstuffed chair in the corner of her bedroom near the bank of newly installed replacement windows, and sat. With her feet pulled up onto the cushion, she wrapped her arms around her legs and attempted the impossible task of clearing her mind while awaiting relief. She hadn't eaten since this morning, so with any luck at all, it would take no more than a few minutes for her to feel the calming, soothing effects of the antianxiety medication.

From the sound of things in the bathroom, Ash busied himself by restoring order, no doubt taking his time to give her a few moments alone to pull herself back together. Or cool down. No, she wasn't angry with him, only disappointed. As much as she hated to admit it, his thinking her capable of pulling her own plug hurt like hell.

She rested her chin on her upraised knees and caught

sight of Eula's fat white rump poking out from beneath the bed. "You gonna hide under there all night?"

In an uncharacteristic display of canine pleasure, Eula wagged her tail. Or rather she swished her portly bottom on the unfinished planks of the hardwood floor.

"Keep that up and I'll be plucking splinters out of your ass again," Greer complained to the dog.

With a sound that bordered somewhere between a whimper and a disgruntled moan, Eula came out from under the bed and waddled over to Greer. A far cry from the epitome of canine fitness, Eula lacked the verve to actually hop onto the chair with her. Instead, she rustled up enough energy to plant her paws on the seat cushion and nudged Greer's bare leg with her wet, snubbed nose, demanding attention.

Greer obliged, rubbing the dog behind the ear. Eula tipped her head sideways and snorted.

"Let me guess. Eula?"

Greer glanced up at the sound of Ash's deep, resonant voice, tinged with amusement. He stood with his shoulder propped against the bedpost. Concern lingered in his gaze, making him appear more weary than the last time she'd seen him. Still virile and as damn appealing as ever, she thought. With his tie loosened and the sleeves of his light blue dress shirt rolled back, to her he looked . . . perfect.

"In the flesh," she said.

"Not much of a watchdog, is she?" He glanced at the bedside clock. The deep teal digits indicated the time at half past seven. "I've been here for almost two hours and this is the first I've seen of her."

"Pathetic, I know. She only plays the big bad pooch with people she knows. She's putty in a stranger's hands."

"Why a dog? You were always more of the goldfish type."

She offered up as much of a smile as she could muster. "A momentary weakness," she said, returning Eula to all fours.

He pushed off the post and couched, extending the back of his hand toward the dog. Eula waddled over, snorted, then shook her fat rump like a hussy.

"She's friendly," he said.

"Don't let her fool you. She's mean and cantankerous and farts like a howitzer."

Ash chuckled as he patted Eula's rotund little body. "Look, Greer," he said suddenly, "I'm sorry about earlier. I didn't mean to imply—"

"Forget it." She came out of the chair and walked to the closet. "I already have." A lie, bigger than Eula's swinging-with-delight hind end.

He let out a sigh and, for a moment, she thought he'd push the issue. There were any number of topics they should discuss, but her mental health came in dead last as far as she was concerned.

"Dr. Endicott said you shouldn't have too heavy a meal tonight, so I threw together a light supper while you were in the shower. Some premade thing you had in the fridge, and a salad?"

"Spinach and seafood quiche," she told him on her way to the closet for a lightweight cardigan. "Don't you think we should talk first?" A bold statement for a woman who made a habit of running at the first sign of distress.

"Later," he said. "You should eat something."

"We'll multitask," she suggested as she shrugged into the cardigan. "Talk while we eat."

The conversation promised a record-setting case of indigestion, but for her own peace of mind, she needed to know why he'd chosen now of all times to come looking for her. Most people had opportunity knocking on their doors. Not her. She had trouble pounding on hers with a battering ram. She had enough to deal with now that she had a possible serial offender trolling for victims. A full-scale investigation to head was more than enough for anyone to handle, but she also had to deal with a marriage to . . . what?

Dissolve?

Resolve?

She blew out a relieved breath when Ash agreed. After she promised to join him downstairs in a few minutes, he left the bedroom. Dragging a brush through her hair, she secured the still-damp mass with a claw clip, then headed down to join him.

He had come to town because of a possible serial offender? In her dreams. With only two confirmed kills, the investigation failed to meet the Bureau's criteria for a serial offense, so she wasn't completely buying Ash's excuse for showing up on her crime scene. The man had the instincts of a coonhound and, as much as she'd prefer otherwise, she simply could not discount his sudden appearance as a coincidence, or that his motives were purely professional.

So much for her steering clear of the Stewart investigation, or anything else that made her uncomfortable. The warranty on her meticulously planned and executed avoidance of dead bodies, profiles and estranged husbands had apparently expired when she was otherwise occupied fending off anxiety attacks and flashbacks.

Since outrunning her past was no longer a viable option, especially not with said past currently under her roof, she had no choice but to determine the least emotionally painful method of surviving the next few days. No easy feat, she mused, as she walked into the kitchen, when all she'd studiously avoided had shown up to bite her in the ass with one gluttonous chomp.

Baby steps, she reminded herself. Wasn't that what the shrink she visited twice a month told her? When overwhelmed, strip down each complication and conflict to its most basic element and deal with it one at a time until resolved. How was she supposed to manage a few simple steps when she'd already suffered two anxiety attacks within hours of each other, one even landing her in the hospital emergency room with a mild concussion?

"Good question," she muttered to herself.

"Excuse me?" Ash asked as he carried two glasses of iced tea to the table.

"Nothing," she said. "Just thinking out loud."

Her marital status, or lack thereof, would just have to wait. She hadn't been away from the Bureau long enough to forget how to track down an UNSUB, hopefully before he struck again, and that took priority. The bitch of it was, he may have already killed again and no one, least of all an overworked, understaffed, small county Sheriff's Department, would be the wiser.

There might not be such a thing as the perfect crime, but the bastard sure had come close. The Stewart woman's body would never have been found if it hadn't been for the Archer exhumation. If the killer hadn't been interrupted, Joanna Webb's body never would've been discovered, either. Was there some connection between the Webb girl and the deceased, Thomas Gartner, or was the UNSUB's choice in disposing of his kills in Gartner and Archer's graves a random one? Or was the connection between the victims?

She took a long drink of sweet tea. To piece together the killer's motivation, she'd need to know more about his victims. Crawling inside the heads of innocents was preferable than going anywhere near a killer's whacked psyche. Unfortunately, the job didn't work that way. But, once she knew her vics, then she might have a better understanding of her UNSUB.

She looked up as Ash set the seafood quiche that she'd made that morning on the table. He added a bowl of canned fruit cocktail from her pantry and a loaf of crusty French bread he'd warmed in the oven, along with the garden salad. Twice the amount she usually ate—when she remembered to eat.

The gold wedding band he still wore caught her attention, flashing like a neon indicator of her failure to hold up her end of the bargain. The symbol mocked the promises she'd made. She had no problem with the loving, honoring and cherishing parts, but she'd clearly breached the *for better or worse* clause of their marital contract.

Baby steps, she reminded herself again. One problem at a time.

She set the glass of tea back on the table and waited for Ash to be seated. "Do me a favor?"

His mouth curved into a smile bordering on sexy. "Name it."

"Keep that goddamn wedding ring out of my sight."

Chapter 9

ASH DIDN'T BELIEVE it possible for his ego to take a direct hit twice in the same day, but in the space of a few hours he'd discovered he no longer knew jack. Particularly when it came to dealing with his wife.

With one last, deep drag on the cigarette, he tossed the butt over the porch railing into the garden of mixed annuals and perennials. The investigation he knew how to handle, and planned to start with the ME just as soon as he received word from Cantrell that the autopsy on the most recent vic had been performed. Under normal circumstances he'd have been present during the postmortem, but since his arrival in Magnolia, normal no longer existed in his vocabulary.

Handling Greer, however, was another matter entirely. He hadn't let himself believe for a second she'd be happy to see him, and her anger with him for showing up unannounced made sense. If the situation was reversed, he'd be mad as hell, too. He just hadn't expected to find her so emotionally fragile. Or rather, he'd hoped not to.

In the two years since Phoenix, she hadn't made any strides toward emotional recovery, at least that he could see, and that had him worried. The woman he'd known had been strong and determined. Fearless in many ways. The woman he'd encountered today was nothing more than a bleak shadow of her former self.

The fault lay with him that Greer was in such bad shape. He didn't have a clue how to help, what to do to fix what he'd destroyed, and the guilt rode him hard. If only he hadn't suggested they use her as bait to draw Vicar out, exploit his fixation with her . . .

Life was too short for a laundry list of what-ifs that couldn't be changed. Clocks weren't made to be turned back, but dammit, how he wished he could relive that one split second in time.

Would he really do things differently if given the opportunity? He had his doubts. The job came first, even before the safety of his own wife, apparently.

Greer was an emotionally unstable train wreck looking for a place to happen and, in his estimation, that put her in over her head professionally now that she had an UNSUB in her own backyard. If an innocuous wedding band upset her, hunting a serial might send her over the edge for good.

Although he'd essentially walked into this case blind, he had enough of the facts to know that this UNSUB was a highly organized killer, and that made him more dangerous than most. There might be only two confirmed victims but, based on the information he'd received from Faith, he suspected Stewart and Webb weren't the UNSUB's only kills. Unless they dug up every grave in the county, their chances of determining exactly how many victims the UNSUB had claimed thus far were nil.

Christ, he hated cases like this one as much as he thrived on the challenge. So had Greer. Once.

He shook another cigarette from the half-empty pack, but slipped it back inside when the hinges of the screen door squeaked. Greer emerged from the house with her useless excuse for a canine waddling past her. Eula labored down the wooden steps and disappeared into the yard.

"You can stay in one of the guestrooms tonight," Greer said, "but I'd appreciate it if you'd check into the motel tomorrow."

He nodded his agreement for the sake of avoiding another argument that would lead them nowhere, but had no plans of leaving anytime soon. He knew what she was up to, asking him to get rid of his wedding band, suggesting he check into the motel—running. Damn telling, he thought, but so was the way she still responded to him. He'd never been a silver-lining, best-case-scenario-kind of guy, but he recognized a slim hope when he saw one. For once in his life, he decided it might be wise to hang on to that tiny sliver for all he was worth.

"Come sit with me," he suggested, not that he thought for a minute she'd willingly get close to him anytime soon. A woman steeped in denial wasn't about to tempt fate, or herself, twice.

Her wary gaze darted between the vacancy on the padded vinyl cushion next to him and the wooden porch railing. As he expected, she opted for the railing.

"How are you feeling?" he asked lamely.

She shrugged, then propped her backside against the porch rail. The scoop-neck top she wore fluttered in the gentle evening breeze, drawing his gaze to the outline of her breasts against the filmy material. She always did have great tits.

Her cotton shorts showed off her long legs. Lean. Smooth. Perfect. His testosterone level spiked.

"Headache's gone," she said. "Finally."

His hand shook as he reached for the pack of cigarettes again. "That's good."

"I thought you quit."

He had, but when she'd left without warning, he'd started up again. Beat drowning in the bottom of a bottle of Scotch, which he might've attempted if it hadn't been for his aversion to not being in control. Besides, he wasn't his old man. First a bottle of Scotch, then the wrong end of a .38. No thanks.

"Some habits are tougher to break than others." He lit up.

Her gaze slid to his left hand. "I can't deal with both of you," she said suddenly. "I know my limitations, Ash. It's you or the UNSUB, but not both."

He drew on the cigarette and considered her admission. From his observations, he tended to agree with her self-analysis. She'd already suffered one panic attack and had been on the verge of another when he'd gone looking for her to tell her he'd thrown together a light supper while she'd been in the shower. The woman he'd known had never run from her problems, but faced them head-on without fear. So, did he play it safe and enable her to keep running? Force her to confront her past before she was equipped to handle the fallout? That could cause more harm than good, but he was sick and tired of waiting around for her to take action. He wanted his life back, too.

"One has nothing to do with the other." From her deepening frown, he had a feeling she understood his point, even if it wasn't *her* point.

"Not the way I see it."

No, she wouldn't. Because she didn't want to, he thought. "And your vision is so crystal clear these days," he said irritably.

"I didn't say that," she snapped testily.

"Then, for God's sake, why the hell don't you tell me how you do see it, Greer? Because I don't know what you want." So much for avoiding an argument.

She looked at him, her eyes filled with confusion and a shimmer of fear. He wanted to help her sort out the confusion, wanted to erase her fears.

"I want you to go away," she said. "Pretend you never saw the report I had to file with VICAP."

"I can't do that."

"Yes, you can," she said.

The pleading note in her voice tugged hard on his heart. He almost considered giving in to her demands. Almost. But not quite.

"Just get in your car and drive back to Virginia until I'm ready to deal," she added. "Your being here is an emotional roller coaster I'm not ready to ride, Ash. Not yet."

He blew out a frustrated breath, then chucked the half-finished cigarette over the railing into the flowerbed again. "I can't do that, either."

One corner of her mouth tipped upward in a half-smile. "Now, how did I know you were going to say that?"

Because they knew each other too well.

He leaned back against the cushion and scrubbed both hands down his face. "You can't keep hiding. Sooner or later you're going to have to talk to me about what happened in Phoenix."

"Wanna bet?" She tugged on the hem of her shorts, then pulled the little cover-up more tightly around her. "I don't process stressful situations well, if you haven't noticed."

Oh, he'd noticed all right. "Then what are you doing wearing a badge?"

"Magnolia isn't exactly a hotbed of crime," she reasoned. "Besides, I got talked into it."

He made a sound that might have passed for a short burst of laughter, if it wasn't for the underlying bitterness. "Is that the load of crap you've been feeding yourself all this time?"

If she tugged any harder on the white cotton sweater she was wearing, the stupid thing would tear. "It's true," she said a tad too defensively.

He leaned forward and braced his hands on his knees. "And since when have you ever done anything you didn't want to do?"

She started plucking at the sleeves. "Which just goes to you show how irrational I've become."

"Sounds like a convenient excuse to avoid the truth."

"Whatever works."

"You want to know what I think?"

"Not especially."

"You're afraid."

"Gee, you think?"

He ignored her sarcasm. "You took the job because you're a cop, Greer. Some people can walk away and never look back, but you're not one of them. You'll always be a cop, whether you're hunting serials or citing little old ladies for jaywalking."

Eula started barking.

Greer pushed off the railing and walked across the porch to the steps. "Been reading the psyche journals again, haven't you?"

"No. I know you."

"Not anymore you don't," she said over her shoulder. "I'm not the same trusting fool I once was."

He stood to follow her down the steps. Eula came waddling up to Greer, the hair on her rotund little body puffed up so she looked like a swollen marshmallow on short, stubby legs. "I'm not the one that hurt you," he said, coming up behind her. He settled his hands on her shoulders, encouraged when she didn't pull away.

"No," Greer said, without looking at him. "You're not. You're the one who let him hurt me."

His cell phone vibrated at his side, saving him from having to respond. Other than offering her another apology, there wasn't much he could say on the subject. Not when she was dead right.

He stepped away as he flipped open the phone and checked the caller ID. The Magnolia County ME's office. Finally.

"Keller here."

A pair of squirrels bolted across the lawn. Eula snorted, then whimpered and pressed herself against Greer's legs. The dog was afraid of squirrels?

"Thought you might like to know the killer left behind a calling card," Cantrell said.

Adrenaline instantly hummed through Ash. The chase was on. "What have you got?"

Cantrell chuckled. "Nothing will brighten your day like a little DNA."

Too easy, Ash thought. Which meant the DNA evidence Cantrell collected probably wouldn't lead them to the UNSUB, but would at least place him with the vic when they finally nailed the bastard.

"Willows is on his way," Cantrell told him.

"I'll be there in ten minutes." Ash disconnected the call.

"You're leaving?"

The hopeful note in her voice pissed him off. "I hate to disappoint you," he said, "but I'll be back."

"Where are you going?"

"The ME's office," he said, reaching into his pocket for the key to the rental car.

"Not without me you aren't. This is my investigation."

He let out a sigh. "You're supposed to take it easy. I won't be long."

A calculating smile curved her mouth. "I'm not supposed to be left alone, either," she said. "Doctor's orders."

The chuckle that erupted held none of the previous bitterness, only resignation. "That's convenient."

"Yes," she said smugly as she coaxed Eula up the stairs and into the house. "Isn't it?"

Greer could claim she wasn't the same person all she

wanted, but Ash was beginning to feel differently on the subject. After months of no communication, she still knew exactly how to get exactly what she wanted from him, and remained as stubborn as the day he'd first laid eyes on her.

"I'll just be a minute," she said and disappeared into the house, no doubt to change into something less revealing.

He grabbed his smokes and turned on the porch light while he waited. He'd let her have her way—for now. So long as they were working the investigation together, he'd do his best to keep his distance, too. Keep it professional. But once they nailed the UNSUB, all bets were off and he wouldn't back down until he had what *he* wanted for a change.

Greer would rather drink a *Fear Factor* shake than admit to Ash she was having second thoughts about tagging along, even if it *was* her investigation. For half a second she wished she'd stayed behind and allowed him to take charge, but despite her reluctance to get all up close and personal with her second dead body in as many weeks, there wasn't a chance in hell she'd ever play second string to Ash, or anyone, for that matter. Good, bad or panic attacks be damned, this was *her* case.

Besides, she thought, as she led Ash down the corridor to the coroner's autopsy room, if she concentrated on the investigation, then she couldn't possibly have the time, energy or inclination to think about Ash in any capacity other than professional. She'd meant what she'd said. The UNSUB or Ash. From this point forward, her sole focus was in capturing the UNSUB. The lesser of her two evils, crawling inside the head of a sick bastard or being run down by the emotional steamroller she hadn't allowed herself to think about since leaving the Bureau.

Avoiding Ash was out of the question now that he'd barged into her life under the guise of a serial investigation that hadn't officially existed until he'd shown up. She'd just have to deal with him. But, if she applied no more significance to his presence than what his job title encompassed, she just might hang on to what little sanity she had left. Not that she needed his assistance. She was, after all, a profiler.

Correction. She had once *been* a profiler. Big difference, in her opinion. Of course, that excuse failed to explain the old hum of excitement moving over her skin the second she pushed through the metal swinging doors of the autopsy room.

Maybe Ash was right. Once a cop, always a cop.

The doors swung closed and she stopped short. Other than the body of a twentysomething life cut short, the room was deserted. Avoiding so much as a glance in the direction of the metal tray loaded with surgical instruments, she crossed the room to the sink to wash her hands. She simply wouldn't think about the instruments.

"You don't have to do this," Ash said, coming up beside her to wash his hands. "Why don't you wait outside? I'll talk to Cantrell."

She dried her hands and plucked a pair of latex gloves from the holder on the shelf. "It's my responsibility."

"Look, I know this is going to be a bitch for you to get through. It doesn't have to be."

She let out a sigh. While she did appreciate his offer to shield her from the unpleasantness that lay ahead, if she ever hoped to achieve a facsimile of a normal life again, sooner or later she had to just get the fuck over herself. With a psychopathic nut job on the loose, later had become a luxury she could no longer afford.

"This is my investigation," she said, turning toward him. "You're here to provide assistance—to *me*. Remember that and both of our jobs will be much easier."

He pulled on a pair of gloves. "I know what you've been through. Why won't you let me help you?"

She shook her head. "Thank you, but no," she said firmly. "You can help me by letting me do my job."

He didn't look convinced, or happy. She wasn't all that thrilled, either, but she refused to rely on him to do her dirty work for her.

"I mean it, Ash," she warned.

"You're the boss," he conceded, albeit reluctantly.

"Exactly."

The sound of voices echoed in the corridor, signaling the return of Manny Cantrell and Travis Willows.

"And I'd appreciate it you'd keep quiet about what happened."

His brows drew downward. "Your panic attacks?"

She nodded. "No one knows and I'd like to keep it that way."

He couldn't have looked more stunned by her revelation. "How have you kept it a secret this long?"

"By avoiding situations like the one we're in the middle of." She turned away as Manny pushed through the double swinging doors, followed by an out-of-uniform Travis.

Travis chomped on the unlit cigar tucked in the corner of his mouth. "Didn't expect to see you here," he said to Greer. "Not after that circus stunt you pulled at the bone yard this afternoon."

"Very funny," she complained. "And I'm fine, by the way. Thank you so much for asking."

Travis grunted and eyed her suspiciously. Today had been the closest she'd ever come to revealing she had a problem, and she didn't like the fact that she'd lost it in front of an audience. Even she had to admit to being minutely grateful Ash had been around to swoop in and play hero. Not that she would ever be so foolish as to rely on him to protect her. That was another mistake she'd never make again.

She looked pointedly at the large twenty-four-hour clock

on the back wall indicating it was already past nine. "It's getting late." The less time she spent with a DB, the better.

Manny pulled on a fresh pair of latex gloves and approached the body. "If this keeps up, Lattie's going to think I have a girlfriend."

Travis chuckled nervously. Apparently her boss wasn't any more thrilled than she was to be keeping company with a corpse.

"You said something about DNA," Ash prompted Manny. "Any chance you found something on the previous vic that we can match?"

"No such luck." Manny pulled back the sheet covering the body. "There are plenty of similars if you're looking to make a connection, though. Particularly in how the two bodies were treated prior to death."

"Meaning they were prepared for burial while still alive," Ash confirmed.

Manny nodded. "More detail was taken with the Webb girl. Why? I can't tell you. I figure that's why you're here. But I *can* tell you it's probably a safe bet that you're looking for someone with a working knowledge of mortuary science."

Travis chomped his cigar and took a step back from the table. Greer couldn't help notice how he avoided the body whereas Ash performed a much more closer examination of the dead girl.

"So we start by looking at undertakers," Travis suggested. "How many we got around here anyway? Five? Six?"

"Five in our county alone," Manny answered. "I can supply you with a list of funeral directors in the area."

"The UNSUB doesn't have to be in the business," Greer explained to Travis. "Serials aren't necessarily working professionals." The Preacher had been a perfect example. He'd dressed as a priest while hunting his victims but had worked as a surgical nurse. "Could be someone who's trained in the field, maybe couldn't pass the state exam, or even a low-level funeral parlor employee."

"You really think this is the work of a serial killer?" Travis asked. "Right here in Magnolia?"

"Two dead bodies, same methodology." Ash gave Travis a tolerant look. "I'd have my doubts that it's a coincidence if I were you."

Ash's attitude bordered on condescending, but she agreed with his assessment. Unfortunately. She looked to Manny. "The DNA?"

The coroner grinned and produced a small plastic bag containing three individual strands of hair. "It's not much, but should be enough for the lab rats to come up with something for you."

Greer took the Baggie and held it up to the light. The darkish colored hairs were no more than two or three inches in length, straight, with no unusual characteristics. "If our UNSUB has ever been in the prison system, this could give us an ID."

"Good," Travis said. "We need to put this son of a bitch out of business fast."

"It won't be that easy," Ash said to Travis. "My guess is the person we're looking for has been at this for a while. He's avoided detection so far, so it's unlikely he's ever seen the inside of a jail cell."

"What do you mean 'a while?'" Travis asked, obviously offended. "This is a small community, Mr. Keller. We notice things like dead bodies lying around."

Ash pulled off his latex gloves and tossed them in the nearby bin marked HAZARDOUS WASTE. "Had many missing persons been reported in the past few years?" he asked, his tone only slightly accusatory.

"No more than usual," Greer answered, disposing of her own gloves.

"Runaways mostly," Travis added.

"What about the surrounding jurisdictions?"

"I'll have to check it out. What do you know?"

"A total of forty-five unresolved missing persons reports are on file in seven counties over the past three years," Ash said. "Eight of them in Magnolia County alone." He looked pointedly at Travis. "They're not all runaways, Sheriff."

"You don't know that for certain," Travis said defensively.

Ash looked at Greer, effectively dismissing Travis. "You never saw a pattern?"

"I never looked for one," she said, trying hard not to take offense at the deepening accusation in Ash's tone. "There have only been two reports since I've been with the department. One right after I joined and another this past New Year's."

"Tell me."

"Jacqueline Barton," she answered without hesitating. "Thirty-six-year-old single Caucasian female, a nurse practitioner. Never showed up for work one morning, reported missing by a coworker. A search of Barton's apartment turned up nothing unusual."

"And Lydia Monterrez," Ash supplied. "A sixty-eight-year-old Hispanic female, retired, never married, no next of kin. A neighbor reported her missing New Year's Day when she failed to show up for a neighborhood party she helped to organize."

"And how the hell do you know that?" Travis demanded.

"It's my job to know," Ash said. "The others are similar. No indication of foul play. It's as if they just disappeared into thin air."

"No one disappears without a trace," she said.

"No, they don't. Someone, somewhere knows their whereabouts."

She nodded. "The UNSUB."

"And we know what he's doing with them."

"Burying the bodies. But why?"

"To avoid being caught," Travis added.

Ash shook his head. "I don't think that has anything to do with it. You have a skilled killer and he's living out a fantasy. He has a need that can only be fulfilled by killing, by following a certain method of killing."

"What kind of sick son of a bitch can do that"—Travis pointed to the undraped body on Manny's exam table— "to a young girl?"

A chill passed over Greer's skin at the look of pure determination in Ash's eyes. "A monster, Sheriff. One that might live right next door to you, and you'd never know it."

Chapter 10

VIVIEN LEE MUCH PREFERRED to suffer the indignity of an overdue bikini wax than the thought of spending another second pretending interest in the bore seated across from her. By the sheer grace of God she managed to keep a smile plastered on her face and appeared interested as her date waxed on about the intricacies of the tax code. Never again would she go on a blind date with an IRS auditor.

How could an online dating profile sound so much more interesting than the real thing? Regardless of how good-looking the guy might be, she'd been lured by yet another case of false advertising.

Her date checked his watch. A relatively expensive brand, she noted, just not a Rolex.

"Would you excuse me for a moment?" he asked politely, then slid from the booth and headed toward the men's room.

Vivien breathed a much-needed sigh of relief. She glanced around the bar and, rude or not, considered making a quick escape before he returned. She didn't care what the old song said. The girls might look prettier at closing time, but the men certainly did not become any more interesting after last call.

The country music band at Lester's Roadhouse had long since ended their final set, but a small crowd remained, desperate with the hope of not going home alone. She really should have cut her losses and called it a night after her first glass of white wine, but even drinks with Mr. Tax Code beat spending another night with only her pampered Persian, Theodore, for company.

Her date—John? Jared? No, Jason. Whatever, she thought, drawing a total blank. Did it matter? Not really, since she'd likely never see him again. Although he had scored major points in the looks department, a handsome face and great body weren't all they were cracked up to be—a lesson learned from her first of three failed marriages.

The sun-bleached blond bartender with a Clark Gable mustache and mesmerizing bluish-green eyes smiled at her, flashing her with his too-perfect white teeth. Vivi smiled back, because it was the polite thing to do, then took another sip of her wine and admired the tight ass of the lead guitarist packing up his gear. He'd scored big in the looks department, too, but her interest in him had nothing whatsoever to do with a meaningful relationship. At least not one that extended beyond a few hours of nothing more than hot, mindless sex.

Her mother would have a royal hissy fit if she brought home a musician. Not that she would actually do it, but the idea of sparking a minor rebellion did make her smile. She wasn't like her sister, who did what she wanted, when she wanted, and to hell with what Mama thought about it all. Maybe she should try to be more like Greer, and do what *she* wanted for a change, not what Mama expected of her.

She took another sip of wine. Coming to Lester's Roadhouse had been an act of defiance, but what purpose did a minor revolt serve when she hadn't really enjoyed herself or if Mama didn't know? Under normal circumstances, she wouldn't be caught dead in a place like Lester's. A properly bred Southern lady wouldn't dream of frequenting a road-side honky-tonk, but she wasn't about to arrange a meeting with a man she knew only from his online dating profile in a place where she'd likely run into someone who knew her. Why, what would people think?

That she was desperate, that's what. That Vivien Lee Lomax Walker Peters Coleman couldn't meet a man the "normal" way and had to resort to a membership with *findamatch.com* to wrangle herself another husband. Why, it was shameful, just shameful, that's what they'd say.

She drained her wineglass.

The truth was, she hated being single. Unlike her kid sister, Vivien didn't do well à la carte. Greer rambled around alone in that disaster area she called a home, perfectly content with her own company. Vivien much preferred the company of a man. The right man, of course, one with strong Southern values and an even stronger financial portfolio.

She just didn't understand her little sister. They were so opposite, sometimes she wondered if they were even related. Where Greer defied convention, and Mama, for that matter, at every turn, Vivien did exactly what she'd been bred to do including marrying well and divorcing even better. Greer not only finished college, but joined the FBI and became a mindhunter. Vivien hadn't worked a day in her life. She volunteered her time to all the right charities, gave lavish dinner parties, shopped and lunched with friends. Greer bought her own house and was up to her bra straps in renovations, with plans to turn the place into a profitable venture. Vivien's real estate acquisitions were awarded to her via divorce settlements.

She stared into her empty wineglass and let out a sigh. In a lot of ways, she envied her little sister's independence and strong sense of self. Some days she wished she could be more like her, but didn't have a clue how to go about it. Shopping, lunching and charity work weren't exactly skills that would land her a promising career. Better to stick with what she knew best.

She looked up as John, Jason, or whatever his name was, strode toward her. He really was a good-looking man, tall with wide shoulders, narrow hips and a confidence she usually found appealing. His soft brown eyes were gentle and his smile kind, but he did absolutely nothing for her. Not so much as a twitch between her legs. She might have three failed marriages to her discredit, but at least she'd been sexually attracted to each of her husbands, even before she'd confirmed their portfolios.

Gathering her evening bag and creamy shawl from the cheap imitation leather seat, she scooted from the booth. "I should be going. I have an early appointment." She extended her hand along with the lie that fell easily from her lips. "Thank you for a lovely evening."

He took her hand. "The pleasure was all mine," he said, his voice as soft as his handshake. "I'd like to do this again sometime."

A lie. If he was really interested in her, he'd attempt to pin her down to a date and time.

"That would be nice," she said pleasantly.

His smile lacked sincerity. "I'll call you."

Sure you will.

She bid him a good evening and left Lester's Roadhouse—alone. With one last, longing glance at the guitarist with the great ass, she slipped through the door into the warm, sultry, summer-night air, still unable to recall the name of her online date.

June absently adjusted the lace doily on the arm of the wing chair. On the wide-screen television in her special room filled with movie memorabilia, Spencer Tracy fought a losing battle of wits with Kathryn Hepburn. The old Tracy-and-Hepburn movies were some of her all-time favorites, with *Adam's Rib* topping her list. She'd watched the old black-and-white movie three times already this week. No wonder her mind kept wandering.

She used to have to stay up late to watch her favorite old movies whenever AMC or TCM aired them, but with so many of the old classics being released on DVD, she enjoyed the luxury of popping a disc into the DVD player whenever the mood struck. Unfortunately, her nocturnal haunts of the silver-screen era hadn't abated with the birth of the DVD player. Too many years of habit made it next to impossible for her to sleep most nights, so she spent her time in her special viewing room watching anything from the screwball comedies of the thirties and forties to the more recent dramatic films Hollywood passed off as entertainment.

Tonight, though, not even Kate Hepburn getting the better of Spencer Tracy could hold her interest. Not when she was busy worrying that her daughters might never find happiness.

Greer wouldn't appreciate the concern. And although her youngest daughter would more than likely choose to attend the annual spring cotillion put on by the garden club than admit it, they really were very much alike. Probably too much, June thought, considering how often they clashed.

Using the remote, she turned off the television and DVD player. If it wasn't so late, she'd call Greer to check on her, but on the off chance her daughter was actually sleeping, she didn't want to disturb her. Greer might not be aware of it, but June knew all about her daughter's insomnia from Greer's neighbor Thelma Crawford. She wished she could do something to help, but whenever she tried, Greer would throw up her usual barricades and refuse to listen.

With a sigh, June stood and headed to the kitchen for a glass of something cool to drink. At least Vivien Lee listened to what she had to say, she thought, as she tightened the sash on her satin dressing gown. Her eldest daughter was too much like her father, though, and words of wisdom and experience were often ignored in deference to whatever self-ish need had momentarily caught her fancy. Vivien Lee did whatever gave her the most pleasure.

Just like Buddy, she thought. God rest his rotten-to-the-core soul.

She reached into the fridge for the pitcher of pineapple juice. The overhead light suddenly came to life, startling her.

"I didn't mean to give you a fright," Davis said as he crossed the kitchen. He placed a kiss on her cheek, as he did whenever he walked into a room and found her there.

"Did I wake you?" she asked, concerned that she'd disturbed him. He rose every morning at precisely 6 A.M., was the first to arrive at the bank and the last to leave every evening. He really should've retired by now, but Davis insisted he'd continue working at Magnolia Savings and Loan for a few more years. Lord knew they could certainly afford for him to retire, but she supposed his going to the bank every day allowed him to feel useful. Something she understood all too well.

He reached around her to the cabinet where she kept the antacids. "Heartburn," he complained.

"I'll make an appointment for you with the doctor," she said and frowned. "This is the third time it's happened this week."

"It's nothing," he reassured her. "Only a minor inconvenience."

She gave him a look he knew better than to argue with, took the bottle of antacids from him and returned them to the cabinet. She wasn't about to take any chances with his health. Why, if something happened to him, she didn't know what she'd do. Oh, she knew people still talked, but contrary to what her daughters believed, she didn't give a pig's pink patootie what the Magnolia rumor mill whispered behind her back. Maybe she hadn't been in love with Davis when she'd married him all those years ago, and she did feel a tad guilty for that, but she loved him now.

Davis Fulton might not have been the most handsome man in town, or the most rich or even the most charming and debonair, but he was ten times the man Buddy Lomax had ever been. Let them think whatever they wanted, she thought defiantly. They would anyway.

Davis loved her and he loved her daughters as if they were his own. The first time Greer had ever introduced Davis as "my dad" to her friends, he'd been so overcome with pride, he'd gotten all choked up. Vivien Lee still referred to him as "my mother's husband," but that didn't prevent her from running to her stepdaddy for financial advice after every divorce. Thanks to Davis's financial wizardry, Vivien Lee would hardly be considered destitute, even if she did need to curb her spending habits a bit.

She poured herself a glass of juice. "Davis?"

"Hmmm?" he murmured as he scanned the contents of the refrigerator for a late-night snack.

"Was I a good mother?" she asked him.

He pulled a container of leftover Fettuccini Alfredo from the fridge. "Of course you were."

She leaned her hip against the counter. "Then why aren't the girls happy? Greer hardly speaks to me since she's come home, and Vivien Lee runs through men like I don't know what. Those are not the actions of happy women, Davis."

He set the container on the counter, then took her glass of juice and set it aside as well. Clasping both of her hands in his, he gave them a gentle squeeze. "My darling, you are not responsible for Greer or Vivien's happiness. They're both grown women, more than capable of making their own decisions."

"Perhaps, but they're making such poor decisions. I can't help but feel that I'm somehow responsible. Like I didn't provide them with the proper guidance."

He let go of her hands and returned his attention to the leftovers. "No, they're making choices that *you* wouldn't make," he said, taking a pasta bowl from the cabinet. "That doesn't necessarily mean they're poor decisions, June. They're just not yours."

She sipped her juice and thought about that while Davis nuked the fettuccini. He did have a point.

"Maybe you're right," she admitted. She opened the silverware drawer and fished out a knife and fork for Davis, then took a seat at the round oak table in the center of the kitchen. "I never would've purchased that run-down old house. And I most certainly would never throw good money after bad on that money pit. I can only imagine the small fortune it's costing her, even if that friend of hers is doing most of the work."

"Selma," he said with a tolerant smile. "And she's very good."

"A bed and breakfast of all things," June scoffed. "Just how happy does Greer think she's going to be catering to the whims of strangers day and night? I did not raise my daughter to be nothing more than a common servant."

"I thought you were glad she's home."

"I'm happy that she's no longer an FBI agent, if that's what you mean."

The microwave dinged.

"And I am," she said before he could comment, "but only because I constantly worried about her. Honestly,

Davis, I think I aged twenty years when . . ." She couldn't bring herself to voice her greatest fear. She'd died a thousand deaths when they'd gotten the news that her precious baby girl had been victimized by that monster.

Davis carried his dish to the table and joined her. "It's over now," he said gently.

She frowned again. "Is it? She doesn't sleep, she hardly eats, and now that husband of hers is in town."

Davis's salt-and-pepper eyebrows rose a fraction. "Ash? How did you learn this?"

June let out a sigh. "He came here today, looking for her. Vivien was here. She was going to Greer's for lunch, so I made her take me with her, but Greer conveniently ran off, claiming she had urgent police business before I had a chance to warn her."

"Is that what's had you so upset all evening?"

"Well, of course I'm upset," she said as if he was being deliberately obtuse. "She hasn't heard from him since she came home. Why would he show up all of a sudden if it wasn't to try to take her back to Virginia?"

Davis let out a long sigh. "June, that's between them."

She tightened her mouth and looked away. She didn't appreciate the warning note in her husband's voice. Greer was *her* daughter, not . . .

She wasn't being fair. Davis might not have been a contributor to Greer and Vivien Lee's DNA, but in his heart, they were his daughters, too.

She sat quietly and sipped her juice while Davis polished off his snack. There had to be something she could do to help her daughters find peace. Not an easy feat when one avoided her as if she was a bastard at a family reunion, and the other simply tolerated her.

She'd figure it out. As a woman of a certain age, she'd managed to gain a few nuggets of wisdom along the way when it came to dealing with her daughters. She was resourceful, determined and wasn't above resorting to manipulation if it meant protecting her babies, even from themselves.

A slow smile tugged her lips. And if manipulation failed, there was always her favorite secret weapon—guilt.

Parker gently peeled the obituary of Thomas Gartner from the photo album. One torn edge stuck to the black construction paper. Using a small utility knife, he meticulously scraped at the paper until all signs of the torn newsprint were eliminated. He'd disappointed Tommy, and for that he was truly sorry, however he had no choice but to destroy all evidence of his failure before he could continue his work.

He had to right the wrong. With the cops sniffing around Tommy's final resting place, making amends would prove difficult, if not impossible.

He detested failure.

Anger churned in his stomach, simmering in his gut. He crumpled up the obituary and set it inside the ashtray on his desk, then struck the match, destroying the reminder of his inability to grace Tommy with his tremendous gift.

There were others requiring his services. Waiting for what they'd been rightfully denied.

He would not disappoint *them.*

Above him, floorboards creaked. Susan. She'd awakened alone, but he knew she wouldn't be alarmed by his departure from her bedroom. He rarely stayed with her after they made love. Unconcerned that she'd come looking for him, he turned his attention to the large flat-screen monitor and called up the file with the announcement he wanted to delete. There would be no union for poor Tommy.

The floorboards creaked again, followed by a muffled whimper.

"Quiet," he hissed.

The whimpering grew louder.

With a vile curse, he pushed away from the desk and stalked across the cold stone floor to the far side of the basement room that no one, save him, knew existed.

"Be patient," he said, then smoothed the back of his hand down the young woman's arm, stopping a few inches above the insertion point of the IV. "These things take time."

Her vibrant turquoise eyes widened with fright. She had no reason to fear him, yet they always did. They simply did not appreciate how very fortunate they were to be chosen. So few were worthy, so few were perfect.

She strained against the straps that held her to the table where he would eventually perform her transformation. "When the time is right, I will make you ready," he said soothingly. "I promise you."

He didn't want to make her wait like this, but occasionally it became necessary to prolong the inevitable. Unforeseen circumstances had caused a delay, and while he disliked having to stall the union, he had no choice. His true client's arrival had been delayed because of recent activity in the coroner's office. Once Hennessy's received delivery of Jefferson Holcomb and his fire-ravaged body was prepared for interment, then he could fulfill his duty.

Tears pooled in her pretty eyes. Curious, he watched the moisture fall, leading a trail down her alabaster cheek. Because she was so perfect, she deserved extra care.

His fingers lingered over her satiny flesh. "So perfect," he whispered. Trailing his hand along her collarbone, then down to the slope of her large breasts. With his palm open, he rubbed against her nipple until a hard little peak formed.

"Such a rare gift," he said, mesmerized by the rapid rise and fall of her chest.

He slid his hand along her rib cage, then spanned his fingers over her flat stomach, his fingers coming in contact with the bone of her hip. He shifted his gaze to the thatch of dark curls between her legs. She wasn't his to take, she belonged to his client, but he still wanted her and his dick hardened.

Desire clawed at him, burned him from the inside out. But he would not allow himself to have her.

He kept his hand on her stomach and moved lower, threading his fingers through the dark curls. She whimpered, but in his mind he heard her moan of pleasure, of a sharp, stinging need that matched his own.

Dipping beneath the waistband of his silk pajamas, he used his other hand to stroke himself. She belonged to his client, would be united with Jefferson for all eternity, but that didn't prevent him from imagining her bow-shaped mouth, hot and welcoming, sliding down his cock.

He closed his eyes to fully absorb the sensations. Her springy curls entwined with his fingers, her mouth, her lips glistening from the moisture of his need. He thrust his hips, then strained against the tightening of her lips surrounding him, the pull of her mouth milking him.

A shudder overtook his body, and he came into the palm of his hand. Before the ringing of his ears stopped, before his breathing returned to normal, he loosened the strap holding one of her legs, then forced her thighs apart.

She kicked at him, and he swore. Using his body to hold her still, he smeared his seed over her cunt, his fingers lingering a fraction longer than necessary over her downy softness.

She cried more silent tears, her body shaking with an almost-violent force as he tightened the strap to hold her in place until she could be readied. "Be patient," he said to her. "It won't be much longer now."

He left her long enough to wash his hands. He returned with a syringe and inserted the needle into the IV's portal. Pushing the plunger, her eyes fluttered almost instantly. Within seconds, she once more slipped into silence.

Chapter 11

SLEEP ELUDED GREER. Not exactly headline news, more par for her particularly pathetic course. Whether because Ash was in the house or because she was being forced into an investigation she didn't want, she couldn't state with any degree of certainty. She suspected both excuses were partially responsible in keeping her tossing and turning for the past four hours. What snippets of sleep she had managed were colored with disjointed dreams that made little sense. Dreams that, for a change, weren't filled with frightening images that had her waking up in a cold sweat or unable to breathe.

Wearing the same cotton shorts and filmy tank she'd had on earlier, she left her bedroom and crept quietly down the hallway. The door to Ash's room stood open. She paused outside the door, but heard nothing from within other than the gentle whir of the electric fan she'd placed near the window to draw cool air into the room. One of these days she'd have the installation of the big air-conditioning unit completed, but until Selma finished insulating all the rooms, she just didn't see much point.

She continued downstairs, intending to put up some coffee. If she couldn't sleep, then she might as well get a jump on profiling the UNSUB. A to-do list wouldn't hurt, either, especially since she was so out of practice but not necessarily of her element. For as much as she'd pitched a bitch yesterday afternoon with Travis about not wanting anything to do with a possible serial case, she couldn't deny the hum of excitement stirring deep inside her. The thrill of the chase, of putting the pieces together that would lead to the apprehension of the bastard responsible for two known deaths thus far, filled her with a renewed sense of purpose, something she hadn't experienced in far too long.

The light was on over the sink, and a half-empty carafe of coffee already sat on the warmer. Her lips twitched. Apparently ole Mr. Sandman had missed Ash, too. She took her favorite Carolina Panthers mug from the shelf above the coffeemaker and added a packet of sweetener, wondering if she or the UNSUB had kept *him* from getting any shut-eye.

The door to the mudroom stood open. With mug in hand, she went out to the back porch. The screen door thumped closed behind her at the same time she heard the click of a lighter. The pungent aroma of tobacco smoke followed, but she was hardly surprised. Whenever Ash worked a case, the man smoked like a fiend and consumed coffee by the gallons.

"Isn't this a familiar scene?" She spoke quietly in deference to the hour and crossed the rebuilt porch to the steps where he sat, wearing only a pair of battered blue jeans. Beneath the waning light of the moon, a heavy mug in one hand and a freshly lit cigarette in the other, he was as virile as ever. A fine sheen of moisture coated his back and arms, a byproduct of the humidity not even the cooler overnight temperatures could completely combat.

A smarter woman than she would've avoided the temptation of all that exposed male flesh, taken her coffee and found a quiet place to work. *Alone.* Except that when it came to Ash, intelligence rarely entered the equation. Besides, his profiling skills were no doubt sharper than ever. For as much as she'd protested, a part of her reluctantly had to admit to a modicum of gratitude for his presence. Ash was, after all, the best of the best.

In more ways than one.

As if she needed the reminder. The guy had a lot going for him, and so long as she had a pulse, she knew she'd never be immune to him. His brush with perfection didn't end with the job. Traffic-stopping good looks and a body she'd never been able to get enough of were only the beginning. Smart, sexy and sinfully decadent in the bedroom.

Lethal. Her favorite combination.

He glanced up as she joined him on the top step. "Couldn't sleep, either, huh?"

One look into those dark chocolate eyes and her breasts started tingling. She tempted fate, and her dormant libido, and sat beside him. "Too hot," she said, then took a tentative sip from her mug. She moaned in sheer delight. "Oh, God. I missed your coffee."

"Just my coffee?"

She lowered her mug and blew out a breath. Not the conversation she wanted to have at four in the morning, but she had only herself to blame since she'd been the one who opened that particular door. "No," she said honestly. "Other things, too."

Like having someone to comfort her in the middle of the night when the nightmares were too vivid and real, for starters. Eula offered no comfort since she was usually too busy whimpering beneath the bed. And there was the very real issue of her self-imposed celibacy.

"Such as," he prompted, a teasing note in his voice.

"Ash, I don't think we—"

"Aw, come on," he said and nudged her with his shoulder. "My ego could use a boost."

She shook her head, then smiled as she breathed in the spicy scent of the sassafras tree in the backyard. "Yeah, right," she answered dryly. "Like I'd ever believe that."

"You calling me arrogant?"

"If the ego fits."

He chuckled, and her smile widened. "Goes with the territory," he said.

"A convenient excuse if I've ever heard one." She always had found his arrogance just a tad sexy. No, not arrogance, she corrected. Self-confidence. Big difference, in her opinion.

She sipped more of her coffee and sat quietly beside him, not exactly enjoying the peacefulness of the predawn hour, but content . . . more so than she'd felt in months. It was next to impossible to feel completely at peace when she had an UNSUB to stop, hopefully before he killed again, but she'd take what she could get for as long as the brief moment lasted.

"It's nice here," Ash said suddenly, breaking the silence.

She shrugged. "I like it." Who wouldn't? She had her own private nature show happening with fireflies dancing to the serenade of crickets right in front of her. A warm, sultry breeze cooled her heated skin and rustled the leaves of nearby trees. In the distance, a dog barked, then quieted. Yes, she thought, taking another sip of coffee, contentment definitely worked for her.

"Do you miss it?"

"The Bureau?"

He nodded, then took a swallow from his own mug.

"Not especially."

Even in the waning moonlight she could see the doubtful expression on his too-handsome face. "Not even a little?"

She held up her thumb and index finger to indicate an approximate inch. "That much," she conceded. "Maybe." She rested her elbows on her knees and wrapped her hands around the warm ceramic mug. "I probably miss the people the most. Faith, Con. The other agents I worked with in the unit."

You.

As a matter of emotional survival, in the two years they'd been separated, she hadn't let herself think about Ash. Yet, despite her staunch refusal to allow him into her thoughts, occasionally he'd break stubbornly through her erected barriers. In those few, all-too-rare moments of weakness, she'd missed him so badly she ached. There'd been countless times she'd picked up the phone, desperate to hear his voice, but she'd always hung up before she opened a door she wasn't equipped to pass through.

Besides, what would she have said if she had followed through on one of those aborted phone calls? That she loved him, missed him, but couldn't bear to see him? That she was too much of a wimp to face him? Thankfully she'd come to her senses before further complicating an already-complicated existence, remembering why she'd left in the first place, and the feeling would slowly pass—until the next time.

"How are the girls?" she asked, not just to change the subject but out of genuine interest. She adored Ash's two daughters from his first marriage. She harbored plenty of guilt over leaving the way she had, and Kari and Shelby resided at the top of the list.

"Growing up too damn fast," he said. "This will be Kari's last year in middle school."

"That's not possible." The last time she'd seen Ash's eldest daughter, the intelligent young girl—with thick, rich sable hair and intense brown eyes like her father's—hadn't even been a teenager yet.

"She'll be fourteen in a few weeks."

"How did that happen?" When she and Ash had first

started dating, his daughters were little, only eight and five years old.

The tick of her own biological clock echoed suddenly inside her, followed by a sharp pang of regret. She and Ash had discussed having a family of their own, but they'd put it off due to their hectic schedules. She hadn't apologized for the decision to wait, primarily because of her old-fashioned belief that a child needed at least one parent around on a regular basis.

He tossed his cigarette butt into the flowerbed. "I don't know," he told her. "I blinked, I guess. Yesterday she was wearing diapers, now she's wearing makeup."

"What about Shelby?" Shelby had always held a special place in Greer's heart. She loved both the girls, but she knew what it was like to live under an older sister's shadow, always being compared to another sibling. Ash's ex-wife was a good mother, though, so she doubted Shelby would ever be subjected to those "why can't you be more like your sister" taunts she'd all too often endured.

"Last month she wanted to be a pitcher for the Baltimore Orioles. I had to replace two windows in the house while she perfected her pitching skills. This month she wants to be a veterinarian."

Greer laughed. "Let me guess. She's collecting strays now."

"Replacement glass is cheaper than vet bills. I'm screwed if she decides to try auto mechanics."

"If nothing else," Greer said with a smile, "she's enthusiastic and not afraid to try new things."

He drained his coffee and set the mug on the step between them. "She reminds me of you in a lot of ways."

"Her short-term obsessions or her enthusiasm?" She hadn't really been all that different from Shelby when she'd been a kid, except Shelby had parents who nurtured rather than attempted to quash her curious nature.

"Both." He smiled and her heart did a little flip. "You used to be pretty determined, too, you know."

"Still am," she said. "I'm determined to turn this run-down old place into a bed and breakfast."

"Why?"

She shrugged. "I have to do something to earn a living."

"No, why a B&B? It's just so . . ."

"Out of the realm of law enforcement?"

He nodded.

"There's your answer."

"Then why'd you join the local police force?"

"I told you, I got talked into it." She finished off her own coffee. "Besides, the extra money helps pay for sandpaper and paint, so it's not all bad."

He leaned forward and propped his forearms on his thighs. With his hands dangling between his knees, he looked at her, his expression skeptical. "I have a hard time imagining you being talked into anything."

"You don't know Travis," she said. "He was my dad's oldest friend. His football career ended in college and Dad went on to make the pros, but they were still tight. Saying no to him is like saying no to my dad." She shrugged again. "The department was short-staffed and I was available. The job was supposed to be temporary, but a year and a half later, here I am, still citing little old ladies for jaywalking."

"How can you stand it?" he asked.

"What do you mean?"

"Where's the challenge?"

She straightened. "I think that's the whole point," she said defensively.

A hardness entered his eyes. "You don't seriously expect me to believe that after the work you did for the Bureau, you actually enjoy handing out parking tickets."

She looked away. Hadn't she had the very same thought

herself a matter of weeks ago? "Like I said, that's the whole point."

"I don't buy it."

"You don't have to. It's what I want." Or at least that's what she kept telling herself she wanted.

"What if I asked you to come back with me when this is all over? Could you say no to me?"

"Ash, don't." *Don't make me think about everything I've been too afraid to consider. Don't make me wonder if I made a mistake in leaving.*

"Yeah, I know," he said, a sarcastic edge to his voice. "You're not ready to talk about it."

Dammit. She didn't need this shit. "Look who's catching on," she snapped irritably and stood. Why couldn't he just leave it alone? Why did he have to go and ruin a perfectly good, nonthreatening conversation?

She turned to leave, but he took hold of her hand before she escaped. "I've missed you, Greer," he said, coming to his feet. "Is that such a crime?"

She knew what he wanted to hear, but she couldn't bring herself to admit to him she felt the same. Doing so would only give him false hope, and that she couldn't do. Even he deserved better.

She attempted to tug free of his grasp, but he tightened his hold. "Don't run away again." He took the empty mug from her hand and set it on the wide wooden railing behind him, then pulled her to him, wrapping his arms around her and holding her close.

She did want to run, as far away as possible, but the intimate contact with another human being, with him, was too strong of a pull. The warmth of his touch kept her rooted. He was temptation personified and she lacked the strength to resist him.

She looked into his eyes and her pulse took off like a

rocket. Desire burned within the intense depths of his gaze and whatever protest she'd been searching for vanished. Instead of pushing away from him like she knew she should, she reached up to cup his jaw in her palm.

And then she kissed him.

Sizzling shockwaves of pleasure danced enticingly over her skin when his tongue swept into her mouth. He didn't wait for her to set the pace, but teased, coaxed and made her want more.

She wrapped her arms around his neck and leaned into him. He groaned in response to her body aligning with his and tightened his hold. Drawing his hand down her back to her bottom, he then moved upward again, his fingers skirting her nape as he cradled the back of her head in his large hand. He deepened the kiss.

God, how she'd missed him.

She let him know exactly how much, too, by rubbing her breasts against his chest. Her nipples hardened into tight buds beneath the filmy material of her top. Damn, but she ached for his touch. Arousal pulled hard in her belly.

God, how she'd missed him.

He turned and guided her backward. Her bottom met the vinyl siding and suddenly she was surrounded by the heat of him, by his large, looming presence holding her a willing prisoner, by the desire making her dizzy.

His hands were on her bottom and he lifted her. She wrapped her legs around his hips, and kissed him more deeply. She drove her fingers though the thick, rich strands of his hair. With the wall to her back, she straddled his hips and clung to him, not caring that they were getting all hot and heavy where insomniac neighbors might see them if they happened to be looking out their window. Her primary concern was in satisfying the sharp need raking her insides, making her restless and achy. Making her want Ash with such a powerful, primal force, she didn't care who saw them.

His lips left hers, but her protest died a sudden death when the heat of his mouth traveled down her throat to the slope of her breast. With her hands firmly gripping his shoulders for support, she arched her back, encouraging him to take her into his mouth.

He did, his mouth hot and wet through the filmy fabric of her top. But she wanted more. So much more. She tightened her grip on his hips and with his help, eliminated the thin barrier separating them.

Warm, humid air brushed her already-heated skin. She bit down hard on her bottom lip to keep the cry of pleasure from escaping on the early-morning air when he suckled her breast, using his tongue and his teeth to draw her more deeply into his mouth.

Heat spiraled, then burned like an out-of-control wildfire inside her. For the first time in ages she felt alive and, for the moment, she welcomed the incredible, chaotic sensations.

Her desire climbed. She wanted Ash, inside her, satiating the deep, insistent and demanding needs of her body. She rocked against him, against the long, hard length of his erection straining against the confines of his jeans. A shudder passed over her and she pressed herself more fully against him. He groaned, a mixture of pleasure and pain that hiked her desire a couple dozen degrees.

His teeth grazed her nipple. A deep moan she had no hope of holding back erupted from her lips. Moisture pooled between her legs and she kept rocking against him, insistently. He took hold of her hips to still her movements and she whimpered in protest. Widening his stance, he held her suspended, then drew his hand over her bottom to dip his fingers beneath the inseam of her shorts.

She wore no panties and he growled what she was certain was approval as he drew the tip of his finger over the slick, wet folds. She clung to his linebacker-wide shoulders and welcomed the fresh sensations rippling through her as he slowly stroked her. His breath came in short, hard pants that mirrored her own struggle for oxygen. Tension coiled tight, yet it wasn't nearly enough.

Her leg muscles quivered. Her entire body trembled. She dug her nails into the sweat-slicked flesh of his wide shoulders as she strained toward the promise of release.

They weren't in a position that allowed him to increase the pressure her body craved. She felt as if she was suspended between the promise of sweet bliss and the disappointment of frustration. Closing her eyes, she focused on the slow-building intensity.

Was she truly that out of touch with the needs of her own body? Had it been so long she'd forgotten how to reach an orgasm? Too damn long, she thought. Just over two years— since their last sane night together in Phoenix, to be exact.

Suddenly, she went stone cold. The orgasm she'd been inching toward slipped too far out of her reach to call it back. She couldn't do it. For as much as she wanted nothing more than to finish what they'd stupidly started, she couldn't.

"Stop." She struggled to get away. Away from the memories before the darkness closed in on her again. "Ash, stop."

He instantly stilled. The passion clouding his gaze slowly cleared, revealing concern. Slowly, he lowered her to her feet.

"I'm sorry." Unable to look at him, she scooped up her top and quickly pulled it over her head.

"Greer?"

"I'm sorry," she said again, her voice as stilted as her movements. "I didn't want for this to happen."

"What's going on?" Concern laced his voice.

"I can't." She stood, anxious to escape. "I thought I could, but . . . I can't."

"I don't understand."

No, she didn't expect he would. How could she explain to him what she barely understood herself? Vicar hadn't assaulted her sexually, but that had been his intent, among other things. While she had escaped that particular degradation, she had witnessed his evil on others. Those were memories she needed to keep at bay or she would lose it. Maybe even for good.

Maintaining the tenuous hold on her sanity wasn't easy for her under the best of circumstances. She didn't need to make matters more complicated by intentionally blurring the lines of her slim grasp on reality.

"Greer, talk to me."

She walked into the house instead. Talk to him? And say what? That she was now apparently frigid? No, that wasn't possible. She wouldn't have been so completely and thoroughly aroused if that was the case.

She hoped.

She hadn't even made it as far as the kitchen before the screen door squeaked on its hinges, then snapped closed. She put out fresh food for Eula and refilled the dog's water bowl. "I think it'd be best if you checked into the motel as soon as possible."

"Dammit, Greer," he said, his voice rising in frustration. "How much longer are you going to keep shutting me out?"

She turned off the coffeemaker, rinsed the carafe and dumped the coffee grounds into the garbage can without so much as a glance in Ash's direction. She couldn't, *couldn't* face the hurt, anger and confusion she knew she'd find, emotions she'd caused, all because she was too afraid of feeling too much.

She had no other choice. Not if she hoped to keep that tiny thread from unraveling and strangling the life right out of her.

She paused in the doorway and kept her back to him. "I'm leaving for the station within the hour," she said, then took off for the stairs, leaving him standing alone in her kitchen.

Chapter 12

"NO TASK FORCE. It's not going to happen."

"You can't be serious," Ash argued, but recognized a brick wall when he ran into one. From her one slightly hiked eyebrow above eyes filled with distinct challenge to the irritating way she kept tapping her pen against the blank legal pad in front of her, she told him loud and clear she wasn't about to budge on the subject of establishing a task force.

Frustration bit into him. His job was to assist, provide investigative support—period. Sure, there were methods of assuming control without officially taking over an investigation, but Greer was as aware of those same slight-of-hand ploys as he, making his job all that much more difficult.

"We're a small department," she added in a more reasonable tone. "A small county, which, by the way, is currently operating without a budget. We just don't have that kind of manpower."

He drained the last of his coffee and tossed the Styrofoam cup in the garbage can beneath the desk he'd commandeered for himself. If he consumed any more caffeine on an empty stomach, by noon there'd be nothing left of his stomach lining. "Then I suggest you call in the state police."

"Ooh, great idea. We can even send an open invitation to the press while we're at it."

Her sarcasm annoyed the hell out of him. Why was she being such a pain in the ass, going all territorial on him? Definitely not the attitude of someone who wanted nothing to do with an investigation. To the contrary, she was behaving as if she didn't intend to relinquish a single ounce of control. He didn't know whether to feel exasperated or encouraged.

"That's not what I was suggesting," he shot back irritably.

"Look," she said, "right now we have the benefit of a low profile. You know as well as I do keeping it that way for the time being can work to our advantage."

"I disagree."

She gave him a level stare. "That's not my problem."

He pushed away from the desk and paced. The department might be suffering from a shortage of available personnel, but they had other options. Exploring those options, however, required Greer listening to reason. Something he doubted would be occurring anytime soon.

He strode to the window and stared out at the cars parked in the lot—his, hers, a Honda that belonged to a very pregnant dispatcher who'd just come on duty and two empty patrol units. One, he assumed was Greer's and the other for the deputy currently off duty. He was beginning to think he was the only one concerned that a serial was on the loose. The clock on the far wall indicated seven-thirty and the sheriff had yet to make an appearance. There were two other deputies on duty, both out on patrol rather than contributing to the investigation. Out of necessity, or had they learned from their own experience not to encroach on what Greer perceived as her domain and chose not to be involved in the case?

He blew out a frustrated breath as he looked over his

shoulder at Greer. "Are you being intentionally obstinate, or is this some new personality quirk I'm only being introduced to this morning?"

She tossed her pen on the desk. "Don't be a jerk, Ash. It's never been your style."

With her, no. Ask any of the other agents in the Unit and they'd tell a different story. He had a reputation as a hard ass for a reason. Pussies didn't nail serials.

"If we brought in the state police," she said as she stood, "we risk alerting the press. The last thing I need right now is some reporter snooping around, dogging my heels. How long do you think it'd take before they realize I don't have jack on this case? That kind of news leaks out, we might as well wave a green flag under the UNSUB's nose."

"I disagree. He's hiding bodies, Greer. He isn't looking to be immortalized in the press."

"Which is exactly why I don't think we should draw any more attention than absolutely necessary. Let's not give him a reason to think he'll be the lead story on the six o'clock news."

"We can use the press to our advantage."

"No task force, and no press." She glared at him. "If you have a problem with the way I chose to run *my* investigation, then I suggest you trot your ass back to Quantico and let the locals handle this one." She looked as if she wanted to crucify that ass she'd just ordered back to Virginia.

Territorialism was nothing new. He'd been the victor in a few pissing contests in his line of work. In that respect, Greer was no different from any number of cops and detectives he'd dealt with, with a couple of exceptions. She was his wife and her perception was skewed. He should probably zip his lip and let her do her job her way, but he couldn't help his need to protect her.

What a joke, he thought. As if she'd ever look to him to keep her safe again.

"Using the press to draw a suspect out is nothing new," he said, realizing too late what he was saying, but unable to stop the delivery of the direct hit to what he knew was a raw nerve. "Challenge him. Taunt him so he'll make a mistake."

Her gaze turned glacial. "Having tried it your way once before," she said coldly, "let's not."

Before he could form an apology, she walked out of the office and took off down the corridor.

Shit!

Real nice, Keller.

With a grunt of disgust, he walked back to the desk and dropped into the chair. The worn leather and ancient springs creaked under his weight. He understood her reaction. He'd made the suggestion once before, and look how that had turned out. One dead officer and what he now strongly believed was irreparable harm to Greer, a fact he hadn't wanted to face but feared he had no choice. She'd survived The Preacher, they both had, but the cost of survival hadn't been without a price. All because he'd convinced her that taunting the bastard could work to their advantage.

It'd been two years, but that press conference remained as fresh in his mind as if it had happened yesterday. Greer facing a mob of reporters, standing before a podium with dozens of microphones attached, her answers designed to infuriate the UNSUB. The plan had been to piss off the bastard so he'd make a mistake, but all they'd done was draw his attention to Greer until he'd become obsessed with her. The Preacher had taunted them with notes about his crimes, boasting of his superiority—each and every one addressed to Greer, containing nothing that provided them with a single lead.

The body count continued to rise. The public was in a state of panic, elected officials were demanding an arrest from a task force two steps behind the UNSUB. The Preacher had turned the tables on them all right, and his communications to Greer had become more and more bold with every slain prostitute they'd found. He'd lead them to crime scene after crime scene, but they'd never gotten close enough to put an end to the Preacher's destruction of human life.

With virtually no leads, they began holding daily press conferences for the sole purpose of recording the crowd. They'd hoped to spot that one person who didn't quite fit in, someone who remained on the fringes or who appeared a little too eager for information, too smug or even amused by the media circus.

Nothing.

Heavier patrols of the red light districts produced zero results, and The Preacher continued to kill. They'd gotten no closer to putting an end to his reign of terror than when they'd first been called in to assist.

Ash pulled his laptop from the case, set it up and fired off an e-mail to Faith, instructing her to run the small amount of new data he had on the current investigation through the Bureau's computer system. If a link or pattern existed, even with such scant information, Faith would be the one to find it. While his incoming messages downloaded, he did what he'd done countless times. Wondered what, if anything, he could have done differently that night in Phoenix.

The Preacher's final message had been no different than the others. A detailed description of where he would strike next but, as in the past, while the authorities were staking out what they believed was the UNSUB's chosen hunting ground, he'd been elsewhere ripping apart a victim he'd already lured into his clutches.

There'd been no way any of them could've known they were being set up. But, God help them, they'd walked right into a carefully orchestrated trap. Ash could berate himself until the end of time and it wouldn't change the fact that his encouraging Greer to play mind games with The Preacher had been a gargantuan mistake. Not once had he anticipated Vicar would physically come after Greer, but he'd all but unlocked the door and invited the son of a bitch inside. He should've argued against her going undercover with a female officer, not agreed with her, but no one, least of all him, had realized the extent of The Preacher's fixation on Greer until it was too late.

They'd taken every precaution, but in the end, they'd grossly underestimated Vicar. Ash's memory was fuzzy at best, most of what he knew had been told to him or he'd pieced together himself. His final conscious thought that night had been about mosquitoes, of all things, but he'd been wrong about the sharp, stinging bite he'd felt on the back of his neck, too. Vicar had seemingly appeared out of thin air, drugged him and it was lights out Special Agent Keller. When he regained consciousness hours later, Vicar and a female undercover officer were dead—and Greer had been teetering on the outer edge of reality.

Somewhere, in another area of the station house, a telephone rang. The metal door at the rear of the building clanged shut, followed by the sound of a gravelly female voice issuing a "mornin'" to Greer and the dispatcher. He pulled out his cell phone and placed a call to the state crime lab for information on the most recent crime scene, only to be told he'd have to call back in a few hours if he wanted to speak to the lead investigator. He left a message, then disconnected the call as he scanned the headers of the e-mail he'd downloaded. A couple from Faith, one with more data on missing persons in the area and another marked CONFIDENTIAL, wherein she reiterated her opinion on his lack of judgment and even questioned his mental state. Contrary to what Faith believed, he wasn't fucking crazy.

He deleted the e-mail and opened one from his youngest

daughter. Consistent with her latest obsession, Shelby asked him to buy a dog kennel for her upcoming birthday—which was still three months away. He sent her an e-mail telling her he'd talk it over with her mother when he returned to DC, then made a note in his task folder to call his ex to discuss the issue. He didn't see the harm, but he wasn't about to give Shelby the go-ahead without checking with Nancy first. It wouldn't be the first time one of his daughters came to him for something their mother had denied them.

The springs groaned under his weight when he shifted in the chair. He answered a few e-mails on other investigations, sent one to the agents in Idaho Falls requesting a status and started one to Con. As he contemplated how to explain why he was in North Carolina, his cell phone rang.

"Keller."

"Where the hell are you?" came the roaring demand of his superior.

Ash shut down the laptop. "Magnolia, North Carolina." He'd known he'd catch hell for the stunt he'd pulled, but for the first time in a long while, he didn't much care. He'd let Greer down once, and he wasn't about to do so again. She would need him, even if she refused to admit it.

"That's a helluva long way from Boise."

"Idaho Falls," Ash corrected.

"I don't give a rat's ass if it was Timbuktu."

"I sent Burke and Hornbeck in my place. It's being covered."

"*You're* supposed to be covering Idaho," Con snapped. "Not a pair of greenhorns looking to make a name for themselves. Unless you're looking to be busted down to file clerk, you'd better have a damn good reason for going off half-cocked to play Sir Gala-fucking-had."

Ash let out a breath. Faith had a big mouth.

"It's Greer," he said, then explained what little information he had on the case thus far.

Con muttered a string of inventive curses. "How is she coping?" His milder tone indicated genuine concern.

"Hard to say," Ash told him. "It's early yet. There's not a lot to go on." Which wasn't exactly a lie, but he wasn't about to discuss Greer when she could walk back into the room at any moment. The ice he'd been skating on with her was already razor thin. One wrong move and he'd crash through and end up with a brutal case of frostbite.

"The Bureau has no jurisdiction," Con said after a moment. "I'm gonna have to pull you off this one."

"I can't do that." No way was he leaving Greer to work the case alone. Her emotional state was fragile at best, at least in his opinion. If the investigation turned ugly, which was entirely possible once she got closer to fingering the UNSUB, she would need him. And this time, dammit, he'd be there for her.

"The hell you can't," Con barked. "You have two kills and no confirmation they're related."

"The MO is the same. The UNSUB embalms the bodies, then digs up a grave to hide the evidence."

"Two victims. *Two.* Not three."

"Technically we have four vics," Ash argued, even if it was a stretch. "You're forgetting the occupied coffins."

"Don't push it, Keller. You don't even know if there's a connection."

"She can't handle it alone, Con," he said, lowering his voice. Hell, she couldn't handle the sight of his wedding band, which he'd refused to remove from his finger. "It's too soon."

"It's been two goddamn years," Con fired back, then continued with a fresh string of curses. "Besides, that's not ISU's problem."

Not the way Ash saw it. She wouldn't be in her current condition if it wasn't for ISU and, by extension, him. "You don't need me. Burke and Hornbeck are handling Idaho

Falls. I'm monitoring their progress. If they run into problems, they know where to find me. Just give me a few days."

Con swore some more. "I should order your ass back to Quantico."

Ash smirked. "Yeah, but you won't. Not yet. Give me some time here."

"Two days. And you'd better keep me updated."

"Will do."

"A piece of advice," Con said, gentling his tone again. "Don't make it personal."

At that moment, Greer walked back into the office. She went to her desk and sat, refusing to look at him. Not make it personal? Just how the hell was he supposed to not make it personal?

He let out a sigh. "Impossible," he said, then disconnected the call.

Chapter 13

PARKER RETURNED THE cordless phone to the unit on the wall. His insides trembled. Fear? No, never. Not him. He was beyond such weakness.

Anger? Yes. That's what he was feeling. Anger. Soul-deep and white-hot.

How dare that stupid cow do this to him, now, after the arrangements were made? What was that selfish bitch thinking? No wake? No memorial service? Just deliver her late brother's body to the crematory and be done with it, she'd said, as if Jefferson Holcomb's life was meaningless. As if he'd never mattered.

"You okay, Mr. H?"

Parker let out a slow, even breath, then turned to face Opal Jones, Hennessy's cosmetologist. She sat perched on a padded stool as she applied makeup to the face of a middle-aged woman whose name he couldn't recall at the moment. He tried, but remembered only that she'd been a secretary at one of the local law firms and had dropped dead at the candy counter of the Majestic Theatre from congestive heart failure at the ripe old age of forty-two.

Tension radiated from his neck to his shoulders. He flexed his hands. "We lost Holcomb," he told Opal.

Opal's eyes widened and she sat up straighter. "Sweet Jesus," she exclaimed. "How'd we lose a body?"

Under normal circumstances, Parker found Opal mildly amusing. Today, her down-home airs grated on his nerves. "We didn't lose the *body*," he said a tad too snappishly. He let out a short, impatient breath. "The deceased's sister changed her mind about the services. The body is being delivered directly to the crematorium."

Opal clucked her tongue and shook her dark head. "It ain't right," she said, dabbing the makeup brush into a jar of colored powder. "Folks deserve a proper and decent send-off."

"Yes," he murmured absently, his mind whirling. Even in death, Jefferson Holcomb would be denied happiness by the same woman who'd denied it to him in life—his vicious, controlling sister. And he was powerless. Helpless.

As Jefferson had been.

The cow. She deserved a send-off all her own.

"My daddy always said funerals, they was for the livin'. Mournin' gives 'em closure. A chance to say their final good-byes. It ain't right to deprive folks that last chance. Don't know what that uppity Jessica Holcomb is thinkin'," Opal continued as she concentrated on applying more powder to the legal secretary's cheeks. "Her brother might not have been the most upstanding citizen in the county, but he sure as dirt don't deserve to be tossed in the oven like unwanted garbage."

The telephone rang again, saving him from having to contribute more to the conversation. Inside, he continued to seethe. The stupid, stupid cow. He should make her pay for what she was denying her brother. And what of Jefferson's soul mate? What was he supposed to do with her now? She wasn't suitable for anyone other than Jefferson, he'd made sure of it. He always made sure the soul mates he chose were perfect.

Tonight, long after Opal and the others were home for the night, he was supposed to prepare for the final union, and now, now he didn't know what to do. He couldn't keep her indefinitely. He'd have to find a way to dispose of her.

He picked up the phone on the third ring. "Hennessy's," he said, infusing a serenity into his voice he was nowhere near feeling. "How may I be of service?"

Greer returned the receiver to the cradle with a little more force than necessary just as Travis walked through the door, looking as if he hadn't gotten much sleep. Eyes bleary and bloodshot, his face puffy, told her he'd tossed back a few too many last night with the good ole boys down at one of the watering holes in town. From the grim expression on his face, she had a feeling her day was about to go from bad to really shitty.

Since she'd gotten out of bed early this morning, not much had gone right. She hadn't handled things with Ash well at all. Throwing herself at him, then changing her mind, as if she was nothing more than a prissy prick tease on prom night. What the hell was wrong with her? She'd wanted to make love to him. Had she ever. And she'd been so close, but then she'd let the past . . .

No, she thought, frowning suddenly. She hadn't let the past intrude. She never did. She closed down before it could reach up and strangle the life right out of her. And when she couldn't control the memories or stop them from overwhelming her, she took a pill and prayed her heart wouldn't explode while she waited for the anxiety medication to kick into gear.

So why did it matter all of a sudden? that's what she wanted to know. Why did she care that the past had kept her from making love to Ash? She'd never questioned the predictability of her defense mechanisms before today, depending instead on their reliability. Why was today different?

She had no easy answers. That bothered her, too, even if she suspected all she'd be doing was attempting to rationalize the irrational. There was something to be said for moving through life as if she were a zombie, not feeling too much, not thinking too much, not too much anything—period. Keeping the world at bay and skirting through life on the fringes, never really participating, had its perks. It kept her safe.

Ash glanced up from whatever he was doing on his laptop computer. "Problems?"

Travis closed the door to the office she'd commandeered for the duration of the investigation. What the room lacked in space and décor, it made up for in practicality, away from the main area of the station where anyone who walked through the double glass doors might see or hear information she didn't want made public.

She'd already tacked a state map to the wall. Green pushpins marked the graveyards where the bodies were buried, while red pins signified the victims' residences, since she had yet to determine how or where the UNSUB was hunting his prey. Ash had added clear plastic-headed pins to indicate the eight missing persons cases from Magnolia County. She hated to think he could be right, that those eight missing women might already be victims of the UNSUB, but she couldn't discount the very real possibility. She could, however, hope that Ash was wrong.

Travis walked to the chair positioned across from her desk and turned it so he could see both her and Ash. "The crime lab came up with zilch from the crime scene," he said. "No trace evidence. Nothing. Not so much as a fiber."

"We still have the hair samples," Ash reminded them. He clicked a few keys on his laptop, then straightened, rolling his shoulders, no doubt to alleviate the stiffness caused by being hunched in front of the computer for the past three hours, analyzing what little data they had on the case. "I talked with the shift supervisor at the lab about an hour ago. They'll get started as soon as they receive the samples."

"Which won't be until tomorrow," Greer added. "I just got off the phone with Manny's assistant. They're having the samples couriered to the lab via overnight delivery."

"Overnight?" Travis balked. "We need those hairs processed ASAP."

"It's the best we can do. Manny's office is as strapped for personnel as we are and just doesn't have the manpower to have them hand-delivered," she explained.

Travis folded his beefy arms over his wide, barrel chest. "So where are we with this goddamn case?" he asked, his frustration evident by the gruff quality of his voice. "Do you have an idea yet what kind of nut job we're supposed to be looking for?"

She glanced at Ash, but he said nothing, just looked at her expectantly. "We already know he's an organized killer," she said, shifting her gaze back in Travis's direction. "What he does takes time and planning. My first guess is he's a white male, maybe late-thirties or early-forties. And he's good at what he does. He has skills, and a pretty solid working knowledge of mortuary science. According to Manny, this guy knows exactly what he's doing."

"You've just described nearly every funeral parlor employee in the county," Travis said. "Except maybe that old fart, Waxman. He's gotta be nearing seventy, and with his emphysema, he couldn't dig up a rosebush let alone a grave."

Travis had a point, but she wasn't going to cross anyone off her list of possibilities quite so readily. "I'll start paying visits to the mortuaries in the county later today," Greer said, consciously suppressing a shudder. With luck, she wouldn't come across any dead bodies on display, although she wasn't about to hold her breath. She'd end up bluer than the corpses she was anxious to avoid. "I can talk to the directors, employees, see if anyone acts nervous or strange."

"You ask me," Travis said, chomping on his unlit cigar, "those undertakers are all strange. You gotta be a little off to hang out with dead people all day long."

Ash's mouth tipped upward in a little half-grin. "Some people find comfort in communing with the dead."

"If it's all the same to you, I'll do my communing with the living," Travis returned. "What about you, G-man?"

"If Greer has no objections, I thought I'd start by interviewing the families of the previously deceased. We can try to determine if there's a connection between the bodies being buried together or if the UNSUB's choices are random."

"I don't think they're random," Greer said. "He's making conscious choices."

Ash frowned. "How you figure?"

"A couple of the cemeteries in the area have started using burial vaults the last few years. Since it looks like the UNSUB is digging up graves to bury his vics in occupied caskets, he has to know which interment facilities employ the use of vaults and which haven't started yet." She rifled through the growing stack of papers on her desk, articles she'd printed out in researching interment operations. She found the one she was looking for and carried it over to Ash. "The lids on those vaults weigh something like eight hundred pounds. That's an article on a cemetery employee down in Georgia. The guy had his legs crushed when the lid from a vault accidentally fell on him during an exhumation."

Ash's frown deepened as he scanned the article. "He's lucky he wasn't killed."

"So, we're back to someone with knowledge of the funeral business," Travis said.

"Possibly," she said, propping her backside against the desk. "It's really too early to be certain of anything at this point." Which made profiling the UNSUB that much more difficult. At the Bureau by the time she'd been called in to assist, the preliminary investigative work had all but been completed, or at least had been deep in progress. She'd always worked from a larger puzzle, not one where the corners hadn't yet been put in place.

She looked back to Ash. "Hold off on the Archer family interview for now. There's a possible investigation there already."

"Related?"

"Unrelated," she said with a shake of her head. "We discovered the first body because of allegations by the deceased's daughters from his first marriage. They convinced the DA their dad could've been poisoned by his second wife. Reba Archer probably won't even talk to us without her attorney present."

"Then I'll start with Gartner's family."

"No good," Travis said. "Gartner was an only kid and his parents left town a couple of weeks ago."

"For good?" Greer asked.

"'Fraid so. I'll see about a forwarding address and get back to you."

This was news to her, although she couldn't blame the Gartners for not wanting to stay in a house with such sad memories. Tommy had been their only son and had had a brilliant future ahead of him. She could only imagine the devastation and heartbreak his parents must be suffering now that their son had died from a senseless accident.

"Would you mind going to New Bern today?" she asked Ash. "Interviewing acquaintances of Joanna Webb would be helpful. See what you can turn up, where she hung out, if she was seeing anyone, if anyone was giving her trouble. The usual."

Ash nodded and started jotting notes. Obviously he'd taken her seriously last night when she'd warned him to back off and let her do her job. If she had no choice but to work the case with him, at least her job wouldn't be more difficult because she had to fight him for control every step of the way. Besides, she could use the extra manpower.

She looked at Travis. "How do you feel about coming with me to interview Joanna Webb's family members? They live here in town, they know you, and it might make them more comfortable and willing to talk if you're there."

"No problem," Travis said and stood. "But I wouldn't expect too much if I were you. They only found out last night their daughter was murdered."

"I know," she said, but the prospect didn't lessen her frustration. She was no stranger to dealing with the bereaved, so she did understand, but she hoped to make them realize the more they were able to tell her, the closer it could bring her to finding their daughter's killer.

"I've alerted the deputies on patrol to be on the lookout for anyone hanging around the cemeteries that doesn't look as if they belong. The boys know this is your baby, Greer, so if you need anything from them, you got it."

"Thanks," she said and managed a quick grin. She hadn't expected to run into problems, but she appreciated knowing Travis stood behind her.

He'd better, she thought, since he insisted she take on the investigation in the first place.

"Give me ten minutes," Travis said, heading for the door, "and then we'll drive out to the Webb place."

Ash stood and plucked his suit jacket from the peg behind the door.

Greer never thought she'd miss her dark suits, but today

with the temperature and humidity both threatening to soar, she'd have welcomed a nice breathable linen rather than the restrictive deputy's uniform.

"It's been a while since I've done leg work," Ash said as he shrugged into his jacket.

"It'll keep you sharp."

"It'll keep me out of your hair."

She smiled at the light, teasing note in his voice. "Gee, I hadn't thought of that."

"I'll bet," he said with a tolerant expression. "You heading out to interview the vic's family?"

"Yes," she said and walked with him down the corridor to the rear entrance where he'd parked his rental car. "Would you come with me to the funeral homes?" She didn't like asking for help, it went against the grain of her independence, but she disliked dead bodies more. Travis would agree to accompany her if she asked him, but she knew how Ash operated, and although she'd established this was her territory, chances were he'd already begun to form a personality profile of the UNSUB. He had the kind of experience that could prove useful, even if she wasn't foolish enough to trust his judgment completely.

He paused with his hand on the door. An intensity entered his gaze, making her suddenly feel awkward and uncomfortable.

"Whatever you need, Greer," he said, and she had the distinct impression he was referring to more than just the case. "All you have to do is ask."

She took a much-needed step back, but the distance did little to lessen her unease. "We can hit a couple of funeral parlors when you get back from New Bern," she said. "After the Webb interviews, I'm going to see about tracking down a few tombstone-tipping teens. They've been haunting the graveyards lately. Maybe they've seen something unusual."

His mouth slanted into that crooked grin again, and her heart did a flip in her chest. "What isn't unusual in graveyards?" he quipped. "Or teenagers, for that matter?"

She returned his smile. "No kidding."

He pushed open the door and stepped into the bright morning sunshine, then hesitated, his hand holding the door open. The air around them sizzled, crackling with a pent-up energy that felt all too familiar. The sudden urge to kiss him was strong, and equally familiar.

"I'll see you when I get back," he said, and then was gone, the moment passing as abruptly as it began.

The heavy metal door clanged shut, but the anticipation humming in her veins wouldn't be disappearing anytime soon. Ash had wanted to kiss her, too. She'd sensed it, felt it from the tingling of her lips, clear down to her toes and all relevant parts in between. Regardless of how much she might protest that she couldn't handle him and the investigation simultaneously, she still found herself wishing he *had* kissed her. Long and hard and senseless.

Chapter 14

VIVIEN LEE DRUMMED her manicured nails on the gleaming surface of the antique writing desk in her bedroom, impatient as the pathetically slow dial-up connection downloaded her e-mail. Converting to one of those high-speed Internet service providers didn't make sense since she didn't use the Internet all that often, and so was an expense she simply couldn't justify. Although, maybe she should reconsider. She had become somewhat of an e-mail junkie of late.

Her gaze caught the stack of unpaid bills poking out of the oval rose-tapestried holder. She needed to do something about those. If she didn't find herself a husband soon, she'd have no choice but to look into actual employment. The balance from the settlement of her last divorce wasn't going to last forever, even if she had managed to cut a few corners in recent weeks.

She wouldn't think about that now. She had more pressing matters to attend to, like her much-needed hair appointment in less than two hours, followed by a meeting of the cookbook committee she was heading up for the Junior League, a charitable venture to help raise money for the new pediatric cancer center.

The sound of Travis's voice jarred her out of her reverie. "What do you mean?"

"Greer . . ."

He saw right through her stall tactic. She knew exactly what he meant, but she wasn't in the habit of baring her soul and saw no reason to start now. "I tripped and hit my head. No big deal."

She suspected from the telltale expression in his eyes, he didn't believe her. She really hated that about him.

She gunned the engine and sped through the intersection. "Don't give me that look," she said, keeping her attention on the road.

"What look?"

She let out a sigh. "Like I'm fourteen and you just caught Selma and me trying to sneak into the Majestic on a Saturday night."

He didn't chuckle as she'd hoped. She chanced a quick glance in his direction, then flipped on the turn signal to change lanes. Sure enough, he had that "sell it elsewhere, kid" look about him.

"What aren't you telling me?"

God, where did she begin?

"Nothing, Travis," she lied.

"Now why is it that I don't believe you?" he mused aloud. "Maybe because you didn't bother to even mention the fact that you're still married. Kinda makes a guy wonder what else you could be hiding from him, doesn't it?"

She changed lanes to make a left at the next intersection. "My marital status is my business."

"You still could've mentioned it," he said, his tone filled with censure. "Not even your mama said a word about you still being married to Keller."

No, she didn't imagine her mother would. Such things just weren't spoken of in polite company, after all. Greer

She'd much rather surf *findamatch.com* for potential husband material.

E-mail downloaded, she clicked through and deleted the spam, read the contents of a digest of thirtysomething Southern single women on the pros and cons of female condom usage and perused a newsletter from one of her favorite mystery authors. She answered a chatty e-mail from one of her e-mail friends, an acquaintance from Virginia she'd met online via one of her e-mail groups, and sent a note to one of her fellow committee members reminding her to bring the minutes from their previous meeting.

She clicked the SEND/RECEIVE button. More mail downloaded, mostly spam—the first promising thicker hair, the next a new and improved method to fight the signs of aging, then how to grow a bigger penis and a get-rich-quick scheme. She had her own method for getting rich quick—thrice proven.

No note from the guy she'd met for drinks last night. Thank heavens. She wouldn't actually have bothered to send him a reply, which would have invariably evoked a twinge or two of guilt—not that the feeling would cause her any loss of sleep. She didn't like to be rude, but what was the point when the guy was all wrong for her?

A fresh stab of disappointment pierced her. No new inquiries from the male population of *findamatch.com*. More disturbing was the absolute silence from the pediatrician up in Charlotte she'd begun to develop an e-mail relationship with over the past couple of weeks. Since they'd "met" on *findamatch.com*, they had been exchanging e-mail almost daily. Initially their e-mails had been chatty in the getting-to-know-you sense, but lately they'd begun to cyberflirt. She'd been hoping and waiting for him to suggest they exchange telephone numbers, or perhaps even arrange a face-to-face to meet for drinks, but so far, he seemed content with their cyberexchanges.

She considered dropping him a quick note, but thought better of it. Best not to appear too eager. Nothing scared a potential prospect off quicker than a woman coming on too strong. The Internet might have widened the world of dating and provided a new venue for meeting men, but the rules were still the same. And if anyone understood men and relationships, it was Vivien Lee Lomax Walker Peters Coleman.

Greer looked pointedly at her watch when Travis slid his bulky frame into the passenger side of the police cruiser. "Ten minutes was forty-five minutes ago," she complained, firing the ignition.

Travis fastened his seat belt. "The DA called. The tox report came back on Archer."

She paused with her hand on the gearshift. "And?"

"Trace amounts of arsenic were found in Archer's liver."

"Well, I'll be damned." She shifted the cruiser into reverse and pulled out of the parking lot. "I didn't think Reba had it in her."

"Archer sure as shit did. According to the DA, the embalming fluid destroyed much of the evidence, so the fact that even trace levels of arsenic were found means Lowell was probably riddled with the stuff."

She turned left and headed in the direction of Main. "I guess this means Pamela will take the case to the grand jury."

"I bet we have an arrest warrant for Reba before the end of the week," Travis said. He slipped his sunglasses out from the front pocket of his uniform and swiped the frames over his pant leg. "You want to do the honors?"

She made a right on Main Street and cruised five miles under the speed limit. The Webbs lived on the opposite end of town, in the poor section, as it'd been called when she was a kid. "Nothing would give me greater pleasure, but I'd

prefer to focus my attention on the current investigation, if that's okay with you. Grant or Ryan would probably enjoy hauling Reba's ass down to the Women's Detention Center." Greer made a sound similar to a short bark of laughter. "Or even Blythe, for that matter. She's not too fond of Miz Reba."

"Who is? But she's not so bad." Travis frowned. "Those no 'count brothers of hers, that's another arrest waiting to happen. Wanna bet one of them has something to do with Archer's death?"

"Hmmm," she murmured as she rolled the cruiser up to a STOP sign. "I wouldn't be surprised. They've been spelling trouble for years."

She took a moment to take a look around Main Street, but noted nothing out of the ordinary. Regulars Lou, Curtis and Muncie sat on the wooden bench outside of the barber shop on the corner of Main and Walnut. From the looks of the three elderly men, who'd been occupying that same bench for as long as Greer could remember, they were heavy into some sort of debate. Seventy decades' worth of baseball trivia or the weather, no doubt, two of their favorite topics.

A young mother attempted to wrestle a double stroller into the pharmacy across the street. A middle-aged gentleman in a neatly pressed pin-striped suit walked up, stopped and held the door for her, then continued on his way to the bank next door. A trio of little girls skipped along the sidewalk toward the park with rolled-up towels tucked under their arms, on their way to their morning swim lessons held at the public pool, she guessed. Quiet. Peaceful. Quaint. Safe. Not a single one of those she observed going about their business was aware a vicious killer could be lurking in their midst.

"So, you gonna tell me what really happened at the cemetery yesterday?"

knew she was a constant disappointment to her mother, but she figured that was Mama June's problem, not hers. "You could've asked, if it was all that important to you."

"Like a lot of people, I just assumed you were divorced," he said. "Besides, it's not as if you're all that talkative about what happened to you."

"I don't like to dwell on it," she said. "So if you don't mind, I'd like to change the subject."

Travis grunted in response, whether out of agreement or not, she didn't know and didn't much care just so long as he didn't push the issue. How was she supposed to put the past behind her if people kept talking about it?

She frowned. How could she put the past behind her when she refused to even acknowledge its existence?

They drove the last half mile in silence. She parked across the street from the run-down Craftsman-style home where Joanna Webb had spent her youth. The house needed a fresh coat of paint on its weathered clapboard siding and new supports under the sagging front porch. As she and Travis neared the cracked concrete walkway leading to the front steps, the scent of recently cut grass permeated the warm, humid air, mingling with the intoxicating scent of roses from bushes in need of weeding.

Travis's hand touched her arm before she ascended the stairs. "You going to be okay with this case?"

"Oh," she said, injecting a lightheartedness into her tone, "today it matters what I think?"

He had the decency to appear contrite. "I'm sorry about that."

She offered him a brief smile. "Apology accepted." She did appreciate his concern, but the facts were the facts. Out of the five members of the Sheriff's Department, she was the one most qualified to handle the investigation. Travis might have tried to bully her yesterday, but she also understood he'd done so out of fear for the people he'd been elected to protect. "I'll be fine just as soon as the UNSUB is behind bars."

As she turned to go up the stairs, she sent up a little prayer that she was right.

By the time Greer pulled her Escape into the driveway of the old Victorian next to Selma's flame-red Dodge pickup, she was convinced of one immutable fact—she was nothing more than a big fat liar. She wasn't fine. She didn't think she'd ever be fine again.

The interview with Joanna Webb's parents had gone exactly as Travis had predicted—badly. Ray and Ladonna Webb were in shock and understandably devastated by their daughter's death. Ladonna hadn't uttered more than two coherent words the entire time she and Travis were at the Webb home, and all Ray Webb had done was rail at the injustice of it all. Not one shred of information had been gleaned from the interview. All she'd managed to accomplish was a reminder of why she'd walked away from the Bureau—because situations like the one she'd been in this morning were just too damn painful.

Ash had yet to return from New Bern, and she hadn't heard a word from him all afternoon. Travis had more rounds to go with the county's budget committee, so that left her to either visit the funeral parlors alone or wait for Ash. Out of self-preservation, she'd opted for the latter.

She had tracked down a few of the boys she suspected were responsible for the vandalism of area graveyards, and once they realized she wasn't going to bust their asses for tipping a couple of headstones, they'd actually been willing to talk to her. Unfortunately, she'd come away with no leads. The boys hadn't seen or heard anything unusual when pulling their pranks. She'd warned them away from the cemetery, more to protect them than from concern over any real harm they might cause. She didn't want to think about what could happen should the boys run across her grave-digging UNSUB.

Before heading into the house, she walked out to the curb to the mailbox. A high-pitched shriek rent the air. She tensed, not drawing a steady breath until she recognized the source. Two doors down, a group of kids ran through a lawn sprinkler.

She let out the breath she'd been holding. Good Lord, she needed to get a grip. She couldn't keep skirting to the edge and back over every out-of-the-ordinary sound she heard. She was jumpier than a high-strung feline today, and starting to feel pretty damn ridiculous.

Mail in hand, she flipped through the envelopes as she walked toward the house. A couple of utility bills, a credit card statement, the latest issue of *Southern Living* magazine and the usual junk mail. Normal stuff. She liked normal. A lot, since normal had become virtually nonexistent in the past few days. A state she didn't see as a possibility until after she had the UNSUB behind bars.

Entering the house through the mudroom, she walked into the kitchen and dropped her purse and mail on the is-land, grabbed a Diet Coke from the fridge, then went look-ing for Selma. The rhythmic scrape of sandpaper against freshly installed drywall drifted to her from one of the up-stairs bedrooms. She climbed the stairs and walked toward the far end of the corridor where she found Selma hard at work, with Eula sprawled in the middle of the floor sur-rounded by drywall dust.

Eula didn't budge.

"What are you doing here so late?" she asked Selma. Her friend usually rolled up for the day around four and it was half-past six.

Selma swiped the sweat from her brow with her forearm. "I wanted to finish off this room before calling it a day."

Greer propped her shoulder against the doorjamb. "It

couldn't have waited until morning? Like when it's, oh, I dunno, thirty or forty degrees cooler up here?"

Selma tossed the sanding block into a white five-gallon tool bucket in the center of the room and shot her a wry grin. "If I'd done that, then I'd have to wait to ask you about that expensive-looking garment bag in the bedroom down the hall. Taking in boarders already, are we?"

"Not exactly," Greer hedged. She'd been so wrapped up in her own problems she hadn't even considered the ramifications of what Ash's presence would do to fuel the Magnolia gossip mill. Travis had already questioned her, and now Selma was about to give her the third degree. If answering questions from her employer and her best friend made her uncomfortable, she didn't want to think about all the innocent and not-so-innocent questions the people in town would ask her.

Maybe she should just let him stay with her. No sense adding to the feeding frenzy by insisting he go to a motel. Not that she gave a rat's ass one way or another what the nosey old biddies of Magnolia thought, but she did have more important things to worry about and didn't need the added headache. She and Ash could coexist and keep their hands to themselves. They were both adults, after all.

Yeah, consenting adults.

That's what she was afraid of.

Selma's grin widened. "I didn't think so."

Greer frowned. "If you know so much, then why are you asking me?"

"Because it's more fun to watch you squirm," Selma said with a laugh. She crossed the room for the ShopVac and unraveled the electrical cord. "So, the rumor that the hubby's come home does have some teeth to it."

Greer pushed off the doorjamb and walked into the room. "Doesn't take them long, does it?"

"What else is there to do in this town?" Selma plugged in the ShopVac. "They're going to talk about what they *think* they know, and what they don't know, they're going to make up."

Selma fired up the ShopVac. Eula bolted from the room as fast as she could waddle and Greer smiled. She motioned to Selma that she'd meet her downstairs and her friend nodded, then turned her attention to the job at hand.

Greer went to her room to change out of her uniform. By the time she'd showered, dressed and gone downstairs, Selma had finished up in the guestroom and was waiting for her on the front porch, sipping beer from a long-necked bottle. Greer joined her and helped herself to a bottle from the cooler near Selma's feet.

She twisted off the top and took a long drink. "Damn, that's good," she said, then sat in one of the lounge chairs near the door so she could hear the telephone if it rang. She'd been home an hour already and still hadn't heard a word from Ash.

Selma looked at Greer expectantly. "Well?" she prompted. "You gonna tell me what's going on or not?"

"*Nothing* is going on," she said, assuming Selma was referring to Ash being in town.

"Hey, this is me you're talking to. Remember?"

Greer took another drink of her beer, because she was thirsty, not because she was stalling. "I can't talk about it."

Selma's eyes widened. "Work?"

Shit. She really needed to be more careful. She couldn't tell Selma the truth. But her friend wasn't stupid, and all too aware of what Ash still did for a living. It wouldn't take her long to add two and three together to come up with serial killer on the loose. "Don't be ridiculous," she chided Selma.

"So did you finally come to your senses?" Selma asked her. "Or did Ash get tired of waiting for you to wake the hell up and get back to living?"

"Do we have to talk about this?" She wasn't prepared to answer questions about her and Ash. How could she? She didn't have a damn clue what the answers were supposed to be. "And for the record, Reyser, I'm living just fine."

"Greer, honey, you know I love you, but I think it's time you opened your eyes and took a good look around. You're not living, you're existing. You're not even doing a very good job of that, if you ask me."

Greer set her half-empty bottle on the wrought iron table with a snap. "I'm not asking you."

"Maybe you should. That idiot shrink you've been seeing sure as hell isn't doing you any good. Haven't you spent enough time hiding from the past?"

Greer stood and walked to the edge of the veranda. Dusk had started to settle, casting deep shadows around the property. Shadows she fought the urge to hide in to escape the truth of Selma's words.

She tucked her hands into the side pockets of her pastel plaid jumper, which had become too loose since the last time she'd worn it, and leaned her shoulder against the post. Even the tank she'd slipped on beneath it hung on her body. Ash had commented on her weight. He'd given her hell for being too thin.

He'd been right. She was too thin. She could easily stand to put on a good ten to fifteen pounds.

"Don't judge what you don't know anything about," she said, turning to look at Selma. "You weren't there. You don't know."

Selma lifted her bottle in a mock salute, then polished off the remaining contents. "I know you went through hell, even though you won't talk about it, even with me."

"It's not that easy."

Selma stood, grabbed the cooler by the handle and walked toward the edge of the steps leading down to the brick walkway. She stopped on the bottom step and looked up at Greer, her eyes filled with concern. "Nothing worth doing ever is."

Greer didn't know what to say, so she said nothing. Out of habit? Probably, but she wasn't ready. Might never be. She simply wasn't that strong of a person any longer and doubted she'd ever be able to face what had happened to her, never be able to articulate how terrified she'd been, how helpless.

She reached for her cell phone the moment it started vibrating in her pocket. "I'll see you tomorrow," she said to Selma, then she checked the blue-lighted display.

Ash.

Finally.

She pressed the CALL button. "Where have you been all afternoon?" she asked by way of greeting, watching as Selma climbed into her truck and drove off. "You should've checked in with me hours ago."

"Missed me, did you?"

Actually, she had, but not for the reasons his flirtatious tone indicated. She'd wanted to get a start on checking out the funeral parlors in the area. Although that didn't explain the warmth skittering along the surface of her skin at the sound of the deep, husky timbre of his voice. "Don't be cute, Keller. Not while we have a job to do."

"Have you eaten?"

"No, not yet."

"Good. I'll bring dinner and we can talk shop. I'll meet you at your place in, say, twenty minutes."

"I take it this means you had a productive afternoon."

"You could say that," he said. "I tracked down Joanna Webb's roommate. Joanna left to go on a blind date and that's the last time anyone saw her alive."

She walked into the house and flipped on switches as she went from room to room until the bottom floor was ablaze with light. "Please tell me her roommate at least had a name."

"Does Tommy Gartner ring any bells?"

A chill colder than ice slid down her spine. "Oh, my God," she whispered. "Ash, Tommy died over two months ago."

"I know," he said, then disconnected the call.

Chapter 15

"HOW MUCH YOU willing to bet the DNA results won't be a match to Tommy Gartner?"

"If we're lucky enough to get a match," Ash reminded Greer as he tossed empty containers of Chinese food into the white plastic sack. He understood the frustration lining her voice, because he felt the same. It'd been years since he'd collected information and chased down leads, and had forgotten how slow and painstaking this level of an investigation could be. For the most part, he walked in, lorded over the locals with his expert opinion, then took off for the next city with another task force on the hunt for another monster. But Magnolia wasn't just another city. This time was different. This time the stakes were much higher. "There is that possibility, you know."

Greer carried their plates to the sink and turned on the tap. She let out an impatient huff of breath. "Like I don't know that," she said, her voice mildly laced with sarcasm. "I've got a news flash for you—I do have an inkling of what I'm doing."

He scooped up the handful of silverware and started placing it in the dishwasher. "I wasn't suggesting otherwise," he said, his tone bordering on placating.

A frown creased her forehead. "Then stop being so damn condescending," she snapped.

His patience slipped. He jammed a serving spoon into the holder, but bit his lip. He didn't know what had made her so damn prickly all of a sudden. When he'd pulled up to the house, she'd actually appeared pleased to see him. Of course, he had been carrying a large sack filled with a variety of her favorite Oriental dishes. But somewhere between the sexy curve of her mouth when he'd taunted her with Moo Shu Pork and the cleanup, something had crawled up her ass. He wasn't going to allow her to draw him into an argument he suspected was nothing short of a smoke screen for whatever the hell was really bothering her.

She slipped a limp hank of hair behind her ear. She'd worn it loose tonight, and the once-vibrant blonde tresses now hung flaccidly around her face, making her look pale and drawn. He'd never get used to seeing her that way.

"I'm sorry," she apologized, her expression contrite as she looked at him from her side of the dishwasher. She set the plates on the rack. "I'm taking my frustration out on you. That's not fair and I'm sorry. You're here to help, not be my whipping post."

He acknowledged her apology with a brisk nod, then walked back to the table for the bag to carry to the garbage can he'd spied out back behind the garage. By the time he returned, she'd stowed the leftovers, started the dishwasher and had a pot of coffee brewing.

He leaned his hip against the counter near the coffeepot. "We did make some progress today," he said. "Not as much as I would've liked, but it's early yet. At least we have a connection, something to go on."

Her expression turned skeptical. "The victim had a blind date with a dead man. I hardly call that progress," she scoffed, pulling a pair of oversized mugs from the cabinet overhead. "Were you able to determine how the date was arranged or even who arranged it?"

"The roommate didn't know. I get the feeling they weren't all that close. We'll figure it out," he reassured her. "We've got Webb's laptop, which I FedEx'd to Faith before I left New Bern. The New Bern PD has been alerted and they're more than willing to cooperate and help any way they can. We'll have phone records by morning, see who Webb spoke to. A woman doesn't go out on a date without talking to someone about it. We'll find the bastard, Greer. I promise you."

She didn't look convinced. In fact, she looked afraid, he realized suddenly.

His heart twisted painfully in his chest. Once upon a time his wife hadn't been afraid of anything, least of all a murdering sociopath. He'd changed that, and heaven knew he had more than enough regrets to last a lifetime. But how much longer would they both keep punishing themselves for past mistakes? How long would she keep punishing him?

"How many more women have to die before we stop this guy?" she asked, her voice barely above a whisper.

He came up beside her and laid his hand over hers, encouraged when she didn't pull away from him. "I don't know, sweetheart. No one does. We can only do our best."

Moisture pooled in her big blue eyes. "Dammit, Ash," she said, her voice tight. "I told Travis I didn't want the investigation. I can't do it, but I can't stand by while more women die, either. God, I hate being in this position."

"I know you do." He didn't know what else to say.

"I don't even want to think about crawling inside the UNSUB's head. And I sure as hell am not looking forward to putting myself in the victim's shoes." Pain mingled with the dampness of her welled-up tears. "I don't even know if I *can*. Do you have any idea how much that scares me? Or how angry it makes me that more women will probably die a horrible death because I'm too goddamn afraid to save them?"

"You don't have to do this alone," he said, and gave her hand a tight squeeze. He wanted nothing more than to pull her into his arms and comfort her, chase away her fears. But he didn't. Not when he selfishly had his own set of fears riding high, namely rejection. "I'm here to help in any way I can."

She made a sound of disgust and tugged her hand from his. With her hands braced on the counter, she looked forward, her gaze fixed on the darkness outside the kitchen window. "Don't take this the wrong way," she finally said, "but you're not exactly the first person I'd call for help."

Pain sliced through him at the hurt and fear in Greer's sweet voice, followed by the hard bite of anger. He'd accepted responsibility for his part in what she'd suffered at Vicar's hand. That didn't mean he hadn't spent countless hours recounting events or berating himself for underestimating Vicar or the mistakes they'd all made that night. He'd give anything, his own life included, to turn back time, but life simply didn't work that way. You made your mistakes, you did whatever you could to correct them and make amends, and then you moved on before it crippled you. Before you ended up with a fifth of Scotch and a .38 caliber chaser.

He moved in behind her to settle his hands on her shoulders. Gently, he turned her to face him. "Then don't," he said, careful to keep the anger from his voice. "Depend on yourself, Greer. You were one of the best in the Unit. Those skills aren't likely forgotten."

"*Were*," she said, "is the operative word here."

"It won't be easy. God knows I realize that, but did you ever stop to think that maybe you'd finally be able to put the past behind you?"

She shrugged out of his grasp and stepped away. "I have put the past behind me." The defensiveness in her tone said otherwise.

"No," he said bluntly. "You haven't. You've spent the last two years avoiding it, and me."

Her eyes narrowed. "Is that what all this is about? You? Us?"

Irritation shot up his spine and settled in his shoulders, then spread upward. He rubbed at the back of his neck, but the tension refused to ease. "Maybe it is," he admitted. "In part, anyway. What's so wrong with wanting my life back? *Our* life back?"

She spun away, but didn't bolt from the room like he half-expected her to do. Like she'd been doing for too damn long.

"How much longer are you going to keep punishing me for what happened?" he demanded, his tone rising out of sheer frustration. He probably wasn't doing much to further his cause, but couldn't help himself. Her refusal to even acknowledge his existence had essentially rendered him powerless in their marriage. He'd had enough. Regardless of what happened over the next few days, when he left Magnolia, he was either leaving with his wife or the name of a damn good lawyer.

Slowly, she turned back to face him. "Is that what you think? That I've been punishing you all this time?"

"What am I supposed to think?" he fired back. "You haven't said dick to me in two years." He let out a rough breath that did little to calm him. "I can't change the past, Greer, I can only do my best not to make the same mistakes twice. Yeah, I fucked up and it nearly got us both killed, but dammit, we made it out alive. Shouldn't that count for something?"

"So what are you saying? I should just forget what that bastard did to me?"

"I'm not—"

"Forget what he did to Linda Hartley? He butchered a woman, a cop, right before my eyes, Ash." The tears she'd been fighting spilled down her cheeks. "He fucking gutted her and there wasn't a damn thing I could do to stop him. That's not something I'm likely to put behind me, or even forget, anytime soon."

He was beside her, pulling her into his arms before his heart struck another beat. She clung to him and cried—hard, great, wrenching sobs forceful enough to shake her entire body. The words of comfort he uttered he suspected went unheard, but he whispered them anyway, until the dam of tears ebbed.

She didn't protest or put up a fight when he guided her from the kitchen and led her upstairs to her bedroom at the end of the hall. She went directly to the bed and sat on the mattress while he walked into the bathroom, returning with a box of tissues tucked under his arm, a cool rag for her face in one hand, a Dixie cup of water and a bottle of aspirin balanced in the other.

A weak, tentative curve of her lips transformed into the semblance of a smile. "You're still such a Boy Scout," she said quietly, taking the water and aspirin from him. "Prepared for everything, aren't you?"

He set the box of tissues on the nightstand. "I try." He sat next to her and held out the damp cloth.

She tossed back a couple of aspirin, downed the cup of water, then exchanged the cup for the washrag to bury her face in the cool terry cloth. "Oh, God," she said, her voice muffled by the material covering her face. She peeked at him over the edge. "This was not how I envisioned us spending the evening."

"Oh, yeah?" He nudged her shoulder with his. "What'd you have in mind?"

She managed a small laugh, more of a release of pent-up

air than actual laughter, but he'd take what he could get. Her smile deepened a fraction.

"Brainstorming," she said dryly.

He gave her a lopsided grin. "Can't blame a guy for trying."

She played with the frayed edges of the washcloth by running the tip of her index finger over the sewn edge. "Maybe you wouldn't have to try all that hard," she said without looking at him.

Her uncustomary shyness touched him as deeply as her statement took him by surprise. As far as invitations went, the one she'd just issued couldn't be any more engraved, but he wasn't about to take advantage of her when her emotions were so raw.

She lifted her gaze to his. "Stay with me."

"Greer—"

"We don't have to make love," she said hurriedly.

"I can't do that."

"I don't want to be alone tonight," she said, clearly misunderstanding his meaning.

He took her hands in his. "Sweetheart, I'm no saint. If I stay here with you, we *will* make love."

The color of her eyes darkened. "I know."

He couldn't recall ever hearing two more provocative words in his life. "Are you sure?"

She nodded. "I'm sure."

"No regrets?"

She drew in a long, tremulous breath and held him captive with her gaze. "The only regret I have," she said, "is that it's been such a long time."

"It hasn't been all that long," he lied. He could probably count back to the last minute if he tried hard enough.

She slid off the mattress and moved to stand between his legs. "It feels like a lifetime." She looped her arms around his neck. "I probably forgot how."

He chuckled. "I doubt that," he said, his tone wry. She was doing a hell of a job of arousing him. He slid his hands around her waist and pulled her close. "But if you're looking for a refresher course, you've come to the right place."

Ash knew he was on the verge of making a monumental mistake where Greer was concerned. He wasn't wholly convinced she was emotionally ready to make love, but the promise of making her forget everything but him, if only for the time being, was a temptation he had no intention of resisting. There were bound to be ramifications for their actions tonight, but he'd deal with them in the morning.

She leaned into him, pressing her body against his, and kissed him, hard, hungry. Her tongue swept into his mouth, demanding his mouth mate with hers. Cupping her cheeks in his palms, he obliged by angling her head and deepening the kiss until he heard her soft, sensual moan of pleasure.

He wanted to take things slow, willing to let her set the pace. To savor every last moment of making love to her. God knew, the last thing he wanted to do was frighten her, but the hunger he'd suppressed for her for so long clawed at him with sharp and greedy talons, threatening his control.

Her own control must've been in equally short supply. Her hands trembled against his chest as she attempted to unfasten the buttons of his shirt. With a mewl of frustration, she yanked hard, sending buttons clattering all around the room.

He needed no further encouragement. They undressed quickly, their mouths and hands hungrily exploring as they reacquainted themselves with each other's body. And still he wanted more. He wanted all of her, holding nothing back.

She took his hand and pulled him toward the bed. He joined her atop the downy-soft comforter, the muted misty swirls of color the perfect frame against her pale skin. He still thought her far too thin, his hands skimming over the evidence confirming his belief as she brought his mouth down to meet hers in another deep, open-mouthed kiss.

They touched, tasted with an urgency that fired his blood, fueling desire already burning white-hot. His dick throbbed painfully, every brush of her hip against his erection filling him with sweet agony. She took his hand and skimmed it down her side, over her hip and down to the thatch of dark blonde curls between her legs where she parted her thighs and welcomed his touch.

He teased open her folds, sliding his finger inside her slick, wet heat. Her back arched and the moan that escaped her lips felt like a caress to his battered soul, the sound coming from deep within her throat, a purr of supreme satisfaction. He stroked her, long and slow, teasing her clit with the pad of his thumb, the way he knew she liked it. The way he knew would push her past the point of no return.

He coaxed her closer to the edge, then held her there on the brink, close to the white-hot flickering flames of desire that would consume both of their souls. The erotic writhing of her slender curves beneath him made him crazy with need.

God, how he'd missed her. For too long he'd dreamt of her touch, craved the feel of her body beneath his. Reality was heaven—heaven in his arms and he knew, without a doubt, he couldn't lose her again and survive it.

She reached for his hand again, the one between her legs, but he pulled away and slid his body over hers, holding himself poised above her. She wrapped her legs around his waist, her thighs surprisingly stronger than they looked, and lifted her hips to meet his, urging him inside her.

With agonizing slowness, he pushed himself into her tight sheath. Her eyes widened momentarily before his name fell softly from her lips in a whisper filled with awe and wonder. The pleasure-filled sound snapped the final thin thread of his control.

He thrust into her, burying himself inside her, and yet it still wasn't enough. With one hand beneath her bottom, he lifted her, angling her body to take all of him.

Her breath came in short, hard pants, the intensity increasing along with the tempo of their lovemaking, until she finally tensed beneath him as her orgasm claimed her. Her sheath contracted around his penis and she flew apart in his arms, her sweet moans of pleasure as uninhibited as her response.

The last of his control snapped and he drove into her, again and again until he joined her over the edge into oblivion. He'd been to hell and back again during the time they'd been apart and for the first time in two years, he'd been granted the taste of heaven. And he'd be damned if he'd ever let go of her again.

Chapter 16

GREER EASED QUIETLY from the bed, taking care not to awaken Ash. Scooping up his white button-down shirt from the floor, she shrugged into it while casting a quick glance at the bedside clock. Ten after two, and she was as wide-awake as if she'd slept eight hours instead of a mere four. So much for her thinking a phenomenal orgasm or two could do for her what a sleeping pill never could quite accomplish.

A brief smile lifted her mouth and she suppressed a satisfied chuckle. She might not have slept long, but, damn, she'd certainly slept good.

Careful to avoid the creaky floorboard at the foot of the bed, she strolled to the window to peer through the lace sheers into the night illuminated by streetlamps. *He* was out there, somewhere. The UNSUB. The killer. And quite possibly a resident of her own hometown. Someone she'd known for most of her life? She wanted to deny the likelihood, but she had her doubts. Or maybe what she really had was a case of wishful thinking. Even more disturbing to her was the thought that the people she cared about most—her family, friends and others she'd known for much of her life—

might have crossed paths with the bastard while going about their daily activities, blissfully unaware a monster lurked in their quiet, peaceful little world.

Ash's comment to Travis that night at the morgue, that the UNSUB could be Travis's own next-door neighbor, hadn't been an exaggeration. All too often the evening news anchors would broadcast sound-bites of shocked and surprised neighbors explaining how so-and-so was an upstanding member of the community, a deacon of the neighborhood church or the guy who cleared their walkways in the winter out of the kindness of his heart. To Greer, discovering that the UNSUB could be someone who seemed so nice—like Jim Gaynor who'd taken over as pharmacist when his father retired from the town's oldest drugstore fifteen years ago, or Bucky Lassister, the girls' basketball coach, or even a quiet, unassuming guy, like her mother's gardener, Herb Rosemont—filled her soul with terror.

The local citizenry might remain oblivious to the fact that a serial murderer could be walking among them, but *she* knew he was out there. Somewhere. Somewhere relatively close.

For as much as she would prefer to have it otherwise, she couldn't ignore the truth. The people of Magnolia counted on her to keep them safe, whether from a motorist speeding down Main Street or from the local florist, postman or pizza-delivery-guy turned sociopath. She had a job to do and, dammit, the job *had* to come first—even if it was the last thing she wanted to do.

She dragged a trembling hand through her hair, wincing when her fingers snagged on a tangle. Knowing what she must do and actually summoning up enough courage to accomplish it, however, were on two entirely different ends of her emotional spectrum. In truth, she didn't know if she still had the guts. She could barely make a decision between red Victorian rose wallpaper or blue antique stripe for one of the guestrooms. How on earth did she trust her own judgment when it came to tracking down the UNSUB?

She snagged a cloth band from the table and pulled her hair into a ponytail, then sank into the chair next to the window, curling up on the cushion and tucking her feet beneath her. She wasn't looking forward to the life-and-death choices awaiting her. How to best proceed with a case she wanted nothing to do with, yes, but that wasn't all that had her sitting in the dark tonight unable to sleep.

With her elbow propped on the padded armrest, she dropped her chin into the palm of her hand. Moonlight streamed into the room through the patterned lace sheers on the windows, bathing the room in blue-tinted, weblike shadows. She looked over at the four-poster bed, wondering what she was supposed to do with the long, lean, gorgeous male specimen sprawled over her mattress. Her husband.

Making love to Ash should've been a mistake. At the very least, a decision she regretted. She didn't. Not so much as a single ounce of remorse.

Loving Ash had never been the issue. She did. She just couldn't live with him.

She blew out an unsteady breath. What did she know about living, anyway? Maybe Selma had a point, after all. Existing *wasn't* living. Not even close. Putting one foot in front of the other didn't necessarily lead to her actually making forward strides. Quite the opposite. She'd become a pro at remaining firmly in place, like attempting to go up on the down escalator. Stagnant, even. But damn, she'd gotten good at leading a reasonable facsimile of a life . . . even an empty one.

She shifted her position, then crossed her arms over her

upraised knees. Nothing ventured, nothing gained. That was her, all right, the freaking poster child for a tired old cliché that summed up her tired old life to absolute perfection.

No, not her life, she silently amended. Her entire existence. How could she expect to actually move forward if she lacked the balls to put the past behind her? Christ, she knew *that* much. She had a background in psychology, a requisite for her becoming a profiler with the Bureau. She didn't need to be Freud to figure that one out.

Details of what had occurred in Phoenix were never discussed. Period. Not with Selma, Travis, her family. Hell, not even the therapist she saw with regularity. Not a single, gory detail revealed. What she'd gone through, what she'd witnessed, what she'd done to survive was all too horrible to relive. Instead, she'd buried everything inside and kept it locked up tight, never speaking of the events that had taken place. Yet, for all her valiant efforts, the truth still found a way of escaping. In flashbacks so vivid she hardly knew reality from fantasy in those moments when her consciousness was no longer hers to control. In dreams so frighteningly realistic, she awoke gasping for breath and fearing her heart would explode. To escape, she downed antidepressants and antianxiety meds as if they were as innocuous as M&Ms. She lived in a broken-down old house, harboring the illusion of one day running a bed and breakfast. A totally ridiculous notion, since what she knew about hotel management wouldn't fill Eula's water dish. The truth was, her so-called ambition was so far removed from her previous career, she clung to her goal as if it was a talisman, her own special *mojo* with the power to make her whole once again.

Bullshit. All of it, she thought in disgust. She was hiding out in Magnolia because Magnolia wasn't Quantico. The house she'd bought didn't provide her with a sense of purpose, but the Victorian kept her mind occupied so she wouldn't have time to think about all she'd walked away from—her career, her marriage, her way of life. She'd done nothing more than create a haven for avoiding the truth.

Tears of frustration blurred her vision, but she remained seated in the darkness, feeling glum and filled with self-pity. Greer Lomax—fraud extraordinaire.

A warm, sultry breeze blew through the open window, cooling her skin. She swiped at the moisture clouding her eyes and concentrated on watching Ash sleep.

God, how she'd missed him.

The admission took her by surprise and rocked her depleting remnants of confidence. She hadn't allowed herself to think about him during the two years they'd been apart, because doing so never failed to fill her with a deep sense of pain and longing. So she did what came naturally—she avoided the subject completely.

She turned away.

With her attention on the open window, the gentle breeze continued to stir the sheers. Walking out the way she had had hardly been fair to him yet, at the time, her decision had been rational—in her irrational opinion, anyway. She'd been unable to cope. She'd been to hell and back, and fairness and right had been a nonexistent priority. Self-preservation, however, had been, and still remained, her singular goal.

Well, she'd survived. She woke up each morning and made her way through the day, never getting too close, never becoming too involved, never remembering all that she'd once loved . . . because it was too damn painful. Because it inevitably led her to memories she couldn't bear to face.

Physically her scars had healed. A few were still evident

on her body, beginning now to fade with time, but they served an important purpose—a reminder of the dangers of putting her faith and trust in another human being. The emotional scars had been ignored and, in doing so, all she'd done was allow them to fester.

"Come back to bed."

The sound of Ash's voice startled her. She looked over at him—resting casually on his side, his elbow propped on the mattress and his head resting against the palm of his hand—and couldn't help but feel a sharp, mournful stab over the time they'd been apart. She also couldn't help noticing how the sheet hung low over his hip, either.

Her blood stirred.

"Do you really think that's a good idea?" She didn't want to mislead him. The fact that they'd made love didn't change anything. Sure, she loved the man, but that didn't mean she was willing to relinquish her iron-tight grip on the thin thread attempting to unravel what little sanity she had left.

Under the shadows of moonlight, she watched as the corners of his mouth curved upward. "Absolutely."

Tempting, but she couldn't. She pulled in a deep breath and let it out slowly. What was it she'd thought earlier? Oh, yeah. No regrets. What a crock.

"Ash, I'm—"

"Afraid."

She frowned. "No," she said with a shake of her head. "I'm—"

"Sorry," he finished for her as he sat and swung his feet to the floor.

Her frown deepened. She didn't like where this conversation was heading. "For what?" she asked with equal measures of caution and defensiveness. She wasn't sorry they'd made love, if that's what he was referring to.

"You want a list?"

She sure didn't need or want him cataloging mistakes she already knew by heart. "No. And I don't want to argue."

"Neither do I, but if that's the only way to get you to talk to me . . ." He shrugged his broad shoulders.

Defensiveness won out over caution. "Talk about *what*, exactly?" Her tone rose sharply.

"You walking out, for starters. Or we could discuss the last two years of silence." He gave her a level stare. "Not a word, Greer. Not so much as a goddamn whisper, even to let me know you're safe, that you're alive." He shoved his hand roughly through his hair and let out a harsh breath. "That you never had any intention of coming home."

This *was* her home. Now, anyway.

She tugged the ends of his shirt tighter around her and looked away. "I needed time."

"To what?" he asked, his own voice rising. "Punish me?"

She stiffened. "This hasn't been about you." Not exactly.

"The hell it hasn't," he argued. "In case you've forgotten, a marriage consists of two people. A wife *and* a husband."

She stood abruptly. She needed space. A whole lot of it. Her heart rate sped up and if she didn't distance herself long enough to pull it back together, she'd be popping another calming pink pill. "I'm not going to discuss this with you now."

She crossed the bedroom and walked into the hallway. There wasn't anywhere in the old house she could go where Ash wouldn't follow her, but she needed to get away to keep from embarking on yet another journey down Anxiety Avenue. He'd always had the tenacity of a cranky old Bulldog and she doubted he'd changed much since she'd last seen him. In fact, she knew him well enough to know he wasn't about to let the subject drop.

Without turning on the light, she felt her way to the staircase and carefully descended the steps in her bare feet. Not smart with a house under constant construction, but escape, regardless of how momentary it would be, outweighed the dangers of a stray nail or carpet tack.

Guided by moonlight and memory, she made her way into the formal dining room and flipped on the overhead light. Several ten-foot strips of crown molding that needed sanding were spread over a trio of sawhorses near the huge bay window covered with a paint-stained tarp. She picked up a sanding block and got started, scrubbing the sandpaper over the wood, trying not to think of anything except the rhythmic hiss of paper against wood.

Just once it'd be nice if she was prepared to handle life when it crashed into her.

Don't think.

And how, exactly, was she supposed to prepare for life when all she'd been doing was running from it the past two years?

Don't think, dammit.

"Greer?"

At the sound of his voice, she blew out a frustrated breath and tossed the sanding block on the makeshift worktable in the center of the room. "Not now, Ash. Please."

"If not now, when?"

She rested her shoulder against the newly painted wall. "I don't know."

He crossed his arms over his bare chest. He'd slipped into a pair of faded sweatpants, which were slung low on his hips. The man looked positively mouthwatering. And way too determined for her peace of mind.

"You can't run forever," he said calmly.

Watch me.

She pushed off the wall and headed toward the doorway. "I can't talk about this now."

He reached out to stop her. "Why not?" he insisted, gently turning her to face him. "Why are you so afraid to talk to me?"

She took a step back and he dropped his hands to his sides. "I'm not afraid of *you*," she admitted. Of herself? Yes. Of the memories that kept her crippled and locked in the facsimile of a lifestyle she'd created to escape a past too painful and horrific to face?

Abso-freaking-lutely.

"You're scared of something. Why else would you have been hiding out like this, pretending to have a life?"

She couldn't answer. He'd gotten too close to the truth. Dangerously close.

Her heart pounded heavily in her chest. "You're wrong," she lied, backing up another step.

"Am I?" he pressed. Slowly, he moved toward her, closing the distance she desperately wanted to keep between them.

She took another step, her backside coming in contact with the plywood worktable. "Yes."

"Then you'd better explain it to me, because I sure as hell don't understand why you insist on making us both miserable."

He stopped in front of her. Lifting his hand, he lightly traced his hand down her arm. A tremor passed over her skin and she shivered. "Let me help you."

"We are so *not* having this conversation."

He smiled, but the curve of his mouth failed to translate to his determined gaze.

"Oh, we're having it, all right. Right here. Right now."

Her palms began to sweat. How was that possible when her insides felt frozen? "No."

"I'm not letting you run away from me again."

She swallowed, hard. "You can't stop me."

A hard gleam entered his beautiful bedroom eyes. "Tell

me," he insisted, his voice a deceptively low and sexy rumble of sound.

She leaned back in an attempt to get away from his nearness. "Leave me alone, Ash." Why was he doing this to her? Was it his turn to punish her?

He shook his head. "Talk to me, sweetheart. What has you so afraid that you're willing to go on making us both miserable? Vicar's dead. He can't come after you again."

Pain, seeming as sharp and as real as the scalpel Vicar had sliced her body with, ripped through her at the mention of the vicious serial killer. She shook her head. "Don't do this," she begged in a ragged whisper. "Please."

He took hold of her shoulders, his grip firm and grounded in a reality she no longer possessed the strength to face. "He can't hurt you, Greer. He's dead."

She planted her hands on his chest and shoved, but he was immovable. "Stop it," she said and shoved at him again. "I know he's dead, dammit. I killed the son of a bitch."

"Then let him die. Stop blaming yourself for what happened in Phoenix and let him die once and for all."

She stared at Ash, unable to believe what she'd just heard. Stop blaming herself? *Herself?* He was more out of his mind than she, and she was certifiable.

She shrugged out of his grasp. "I don't blame myself." Her short bark of laughter came out caustic and brittle. "No, Ash. If you're looking for blame, then I suggest you take a good, long look in the mirror."

The hardness in his eyes softened, replaced by hurt at her ugly accusation. She hated herself for the stricken look on his face. She felt as if she'd slapped him, and she supposed, in a way, that's exactly what she'd done. She had never wanted to come out and say she held him responsible for what happened that night in Phoenix, but they couldn't ignore the elephant in the room any longer. She *did* blame Ash, because if she'd followed her own instincts rather than his, then just maybe she'd still have a life to call her own, not the sham she'd been existing in since she left him.

"You think I don't blame myself for what that bastard did to you?" he countered, his tone rising. "You're not the only one with regrets, sweetheart. What do you think it did to me to know that I was the one that put you in his path? You're not the only one who nearly died that night."

An image flashed brilliantly in her mind, like a wicked streak of lightening illuminating a moonless night and she saw Ash slumped on the cold stone floor of Vicar's own personal torture chamber where he'd lived out his sick fantasies of power, of mutilation and degradation.

"Don't," she said, her voice but a mere whisper. "Let's not do this."

"You think I don't have nightmares?" he continued hotly, ignoring her plea. "Nightmares. Waking up in a cold sweat. Fear. I know what it feels like."

He let out a short, impatient breath and jammed his hand through his hair. "I understand what you're going through, but dammit," he said, gentling his tone, "you have to move on. You won, Greer. You got your man. You put a vicious sociopath out of business. For good. But every day that you continue to hide out here, he wins. You may have killed him, but you won't let him die."

Tears welled in her eyes, blurring her vision. Tears of anger, frustration and the cold, hard reality of the fear that Ash could be right. "No," she said, but her voice lacked conviction. "You're wrong."

"Am I? What do you call all this?" he asked, sweeping his arm wide.

She looked around the dining room under construction. He couldn't be right. He couldn't. Her entire existence depended on believing her home was her sanctuary, the one place in the world where she felt in control. "It's therapeutic."

"It's bullshit!"

"It's my reality," she fired back at him. She gripped the ends of Ash's shirt she was still wearing and yanked, hard. The only remaining button popped and bounced off the bare Sheetrock. She held open the shirt, standing boldly before him. "*This* is my goddamn reality."

The thick scar running from sternum to midabdomen appeared to gleam under the glare of the harsh overhead lighting. If she touched it, she knew she would feel it pulse as if it were a live thing.

The tension visibly left his body as he stared at the scar The Preacher had left behind, forever marring her flesh with the constant reminder of her failure. Of Ash's failure to keep his promise that he'd keep her safe.

Ash hadn't seen the scar when they'd made love earlier. She'd made sure of it. She'd made certain his hands didn't accidentally skim over the puckered flesh where The Preacher had sliced her flesh with the sharp blade of his scalpel. If Vicar hadn't been distracted by Ash as the effects of the drug The Preacher had injected him with began to wear off, he'd have gutted her as he'd done with Linda while Greer had been forced to helplessly watch.

God, why did Ash have to come here? Why couldn't he have sent some flunky in his place? Wasn't it enough that she had to deal with a serial killer in her own backyard? She shouldn't have to deal with her husband now, too, pushing her to relive the horror when all she wanted to do was forget.

It wasn't fair.

Life wasn't fair. Bad things happened to good people all the time. She knew. She'd dealt with the grief of families of countless victims, uttered all the right platitudes, but nothing she did would ever bring those families their daughters, sons, wives, husbands, mothers or fathers back to them. All she could offer them was justice. It wasn't enough. It wasn't fair.

Life wasn't fair. But it was all she had—along with the scars to prove it.

Chapter 17

GREER'S SKIN BURNED as the tip of Ash's finger trailed the length of her torso, skimming with feather-like softness along the puckered flesh of her scar. Unable to bear the pity she suspected she'd find in his eyes eventually, she guarded against it by closing her own. Instead, she envisioned his touch being powerful enough to cauterize her wound. But rather than breaking through her barriers to free her from the pain, the reverence of his touch further sealed the hurt inside.

God, someone set her free. Please, she silently begged. Why can't the past just die? Why can't she be set free—from the pain, the anger, the constant fear keeping her locked in the past and popping pills to escape? Free her from the disillusion and denial that ruled her every waking moment, from the mockery of an existence she'd created, a make-believe safe haven where she no longer hurt, didn't feel too much . . . couldn't love.

"I'm so sorry, Greer."

In his whispered apology, she detected an edge to his voice she couldn't quite decipher.

Tenderness? Yes.

Compassion? Perhaps.

Hurt?

All of the above?

She'd become so adept at keeping her own emotions shackled, she lacked the insight to interpret his. Opening her eyes, she lifted her gaze to his. Concern filled his eyes.

"Does it still hurt?" he asked.

Not trusting her voice to betray the sudden wave of vulnerability rising up inside her, she shook her head instead. No, she wanted to tell him, the mark left on her flesh was but a permanent reminder of what she'd endured, of what Ash's ego had cost her, but no longer caused her physical pain. Emotionally, well, that was a whole other matter.

"I've never seen this," he said. "I didn't . . . I didn't know it was this bad."

Because until this moment, she'd never given him the chance. A lump lodged in her throat. "I know," she managed hoarsely.

Guilt nudged her vulnerability with a sharp jab.

He moved a step closer, narrowing the minute distance still between them until he stood too close, invading her space, making it difficult for her to draw her next breath. She stared into his luscious dark eyes and caught a glimpse of what they once were—arrogant. Invincible. Crazy in love.

His hand slid to her waist, then slowly eased around to the small of her back, pressing into her flesh, urging her the few final inches remaining between them. "If I could erase the past two years, I would."

"If only," she whispered.

She took that final step toward him. Their bodies touched and her thoughts went flying into a chaotic spin.

"We can never go back," he said. "I don't have the power to erase that scar, or change what happened."

"I . . ." her voice caught. "I know." But God, how she wished at least one of them did.

"All I can do is offer you whatever the future might hold. For us."

The hope in his voice was very nearly her undoing. She closed her eyes again in a vain attempt to ward off the sharp pain slicing through her, hoping to shut off the imminent flow of tears before they had a chance to surface. "Please, Ash. Don't. I can't think about that now."

When could she?

Probably never.

He let out an impatient huff of breath. She held hers, waiting for him to either turn away from her or vehemently start stating his case. Thankfully, he did neither, just dipped his head and brushed his lips lightly over hers.

A tremor chased down her spine, followed by a sharp tug of desire pulling low in her belly. Drawing her in, promising what she hadn't dared think about in far too long. Promising her hope.

"Then think about this instead." He spoke softly, his warm breath caressing her lips.

This consisted of his mouth capturing hers in a hot, open-mouthed kiss that rocked her unstable world, instantly reigniting her libido. She should shove him away. She should insist he leave, now, before they further complicated their relationship—such as it was—by once again giving in to the enticing warmth of his embrace as he held her tightly, perfectly aligning their bodies.

She didn't. She did neither of those things she *should* do, but wreathed her arms around his neck, welcoming instead the fierce, possessiveness of his kiss. Welcoming *him*, if only for this moment in time.

She clung to him and didn't bother to catalog the myriad sensations shooting through her with lightening-fast speed, just lost herself in the rush of emotion and the closeness of their bodies. The way her breasts crushed against his chest, the scent of him, of their earlier lovemaking, still clinging to his warm skin. His heat, his hardness.

Ash.

Later, when she was alone, maybe she'd be able to recall the exciting sensations his touch and deep kisses evoked. Maybe, with any luck at all, she'd be able to recall these stolen moments with Ash instead of the terrifying images constantly haunting her. An exchange of dark pain for the ultimate in pleasure.

She could only hope.

Her fingers toyed with the wisps of hair at his nape as she once again breathed in his scent. Rich, masculine. Ash. Sex. *Oh, God.*

His hands fell from her waist to her bottom and he lifted her. Without hesitation, she wrapped her legs around his waist and clung to him, held on tight, as if he was her only lifeline to another lifetime, one where she was whole again rather than a fragmented imitation. For now, it was enough, even if it was all only pretend.

With her senses heightened, her defenses swiftly abandoned her. She gave into it all and surrendered to the splendor of making love to the only man she'd ever truly loved with all her heart.

Had she been foolish to leave him? she wondered now. Had she made a mistake, or worse, compounded the mistakes they'd both made and ended up ruining their lives for good? She couldn't think. She didn't have any answers. Maybe she didn't want to know, at least not now when Ash's mouth burned a hot trail of kisses along her jaw, down her throat to the valley between her breasts. She jammed her fingers through his hair, holding him to her as his tongue flicked over the pebble hardness of her nipple.

Her head fell back and thumped against the wall. She arched toward him, her body straining to his, filled with need, with desire that burned hot and heavy between her legs. She wanted him inside her again. She wanted him to make her forget everything but the wildness of their love-making.

This was what she hadn't allowed herself to think about; the sweet intoxication, the heated passion, the love they'd shared. The absolute trust.

She struggled to shut down the memories for fear of losing what little of her mind she'd managed to hang on to. She'd forsaken the memories, purged the life she'd once known. Doing so had been her sole means of survival, and now the thoughts and emotions threatening her sanity and racing through her mind were nearly foreign to her.

"Ash," she whispered, urging his mouth back to hers for another soul-stealing kiss. Anything, if it'd stop the flood of memories before she drowned completely.

She lost herself inside the tingling sensations setting her body on fire. Rather than question the wisdom or fallacy of her choices, she simply allowed the flames of desire Ash ignited to consume her mind, her body, her heart and soul. A heart and soul that would never be hers again, or perhaps had never truly belonged to her, because in her passion-flooded mind, they'd always belong to him.

She savored each intensely heightened sensation. For the first time in two years, she felt truly alive. Whole, even. She didn't care if it all was nothing but another illusion. She savored the beauty of their lovemaking, savored the feel of his body as her hands coasted over his shoulders, down the sculpted landscape of his back, the muscle and sinew firm and real beneath her fingertips. Warm. Alive.

Real. A concept she'd nearly forgotten existed.

She tore her mouth from his. "I want you inside me," she demanded. "Now."

His answer was a deep groan of pleasure-filled pain, making her smile. Pressing his body into hers, he held her against the wall with his weight. Capturing both of her hands in his large one, he urged them over her head, rendering her powerless. And she was, powerless to resist him—not that she had any intention of denying either one of them the pleasure awaiting them.

With his other hand, he freed himself and quickly buried himself to the hilt inside her. Her breath expelled on a throaty groan so low and sultry she hardly recognized it as her own. She pulled her hands from his grasp and clung to him. Erotic little sounds of pleasure mingled with each hard pant of breath she expelled. His fingers bit into the soft flesh of her ass as he thrust, withdrew, harder, faster, again and again. She was in awe at the raw openness of their lovemaking.

Her moans grew louder, more demanding until she emitted one long, shouted, "Yessss. . . ." Her body tightened around him, and she flew apart.

With one final, deep thrust, she felt him come in a heated rush, joining her in blissful oblivion.

Too bad, she thought, as her senses and sanity slowly returned, that tonight changed nothing between them. But that would be an argument that could wait until morning. For now, she consciously welcomed the illusion that for once in her life, she was perfectly normal.

Vivien stifled a yawn, then hit the SCROLL button to review the e-mail she'd been composing for the past twenty minutes to her sister, reminding Greer she'd promised to attend Mama's "surprise" birthday dinner tomorrow night. Covering her bases, she also planned to send Greer a text message, as well as leave several voice mails if necessary, until she received a definite confirmation from her sister that she would indeed be present. Vivien loved her mother dearly, but she didn't relish the idea of spending an evening with Mama and Davis, getting lectured by Mama about her poor matrimonial choices.

She read through the e-mail for the third time, then made a few changes to soften the tone. Greer didn't respond well to demands.

Technology definitely had a few perks, she decided. Not that foot-in-mouth syndrome was an affliction she suffered from on any regular basis, but she did enjoy the benefit of perfecting her words even more before sending them out into cyberspace. Even to her overachieving little sister.

She should just pick up the phone and give Greer a call. Greer had become such a nocturnal creature since returning to Magnolia, Vivien didn't worry about waking her. But, that husband of hers was in town, and well . . .

She giggled. Maybe Greer would mellow some now that her hunky hubby was home.

Mama might not show it very well, but Vivien knew Mama liked Ash. In her own way, Mama had expressed her disappointment when Greer returned to Magnolia sans Ash, whom Mama referred to as "a bit of Cary Grant, with a little Errol Flynn and a hint of that bad boy Colin Farrell all rolled into one."

Greer's husband was a nice-enough guy, Vivien thought. And damn good-looking, too. From what little she'd witnessed over the years, he certainly appeared to be wildly in love with her sister, but he was way too intense for her own liking. There just wasn't a thing controllable about that man, and she didn't know how Greer could be attracted to all that tough, alpha-male crap. Vivien preferred her men much more malleable. It made those hefty divorce settlements all the sweeter.

The dialog box for her instant-messaging service popped up on her screen and she immediately heaved a sigh of relief. It was *him*. She hadn't received an e-mail from the doctor from Charlotte in almost two days and worried she'd done something to scare the guy off.

I was hoping you'd be online.

More beautiful words she didn't think it possible to read. Well, except for perhaps her name in conjunction with his, written in delicate, gold foil–embossed script on a wedding invitation.

"Trouble sleeping," she typed into the REPLY bar. She paused, then added, "You?" before hitting the SEND button.

Rough day. Lost a patient.

An excellent opportunity to portray the sympathetic listener. She rubbed her hands together. "I'm so sorry. Do you want to talk about it?"

She hit SEND, then held her breath, waiting.

She drummed her newly manicured nails on the gleaming surface of her antique writing desk. Waiting. Waiting . . .

What's your number? popped up in the dialog box.

She smiled.

Perfect!

Exactly what she wanted. Another perfectly malleable male—with an enviable financial portfolio suitable enough for her to consider becoming the wife of a pediatric surgeon. An excellent way to spend the next few years of her own pathetic excuse for a life.

Parker glanced at the clock on his desk as he hung up the telephone. In little more than four hours, his staff would be arriving for the day and he'd foolishly ignored his body's need for sleep in exchange for spending two hours cultivating Dylan Beaumont's ideal match. He knew he was getting ahead of himself, but "diamondgirl" was exactly right for poor Dylan, dead from a coronary at the age of forty-two. A dutiful, beautiful, well-bred Southern woman with impeccable manners and grace. The perfect hostess, the ideal doctor's wife. From the photograph she'd posted on *find-*

amatch.com, she looked as if she'd stepped off the pages of *Southern Living* magazine. In another time, she'd have made a perfect belle.

Parker despised her.

He couldn't wait to have her.

A soft, mewling sound penetrated the anger coursing through his body, drawing his attention away from his preparations for the good doctor.

Her.

He still hadn't disposed of his last conquest. The opportunity had been robbed from him, causing his anger to mount. She simply wasn't suitable for another. The bitch responsible should pay, but she wasn't worthy of any of his clients.

Still . . .

He rose from the inexpensive task chair and crossed the uneven floor to the embalming table, where she pathetically clung to life. He should simply end her, but he wasn't permitted to until he located her perfect mate.

She looked up at him, her gaze no longer filled with terror, but pure hatred. He wanted to slap her. He fisted his hands at his side and stared down at her. "Bitch," he hissed at her. "You're ruined."

Fire burned in her gaze.

He drew his hand back, but instead of fulfilling the fantasy of putting out that fire for good with his bare hands, he reached over her to the shelf above for the bottle of Ketamin and a syringe. He filled the syringe with a dose strong enough to render her unconscious for several hours and injected it into the IV portal. He then changed the bag of dextrose and water that kept her alive.

Waiting until her hate-filled eyes fluttered closed, and assured all was well, he locked away his files, shut down the computer, then climbed the stairs. He left the subbasement to the official work area of Hennessy's. After closing the door to the hidden room below, he stopped to listen. Nothing but silence and the strong, steady thud of his heart.

He approached the staircase and made his way to the kitchen for a drink, then headed up to his bedroom on the second floor of the house, still undecided what to do with *her*. He had to make a decision soon. Very soon, in fact, because it wouldn't be much longer until diamondgirl would be ready to join him.

She was going to die.

This wasn't how she'd envisioned the end. Wasn't she supposed to be surrounded by family—her sister, some kids would be nice, even a few grandchildren and maybe a great-grandchild, as well? And what about a loyal cat or two, curled up in that upside-down way of cats, on an antique sleigh bed she'd refinished herself years before, atop the folded, aged and faded-with-time quilt at the foot of her bed, handmade by the Ladies of Polite Southern Society?

She was going to die. No one would witness her passing, other than the sadistic bastard responsible for her death. He'd made sure of it.

His fetid breath filled her nostrils. He was calm, eerily so. No beads of perspiration marred his waxy forehead as he bent over her. A slight crook to his mouth, not quite a smile, more like a satisfied twist, yanked up the corners of pencil-thin, almost nonexistent lips. His clawlike fingers skimmed over her bare skin and she prayed the end would be swift, but she knew otherwise. She'd studied the bastard and knew a quick, merciful end could never be hers now. He had a fantasy to fulfill. A fantasy of unspeakable horror,

horror she'd witnessed over and over again for weeks.

She tried to close her eyes, but her lids refused to cooperate. All she could do was stare into the black, blank sockets where her killer's eyes were supposed to be.

He drew the scalpel over her skin.

She opened her mouth to scream, but couldn't pull enough air into her lungs. She felt as if her face was covered, but that wasn't right. How could she see everything so clearly if he'd covered her head? How could she witness his horror?

But she couldn't breathe. She couldn't draw a shred of oxygen into her lungs. Her heart pounded so heavily she knew it would burst any second now, then she wished to hell it would, to save her from the slow, painful death awaiting her.

A soft groan came from somewhere below her to her left. Vicar's eyeless, waxy complexion momentarily froze, but the fear she'd glimpsed slid away, replaced by cool serenity.

The instrument in his hand fell from his grasp. The cold metal glanced painfully off her rib, slicing more of her flesh before clattering to the metal table where he'd bound her. Helplessly, all she could do was watch as he calmly lifted a crowbar from the bracket on the wall behind him. He slowly crossed the dank space, not walking, but floating like a strange and horrifying apparition, until he finally drifted to a stop. He lifted the deadly tool over his head.

She struggled furiously with the restraints binding her. The thin leather straps cut viciously into her wrists and ankles like a thousand razors slashing at her tender flesh. She tugged harder, twisted more violently until she felt one of them give. She prayed for strength to close her mind to the excruciating pain and pulled even harder.

She had to free herself. Save herself. Save all of them.

As if watching a movie frame by frame, Vicar slowly swung the crowbar back as if he was a golfer preparing to take a perfectly measured stroke, his aim on the body struggling to rise from the stone floor.

She had to save him. Save herself. Save all of them.

She yanked so hard on the restraints, she heard a crackling sound, then a snap. A blood-curdling scream ripped from her throat, momentarily stunning him, unwittingly granting her a few precious seconds and a shot at freedom.

Fighting against the agonizing pain in her wrist, she grabbed the abandoned scalpel and sliced away the thin leather strap wound around her other wrist, then her ankles. Without a thought for the deep wound laying open a layer of her flesh or the bones in her wrist she was certain were shattered, she dove for Vicar.

Using her shoulder, she hit him hard. He flew back against the wall. The weapon fell to the ground with a clang that sounded like a death knell.

She didn't think. She didn't have time. She reached for the crowbar. As she gripped the cold steel and lifted it from the ground, it transformed in her hands, morphing into the sure grip of her 9 mm.

She stood over him, nude and bleeding. She lifted the weapon and aimed the gun at the kill spot right between those soulless black holes where his eyes should've been.

And then she released the safety . . .

Chapter 18

CLICK.

The sound jarred Ash awake, leaving him momentarily confused. But there'd been no mistaking the distinct, albeit subtle, click of a safety being released.

He'd stared down the wrong end of a gun more than once in his line of work. A feeling he hadn't appreciated one bit. The fact that his wife now had a weapon trained on his forehead did nothing to change his opinion any, either.

Blood raced through his veins, sending a surge of adrenaline rushing to his heart. "Honey." He forced himself to speak softly so as not to startle her. "Lower your weapon."

She didn't move. She stood perfectly still. And kept the gun pointed directly at him.

"Greer?"

No response. Was she asleep? Locked in some nightmare?

"Greer," he called again, only louder.

Nothing. She stared at him with those unseeing eyes, unnerving him. He'd lay odds it wasn't him she was seeing, but some monster holding her prisoner in her mind. Bonus points for knowing which one, too. The same one who'd essentially destroyed her life. Their lives.

Shit!

With dawn barely breaking the horizon, it cast the room in murky shadows, making it impossible for him to determine if the gun's clip was in place. By the time he untangled himself from the bed linens, she could have a bullet sunk into his brain.

Waking a sleepwalker was dangerous business. Waking one that quite possibly had a loaded weapon in her hands was nothing short of suicide.

He didn't have a choice.

"Greer," he said more forcefully this time. He eased the covers aside and slowly swung his feet to the floor. "Greer, wake up."

She remained silent and immobile. By sheer luck, his movements didn't have her pulling the trigger.

He moved swiftly then, leaped off the bed and side-stepped the direct aim of the gun. He made a grab for her arm, aiming the weapon toward the ceiling.

"No!" she cried, then pulled the trigger.

Greer sat at the table in her kitchen, staring into the murky depths of the mug of coffee in front of her. Her body had finally stopped shaking, but the horror of what she'd nearly done remained, and probably would for some time.

Good God, she could've killed Ash. What the hell was wrong with her?

She'd never walked in her sleep before. Never awoken thinking she was in a strange place. Never discovered her things out of place as if she'd been haunting her own house in the few hours of sleep she did manage during the night. The dreams were always vivid, yes, always terrifying, but never had they driven her to the point where she was in danger of losing anything but her mind.

She couldn't keep going like this. She had to do something, but what? Two years of therapy certainly hadn't provided her with answers. The old "keep busy and give your mind time to heal from the trauma" bullshit wasn't cutting it any longer.

She was a reasonably intelligent woman. She'd figure this out. She had to, and hopefully before she hurt someone.

Eula's impatient *woof* at the back door made her flinch. She pushed away from the table just as Ash walked into the kitchen, freshly showered and impeccably dressed in a charcoal suit that did heart-stopping things for his physique. He hardly looked like a guy who'd nearly kissed death less than an hour and a half ago.

She turned away and went to the back door to let Eula inside. Why couldn't Ash just go away and leave her alone? She'd avoided him all this time for a reason, and this morning's incident served as solid proof she'd made the right decision. She'd been sitting downstairs staring at her coffee, dreading having to face him after what she'd done even more than she hated having to visit the local funeral parlors that morning.

Eula waddled over to Ash and sniffed his highly polished dress shoes. The cantankerous old dog wiggled her bottom and looked up at Ash adoringly as he poured his own mug of coffee.

Greer shook her head in disgust. The ill-mannered old dog never greeted her with an ounce of enthusiasm.

Eula finished paying homage to Ash, then trotted to her food bowl, snorting her enjoyment at the sight of fresh kibble.

"What'd you do? Sneak her a T-bone when I wasn't looking?" she complained. She didn't know what to say to him that didn't include yet another apology for her appalling behavior this morning, so she opted for safe territory and totally off-the-subject sarcasm.

Ash turned, mug of coffee in hand, looking way too handsome for her fragile peace of mind. "I thought I should warn you, I'm talking to Travis first thing. You're off the case."

Her ploy to avoid reality failed miserably. She blinked, several times in fact, and stared at Ash in stunned disbelief. He couldn't be serious?

"The hell you are," she argued when her voice finally returned.

What kind of first-class idiot was she, anyway? This was exactly what she wanted. Wasn't it? Hadn't she just a few days ago essentially told Travis to take her badge and stick it elsewhere? She'd wanted nothing whatsoever to do with crawling inside the head of a sick sociopath, so why on earth was she bristling at Ash's high-handed attitude?

Because, dammit, whether she wanted it or not, this was *her* case. Her responsibility. To hell with her mental state, or her fears. She had a job to do, and the job always came first. Some sick bastard had elected to play his twisted game in her backyard, and she'd be damned if she'd let him get away with it. Magnolia was her town, and she'd taken an oath to protect and serve its citizens.

Ash set his mug on the counter. "You're in no condition, emotionally or physically, to handle the investigation. Christ, have you looked in the mirror lately? You look like hell, babe."

"Gee, thanks," she muttered. "And to think I once fell for your charm."

"I'm serious, Greer. You're off the case."

She didn't appreciate his my-way-or-forget-it posturing, or the steely determination in his eyes. "You can't do that," she told him. "You have no authority here."

The tolerant look he gave her bordered on superior. "Wanna try me?"

"The investigation hasn't yet met the legal requirements for ISU's involvement." She held up two fingers. "Two bodies," she said. "Two. Not three."

"Four."

"You're counting Archer and Gartner?"

"If I have to."

"That's a stretch and you know it. Archer was already deceased and Gartner's grave was merely disturbed."

He shrugged in that smug way he had, which never failed to set her teeth on edge. "You forget the eight missing women in Magnolia County alone, not to mention those from the surrounding counties."

"Oh, go to hell," she snapped irritably. "There's no solid connection."

"Yet. But you know it's there. We just haven't found it yet."

God, she hated it when he was right, but he did have a valid point. She'd be insane not to admit the possibilities had her scared shitless. The UNSUB could've been wracking up dead bodies for months, years in fact, and they'd never know it, considering his method of disposing of the bodies.

The perfect crime.

Almost.

She strode to the table for her mug, then back to the sink to dump the now-cold contents. "Travis will never agree to remove me from the case," she said, sounding more confident than she felt. If Ash squealed about her nocturnal behavior, Travis wouldn't only remove her from the case, he'd quite likely kick her off the force as well.

And, again, why was she protesting?

"For one, we're fighting budget cuts and simply don't have the manpower. There is no one else. And secondly, I'm the only deputy on staff with the experience to handle this type of investigation."

She couldn't believe she was seriously arguing in favor of remaining on the case. She needed more than therapy. Better yet, she needed to be locked up in the local nut ward.

She set her empty mug inside the dishwasher. "I'm going to work."

Before she could make good on that particular threat, Ash's hand settled on her arm. "Have you thought about what's going to happen to you when you do attempt to crawl inside this guy's head?"

She wasn't a complete idiot. For that very reason she'd tucked a few pink pills into the pocket of her uniform this morning when she'd dressed.

"How can you even think about putting yourself in the victims' place?" he continued. "Don't seriously think for a second you're going to be able to cope with this thing, Greer. Experience alone should tell you it'll get uglier before it's over."

She tugged free of his grasp. More silliness on her part, when she had the unexpected urge to wrap her arms around him and let him have his way. Let him protect her, keep her safe once and for all. A stupid, moronic even, proposition for her to consider when she knew better. He'd failed her once, how could she possibly trust him? She barely trusted herself.

"I can do my job," she said and turned away to close the dishwasher.

He grabbed hold of her shoulders and spun her back to face him. "No, you can't. Christ Almighty, Greer," he said, his voice rising. "You either turn as green as the walls in Cantrell's autopsy room, or have a panic attack after you've been within twenty feet of a DB. You've only scratched the surface on the investigation and your nightmare became so real this morning, you nearly blew my fucking head off."

Guiltily, she looked away. "I said I was sorry about that."

"Sorry?" He laughed, the sound bitter and caustic. "How sorry are you going to be when you actually do hurt someone because you can't put the past behind you? People do go to jail for accidents, you know. It's called involuntary manslaughter. You know what they do to cops in those places?"

"Okay, now you're really reaching. Look, I'm sorry about this morning. It won't happen again."

"How can you say that? You didn't even know what you were doing."

She shrugged out of his grasp. "Then maybe you'd better check into a motel," she fired back.

"This isn't about me. It's you I'm worried about."

She made a sound filled with frustration and put much-needed distance between them. "I'm doing the best I can."

"Your best isn't what it used to be, Greer. At least admit that much."

And give him the ammunition he wanted to have her taken off the case?

Hardly!

"What do you want from me?"

He let out a long, slow breath. "I want my wife back," he said, his tone gentling.

He'd switched gears so fast, she had trouble keeping up. "I told you, I can't deal with both of you. Not now."

"My point exactly."

"I can do my job, Ash."

"At what cost?"

Oh, just what little sanity she'd managed to hang on to. "I can handle the investigation."

"I have my doubts."

"That's just too damn bad. I suggest you get the hell over it, because I refuse to have this discussion again." She turned and stormed out the back door. She could continue to argue with him all morning over her right to remain on the case, but she wasn't about to go into battle over their relationship. She had only so much emotional energy at her disposal, and she knew exactly where she needed it most.

She had an UNSUB to stop, hopefully before he killed again.

"Get over it," she muttered, unlocking the door to her Liberty. As if she even knew what she was talking about. If anyone was ever awarded a prize for knowing how to harbor a grudge, she'd win—hands down.

The trouble with mortuary-hopping was in avoiding all those pesky dead bodies. It simply couldn't be helped. The places were rife with them. But, she'd held it together so far, and culled only a case or two of the heebie-jeebies all day.

By the time Greer steered her cruiser up to the fifth and final funeral home on their list, she didn't know whether she should thank her lucky stars or curse her rotten luck. Ash hadn't been able to speak with Travis about having her removed from the investigation, since her boss had been pulled back into the fray with the council members, attempting to wrangle enough funds to keep the Sheriff's Department operational.

She decided not to think about her luck, good or bad. All she wanted was to have this last visit behind her so she could go back to the department and start assimilating the information they'd gathered today. And with any real luck at all, she'd be drowning her sorrows in a chocolate donut—or three—within the hour.

"How are you holding up?" Ash asked when she killed the engine.

How do you think?

"Fine," she said for the fifth time that day, and reached for the radio to call their location into dispatch. "Let's just get this done, okay?"

She'd freak out later. Hopefully when she was alone, although she doubted the possibility of that fantasy. Ash didn't appear to be in any hurry to leave her alone and, quite frankly, she was out of energy to argue with him.

Actually, other than discomfort, she thought she'd done a bang-up job of coping today. Ash deserved a great deal of the credit, however, because while she interviewed employees, he ventured into the actual working areas of the mortuaries. Luck had to be on her side for a change, because she'd encountered only two dead bodies all day long.

She couldn't count as wasted the time they'd spent today interviewing mortuary employees, even if they hadn't discovered anything out of the ordinary, as least as far as funeral parlors went. She'd confirmed what she'd always suspected—it took a special kind of individual to work in the field—a strange kind of person. Most could be broken down into two categories—either creepily somber or possessed by a dark sense of humor, not unlike those in the medical and law enforcement fields.

They left the coolness of the interior of the cruiser and stepped out into the blazing sunshine. The humidity had climbed as the day wore on, but relief would be coming shortly if the thunderheads forming in the distance could be counted on for a good summer storm.

Greer headed up the concrete walkway to the front steps of Hennessy's, keeping two paces ahead of Ash. The building looked charming and inviting, not at all like a place that prepared the dead for their final resting place. She supposed that was the point, after all. How much business would be attracted if funeral homes looked like a haunted mansion in a horror flick?

Regardless, she wasn't fooled by the wide veranda wrapped around the front porch, or the baskets overflowing with summer flowers in full, vibrant color hanging from wrought iron hangers on each of the pristine white supports. A mixture of low-cut shrubs and perennials filled the brick-edged flowerbeds running the length of the porch. The place didn't look like a parlor of death, just an ordinary, large, rambling old house, probably built before the Civil

War—or, as her mother was fond of saying, "that nasty business with the Yankees."

Nope, she wasn't fooled one bit. There were dead bodies inside. And that was enough for her to hesitate for a split second.

Ash's hand landed momentarily on her arm, but she shrugged off his touch without looking back at him. She didn't need or want his comfort. Dammit, she could do her job.

She hoped.

A movement out of the corner of her eye had her stopping her ascent up the steps to the porch. She turned to see a woman approach, a flowing, floral skirt swirling around her ankles. A simple white cotton sleeveless blouse showed off her tanned, slender arms. She carried a pair of gardening gloves and pruning shears in one hand along with a basket filled with fresh-cut flowers, the handle slung on her forearm. She shielded her eyes from the brilliance of the noonday sunshine with the other hand, preventing Greer from seeing her face clearly.

"Greer?" she called out, a trace of warmth in her voice. "Land sakes, is that really you?"

Greer pasted a smile on her face as the woman neared. "Susan? Susan Nichols?"

"It's Hennessy now," she corrected, and smiled shyly. "Goodness, it's been ages."

Greer looked to Ash. "Susan and I went to school together," she explained, then took care of the introductions. Actually, they'd been quite close when they were younger, but for some reason had drifted apart when they'd hit high school.

A slight frown creased Susan's forehead. Making the connection between Greer and Ash, no doubt. But Susan was too much of a Southern lady to question Greer on such a personal matter, at least that's what Greer hoped.

"FBI?" Susan questioned. "Is this an official visit?"

"Unofficially official." The lie slipped easily from Greer's lips. "There have been some disturbances at the local cemeteries."

"I heard about some of the pranks," Susan said with a nod. "Why, it's scandalous what those college boys have been up to this summer."

She didn't know the half of it, Greer thought. Before the day was out, she figured most of the county would be buzzing with speculation. By breakfast tomorrow, their visits to the funeral parlors throughout the county would not only be common knowledge, but *the* hot topic of conversation. Rumors would no doubt fly, too. There was just no avoiding it – especially in a town the size of Magnolia.

"You'll be wanting to speak with Parker, then?"

"If it wouldn't be too much trouble," Ash said.

"Of course," Susan said and smiled sweetly. "Let's get out of this heat, shall we?"

Greer followed Susan up the steps. "How long have you and Parker been married?" she asked. She didn't know Parker Hennessy personally, but everyone in Magnolia knew the Hennessy name. The family had been operating a funeral home in the area practically since the town's inception. In fact it was Hennessy's that had handled her father's interment all those years ago.

"Shortly after Parker returned to Magnolia following the accident. A little over four years ago."

"Accident?" Ash questioned.

"Yes. It was quite tragic," Susan said as she opened the wide front door and ushered them inside. "A hiking accident. Parker had been living in Colorado. His father had gone for a visit. They'd been hiking in the mountains. I don't know all the details, but his father and the guide they'd hired were both killed."

"I'm sorry," Ash said.

"Thank you." Susan set the basket of flowers along with her gardening gloves and pruning shears on a highly polished table in the center of the foyer. "I'll get Parker." She indicated a sitting room to the left. "Please, make yourselves comfortable."

"She seemed nice," Ash said in a hushed tone once they were alone. "Too nice, if you ask me. Did you get the feeling she was expecting us?"

Greer crossed the thick rug to view an abstract print in subtle hues hanging over the settee, and to distance herself from Ash. "She probably was," she said. "This is a small town. Before we left our first stop, no doubt all the other funeral directors in the area were expecting us, too."

Ash didn't looked convinced, but that wasn't her problem. Gossip flowed faster than water in Magnolia. All she wanted was to get through this final interview and head back to the department, where there'd better be a chocolate donut with her name on it.

She turned as Parker Hennessy walked into the receiving room, a term she'd just learned from her mortuary visits. The room where directors spoke in hushed tones to the bereaved, bilking them out of thousands to bury their dead. The hairs on the back of her neck stood at attention as she took in the absolute, pure perfection of Parker Hennessy.

Chapter 19

"WELCOME," PARKER SAID warmly, extending his hand to Greer. "I've been expecting you."

She hesitated briefly before taking his hand. "Have you, Mr. Hennessy?" she asked, suspicion conveyed in her tone.

She had a strong voice. He liked that, but the clamminess of her hand took him mildly by surprise. Interesting, he thought. The heat? Entirely possible. Nerves? An unusual reaction for an officer of the law.

"Yes," he said. "I received a call from Don Maier. He informed me of your visit. Call me Parker. Please."

He noted that she shot an I-told-you-so look at the FBI agent with her.

"I understand there have been some disturbances at our interment parks in recent weeks."

"And did Mr. Maier tell you that, too?" she asked.

He smiled at her. "But, of course, Sheriff." The only difference was, he knew precisely what type of disturbances they were investigating, and it had nothing to do with panty raids or tombstone-tipping as Maier had implied.

Fools, he thought. All of them. Did they not realize the implications of the FBI's presence in Magnolia? He didn't doubt for a second they were here because of his failed match for Tommy Gartner. Not that he was the least bit concerned. They'd never connect him to the Webb girl, or Gartner, for that matter.

"Deputy," she corrected him, as he knew she would. No one judged character as well as he did. "Deputy Lomax."

His smile never faltered. "Please, make yourselves comfortable. Can I offer you something cool to drink?"

"No, thank you," she said.

He looked at the FBI agent.

"I'm good," Ash said.

"I'm afraid you have me at a disadvantage, sir," he said to Agent Keller. Yes, he knew their names. Not only had Susan informed him, but so had Maier during their brief conversation earlier, shortly after Lomax and Keller had left Maier's establishment. But in pretending ignorance, it allowed him a few more precious seconds to observe the pair.

"Keller," the man replied, then offered his hand.

The firm, solid grip of a formidable opponent. A challenge he would enjoy greatly.

"Special Agent Keller is with the FBI," the deputy supplied.

Parker simply offered a small nod of acknowledgment, otherwise he showed no outward indication that her announcement concerned him. She watched him closely, too, hoping for a reaction, no doubt. Did she think she was dealing with an amateur? Foolish, ignorant woman.

He waited until his guests were seated before taking the wing chair for himself. Deputy Lomax sat on the far corner of the settee. Keller chose to remain standing, close to the deputy, he noted with interest. Almost as if he was hovering.

Fascinating, indeed.

"How may I be of service?" Parker asked them.

Agent Keller spoke. "If it's not too much trouble, we'd like to speak with your employees. We're just trying to dis-

cover if anyone has seen or perhaps heard anything unusual."

"Certainly."

"Can you account for your whereabouts Tuesday night?"

Keller frowned at the deputy, a look she ignored, since
she kept those mesmerizing eyes trained on him. She was
trying to read him.

*Go ahead and look, my dear. You'll only see what I allow
you to see.*

"As I do most evenings," he addressed her calmly, "I
spent it at home with my wife."

She didn't like him. He could tell by the iciness creeping
into her blue-eyed gaze. She did have beautiful eyes, he
thought, particularly when they softened ever so slightly
whenever she glanced Agent Keller's way. He detected a
connection between them, one that transcended any professional relationship.

He sensed Susan's approach before she appeared in the
doorway. "Pardon me for interrupting," she said, her sweet
voice apologetic. She cast him a serene smile before shifting
her gaze to the deputy. "Greer, you have a phone call."

Parker immediately indicated the phone on the side table.
Greer? So Susan was well-enough acquainted with the
deputy to be on a first-name basis with her. How fortunate
for him.

Greer stood, and with her back to them, picked up the
blinking line. "Lomax."

"How many people are in your employ?" Keller asked
him.

"Three," Parker answered once Susan quietly disappeared. "I'm afraid Opal Jones and Carl Sanderson are the
only ones available at the moment. David Knox has the afternoon off. Business has been rather quiet today."

"Are you sure about that?" Greer spoke into the phone,

a distinct note of excitement filling her voice. She pulled a pen from the pocket of her uniform. "Okay. Give it to me again." She made use of the pad of paper next to the phone and jotted something down. "We'll be in soon. Thanks, Blythe."

She hung up the phone and tore off the sheet of paper, folded it, then tucked it in her pocket along with the pen. Parker watched her closely. Her attempt to remain stoic failed when she glanced in Keller's direction. A look passed between them, another silent communication, further confirming his suspicion that there was more to their relationship. A familiarity existed between them, he knew it as well as he knew his beloved Susan would tell him all he needed to know about Deputy Greer Lomax—and perhaps even her relationship with Special Agent Ash Keller.

Parker stood. "If you'll come this way, I'll take you downstairs so you may speak with Opal and Carl." And while they were busy interviewing his staff, he'd have a little chat with Susan.

"We have an ID."

"It couldn't be that easy," Ash said, fastening his seat belt.

Greer huffed a chuckle and pulled the sheet of paper with Eric Fieldler's name from her pocket to hand to Ash. "No such luck," she said, firing the ignition and shifting the cruiser into REVERSE. "But we've got a current address. Minnesota State Pen."

She glanced in Ash's direction before pulling out of the parking lot. He frowned.

"That's not possible."

"You think?" She slowed the vehicle as she pulled up to the STOP sign at the corner. "Any ideas how a current resident of the Pen left his DNA at a crime scene in North Carolina?"

Ash was thoughtful for a minute. Greer drummed her nails on the steering wheel, waiting for an eighteen-wheeler to pass.

"DNA could be a plant," Ash finally said.

Greer considered his suggestion, but just as quickly disregarded it as a possibility. "This guy is smart," she said, pulling away from the STOP. "But not that smart."

"It's entirely possible. Think about it. The UNSUB is a highly organized killer, plus he has a working knowledge of mortuary science. We've established that much. He handles DNA all the time. A strand of hair here or there could easily be planted."

"Then we need to come up with a connection between Fieldler and the UNSUB."

"Provided they aren't one and the same."

"Which isn't possible if Fieldler is a resident of the Gray Wall Hotel," Greer reminded him. "We need to interview this guy."

God, she hated everything about this investigation. The more they learned, the less that made sense. Other than the creepy feeling she got while in Parker Hennessy's presence, there hadn't been anything all that unusual about any of the funeral home employees they'd interviewed today, other than their choice of profession. But Hennessy? The guy was just too perfect. Too polished. Too cordial. Too—everything, for her comfort. And as far as she'd witnessed, Susan apparently worshipped the ground he walked on. Even his employees thought the guy walked on water.

"I'll place a call to the Minneapolis field office," Ash said, pulling his cell phone from his pocket. "See if they can spare a body to take a trip out to the Pen to check it out. Any idea what the guy was sent up for?"

"No. Blythe said the crime lab faxed the report. She figured we'd want to know about the DNA match ASAP, so she called."

"You didn't like Hennessy. Why?" Ash asked.

Greer shook off the chill chasing down her spine. "I don't know," she said after a moment. "Show me something perfect and I'll show you something that isn't."

"Like his wife."

"Susan?" She thought about that for a moment. "I wouldn't be putting her on the list of suspects, if that's what you're thinking."

"Eliminating possibles already?"

"Hardly," Greer said, changing lanes. "It's just that she's harmless. Doesn't fit the profile, either. Her devotion to Hennessy is obvious, though."

"You picked up on that, too."

"Yeah, but I'm not surprised," she said, slowing as she reached another STOP sign. Greer knew the type, understood it all too well, in fact, having borne witness to it in the years before her father died. Her mother had essentially worshipped the man, who in turn did nothing but continually humiliate her. She didn't know if Hennessy was out banging twenty-dollar prostitutes, but her gut told her the marriage wasn't anywhere near perfect. Greer sensed it in the submissive way the other woman behaved in Hennessy's presence. It made Greer dislike the guy even more.

Ash pushed a few buttons on his cell. "Nothing from Faith." He pushed a few more buttons. "Damn."

"Hopefully she'll find something on Webb's laptop soon," Greer said. "Didn't Hennessy bother you?"

Ash shrugged. "No more than any of the others we talked to today. That Opal Jones is a character."

Greer's lips twitched. "My mother went to school with Opal, back before integration was considered illegal. She hasn't changed much in the years I've known her, except for maybe being even more outspoken the older she gets. Whatever's on Opal's mind comes out that woman's mouth."

"So I noticed," Ash said with a chuckle. "She didn't buy for a minute I was there because of a few tipped headstones."

Greer shot him a quick glance.

"Don't worry," he said. "I've done this before, you know."

Yes, he had, and for the first time since he'd arrived she was truly grateful for his presence. Not that it meant anything. Still, she had some difficult decisions ahead, but those would have to wait until they'd nailed the UNSUB. She could handle only one disaster at a time.

"I'd just like to keep this quiet until we know more," she said. "We don't know how the UNSUB is hunting his vics, we don't know why he's choosing to dispose of the bodies in such a gruesome way—"

"To remain undetected," Ash supplied. "No body, no crime."

"We have a DNA match, but the guy is behind bars. Nothing is making sense. I'm not about to take this to the press yet, and we sure as hell don't want it leaked at this stage." With more questions than answers, the department would look like a sorry group of inept amateurs.

"You realize you may not be able to avoid the press sniffing around for much longer. You said yourself, this place is going to be buzzing with gossip by morning."

Greer let out a weighty sigh as she pulled her cruiser into the department's parking lot. She parked and cut the engine. "Aren't you going to call Minneapolis?"

"I want a secure line," he said. "I'm not about to take any chances that this thing gets leaked." He placed his hand on her arm before she could exit the vehicle. "You might want to consider setting up some extra patrols tonight."

Greer nodded her agreement, then stepped from the cruiser. Their interviews might not have gleaned any solid leads today, but odds were their presence had rattled the wrong cage. The UNSUB could very well strike again, just to prove he was the one in charge.

Parker pulled the pad of paper Greer Lomax had used from the pocket of his jacket and set it on his desk. With a soft-leaded pencil in hand, he lightly traced back and forth until the depression was clear.

He stared at the name. Anger burned inside him. White-hot anger, blurring his vision.

Eric Fieldler.

Fuck!

Apparently Deputy Lomax was a lot closer than he'd anticipated.

Too close. And that was extremely unfortunate—for her.

"Greer?" Addy's voice crackled over the intercom. "Line one, Sugar."

"Lomax."

"Don't you return phone calls any more?"

Greer let out a sigh and sank into the chair behind her desk. "Vivi," she said. No chocolate donuts, two dead bodies and now her sister. Talk about a crappy afternoon. "Sorry. It's been hectic."

"Mama's birthday dinner is tonight. Don't forget."

Damn. She had forgotten. She didn't see how she could attend. In stepping up patrols in a department already operating with a skeleton crew, that meant she'd be pulling an extra shift, patrolling the local cemeteries herself. Not exactly the best duty she'd ever pulled, but it couldn't be helped. They simply lacked manpower.

"Vivi—"

"Don't you dare cancel, Greer. It's important to Mama."

Not as important as finding a homicidal maniac.

"Maybe I can stop in for a bit. But I can't stay long."

Sometime between now and her next shift, she'd need to catch at least a couple hours' sleep. "I have to work tonight, Vivi. It can't be helped."

"Surely you can find someone else to take your shift."

Christ, she didn't need this crap now. "Not really."

"Will you be bringing Ash?" Vivi asked.

Now *that* she really didn't need, but she didn't see how it could be avoided, either. At least not without some heavy-duty explaining to Mama, and Ash was not a subject she wanted to discuss. Even with herself.

Greer let out another hefty sigh. She'd rather eat ground glass. "Fine. We'll be there," she said and hung up the phone, unsure which she dreaded more—cruising grave-yards or spending an evening with her mother—and Ash.

Chapter 20

GREER TURNED AWAY from the map Ash had tacked to the wall. She'd been staring at it for the past twenty minutes, and as hard as she tried to see something, anything, all she saw was a random series of colored pushpins that held no clue. There weren't even enough bodies for her to formulate a pattern, for that matter. She knew she should be grateful for that much, but instead, frustration bit into her, hard.

"I hate this damn case," she muttered to herself. "I hate this freaking UNSUB."

"You sure it's even a serial?" Tate Orson occupied the chair opposite the desk Ash had claimed. "At the academy, we learned it takes three murders to even be considered a serial."

"The MO is too similar for them to be random acts," Ash patiently told the young deputy. "Too much attention to detail. You have a repeat offender on your hands. Trust me."

Orson nodded slowly. He bent his head, studying the notes he'd been taking copiously since the meeting started over an hour ago.

What she wouldn't give to have a group of well-seasoned detectives and agents at her disposal. A real task force to increase their odds of stopping the UNSUB before he killed again. She needed officers on patrol keeping their eyes open for anything suspicious, detectives doing the leg work, agents to analyze and dissect the information collected so she could develop a solid profile that would put them that much closer to capturing the monster. But all she had were four street cops and Ash. If they didn't come up with a solid lead soon, she'd have no choice but to call in the Staties and let them take over jurisdiction.

Kyle Norton, another of Magnolia's overworked deputies, leaned his shoulder against the window frame and let out a weary sigh. Brackets of exhaustion framed his deep blue eyes, compounding Greer's guilt. He'd just come off a double shift not five hours ago, and with Blythe refusing to take maternity leave until she was ready to deliver, no wonder the guy looked so beat. Double duty at work and at home.

Greer hated that she'd asked Travis to call every available uniform in tonight, but she'd had no choice. Even Grant Mitchell, still officially on medical leave and hobbling around on crutches, had agreed to come in and work dispatch tonight, coordinating patrols. She'd needed bodies, live ones, in order to step up patrols around the area cemeteries. Thankfully, the men she'd worked with for the past two years hadn't hesitated a second.

Odds were she and Ash had rattled a cage by paying visits to all the local funeral homes. Their UNSUB would want them to know he was smarter than they were, and what better way to prove his point than with a body dump right after she and Ash had walked through his door. She knew the ramifications, understood how it could cost another innocent life.

Her stomach tightened with equal amounts of dread and anticipation. Her only hope was that the UNSUB, in his haste to prove he was the one in control—if she had any luck whatsoever—would get sloppy and make a mistake, giving them the break they needed in this case.

The big metal back door to the department clanged shut. A moment later, Travis Willows walked into the office, the ever-present unlit cigar clamped between his lips. "Sorry I'm late," he said around the cigar. "Damn council meeting ran over again."

"Any luck?" Kyle asked. "I'd like a raise, but I'll settle for a couple less shifts a week."

"Cheap pricks," Travis complained, lowering his bulk into the chair behind Greer's desk. "We'll be lucky to keep the lights on with the pittance they're wanting us to operate on this year. I've never seen a bunch of idiots whose asses didn't pucker up tighter than a snare drum when the subject is money than these jerks."

"Guess that's a no," Grant said with a chuckle.

"What do they expect us to do?" Tate asked. "Work for free?"

"Don't give them any ideas," Travis groused, then looked over at Greer. "What have you got on this bastard so far?"

"Not as much as I'd like. We still don't know how he's hunting for his victims. Until we can determine that, it won't be easy to stop him."

"But we know what he does with them," Travis said.

"Unfortunately," Greer said, "our UNSUB is what we call an organized killer. He knows what he's doing and he's good at it. According to Manny, he's extremely methodical. I'm convinced there's a reason he prepares the vics for burial while they're still alive, but all I keep coming back to is his knowledge of mortuary science."

"He's a twisted fuck," Grant said. "That's why."

Greer didn't disagree.

"What about disgruntled employees?" Kyle asked. "Anyone been fired for not passing the funeral directors' exam?

Any chance this is a wannabe nut job pissed off at the world?"

"Could be someone with an unusual interest in dead bodies," Tate added.

"It's more involved than that," Ash said to Tate, then looked at Kyle. "Maier's Funeral Home had an employee they let go about a year ago for incompetence. He mixed up a couple of bodies, which, from what I heard today, was fairly devastating for the families."

"Where's this clown now?" Travis asked.

Ash checked his notes. "Relocated to Oregon shortly after he was terminated. I've got the Portland office checking it out. My best guess is, it'll be a dead end. I didn't get the impression the guy had an axe to grind."

"Did I hear right, that you had DNA?" Travis asked.

"Yes," Greer said with a nod. "I'm betting it's another dead end, though. The DNA matches an Eric Fieldler, a prisoner in the state pen in Minnesota. Anyone care to tell me how the DNA from a prisoner eighteen hundred miles away ends up on a DB in Magnolia?"

"We're waiting to hear back from the feds in Minneapolis," Ash added.

"There's a connection that I can't figure out," Travis spoke. "Archer and Stewart. Webb and Gartner."

"We don't know that there is a connection," Ash said.

"Oh, give me a break," Travis argued. "If this whacko is a serial, then there's a goddamn connection."

"I didn't say there *wasn't* a connection, we just haven't figured it out yet."

"But you have a theory."

Ash glanced at Greer. Apparently he'd forgotten about talking to Travis about having her removed from the case.

She let out a sigh. "We have Joanna Webb's laptop. Ash sent it to Quantico. The geeks should've gotten it by now.

Hopefully that'll tell us something soon. Did you talk with Trina Stewart's son? Can we get into her place, or do we need a warrant?"

"As soon as I know, you'll know," Travis said.

"If you don't have his consent by noon tomorrow, let's get a warrant."

"What's your theory, Greer?" Travis pressed.

"I'm working on it."

"There's a reason he's selecting the graves where he's buried, or attempted to bury, the vics. What is it?"

She didn't have a clue. "As soon as I know, you'll know."

"I don't care what it takes," Travis said, pushing out of his chair. "Let's nail this bastard to the wall. The sooner, the better."

Greer couldn't agree more. She looked to the men. "You know where you'll be tonight?"

With the aid of his crutches, Grant stood. "Yeah, dull dispatch. You guys better keep the chatter up," he said, hobbling toward the door. "I forgot to bring a book and I need something to keep me awake all night." He looked at Greer. "I wish I could be out there with you."

She managed a small smile. "I know. But I appreciate you manning the desk. You need anything, just let us know."

"Coffee. And a lot of it," Grant said before he disappeared down the corridor to the dispatch room.

Kyle wearily pushed off the window frame where he'd been leaning throughout the meeting. "I've got the northwest side of the county covered," he said. "I'll be in touch."

"I'm northeast," Tate said and stood.

"Travis, you'll take the southwest side?" Greer asked. At his nod, she added, "I've got the southeast quadrant. I wish we had more bodies."

"Live bodies," Travis corrected. "Dead bodies, we've had more than enough of already." He looked to Ash. "What about you?"

"I'll be riding with Greer. We can brainstorm while on patrol."

Travis looked closely at Greer.

He knows. He knows I'm close to losing it, she thought.

He *had* to know. She'd never been a fan of graveyards and the thought of cruising cemeteries, especially at night, made her antsy. Travis wasn't a fool. He probably suspected she was teetering on the edge of sanity and it wouldn't take much to send her plunging over the edge.

He finally nodded his assent. "Good idea." He tucked his cigar back in the corner of his mouth. "Keep your eyes open," he said, "and let's all add a prayer for a silent night."

"You ever think about retirement?"

Ash looked over at Greer. She'd asked the question in an offhand manner, but he doubted there was anything casual about her query. They'd been driving around for the past three hours, seeing nothing out of the ordinary. The radio crackled to life occasionally whenever one of the officers changed his location, but otherwise, all was silent. Even the moon had taken a night off, hidden behind the clouds rolling in from the Atlantic, promising another late-night storm.

"Sure, I've thought about it," he told her honestly. "Everybody does eventually."

Retire to Florida. Buy a fishing boat. Down a fifth of vodka for courage before swallowing the wrong end of a .38 Special.

She blew on the service-station bargain cappuccino before taking a sip from the tall Styrofoam cup. "You've got, what? Another four, five years before you're eligible?"

"More like eight," he answered.

She looked at him sharply. "You really think you can do this for another eight years? Keep chasing after monsters?"

He was thoughtful a moment. They were parked on the street side of some cemetery he didn't know the name of on the outskirts of the Magnolia city limits. The lights of the dash illuminated the interior of the police cruiser in eerie shadows of LED blue.

He'd considered getting out, more so since Greer had left. What would happen if he did retire from the Bureau? Wouldn't the Earth stop spinning?

"It isn't that easy to walk away," he admitted. He didn't know what he'd do if he wasn't an agent. The Florida scenario certainly held no appeal.

She took another sip of her cappuccino. "I did."

"Yeah," he said, then took a drink of his own strong black coffee. "You did. But if Phoenix hadn't gone down the way it had, you can't tell me you wouldn't be chasing the same monsters I still do."

She let out a sigh. "You're probably right." She surveyed the darkness through the open side window, then rolled it up as the wind kicked up a notch.

"Don't you miss it?" he asked her.

She let out another sigh, followed by a shrug of her too-slender shoulders.

"Be honest," he pressed. "You do miss it, don't you? You miss the rush of adrenaline when you're close. The satisfaction of knowing you were right. That one less monster is out there because of your ability to outthink, outsmart the bastards."

The hint of a grin tugged at her lips. "The old God complex. It never goes away, does it?"

He shook his head. "I don't think so."

She drew in a deep breath and turned to face him. In the dim lights of the dash, her blue eyes were bright. "I've missed you," she said, her voice so soft he wasn't certain he'd heard her correctly, but hoped like the devil he had.

Hope. A concept he rarely indulged in on any regular

basis. In his line of work, all too often hope was an illusion. A wispy, illusive apparition. A goddamn fallacy.

His heart started thumping wildly in his chest. Hope. It was all he had, so he hung on to the thin thread for dear life. And hoped.

"Enough to come back with me when this case is closed?"

She turned away and looked out the windshield. "How can you ask me that after what happened this morning?"

His grin turned wry. "Nothing will get your heart pumping in the morning like a nine mil pointed at your skull."

She looked at him again and frowned. "That's not funny, Ash."

"I know," he said, sobering.

"I've built a life here."

He let out a sharp, caustic laugh. "What life?"

She handed out jaywalking tickets and sank probably every dime she'd saved into that monstrosity she had the nerve to call a home. She worked double shifts, didn't eat right and he hadn't seen her sleep more than three or four hours at a stretch. That wasn't a life. Hell, it was barely an existence.

Her frown deepened before she looked away again. "You sound like Selma."

"I always did like her."

"The Bureau would never take me back," she said. "I'd have a better chance of winning the Kentucky Derby on foot than passing the psyche exam."

"You don't know that."

The look she gave him told him otherwise. Yeah, but maybe it wasn't quite the leap she believed.

"Who says you have to go back into the Unit?"

From the surprise flickering in her gaze, he could tell she hadn't even considered not returning to the Unit as an option.

He pressed the advantage, regardless of how small. "You could teach."

She let out a small puff of air. "Those who can't, teach, huh?"

"No one's saying you can't, Greer. I'm just saying it's an option."

She shook her head. "My family is here."

In all the time they'd been together, they'd made only a handful of trips to Magnolia to visit her family. And even those were short, two- or three-day trips. "That's never bothered you before."

"Dammit," she said, and smacked the steering wheel with the heel of her hand. "Oh, God. Vivi's going to kill me." She looked at the clock on the dash, the blue digits indicating half-past ten. "Hopefully Mama's still up."

"What is it?"

She fired up the cruiser. "Mama's birthday dinner. It completely slipped my mind." She reached for the radio and waited for Grant to acknowledge. "I'm heading into town," she told the other officer, then rattled off the phone number to her mother's house.

"You're going to your mother's? Now?"

She shifted the cruiser into gear. "I know, I know. The job always comes first. Thirty minutes, tops. That's all I need."

She pulled away from the curb and drove a little too fast toward the city limits. "Birthdays are important to Mama June. Not that she counts them," she explained while negotiating a turn, "but she does celebrate them. Birthdays are the one thing Mama always got right. Even those first few months after Buddy died."

Ash reached into the backseat and pulled his laptop case over the seat. Within a few minutes, he had it powered up, the portable printer attached, and an Internet connection made through his cell. "Perfect."

"What are you doing?" Greer asked.

"Improvising." He clicked to the site he had in mind and ordered a hefty gift certificate to a national video-store chain. He wanted Mama June on his side if he needed her to help him convince Greer that returning to Quantico was a good idea. No way was he going in empty-handed.

Chapter 21

PARKER CONSIDERED HIMSELF an expert at most of his endeavors, but timing in particular he considered his specialty. He didn't believe in luck, he believed in opportunity. Another expertise he'd perfected over time. Being in the right place at the right time didn't occur by happenstance, but from successful planning. Well-thought-out strategy and methodical attention to every minute detail were key, as was his ability to develop a contingency plan at a moment's notice. The closely guarded secret of his superior success.

The loss of Jeffrey Holcomb's burial had angered him. The possibility of such a perfect mate going to waste had infuriated him, but he'd refused to panic. He'd been confident that the ultimate solution would present itself if he was patient. Patience, the paramount ingredient in answering his true calling.

He'd kept her longer than most, a rarity, but oh, how he'd enjoyed her company. She'd been especially beautiful. Sweet. An innocence about her so uncommon in such a decadent, narcissistic world. She'd been the ideal mate for the poor, misguided Jeffrey who had barely been capable of writing his own name. She'd been an elementary school teacher. She would've served dear Jeffrey well in eternity. The perfect match, as were all his eternal unions.

Slowly, he removed his protective gloves, tossed them into the hazardous waste container and took a step back to admire his excellence. His ability to complete such a flawless transformation pleased him. Sweet, sweet Sarah, no longer recognizable, a mere facsimile of her former self. She'd been readied, prepared for her new eternal union. He only wished he could personally witness their reaction when they found her.

Donning a pair of leather gloves, he carefully prepared Sarah for transport. He'd been listening to the police scanner as he'd completed her transformation. The fools were keeping close tabs on the cemeteries tonight, but he wasn't worried. He had no reason for concern, because timing was, after all, one of his very special gifts.

He smiled as he tugged closed the zipper to the body bag. They were looking for a gravedigger. Oh, but they would certainly be surprised when they realized their mistake. He smiled as he imagined them scratching their asses, wondering how he'd gotten past their diligent, yet useless, efforts to capture him.

He quietly opened the door to his private domain and listened for the sounds of activity on the floors above. As he expected, silence. Susan would be sound asleep by now, the additional sleeping pill he added to her evening glass of wine, combined with the pill she'd take herself at bedtime, would most certainly have rendered her unconscious for the night. He had much to do, thanks to the valuable information Susan had shared with him.

Deciding it safe to remove Sarah undetected, he rolled the gurney carrying her body out the side door to the van, then carefully transferred her into the back, closing the doors as silently as possible. He checked his watch. He had to leave now. There was no time to spare. Not tonight.

Tonight his timing would be perfect. As perfect as his plan to end Greer Lomax.

Her daughter looked as if she wanted to be anywhere in the world, except sitting at the kitchen table with an untouched slice of strawberry-filled birthday cake in front of her. Her son-in-law, however, having just polished off his second helping, appeared as if he was seriously considering a third slice of the cake Vivien Lee had brought for the small dinner party, which had ended hours ago.

"The market will shift again," Davis was saying to Ash. "These things have always been cyclical."

"And political," Ash said, finally setting down his fork.

Davis considered the mug of decaf in front of him. "I don't believe politics has as much influence as people like to think. Or lay blame."

Greer toyed with her uneaten slice of cake and June's heart squeezed with a touch of anxiety and a flash of pain. Of all the hopes and dreams she'd had for her daughters, in truth, all she'd ever really wanted, all any mother wanted, she theorized, was for her children to be happy.

Lord knew, she'd failed both of her girls on that score.

Davis had told her Greer's and Vivien Lee's happiness wasn't her job, but she begged to differ. Guilt gnawed at her constantly, and she wasn't even a Catholic.

She hadn't done the best she could by them. She hadn't done enough. If she had, Vivien wouldn't run through men like water and Greer wouldn't be sitting across from her looking as if she hadn't eaten or slept in a month. She worried about her girls, worried they'd never be happy.

Greer had been once, a thought that gave June hope. To her way of thinking, what once had been achieved could be regained.

How on earth did she make a daughter who barely communicated with her see that bit of wisdom? Especially one as stubborn and willful as Greer? With a twelve-inch cast-iron chicken fryer upside the head, if necessary, that's how.

"I'm really sorry I was so late," Greer said for the third time in the twenty minutes since she and Ash had arrived. She dragged her fork through the rich butter cream frosting. "It couldn't be helped."

June attempted a gentle smile, but she was too concerned for her daughter's welfare for it to be genuine. "I'm sure what you're doing is important to you."

Greer's lips thinned into a tension-filled line.

Damn. She hadn't meant for that to sound so judgmental.

"It is, Mama," Greer set the fork aside and pushed the china plate away from her. "That's why we can't stay," she said, rising. "I'm on duty tonight."

"But you just arrived." They'd barely spoken in the short time she'd been there. In fact, if it wasn't for Davis and Ash, the only sound in the kitchen would've been the rhythmic tick of the sunflower-shaped clock above the stove.

"I'm sorry," Greer apologized. To Ash she said, "We need to get back out there."

"Come for dinner on Sunday," Davis invited. "Both of you. Maybe your mama will make her famous cornbread and beans. I'll grill up some steaks."

"We'll see," Greer said in her usual noncommittal fashion.

Ash shook Davis's hand. "Good to see you again, Davis."

"Greer—"

"Mama, I can't make any promises right now."

Something had her daughter worried. Not only worried, but scared. She could see it in her eyes, eyes that revealed so much. Her pain, her fear, even love—whenever she looked in Ash's direction, even if those glances were fleeting.

June didn't understand why Greer had left Ash when it was so painfully obvious her daughter and son-in-law were still very much in love. Not that Greer would ever confide in her. Since she'd returned to Magnolia, their conversations were superficial at best.

"If you'll excuse me," Ash said. He kissed June on the cheek. "Thank you for the cake. It was delicious."

She summoned up a smile. "It's always a pleasure having my favorite son-in-law for a visit. Come back soon. Promise?"

"I promise." To Greer he said, "I'll wait by the car."

Greer gave June, then Davis, a quick hug before stepping onto the porch. "Please try to understand, Mama. What I have to do right now is too important."

A trace of fear crept into her daughter's voice that concerned June. Whatever Greer was involved in at the moment had frightened her. Call it mother's intuition, but something was terribly wrong. She wondered if her daughter realized how brave she was, or how proud June was of her. Greer was tough, a survivor, and whatever she was dealing with, she'd come out on top. But that didn't lessen her apprehension over her daughter's safety or her worry over the haunted shadows in her daughter's clear blue eyes. How could it? After what Greer had suffered at the hands of that monster . . . She could only imagine the worst, and those thoughts kept her up late most nights.

June let out a sigh. "I'm trying, Greer, but it would help if you told me what was so important."

"I can't discuss an ongoing investigation, Mama. I'm sorry."

She glanced over at Ash. He didn't look any more rested than Greer, standing next to Greer's police car, speaking into his cell phone. "Is that the only reason Ash is in Magnolia? This investigation you're working on?"

Greer shrugged. "Mostly."

June shook her head. "If you truly believe that, then you're a bigger fool than I ever was."

"I don't want to discuss Ash," Greer said and looked away.

"You haven't wanted to discuss anything since you've been home," June said, sounding irritable and judgmental—again.

"Mama, don't," Greer said quietly. She let out a sigh and added, "Not now."

June left the doorway and approached her daughter. Gently, she placed a kiss on Greer's cheek. "I only want you to be happy."

And safe.

Both of her daughters possessed the danger gene, something they'd obviously gotten from their no 'count father, God rest his rotten-to-the-core soul. Greer put her life on the line to make the world a better place. Vivien chased men, so desperate to find a new husband she was endangering her own life, in June's opinion. She most certainly did not approve of her eldest daughter's current quest of dating strange men she met online. It wasn't that she didn't approve of blind dates, but they should be arranged through the friend of friend, or the third cousin of an acquaintance. But like Greer, when Vivien set her mind to something, there was no talking to her.

Greer took a step back, a deep frown creasing her forehead. "Why is everyone so concerned about my happiness all of a sudden?"

"Because people care about you."

"I have to go."

The burst of emotion dissipated as quickly as it arose. Shut out again, June thought. She felt Greer closing down her emotions as physically as if she'd slammed a door in her face.

"Ash is a good man, sweetheart," she said as Greer reached the porch steps. "He loves you. Take it from me. That's not an easy thing to find."

Greer stopped at the foot of the steps, but didn't turn to face her. "I know."

"But?" June prodded.

"But I just can't think about that now, Mama," she said, then hurried across the brick path to the driveway.

"Well, that went well," June murmured sarcastically, then turned to go back inside the house, wondering where she'd put that damn cast-iron skillet.

"Fieldler's dead."

Greer pulled the cruiser to a stop at the curb and turned to look at Ash. She needed to focus. The argument with her mother still rang in her ears. Well, not an actual argument, but she certainly left with her mother's disappointment weighing heavily on her shoulders. Nothing new there, she thought.

"Say that again?"

"Fieldler's dead. That was Covington from the Minneapolis Field Office with the latest. He would've called sooner, but they've been swamped."

Not an usual occurrence since 9/11. There wasn't an agent who hadn't been putting in serious overtime since the attacks.

"Any chance the body's been shipped here for burial?" she asked hopefully.

Ash shook his head. "No. The body was claimed by a Thea Wesley—five years ago."

Greer stared at Ash in stunned disbelief. "Five years?"

He nodded. "Someone, somewhere dropped the ball. Fieldler was shanked in the prison shower. Who knows why. Covington's e-mailing the rap sheet in the morning. He doesn't think he's our guy."

"Well, yeah, for one, he's dead."

"Not only that, but his rap sheet is long. Strong history of violent crime. Armed robbery, assault with a deadly, a few battery charges—just to name the highlights. He was pulling a twenty-to-life stretch that lasted less than eighteen months."

"Doesn't fit the profile," Greer agreed. "But it's just another dead end if the guy's been six feet under for five years."

"I've already booked a morning flight to Minneapolis. I'm going to talk to this Wesley woman myself and see what I can turn up."

Greer nodded her agreement.

Ash was leaving.

She should be relieved. She should be grateful. Out of sight, out of mind. Her specialty.

She pulled away from the curb with dread churning in her tummy like a ball of fire.

Ash was leaving. And, God help her, she didn't want him to go.

Chapter 22

ASH WAS LEAVING.

Greer propped her shoulder against the doorjamb of the spare bedroom, watching him throw a few items into an overnight bag. He'd walked back into her life when she'd least expected it, his presence the equivalent of tornado-force winds stirring up her chaotic landscape, when all she'd wanted was peace, quiet, boredom . . . and now he was leaving.

He'll be back.

Oh, really? she thought. How is that, when she'd given him no reason to come back to her?

Is that what she wanted?

Yes.

No.

God, she didn't have a clue.

He'll be back. Of course he will. The bad guy was here, after all.

So are you.

She let out a sigh. Her conscience was really starting to work her last nerve today.

"Try to get some sleep on the plane," she told him. "You look like hell."

He turned and gave her one of those smiles that still had

the power to make her heart skip half a dozen or so beats. "Coming from someone refreshed and ready to start the day?"

She dredged up a small smile in return and shrugged. "I don't sleep much."

Truth was, she was exhausted and, as soon as Ash left, she planned to catch a few hours' sleep before heading back to the station. The night of patrols had been a wasted effort. Or perhaps not, depending on whether she was feeling optimistic. Their presence may have scared off the UNSUB, but that didn't mean he hadn't been prepared to strike. Or perhaps he had, and they'd thwarted his opportunity to dispose of a body.

Ash tossed his shaving kit into the overnight bag. "You have my cell phone number, right?"

She nodded, but he didn't see her, since his back was turned as he zipped closed the overnight bag. "Yeah, I've got it."

"Call if you need me."

"I will."

She wanted to tell him not to go. She wanted to tell him to hurry back, wishes that had nothing to do with any investigation. She wanted to tell him that without him, her life had been nothing but an endless series of dull, gray images. He brought vibrant Technicolor back into her world. She didn't want gray any longer, she realized. She wanted, needed, that color.

She wanted, needed Ash.

A lump formed in her throat, damming the words so they welled up inside her, unable to escape. She'd once been articulate, an excellent communicator. What she wouldn't give for one iota of those skills now. Instead, she stood there with her back pressed against the doorjamb, as silent as a stone.

Fear? Yes, but not because she thought for a second he'd reject her, but because she wasn't certain she could go back with him. Back to an endless series of body bags in one nameless city after another, bad coffee, crappy flights, lousy hotels, and sick and twisted sociopaths lurking in every dark corner waiting to perform unspeakable acts.

And then there were the nightmares, so vivid and real. She could've killed Ash yesterday, and that frightened her more than the night terrors.

Fear? Absolutely. They kept her running, from the past and the future. She was sick and tired of being afraid all the time.

Baby steps, she thought. Her shrink kept reminding her she needed to take small steps if she ever hoped to put her fears and anxiety to rest. Solve the case, then solve her life. In baby steps.

Yeah, right. Impossible, especially when she desperately wanted to take a flying leap right into Ash's arms and beg him not to leave her.

With the overnight bag in hand, Ash walked toward her. She kept her hands behind her, afraid she'd latch on to him and never let go.

"I'll be back tonight," he said. "Tomorrow morning at the latest."

She nodded. "I'll be fine."

His smile was gentle, yet no less breath-stealing. "I know you will."

"Blind faith?" she teased. "Since when?"

He reached up and cupped her cheek in his warm palm. "Since the day you walked out," he said. "I always had faith you'd come back to me."

Her heart gave a painful lurch. She'd caused them so much pain. She hadn't been fair, to either of them. And since she was being honest with herself for a change, she regretted her decision to run. But, at the time, total detachment had been her only means of emotional survival.

The lump returned. Moisture blurred her vision. "I'm sorry," she whispered.

"Me, too," he said softly, then dipped his head and brushed his lips gently over hers.

The kiss had no hope of remaining gentle for long. Not when she wrapped her arms around him and held on for dear life. All she had left to do was beg him not to leave her.

The overnight bag hit the unfinished hardwood floor with a loud thud and he pulled her tight against him. Her chest hurt from the fierce and overwhelming emotions crowding her heart. She'd been a fool. She understood that now. How could she have believed for a second, not to mention two years, that she was better off without Ash by her side? He was her husband, the man she'd vowed to spend the rest of her life with, for better or worse, and she loved him.

She'd blamed him that she'd become a victim of The Preacher, but she'd been so very wrong. The blame belonged to her, for thinking herself invincible. She'd believed she could conquer the world, that it was her job to make it a better place. One bad guy at a time. Because in the back of her mind, she knew Ash would keep her safe. And when he hadn't, she'd laid the blame at his door rather than at her own.

God, she'd been such an idiot. So much time wasted.

She ended the kiss, wanting to say so much but not knowing how or where to begin. "You'll miss your flight."

"I'll call when I land, so keep your cell turned on," he reminded her, then planted one last, hard kiss on her lips before he picked up his bag and headed down the stairs.

She nodded, not trusting herself to blurt out what was in her heart. Now was not the time. They had an UNSUB to nail, and dammit, the job had to come first.

* * *

Greer couldn't exactly say she was well rested when she walked into the Sheriff's Department a few minutes before eleven, but at least she'd slept for three solid, dreamless hours. An amazing feat, considering Selma and her small crew had arrived minutes after Ash had departed for the airport and had been framing the walls for the attic rooms all morning.

She'd spoken to Ash just before she left the house. He'd landed safely in Minneapolis and had been on his way to the field office, promising to call when he had news.

She missed him already.

She stopped for a mug of coffee, then headed down the corridor to the task force room across from the small dispatch center. Blythe was working the desk today, sitting with her feet propped on a pillow. "Quiet morning," Greer said by way of greeting. "I hope."

"Nothing out of the ordinary," Blythe answered. "We've only got Tate out this morning. Kyle's home catching up on sleep for his double shift later."

"Where's Travis?" Greer asked before taking a much-needed sip of coffee.

"Just checked in," Blythe told her. "He's having lunch with a couple of the 'tightwad bastards,' then he'll relieve Tate. Probably another hour or so."

"Tate's been on since seven last night. Call him in," Greer said. "I'll take his patrol until Travis is free." Things were quiet, and with Ash out of town for the day, she didn't see any reason she shouldn't handle a patrol for a few hours to relieve one of her fellow officers who'd been on duty for over sixteen hours.

Blythe nodded. "He'll appreciate it," she said. "Check with Addy before you head out. I think she might have a couple of messages for you. Oh, and Grant called. He wants to know if you want him to man the desk again tonight."

"If he calls back, tell him I'll be in touch later," Greer said, then left for the front office. Addy wasn't at her desk, but a small handful of pink message slips were waiting for Greer. One from the crime lab indicating a preliminary report on the Webb crime scene would be faxed to her by the end of business today, one from her mother marked IMPORTANT and another from Faith.

Her mother would have to wait. Mama's interpretation of important was probably nothing more urgent than an attempt to cull a commitment for Sunday supper.

She went into the task force room and immediately placed a call to Faith's direct line at Quantico.

The agent picked up on the second ring. "Faith? It's Greer."

"Well, hello stranger," Faith said in a somewhat cheery tone. "How the hell are you?"

Confused. Anxious. Wishing Ash was here. "I wish I could say it was good to hear your voice," Greer said.

"Under normal circumstances, huh?"

Greer's lips twitched. "Exactly."

"Hey, where's that superagent hiding out? He isn't answering his cell. Any idea where I can find him?"

"He's in Minnesota following up on a possible lead." Figures, Greer thought. The man tells her to keep her cell on, but doesn't practice that of which he preaches.

"Oh?" Faith prompted. "What's so important in the frozen North?"

"We found DNA at one of the crime scenes, of a guy that was murdered in prison five years ago."

"Planted evidence?"

"Doubtful," Greer said. "The body was claimed and buried eighteen hundred miles away."

"Well, when you talk to the great one, tell him Con's seriously on the warpath. He was supposed to be back today."

Greer hadn't been aware that Con had put a time limit on Ash's stay in Magnolia. She didn't like the thought of him risking his job for her. "I'll tell him. Is that all?"

"Not really," Faith said. "Ever hear of an online dating service called *findamatch.com*?"

Greer's stomach bottomed out. Wasn't her sister using online dating services for her latest method of catching husband number four? "Not specifically, but I'm aware of the services."

"Well, Joanna Webb was a subscriber. So was one of your dead bodies, Gartner. But here's the catch, Gartner's subscription didn't begin until two days after his death."

"You're sure?"

"Absolutely," Faith said. "The site has one of those BEEN A MEMBER SINCE indicators on their public profiles."

"Did Gartner and Webb exchange e-mails?"

"Yes. We uncovered Webb's deleted files. She corresponded with him on several occasions before they arranged to meet."

"That's how he's hunting for his vics." She didn't have concrete proof, but her instincts were screaming at her. "Can you track the ISP? That could at least give us a location."

"We're working on it, but Gartner, or whomever was posing as Gartner, used a dummy e-mail account and a whole lot of rerouting. It could take a few days."

Methodical. Patient. And damn intelligent.

They didn't have a few days. She wanted the UNSUB stopped—now. "What about this matchmaking website? They'd have to have payment records."

"It'll take time," Faith said again. "I tried talking to these people, but they're pretty tight-lipped when it comes to protecting the confidentiality of their customer base. We're going to need a court order."

"Get one," Greer told her. "And while you're at it, check out Lowell Archer and Trina Stewart. See if they have any connection to *findamatch.com*."

"You think your UNSUB is using online dating services trolling for vics?"

"Call it a hunch. A big one."

Despite the gravity of the situation, Faith still chuckled. "You can take the girl out of the ISU . . ."

That's what had her worried. "You're a riot. I'd forgotten what a comedienne you were."

"I'm here all week," Faith said. "I'll get back to you as soon as I have something solid."

"Thanks, Faith," she said. "You're still the best."

"Tell that to Con. I'm due for a raise soon."

"Hold on a sec," Greer told Faith as Blythe waddled into the office wearing a frown.

"This just came in," she said, handing Greer a call form. "Orson's on his way out there now."

"He's supposed to be coming off duty."

"Thought you could use the backup," Blythe said.

Dread filled Greer as she noted the location. She looked up at Blythe. "You're sure this is a DB?"

Blythe nodded. "I'm sorry, Greer."

"What's going on?" Faith asked.

"Faith? Give Con a message for me?"

"Sure thing."

"Tell him I'm pretty sure the Bureau now has official jurisdiction."

"That's what I was afraid of."

"Yeah," Greer said. "Me, too."

They'd done it. They'd rattled the wrong cage, all right. And it'd just gotten personal.

The dead body discovered by Munroe Younger this morning had been dumped at Upland Hills Memorial Park—at the tomb of the legendary Buddy Lomax.

Chapter 23

THEA WESLEY'S WELL-KEPT, modest home was located in one of the many quiet suburbs of the Twin Cities. The paler-than-butter Cape Cod style with dark teal shutters and trim, window boxes overflowing with summer annuals and a bordered walkway with low-lying evergreens pulling double duty as ground cover, held a cozy, welcoming appeal. Large red clay pots, filled to the brim with more summer blooms, flanked the concrete stoop.

Ash rang the bell and waited for someone to answer. Moments later, a woman he'd never classify as elderly appeared. She was a large-boned woman who didn't look a minute over fifty-two.

"Thea Wesley?"

She peered at him through the screen door while wiping her hands on a paint-stained rag. "Yes? May I help you?"

Ash introduced himself and pulled his credentials from his suit pocket, holding them up against the screen for her inspection. "Mrs. Wesley, I was hoping you could answer some questions for me about Eric Fieldler?"

Even through the screen, Ash could tell she was turning pale. The hesitant smile on her face faded. "He's dead," she said coolly. "There's nothing left to say."

"Yes, ma'am," he said. "Just a few questions."

Her lips thinned into a tight line. "I have an appointment. I'm sorry."

Sure she did. That's why she was dressed in a pair of faded, loose-fitting denim slacks and a paint-splattered shirt with a pair of bifocals hanging around her neck from a gold chain.

"I promise this won't take long. A few moments of your time. Please, ma'am. It's important."

She hesitated, then unlatched the door and held it open for him. "It must be if you're asking about a man who died over five years ago."

Ash followed her through the home, which was larger than he'd expected, given how it looked from the outside. He took note of a formal living and dining room combination, furnished with several heavy pieces that were probably antiques. She led him through a brilliant yellow kitchen, complete with breakfast nook, to a sun porch at the rear of the house, overlooking a meticulously landscaped backyard. An easel sat in the corner of the room with a table covered with an array of brushes, dozens of paint tubes and a fat gingersnap-colored cat lazing in the rays from the midday sun. A photograph of a seascape was tacked to one corner of the canvas, obviously her inspiration for the painting she'd been working on when he'd interrupted her.

She indicated a pair of white wicker chairs, taking one for herself. "Why are you asking questions about Eric?"

"Prison records indicate you were listed as Fieldler's emergency contact," Ash said, citing the information he'd received from the agent in the Minneapolis office.

"Yes," she said. "Eric had no family."

"What was your connection to him?" In other words, what ties did this woman, by all appearances an upstanding citizen, have to someone like Fieldler?

"I was his social worker."

Her answer surprised him. From the background check

conducted, he knew she was a retired Children's Services employee with a thirty-five year career behind her, widowed with two grown children, a daughter with two kids of her own who lived in a neighboring community and a son in Miami working in broadcasting. "Fieldler had no history of mental incapacity."

"No," she said with a shake of her head. A thick strand of chocolate-brown hair, sprinkled with gray, fell across her cheek. She pushed it away impatiently. "He was a ward of the state until he reached the age of eighteen. I was Eric's case worker while he was under the supervision of Children's Services." She eyed him curiously. "You never answered my question, Agent Keller. Why are you asking about a man who's been dead for half a decade?"

"Because I don't believe he's dead," Ash admitted. "But you buried him, didn't you?"

Her gaze turned shrewd. "Why do you think he's still alive?"

Ash's instincts went on high alert. This woman knew something. And he knew an evasive tactic when he heard one in the way she kept answering his questions with questions of her own.

"Did you view the body prior to burial?"

"Yes."

"And was it Eric Fieldler?"

"That's what the death certificate said."

"But it wasn't Fieldler, was it Mrs. Wesley?"

"What makes you think it wasn't?"

"Because I have DNA evidence which indicates Eric Fieldler was in North Carolina just two days ago."

She looked away.

"It's possible, isn't it?" he pressed.

She gave a subtle nod. If Ash hadn't been watching her closely, he might have missed it. "Who did you bury five years ago?" he asked her.

She let out a long, even breath. "I don't know," she admitted.

"Yet you paid for the funeral of a stranger. Why?"

"Someone had to," she stated evenly.

Not necessarily. Each state had its own version of Potter's Field, or a like method of disposing of the bodies of the unclaimed or unwanted members of society.

"Do you believe evil is born, Agent Keller?" she asked suddenly.

"I'm not sure what you're asking." He knew exactly what she was asking. Were serial killers natural-born killers? Which came first? he thought.

"I always believed evil was made, until I was assigned Eric's case. You see a lot working in Children's Services," she said. "I've dealt with a lot of disenfranchised children in my line of work, and so many of them could've been capable of horrific crimes, considering their backgrounds. But they didn't. Oh, sure, there were a few petty crimes, but most of the kids I worked with turned out fine. I've even witnessed a few true success stories."

"Except Eric," Ash surmised.

"Except Eric," she agreed. "At first I maintained my belief, based on his history, but the more I learned about him, I realized that evil, true evil, is born."

"How so?"

"At first glance, Eric really wasn't all that different from any number of the sad cases any social worker has dealt with in their career. A history of severe abuse, neglect, extreme poverty—you name it, we've seen it, and Eric Fieldler lived it. You try to develop a thick hide, but I never could help being shocked by the terrible things that people will do to their own children."

"What happened to Eric?"

"He was only nine when he witnessed his mother murder his father. She escaped conviction. Her lawyer, a young, ambitious public defender, employed the battered-wife defense, but the truth was, those arguments and the violence reported by several neighbors wasn't Paul Fieldler abusing his wife, but vice versa. Eric never forgave his mother for killing his father, and the parade of drunks, drug users and just plain mean sons of bitches to follow did nothing to soften Eric toward his mother."

"She was Eric's first victim, wasn't she?"

Mrs. Wesley nodded. "Not that anyone had been able to prove it," she said. "They were living in a two-room walk-up above a bingo hall in downtown Minneapolis. The police report said Renee Fieldler fell asleep with a lit cigarette. The building was a fire hazard waiting to happen anyway, and the place went up in flames. The autopsy showed heavy traces of Ketamin in her liver."

"Horse tranquilizer?"

"Two days before the fire, the veterinarian's office in the area had been burglarized. No one was ever charged with the burglary."

"You don't believe her death was an accident, do you?" he asked her.

"I don't care what the official reports indicate," she said firmly. "No one looked too closely, either. Renee Fieldler wasn't a good person. She was a junkie, and no one really gave a damn what happened to her."

"What became of Eric?"

"Foster homes, mostly. A couple of group homes. He never stayed too long in one place. He scared a lot of people. More than one family pet turned up missing when Eric was around, too. No one could ever prove anything, mind you, but I knew. In our line of work, we rely a great deal on our instincts, don't we, Agent Keller?"

"Yes, ma'am."

"When I exhausted the list of families and group homes, there was nothing left to do but place him in a state-run juvenile facility. From there, I'm not sure what happened to him, but I imagine it hasn't been good." She gave him another of those shrewd looks through narrowed brown eyes. "I'm right, aren't I?"

"You wouldn't happen to have a photograph of Fieldler, would you?" he asked, employing her own evasion tactic.

"No," she said and stood. "You can try the Children's Services office, but the file is so old, I don't know that you'll have any luck."

"It's worth a shot," he said, standing. "Thank you for your time, Mrs. Wesley."

She didn't say anything, but led the way back through the house. Instead of going to the front door, she turned right into the living room, coming to stop before a large oak sideboard. She reached into a drawer and withdrew a stack of colorful envelopes tied together with a faded, well-worn blue silk ribbon. "Here," she said, handing the envelopes to him. "Take these. Maybe they'll be helpful to you."

Ash took the envelopes, untied the ribbon and scanned them. There were no return addresses with the exception of one from the Minnesota State Penitentiary. The others carried a variety of postmarks, both before and after the one from the State Pen, all mailed on the twentieth day of December each year. El Paso, Texas. Port Orchard, Washington. Fort Riley, Kansas. Bangor, Maine. Aspen, Colorado. Crescent City, California.

The hair on the back of Ash's neck rose.

The last four envelopes all carried the same postmark: Magnolia, North Carolina.

Greer.

He had to get back there, today.

"I don't know why I saved them," Mrs. Wesley said, "anymore than I know why he sent them to me. Maybe I hung on to them because I figured they might be important to someone someday."

"You tried to help him," Ash said. "You were probably the only person who ever cared what happened to him."

"No," she said, her tone firm. "I did my job, Agent Keller. That's it. Quite frankly, I was never more thrilled to close a file in my life. Eric Fieldler scared the hell out of me."

The case had gone from personal to in her face.

Greer slipped her cell phone back into her pocket. She'd left three messages for Ash while waiting for Manny Cantrell and Travis to arrive on the scene. She paced the corridor, doing her best to avoid the body until the others arrived, while Tate marked off the entrances to the mausoleum with yellow crime scene tape.

"You okay, Miss Greer?"

Greer turned to look at Munroe Younger. A frown creased his forehead. His hands twisted the bill of a dirty ball cap. She hadn't even heard him approach.

"Just impatient," she said, her gaze drawn back to the young woman lying on the cold marble floor in the Lomax alcove.

She was impatient, all right. Impatient for this entire mess to be over and done with, once and for all. Anxious for Manny to arrive and take the woman away so she wouldn't keep staring at the bad Dolly Parton wig; the thick, garish makeup; or the choker tied at the base of her throat—black silk with a cheap, dime-store cameo pinned to the center. A micromini red leather skirt and black bustier barely covered the essentials.

Dammit, where were they? She started pacing again and counting to ten repeatedly. She was determined to try to get through the next few hours without any chemical assistance, but she didn't know if she was actually strong enough to pull it off. She patted her pocket and felt for the pills she'd tucked there before leaving the house. Maybe just knowing she had them would be enough today.

She hoped.

She doubted it.

Her cell phone rang. The sharp trill echoing off the marbled walls and floor made her jump. With trembling hands, she fumbled with the phone and finally managed to pull it from her pocket. She flipped it open, hoping it wasn't her mother again. She'd called twice already, but Greer didn't have the time or the patience to deal with Mama June today.

She checked the display.

Ash.

Thank you, God.

"Where the hell have you been?" she snapped in a sorry excuse for a greeting.

"Interviewing a material witness," he said. "What's wrong?"

She walked back toward her daddy's tomb. "We're close," she told him, keeping her voice low.

"How close?"

"Damn close." She let out a pent-up breath. "Ash, he's playing with me. He's dumped a body outside my dad's tomb." She dragged her shaking hand through her hair. "A hooker, from the looks of her." Her heart started to race.

"I don't get it."

She dropped her head against the cool, marble pilaster at the entrance of the Lomax alcove. She caught sight of a black fishnet stocking and closed her eyes. "My dad died in a hotel room with a prostitute," she said quietly. "Whoever did this *knows* me. It's personal."

It was in her goddamn face.

Ash swore vividly. "I'm on my way back. Don't do anything until I get there."

"I'm at the crime scene now, waiting for Manny and Travis to show up."

"Just don't do anything stupid. I'll be there as soon as I can catch a flight."

As if he had the power to keep her safe? She'd mistakenly believed so once and look how that had ended.

Or save her from herself?

"Promise me," he said when she remained silent.

"Just get here as soon as you can," she whispered.

Monroe cleared his throat. Greer looked up to see Manny appear at the opposite end of the corridor. Travis trailed behind him.

"Did you have any luck with Thea Wesley?" she asked.

"Yes and no," he said. "We have a name, but it won't do us much good because he's obviously operating under an alias. Eric Fieldler *is* our UNSUB, and we already know he's in Magnolia."

"No shit, Sherlock," she said irritably. "What's Wesley's connection?"

"She was his caseworker. He was a ward of the state as a minor. I already tried Children's Services, hoping for a photograph, but the record was destroyed years ago."

"They don't keep them very long," she said, nodding a greeting to Manny and Travis. She gave them the 'I'll be a minute' signal, then walked over to the stained glass window for some privacy. "So we know who we're looking for, but we don't have a physical description."

"You grew up there, Greer. You know those people."

"Only in passing. I didn't exactly play in the backyards of the funeral homes when I was a kid, you know."

"Think on it," he said, ignoring her sarcasm. "Anything at all that doesn't seem right, we'll check it out when I get back tonight."

Which wouldn't be soon enough to suit her.

"I've FedEx'd Faith the Christmas cards Wesley gave me.

She'll get them to the lab. If nothing else, we might be able to confirm DNA."

"She called, by the way. She couldn't get in touch with you." She let out another breath that did little to calm her. "We think we know Fieldler's hunting grounds. The online-dating circuit. She's checking for a connection between Archer and Stewart before we're sure."

The call waiting signal interrupted just as Manny appeared at her side. Her mother was calling—again. She'd just have to wait. "I've got to run. Manny needs me."

"Greer, be careful."

The concern in his voice slowed her racing heart a fraction. "I will. Just hurry back."

"I'll see you soon," he promised, then added, "I love you," before disconnecting the call.

Greer slid the cell back into her pocket. For now it would have to be enough.

Chapter 24

WITHIN A MATTER of hours, Manny called with an ID on their most-recent victim. A fingerprint match for Sarah Rhodes, who was no prostitute, but an elementary-school teacher from Buxton who'd been reported missing four days ago when she failed to report for work. Greer was still waiting to hear from the Buxton PD once they'd completed their search of Rhodes's apartment, but Greer was laying odds Ms. Rhodes was a client of *findamatch.com*. She had Faith checking it out as well.

As with the previous victims, Sarah Rhodes had been meticulously prepared for burial while she'd been alive. It'd be days before the toxicology report came back, but Manny's initial impression indicated traces of Ketamin in the victim's liver. For some reason, that made Greer feel a little better. At least the victims were heavily medicated and, with any luck whatsoever, not fully aware of the horrors being perpetrated on them.

Greer leaned back in the worn leather chair across from Travis's desk and rubbed uselessly at her throbbing temples. Too bad she didn't put a whole lot of stock in something as obscure as luck, because she could certainly use a dose of it now.

"So we know he's keeping them alive for several days,"

she said to Travis and Kyle. "That tells me he has an isolated location where he does his work. What he does takes time."

"And privacy," Kyle interjected from the chair beside her. "Mortuaries aren't all that isolated. There are employees coming and going all day long."

"In some cases, the family even lives on the premises," Greer added.

"That would eliminate the Oakmont Funeral Home, Hennessy's Mortuary and After Care Memorial Home," Travis said thoughtfully. "The Hennessy family has lived on the upper floors for years."

"Charlie and Nadine Oakmont live behind the business in a separate residence, don't they?" Greer asked.

"Yeah. Phil Dickerson is a widower," Kyle said helpfully. "He'd have a lot of free time on his hands after hours."

"He could be keeping the vics in his home," Travis added, "then make use of the facilities after the staff has left for the day."

Greer shook her head. "It's a possibility, but doubtful. Dickerson doesn't fit the profile. For one, the guy's in his mid- to late-sixties. No way could he dig up a grave in a matter of hours."

"What about Oakmont's son? What's his name?"

"Billy," Greer answered. "No, Bully. Some sort of nickname for Buford, I think."

"Yeah. That's the one." Kyle said. "He's an odd duck. Young enough."

"Strong enough, too," Travis added. "But so is Parker Hennessy. Now there's a strange cookie."

Greer agreed, but wondered if she did so because she hadn't liked Parker Hennessy. "Married," she said. "And Susan is no murderer. I've known her all my life. We were pretty good friends in school."

"Wasn't she the shy one?" Kyle asked. "I never quite got

the three of you. Susan was so sweet and quiet compared to you and Selma."

She shot Kyle a dirty look. "Gee, thanks."

And Susan was totally devoted to her husband, Greer thought. Devoted enough to turn a blind eye to her husband's extracurricular activities?

Why not? Wives did it all the time. Hell, her own mother was a perfect example. Mama June had chosen to remain oblivious to Buddy's gambling and screwing anything in a skirt, while keeping up appearances—maintaining their stately home, hosting elaborate ladies' luncheons and formal dinner parties, and sending her daughters to a high-priced Eastern boarding school.

Damn. She still hadn't returned her mother's calls. Once she wrapped up her meeting with Travis and Kyle, she'd return Mama's calls. She'd be going home shortly to catch some sleep before Ash returned. She'd talked to him a couple of hours ago and knew he wouldn't be back in town until after nine tonight.

Sleep—as if it was even possible after the day she'd had today. She needed to try, though, since she'd be on duty later. Tate had the night off and Grant would be in to cover the graveyard shift again, coordinating patrols between her, Kyle and Travis.

Not that their efforts had proven successful, considering Fieldler had managed to slip past them undetected. Thanks to Munroe, though, they'd discovered an access road that hadn't been used in decades, one that would make it easy to come and go from Upland Hills Memorial Park without being detected.

A vision of Sarah Rhodes's body decked out as the Happy Hooker unexpectedly flashed through her mind. She saw the wig, the disgusting display of makeup, the choker draped around her throat, the tiny wire poking through her upper lip.

She had to find a way to block those images from her mind, or else she'd go off the deep end again. At least she'd managed to keep her panic attacks at bay for a change. But, Lordy, she'd been tempted several times to dip into her secret stash for a little pink pill, just to take the edge off her climbing anxiety.

The phone on Travis's desk rang. He plucked the unlit cigar from his lips and answered. "Sheriff Willows," he barked into the receiver.

"June," he said jovially, his expression instantly softening.

Greer cringed. Her mother was nothing if not persistent.

"It's good to hear—" The smile faded from Travis's face. "When?" He paused. "You're sure?"

Greer frowned. The sinking feeling that she'd had all day began to make her stomach roll, like waves crashing into the shore, then slowly creeping back out to sea, only to come crashing in again.

"We're on the way," he said and hung up the phone.

"What is it?" Greer asked.

Compassion weighed heavily on Travis's features as he looked at her. "Vivien Lee is missing."

Sleep remained out of the question for Ash even though he was dog-tired. An active mind could be a curse, especially when he continued to mentally sift through facts, evidence, supposition and possibilities with no clear answers. He wanted to view the various crime scene photos, spread them out and thoroughly examine each one. Together as a group. Separately. Do what he usually did when working a case, until some small detail clicked in his mind, anything that would bring them closer to putting an end to the reign of The Matchmaker, as Faith had dubbed the gruesome killer.

What did he know about this case? After three days,

nowhere near as much as he'd like. They now knew *how* The Matchmaker was hunting his vics, through the online dating service *findamatch.com*, and possibly others as well, but they still didn't have the first inkling as to *why* he chose certain victims.

Desperate women, dying, literally, to meet the perfect man?

Not so much, he thought. The two victims they were aware of thus far had taken the standard precautions. They exchanged e-mails with their supposed "date," but the paper trail had been obscured by a complicated rerouting technique that had led them nowhere.

Joanna Webb had told her roommate she was going on a blind date with Tommy Gartner and on three occasions prior to meeting him had spoken to the man she knew as Gartner.

Another dead end.

The cell phone Webb had called was traced to one of those disposable, pay-in-advance services, paid with cash at a place that didn't look too closely at identification. Surveillance tapes would prove useless since they didn't even have a photograph of The Matchmaker to use as a comparison.

From his briefcase he pulled the copies he'd made of the Christmas cards and the corresponding envelopes Fieldler had been sending to Thea Wesley for the past eighteen years. Prisoners weren't permitted to send mail without a return address, complete with their identifying prisoner information. The return address on the holiday card sent from the Minnesota State Penitentiary matched the prisoner information Ash had on Fieldler. At some point Fieldler must have been incarcerated in Minnesota, but the rap sheet associated with him didn't fit the profile of a serial offender.

Perhaps Fieldler, the real Fieldler, never had been in

prison, he thought. But that didn't make sense, either, or else Thea Wesley's name never would've been listed as an emergency contact. So exactly what was Fieldler's connection to the prisoner Thea Wesley buried? They might never know the answer to that particular question.

Greer was right. This case made no sense.

Yet. But it would, eventually, of that he was certain. And when it all came together, they'd have the bastard.

Ash understood why Fieldler would've listed Thea Wesley as an emergency contact or next of kin. Despite the social worker's fear of Fieldler—which resulted in her misguided silence—and Fieldler's apparent hatred of women, Ash believed The Matchmaker considered Wesley the one person in the world who'd tried to help him. Even in a twisted killer's mind, an odd sort of loyalty was entirely possible. Oftentimes it was the driving force behind their heinous actions. A righting of some horrible wrong.

Ash sat upright. That's it, he thought suddenly. *A righting of some horrible wrong.* That was the reason behind the dates, the matchmaking. In Fieldler's mind, he was correcting some perceived wrong.

He was making the perfect match. For the deceased.

Ash motioned for the flight attendant. "How much longer until we land?" he asked the woman when she appeared at his side.

"Another forty minutes," she told him with a plastic smile. "Would you like some more coffee?"

"No, thank you," he said, already pulling out his laptop in an effort to put his thoughts on paper, as it were.

Why Archer?

Why Gartner?

What had been wrong in their lives that Fieldler was attempting to rectify? he wondered.

He'd have to ask Greer for insight on Archer and Gartner since she knew, or knew of, them. The wild card was her old man, Buddy Lomax. Ash understood the purpose of Fieldler's dumping the corpse of a prostitute outside Buddy's tomb, and suspected the choice had nothing to do with righting some perceived wrong. No, the reason was far simpler—to rattle Greer, a sick calling card to let her know that Fieldler knew she was close to the truth.

The closer she came to identifying Fieldler as The Matchmaker, the more dangerous the game. Her hunch had been spot-on—The Matchmaker was more than likely one of the funeral home employees they'd interviewed. The fact that he'd struck again so soon after they'd visited the local mortuaries was proof enough for Ash. But which employee? Which funeral home? They needed something solid in order to obtain a search warrant and, so far, they had zilch to convince a judge to put his John Hancock on a warrant.

Damn. He wished he was on the ground *now*—with Greer. He hadn't spoken to her in a couple of hours and worried how she was holding up under the strain.

God, please don't let her do anything stupid. Heroic and stupid.

However Freudian, he knew in his gut there was a damn good chance she'd try to right her own wrong on this case by attempting to take down The Matchmaker herself. Now that the case had gotten personal, her judgment could easily be skewed. Reminding himself she was a highly trained professional did little to ease his mind, either. Another place, another time, maybe, but she had far too many open wounds, too many emotional scars she had yet to heal.

He scrubbed his hand down his face, then let out a harsh breath. He fucking hated ticking clocks.

He flipped through the photocopies again of the Christmas cards and envelopes Fieldler had sent to Wesley. He made a list of the cities shown on the postmarks. A map would be useful to see whether a pattern could be established and he had instructed Faith to look for one as well.

Local jurisdictions would be contacted in an attempt to determine whether similar crimes had been perpetrated in each of the areas. Unsolved crimes would be stirred up, too, which wasn't necessarily a bad thing to have happen. All too often, a fresh perspective did wonders for solving a cold case or two.

Other cases were his last concern. His only priority at the moment was the safety and well-being of his wife.

God, please don't let her do anything stupid.

Greer sat at the formal dining table next to her mother, holding her hand as June explained once again how Vivi had failed to arrive for a shared appointment with the hairdresser this morning. She'd tried several times to reach her, but Vivi hadn't answered her cell phone or her home phone all day long. Having a key, she'd finally gone to Vivi's after supper and there'd been no sign she'd been at home. Her mail remained untouched in her mailbox and a dozen unanswered phone messages were on her answering machine.

Although Greer was a cop, and a former profiler for the FBI, right now she was only a daughter and sister—concerned for Vivi's welfare and consumed with guilt that she hadn't answered her mother's many calls today. Her mother was understandably distraught, and Greer tried to offer what little comfort she could. Which wasn't much, for the simple reason that she feared the worst. Fieldler had already made a point of making the case personal.

She glanced over at the ticking grandfather clock in the corner of the dining room. Ash wasn't due to arrive for another hour or so. Dammit, she needed him now. She needed his wisdom, his expertise. His objectivity.

Hell, she needed him to hold her. Needed to hear his strong, velvety-smooth voice promising her they'd find her sister, to give her a sliver of hope that Vivi wasn't about to become Fieldler's next victim.

A cell phone rang and everyone in the room instantly checked their own cell phones. Disappointment drifted through Greer that it wasn't Ash.

"It's mine," Kyle said, then quietly stepped out of the formal dining room into the kitchen to take the call. He returned a few seconds later. "It's Blythe," he said, his tone apologetic. "She's in labor."

"Go," Travis told him without hesitation. "We'll handle this."

"I . . . I'm sorry," he said to Greer.

"It's okay," she told him, and offered him a weak smile. "Give Blythe my best."

Kyle nodded. Davis made some effort to wish Kyle luck, but the words were flat and unemotional. For once Mama didn't even make an attempt to be the perfect hostess. She simply sat and stared at the elaborate floral arrangement centered on the gleaming surface of the dining room table, worry encompassing every feature on her face. She looked so old suddenly, and Greer's guilt climbed another notch.

"We'll find her, Mama," she said. She wanted to add, "I promise." But the words simply would not come. How could she make a promise to her parents she didn't know she could keep, even if she knew it might bring them a modicum of comfort?

She couldn't. And that hurt.

"When did you last see Vivi?" Travis asked June for the third time since they'd arrived.

June kept her gaze on the floral arrangement. "Last night," she repeated, her voice hollow. "She was here for my birthday dinner and left about nine thirty."

"Did she mention any plans she might have made?"

June shook her head. "I don't know."

"Think hard, Mama," Greer encouraged her. "Did Vivi have anything going on? What about one of her clubs? Is she in the middle of planning some event that could have taken her out of town for a day or two?"

"She's on some cookbook committee," Davis offered, turning his grief-stricken eyes to his wife. "We talked about it, June. Remember?"

Her mother remained stoic.

"I can't recall which organization is doing a cookbook this year," Davis said. "Junior League? I . . . I don't remember."

"Does Vivi keep a date book we can check out?" Travis asked.

"A palm," Davis supplied, "but it's her bible. She keeps it with her at all times."

Greer stood. "I'm going over to Vivi's. See if I can find anything that might tell us where she is."

"That's not a good idea," Travis said.

Greer frowned. "Why not?"

Travis's answering frown made Greer's feeble in comparison. "A word, Deputy," he said using his I'm-the-boss tone.

Greer gave her mother's hand a gentle squeeze. "It'll be okay, Mama." She still refused to add "I promise." Instead she said, "I'll be back," and followed Travis into the kitchen.

"What the hell is wrong with you?" Travis said in a sharp whisper. "Vivi's place has to be treated as a crime scene."

"And I'm the investigating officer on a serial murder case. I have every right to search a possible victim's residence."

"A case that just got personal as of this morning."

"My sister has been using online dating services the past couple of months. This sick son of a bitch could very well have his hands on Vivi."

"Which is exactly the reason you're not going over there," he argued.

"I know what I'm doing, Travis."

"Your objectivity is in question, Deputy. I don't give a damn how much experience you have."

"I know my way around a crime scene. I know how not to disturb physical evidence. Besides, Mama said Vivi's place was deserted."

Travis let out a rough sigh. "Will you at least wait until Ash gets here?"

Greer shook her head. "That won't be for another hour or so."

"Just wait, Greer," Travis said again.

She looked up at him, but didn't really give a rat's ass if he understood or not. "I can't," she said. "She's my sister."

Chapter 25

COLD. SO COLD.

Vivien's entire body trembled. She'd given up attempting to differentiate from cold or fear hours ago. All she knew for certain was that she was going to die.

How could she have been so incredibly stupid? She'd told no one where she was going. Days could pass before anyone realized she was missing. And by then, it'd be too late. She'd be as cold as the slab she'd been tied to.

She had no idea where she'd been taken. Not that she had the power to let anyone know where to find her. Her arms and legs were secured by thick leather bindings. And her head felt fuzzy, as if it'd been stuffed with cotton. She didn't know what the bastard had shot her full of, but her body felt leaden. She could barely wiggle her fingers and toes, let alone keep her eyes open or manage an escape.

She struggled to gain her bearings, but the light was so dim, she could make out only obscure shapes and out-of-focus images. Slowly, as if her head weighed a ton, she managed to turn to look to her right. A shelf loaded with bottles and tins carried labels she couldn't make out in the darkness. An IV apparatus hung above her. She followed the line with her gaze and was shocked to see that it led directly to her arm. Upon further inspection, she noted a sheet covering her body. She was naked.

Another round of fear climbed up her spine. This simply could not be happening to her. Any second now she'd awaken from this horrible nightmare. She'd be home, safe in her own bed with the television blaring in the background. She had watched some old horror movie and fallen asleep, that was all. This was just a bad dream. A really bad one.

Only it wasn't, and she knew it.

She closed her eyes to stop the tears from flowing down cheeks she couldn't wipe clean. She concentrated on the sounds around her, but all she heard was a dull humming in her head.

No, that wasn't right. She kept her eyes closed and tried to concentrate. A distinct hum. She was certain of it. An air-conditioning unit?

Yes. Definitely. A large one, too, industrial size.

Hello, Greer? Can you come get me please? I'm in a building with a big air conditioner.

She had no phone, couldn't move, had no chance of escape and was certain she'd be dead before long.

She was screwed.

Not yet, baby.

Hold on to that thought.

"I'm trying," she whispered. Christ, even her tongue felt weighted down.

How the hell did she get into this nightmare? She'd walked right into it, that's how, not suspecting for a second that Dylan Beaumont, the studly pediatric surgeon, wasn't who he claimed to be. Or, rather, that Dylan Beaumont wasn't Dylan Beaumont at all, but a man claiming to be Parker Hennessy.

Hello, Greer? Can you come get me? Some sicko who

thinks he's my old friend has kidnapped me, but I don't know who this fuck nut really is, except he ain't Parker.

She *knew* Parker Hennessy, and this guy was not him. Not by a country mile. Sure, he looked a lot like Parker, so much that it was creepy. He talked like Parker, walked like Parker, even managed to cultivate Parker's innate charm. But she *knew* Parker, had gone to high school with him. They'd run in the same crowd, for crying out loud. Granted, they'd not been in touch in who-knew-how-many years, but this guy couldn't hold a matchstick to the real deal.

Susan Nichols had never been the brightest bulb on the Christmas tree, but even she had to know the man she was married to wasn't who he said he was. How was it possible an entire town did not even know he wasn't Parker?

Because Parker had left town and hadn't returned for a very long time. There'd been no family members around to say who-the-fuck-are-you-asshole?—that's how.

Lord, she was confused. She'd been kidnapped, was being held prisoner by a madman who intended to do God only knew what with her. She'd been drugged, heavily, but she'd bet her last breath—ooh, bad turn of phrase. She'd bet the art collection she'd received in her second divorce settlement that the man holding her captive was absolutely *not* Parker Hennessy.

So who the hell was he? And what did he want with her?

She didn't know the answer to either question and, God help her, she didn't care to find out, either. She just wanted out of this horrible situation. She wanted to be home, safe in her own bed with a pile of bills staring at her from the antique Queen Anne desk.

Safe. She doubted she'd ever feel that way again. Was this how Greer felt all the time? she wondered. Her sister had survived unspeakable horrors at the hand of a lunatic. She only hoped she would be fortunate enough to live through this ordeal. But Greer was the tough one. She'd always been the stronger one. The smarter one.

Mama always said, "Why can't you be more ambitious, like your sister?" Indeed. She could definitely use a dose of Greer's smarts right about now.

Think, Vivien Lee. Think. There has to be a way out of this mess.

What would Greer do?

Pull a gun out of thin air and blow the son of a bitch straight to Hell, where he belonged.

Greer wouldn't panic. She'd look for any opportunity, no matter how small, to save herself.

That's it, she thought. Don't panic. Don't let the bastard know you're scared to death.

So where was the son of a bitch? Why did he have her trussed up like Dr. Frankenstein's monster about to be cranked up to the tower to wait for a bolt of lightening? What did he plan to do with her?

It wasn't good, that's for damn sure.

What would Greer do?

She wouldn't wait for someone to come save her. Greer would do the job herself.

She wished she was more like her little sister. Tough as nails with cold, hard logic on her side.

Hello, Greer? Can you come get me, please? I really don't want to die today.

By the time Ash's flight touched down, he would've welcomed one of Greer's sweet little antianxiety pills. Although he couldn't be one hundred percent certain he knew Fielder's identity, he had a bad feeling, and that was enough for him.

The evidence, as thin as it was, had been staring at him

during the entire flight, but he hadn't put it together until he started going over their visits to the funeral homes. He recalled the brief conversation Greer had had with Susan Hennessy yesterday afternoon and that's when the pieces started clicking into place.

According to Susan, Parker had been living in Colorado. Old man Hennessy goes for a visit and on a hike in the mountains, a freak accident kills old man Hennessy and the guide, a supposed expert. Parker Hennessy has been away from Magnolia for a number of years and, if Ash's instincts were to be trusted, Fieldler returns to Magnolia impersonating the real Parker Hennessy and no one is the wiser.

Was that how Fieldler managed to escape prison? Had he impersonated another prisoner? But why would a prisoner willingly exchange places with Fieldler?

Money, Ash thought, as he hurried through the airport to the parking lot where he'd left his rental car. Money, threats, any number of possibilities.

The dates on the Christmas cards Thea Wesley had provided him confirmed the timeline. Nowhere near enough evidence to convince a judge to sign a search warrant, but probable cause could be argued. To be absolutely certain, they'd have to exhume the body of the guide, which Ash believed was actually Parker Hennessy. If a body even existed. Fieldler could've had it cremated.

He threw his gear in the trunk, pulled his cell from his pocket and dialed Greer. Voice mail. Dammit, she'd turned off her phone.

His cell beeped three times. Low battery, the display read. *Shit!*

"Greer, listen, it's me. Fieldler's really—"

Three more beeps. The damn thing died.

Okay, so maybe going off half-cocked to Vivi's place without backup hadn't been the smartest move she'd ever made, but in Greer's opinion, she'd had no other choice. They simply lacked the manpower.

She didn't have a shred of evidence to indicate Fieldler even had Vivi, but Greer's instincts screamed otherwise. Once upon a time she'd always trusted her gut. For too long she'd overanalyzed every minor decision until she'd chewed the flavor out of it. Well, no more, she thought, slipping her key into the lock of Vivi's back door. She was tired of being a prisoner of the past. Her sister's life depended on it.

With her weapon drawn, she slowly pushed open the back door and listened for any sound to indicate a presence. Only a distant rumble of thunder.

Moving steadily, she entered the house, keeping her back to the wall. With her heart hammering in her chest, she methodically swept each room, turning on lights as she went, until she determined the house was clear of intruders.

There were no signs of any struggle in any of the rooms. If Fieldler did have Vivi, and Greer was dead certain he did, he hadn't taken her from her home. He'd lured her to some other location. How?

A blind date. They knew Fieldler's MO, and Greer was damn sure Vivi had fallen victim to Fieldler's sick matchmaking game.

Like the lightning firing up the night sky, a brutal image flashed in Greer's mind. Only it wasn't Sarah Rhodes's body she saw, but Vivi's.

She felt physically ill. Several deep breaths quelled the nausea ever so slightly.

Greer moved to Vivi's antique writing desk and powered up her sister's computer. While the laptop booted up, she looked around the room, searching for a sign, some indication of what might have happened to her sister.

The four-poster bed with a dozen lacy throw pillows in various sizes and shapes were artfully arranged. The bedside table held a lamp, a small tray with an empty crystal water decanter and a book, a pair of reading glasses tucked between the pages, holding Vivi's place.

On the dresser sat Vivi's jewelry box. Greer walked across the room and peered down at the contents. This wasn't Vivi's real jewelry box. Her sister kept the good stuff locked in a safe behind the Picasso in the study downstairs.

A piece of faded black ribbon poking out from one of the tiny drawers caught her attention. Curious, she opened the drawer and pulled the ribbon from the rich blue velvet compartment. Pinned to the center of the ribbon was a cameo. God, she hadn't seen this thing in years, had thought she'd lost it. She'd even forgotten the choker existed. She didn't know Vivi had the damn thing, or that her sister was even aware it existed.

She stared at the cheap, dime-store piece of costume jewelry in her hand. An exact replica had been around Sarah Rhodes's throat.

Only two other people knew the choker existed. Only two others understood the significance. Her hand started to tremble.

She walked over to the bed and sat on the edge, the choker still clasped between her fingers. God, it'd been so long ago, but she remembered that day so clearly.

They had come back to the house from Buddy's funeral. No one had been paying much attention to her or Vivi, certainly not her mother, who'd been zoned out on prescription medication. Greer had been sitting on a padded bench in the foyer when the mailman showed up at the door with an envelope addressed to her along with a stack of condolence cards addressed to her mother. No one had ever sent her mail before. Even though they'd just buried Buddy, she couldn't help but be a little excited she'd received her first-ever piece of mail.

She'd taken the envelope up to her room and opened it—a choker. It was from her father. The night he'd died, he'd said he was with a jewelry saleslady and was sending her a present. She hadn't realized at the time it'd been the prostitute he'd been with that night. She'd figured *that* one out a few weeks later after she'd overheard some ladies in the drugstore talking.

She'd been so hurt. And embarrassed. She'd carried the stupid thing with her for weeks, afraid her mother would find it. One day she was walking with Selma and Susan and it fell out of her pocket. Selma questioned her about it when she started to cry and she'd ended up revealing her horrible secret to her two friends. She'd sworn them to secrecy, then hid the choker in her closet and forgot about it.

Until now.

Susan knew about the choker, understood the significance. And Susan was married to Parker Hennessy, a man with a background in mortuary science and a wife who knew Greer's dirty little secret. That Sarah Rhodes's body had been dressed up like a prostitute, complete with the same-style choker was no coincidence.

She stood and walked over to Vivi's computer. She knew with absolute certainty that if she checked, she would discover Vivi was a subscriber to *findamatch.com*. She also knew that whomever Vivi had arranged to meet was probably already dead, and that Vivi had been chosen for a horrible match, a deadly match.

She looked down at the screen and her heart took off at a speeding gallop. A dull ringing in her ears started and before she could stop it, her throat closed, cutting off her oxygen supply. The room tilted, and she stumbled, gasping for breath.

Not now. Please, not now.

The ringing continued, growing louder by the second.

She groped for the pills in her pocket, but her fingers refused to cooperate and they spilled onto the floor.

The last thing she saw before she hit the floor with a thud was Vivi's body tied to a slab, a sheet covering her body. Her image visible through a webcam.

Chapter 26

A LL HE HAD to do was wait. He'd known she'd come
to him. As usual, his patience was greatly rewarded.

Slowly, Parker lifted the access panel to the attic and lowered the foldaway ladder. He descended quickly and entered
the bedroom where Greer lay crumpled on the plush, crème
carpeting. He didn't waste time enjoying how easily it'd
been to push her into a panic attack so severe she'd been
rendered unconscious, but immediately bent to inject her
with enough Ketamin to keep her that way for a while.

His grand finale. The ultimate union awaited, and then
Magnolia would become nothing but a distant, but oh-so-
pleasant memory.

He still hadn't decided what to do about his beloved
Susan. Leaving her behind was not an option. He despised
loose ends.

Dear, sweet Susan, so shy, so timid. She needed a strong
man to guide her through eternity. Her perfect mate.

There was no one stronger or more perfect for Susan
than himself. Perhaps he would keep her with him—for a
while longer. She'd proven herself so very useful. Although
she'd been unaware of his true purpose, she'd given him all
he would need to ensure the nosy little deputy and her FBI
man would be joined forever in eternity.

With ease, he lifted the deputy into his arms and carried her from the house to the garage, where he placed her in the back of his van. He'd watched her arrive while in his hiding place in her sister's attic. The foolish woman had never checked the garage. Her mistake would be her reward, he decided. He'd make certain she spent her final hours fully aware of her fate. And that of her social-climbing sister.

It'd been so simple. Too easy. Hardly a challenge at all, he thought with a smile as he pulled out of the driveway and sped away in the rain-soaked night.

Damn it. He should've gone back into the terminal to find a pay phone because he sure as shit wasn't having a bit of luck on the highway. Through the slap of the windshield wipers, Ash spied the neon glare of a convenience store and immediately pulled off the highway. He cut the engine and darted from the rental car, only to find the public phone out of service.

Screw it. He was a federal agent, for Christ's sake. That had to afford him a few liberties.

He stormed into the store, but the counter was deserted. His frustration mounting, he did a quick search of the area. Two rows in, he found a pimply faced clerk in a ridiculous green- and white-checked shirt and red ball cap, humming to himself as he knelt on the floor restocking tortilla chips on a metal wire shelf.

"Where's your phone?"

The kid looked up at him. "Sorry, dude," he said. He stood slowly, his gaze cautious. "It's busted."

Ash's patience was already stretched to the limit. He pulled his badge. "FBI. This store got a phone?"

The kid's eyes widened. "That thing for real?"

"As real as it needs to be to bust your ass for selling drugs out the back door."

"Hey!" The kid lifted his hands as if Ash held a gun to

him. "I don't do drugs, man." He grinned. "I gotta get a scholarship."

"Where's the goddamn phone?" Ash barked. He didn't give a damn if junior here was related to Einstein himself.

"Chill. Out. Dude. It's under the counter."

Ash turned and bolted for the counter.

"You can't dial out," the kid called after him. "Manager don't trust nobody."

"Shit. You got a cell phone?"

"Uh-huh," the kid nodded.

"Well?" Ash snapped.

"Oh, you wanna use it?"

God save him from brain-dead honor students. "That would be the case. Yes." A candidate for MIT junior wasn't.

The kid dug into a dirty backpack stowed under the counter and produced a neon-green cell phone. "Just don't be too long. My mom will kill me if I go over my minutes again this month."

Ash dialed the Magnolia Sheriff's Department and reached Grant Mitchell. "Mitchell, it's Special Agent Keller. I need to talk to Greer or Willows."

"Where are you?" Mitchell asked. "We need as many bodies as we can get here tonight. Kyle's wife went into labor, Tate's off duty after pulling nearly twenty hours. Only Travis and Greer are on duty."

"Where's Greer now?" With any luck, Mitchell could patch him through to her, or at least run a relay.

"At her sister's last I heard. Vivien Lee went missing."

A cold chill settled over Ash. "Fieldler," he said.

"You think? Could just be a coincidence," Mitchell said, but the tone of his voice said otherwise.

"There are no coincidences," Ash told him. "After the stunt this morning, what else could it be? Is Willows with Greer?"

God, please. Don't let her have gone off alone. With the body this morning and now her sister missing, she had to realize she'd be walking into a trap. Again.

"He's still at June's place."

"Can you patch me through to him?"

"I can give it a shot. Hold on."

Ash stood next to the cigarette rack and fought off a sharp craving.

Mitchell came back on the line. "Okay, go ahead," he said.

"Willows? I know who Fieldler is. It's Parker Hennessy. He's our UNSUB."

"You're sure 'bout that?" Travis asked. "The Hennessys have been a part of this community for years."

"Maybe the Hennessys have, but that isn't Parker Hennessy, it's Eric Fieldler," he said, then quickly explained the connection he'd made. "It's the best we've got."

"Good enough," Willows said. "I'll call in the state boys, but it'll take some time to get them out here."

"He has Greer's sister." And quite possibly Greer.

"You don't know that for certain," Willow argued.

"Call it a hunch. When was the last time you talked to Greer?"

"It's been a hour. She's at Vivien's now."

"I'm about ninety minutes away. Goddamn weather," he complained and checked his watch. "Get over there and make sure Greer's safe. If Fieldler has Vivien, he could've been waiting for Greer."

"Dammit, I told her not to go alone. I'm leaving now."

"I'll meet you," he said and disconnected the call, praying they weren't too late.

"So, dude, was that like official secret-agent stuff?"

Ash handed the kid the phone. "Wrong agency," he said and slipped the kid a twenty. "Chat it up, junior."

"Fresh," the kid said and had the twenty pocketed before Ash hit the door at a run.

Pain seared her brain. Her arms ached and her wrists felt as if they were secured with a vice. Her head felt fuzzy. She attempted to open her eyes, but they weighed a ton.

Greer had no idea where she was or how she'd gotten there. Although she did have a pretty good idea who was responsible for her being tied up like a calf at a rodeo.

"I know you're awake, Deputy. Or is it Special Agent Lomax?" He chuckled, the sound eerily confident. "Or perhaps you prefer Mrs. Keller?"

Greer opened her eyes, but had trouble focusing. A dark vision swam before her eyes.

Fieldler.

Dizziness swamped her. The room tilted at a strange angle. He must've given her something. Ketamin, she surmised. His drug of choice.

"Go to hell," she spat, but the epithet fell short due to her raspy voice and leaden tongue. Her throat was on fire, as if she'd swallowed gasoline.

"After you," he said in a congenial tone. "And your sister."

Greer tugged on her bindings. Her feet were bound as well, but not secured to the office task chair he'd tied her to. If she could free her hands, she might stand a chance of getting her and Vivi out of this nightmare.

She didn't know how he'd gotten to her or how much time had passed since she'd blacked out. She remembered being in Vivi's house, in her bedroom. She'd searched every room. He must've snuck in when she'd been distracted with that damn choker, but she hadn't heard anyone enter the house. The last thing she remembered was seeing the webcam with Vivi's image.

Greer shook her head in an attempt to clear it, but the

room only swam in dark swirls of colors and muted light. She needed every ounce of her wits if she and Vivi were going to survive. She blinked her eyes and tried once again to focus.

Her weapon, with the clip removed, lay on the desk, not three feet to her left. A fat lot of good it did her now. She saw Fieldler, standing next to the metal slab where he'd tied Vivi. He held a syringe in his gloved hand and reached for the IV tube above Vivi's head. From what Greer could see, it appeared Vivi was unconscious.

"Let her go," she told him. "You know she's not the one you really want."

"Oh, but you're wrong. I've had plans for Vivien Lee for some time now, although I didn't know then she was your sister. My client, her perfect mate, has been waiting for her, you know. And I don't like to keep my true clients waiting. You, on the other hand, are a welcome bonus I hadn't counted on at the time."

He applied the needle to the IV portal.

"Wait!"

"Don't fret, my dear. I'm not going to kill her." He smiled, a cold one that sent a chill racing down her spine.

"Yet," he added, menacingly. "I'm just giving her a mild adrenaline boost so she can join our little party."

So she would be awake for his horrific fantasy.

He pushed the plunger.

I'm sorry, Vivi. God, I'm so sorry.

He smoothed his latex-gloved hand over Vivi's brow. "Wake up, my sweet," he crooned. "We have a guest."

Greer knew the instant Vivi awakened. Her sister's body tensed, straining against her restraints.

"Why are you doing this?" Greer asked him uselessly. She already knew the whys of his actions. For sociopaths, who had no regard for human life, they were always the same—to live out dark, twisted fantasies.

He turned to face her and slowly walked toward her. "Because it is my calling," he said conversationally. "It's no different than any other, really. Your need to rid the world of evildoers, a musician's need to create music, a doctor's calling to heal." His smile widened to an ominous grin. "Or a priest answering the call to serve God. You know all about that, don't you, Special Agent Lomax? And you know what happens when a calling cannot be fulfilled, too, don't you?"

He was referring to Vicar, aka The Preacher. He'd been a surgical nurse by profession, but what hadn't come out until the aftermath was that Vicar had been a defrocked priest.

"You seem to know a lot, don't you, *Eric*?"

He blanched. "Eric is dead."

She'd rattled him. Good. Maybe if she pushed him off balance, he'd make a mistake. Maybe then she stood a chance of getting her and Vivi out of this hell.

"Greer?" Vivi called out. "Oh, thank God."

"It'll be okay, Vivi," she said to her sister, never taking her eyes off of Fieldler. "Who did Thea Wesley bury, Eric?"

"Leave her out of this," he spat viciously. In two strides, he was in front of her, his hands on the arms of the office chair he'd tied her to, his cold, hard face inches from hers. "This is between us."

Her smile turned condescending. "She gave you up, Eric. She told us all about you. All about your slut of a mother."

"Shut up."

"Awww, what's the matter, Eric? Mommy loved the needle more than you?"

"Shut the fuck up," he snarled. He drew his hand back and slapped her hard, across the face.

She refused to cry out. "Is that why you hate women so much?" she taunted him, struggling to ignore the metallic taste of blood in her mouth. "What'd Mommy do, Eric? Pimp you for a fix?"

He pushed away from her. "You don't know shit, bitch."

"Oh, you're wrong. I know all about you," she continued. "I've known about you for years."

"Like hell."

He started pacing, his movements agitated. She took advantage and explored as far as her fingers would take her. She brushed against the backrest of the chair.

She slouched down slightly to use the post of the backrest to loosen, or hopefully cut, the IV tubing he'd used to tie her to the chair. "She beat you, didn't she? Left you alone for hours. Brought home whichever piece of shit paid her the slightest bit of attention."

"You don't know anything."

"Yes, I do," she said. "It's the same old story, Eric. Poor little abused boy acting out the same fantasy over and over again. There's nothing special about you, Eric. I've seen it before." She laughed. "You're as predictable as all the others."

Eric approached Vivi. Her sister began to sob. "Please," she begged, her voice a ragged, terror-filled whisper that tore through Greer.

"Don't worry, Vivi," she said, and prayed she wasn't offering false hope.

She found the edge and worked the tubing back and forth in slow, surreptitious movements while his attention remained focused on Vivi. She seethed as his hand glided over Vivi's bare arm.

"Are you thinking about Mommy now?" she asked him in the same taunting tone. "How she betrayed you?"

"He never should have married her," he said.

His eyes were on Vivi, but Greer suspected he'd slipped into the past.

"She was nothing but a whore. He deserved so much more."

"A whore who used her little boy for drugs," Greer said. The tubing gave slightly, but not enough for her to free herself. She was closer, but would she be free in time to save Vivi?

She hadn't been able to save Linda.

Don't think about that.

She couldn't help herself. In her mind, she saw Linda's body, brutally gutted before her eyes by Vicar while she'd lain helpless, unable to save her fellow officer.

"How many more women do you have to kill before you no longer hear the cries of that little boy, Eric?"

He turned on her and she stilled. "Shut up!"

"Mommy . . ."

"Shut the fuck up!" he shouted at her. His actions jerky, he plucked a barbed wire from a tray near the table. "Shut up now."

Greer's heart thundered in her ears. She had to distract him before he hurt Vivi.

"Is that what the bastards said to you when they fucked you in the ass for payment of Mommy's smack? Shut the fuck up, little Eric?"

"You don't know," he said. His hand shook and the wire slipped from his trembling fingers.

"Did Mommy watch?"

He turned, his face filled with rage.

"Did you cry for Mommy to make them stop? She couldn't help you. She had a needle in her vein."

He charged her and she was ready. She lifted her bound feet and planted them hard in his chest. He stumbled backward. The tray holding the implements of his evil trade clattered to the floor. With one final jerk, the IV tubing snapped and gave way, freeing her hands.

Her fingers were nearly numb. Instead of struggling to untie the bindings at her ankles, she reached for her Glock.

Her fingers trembled. She struggled to slam the clip into place.

Too late; he charged her. They fell to the hard, cold stone floor. Her grip on the Glock loosened. He reached for the gun—and it fired.

They had Hennessy's Mortuary surrounded. Ash, Travis and a dozen state troopers. Ash's heart stopped when he heard the muted but distinct pop of gunfire.

Without hesitating another second, he stormed through the back door with a state trooper on his heels. Susan Hennessy screamed and dropped the teacup in her hands, the china shattering when it hit the floor.

"Where is he?" Ash demanded.

"I . . . I don't know."

"Cuff her and read her her rights," he told the trooper with him as Travis and three more troopers charged the kitchen.

"The basement," Travis said, but Ash was already heading in that direction when he heard another muffled pop.

She hadn't killed him, but the son of a bitch wasn't going to hurt anyone else anytime soon. She didn't give a shit if he bled out, either, she wasn't taking any chances. She cuffed the prick.

Slowly, she rose to her feet and holstered her weapon. She felt mildly woozy, but she reached Vivi, who cried softly, and began to loosen the restraints. "It's okay, Vivi. He can't hurt you now."

"Oh, God, Greer," she said between sobs. "I'm sorry. I'm so sorry."

"Shhh," she said and freed Vivi. "You have nothing to be sorry about. It's over."

Fieldler remained unconscious, motionless on the floor, a dark puddle of blood forming around his torso, staining the concrete floor. She'd shot him only in the shoulder. The bastard would live, until a jury got through with him.

"Can you stand?"

Vivi nodded. "I think so."

Greer helped Vivi up and wrapped the sheet around her. And then she heard shouts above her.

Ash.

"Down here," she yelled. She looked at Vivi and smiled. "The cavalry's here."

Vivi's answering smile was weak and tremulous. "Who needs the cavalry when I've got you to save me from the blind date from hell?"

Greer started to laugh, but her laughter quickly turned to tears and she wrapped her arms around her sister and let them flow. Tears of joy that her sister hadn't been harmed, tears of relief that the nightmare was over, even tears spurred by anger that a monster had terrorized her hometown.

Physically Vivi would be fine. Emotionally, her sister would have a lot to deal with, and Greer would know. She'd been battling her own demons for two solid years. Probably always would, too, she realized. Just because she'd been able to save herself and Vivi didn't mean she'd been miraculously cured, but damn if it didn't make her feel a whole lot better at the moment.

She hugged Vivi close. "I'm sorry I've been so distant," she told her.

"Me, too," Vivi said.

Greer didn't know if Vivi was apologizing, too, or agreeing with her. It didn't matter, she decided. What mattered was that they still had an opportunity to be sisters.

"God, I need a job," Vivi said. "Take care of myself for a change instead of letting someone else do it. This stuff can get dangerous."

Greer had the perfect solution, but before she could tell

Vivi, she heard the creak of a heavy door. The room suddenly filled to capacity with large male bodies. There was only one she was interested in, and she immediately found him.

She left Vivi to the care of a strapping state trooper and rushed into Ash's arms. The tears she'd thought she'd spent came flooding back and she clung to him. She'd wasted so much time, precious time. She, more than anyone, knew how short life could be, and she was tired of wasting what little time she might have left. Whether she had twenty minutes, twenty years or another fifty, she wasn't about to squander another second.

She didn't know what the future held, but one thing she knew for certain—her future was with Ash.

He held her face in his palms. "Are you all right?" he asked, his gorgeous brown eyes filled with concern.

"I'm okay."

"Let's have a doctor make sure."

She shook her head. "I'm fine, Ash."

He let out an impatient sigh. "Would you please not argue with me? For once."

"Take me home."

"Home?"

She nodded.

"Where?"

She gave him a tear-filled smile. "Whereever you plan to be for the next fifty years."

He kissed her, nowhere near as long and hard as she wanted, but it was enough for now. She had the rest of their lives to make up for the time she'd foolishly kept them separated.

"I love you," she whispered, when he ended the kiss way too soon.

He grinned. "You can't help yourself. I'm just too irresistible."

"I was thinking arrogant."

"Don't forget incredibly charming," he said as he led her from the subbasement and away from the nightmare.

By the time they reached the outside of the funeral home, they were met by a blaze of lights from police vehicles and ambulances along with several emergency medical personnel. She saw Vivi being led by the state trooper to an ambulance.

"She's going to be all right," Greer said. "It'll just take her a while to put this behind her."

She let out a sigh as a pair of paramedics approached her, insisting on taking her vitals. "If there's one thing we Lomaxes do well, it's milking a tragedy for all it's worth."

They also knew how to survive, she thought. Sometimes, it just took a while to figure it all out.

Epilogue

Six months later . . .

THE UNOFFICIAL GRAND opening of Magnolia House, a gathering by invitation-only to family and friends, had turned out even better than Greer anticipated. Of course, with Vivien Lee running the show now, she really shouldn't have been surprised. Whether or not her sister realized it, Vivi was a born hostess.

When she'd first approached Vivi about becoming a full partner, her sister had been hesitant. But Greer hadn't let up. She knew how important keeping busy could be to Vivi's emotional recovery. It hadn't taken too much prodding, and after a successful auction to sell off some of Vivi's jewelry and most of her art collection, the Lomax girls were in business together.

The oak table in the formal dining room held an array of traditional Southern dishes as well as more artful culinary fare, from down-home fried chicken to the most exquisite caviar Greer had ever tasted. She'd probably choke when she saw the monthly statement Vivi would send her, but everyone was having such a good time, she didn't much care. From her conversation with Vivi last night when she and Ash had first arrived in town, once Magnolia House officially opened for business next month, they'd be operating at eighty-percent occupancy for most of the spring and summer.

Greer was glad she and Ash were able to take time off for the opening. The weather was a definite improvement from their home in Virginia, too. Not quite as warm as she'd hoped, but at least she'd managed to escape the snow for a few days. Unfortunately their trip wasn't all pleasure. Monday morning she'd be appearing in court for the penalty phase of Eric Fieldler's trial. Whether or not the jury who'd found him guilty after only two hours of deliberation would sentence him to death by lethal injection, she couldn't say. She supposed what really mattered was that his reign of terror had ended.

No one had seen Susan since the trial began. According to what Selma had told her, Susan had obtained an annulment and had moved West. Greer wished her luck.

She shook off the morose thoughts and helped herself to a glass of sparkling wine, then went in search of her sister to congratulate her on such a fabulous party. She found Vivi in the kitchen, giving more instructions to the catering staff. Her mother and Selma were involved in some debate Greer decided she wanted no part of, while Blythe watched with amusement from the kitchen table as she bottle-fed little Kiera.

Her mother spied her first. "Greer, come here a moment. We'd like you to settle something for us."

"Not a chance," she said with a laugh. "Sorry, Mama. You're on your own."

"Chicken," Selma taunted her.

Greer nodded and took a sip of champagne.

"Wise move," Davis said, coming up behind her. He slipped his arm over her shoulder and gave her a gentle squeeze. "Those two have been at it ever since your mama hired Selma to remodel the upstairs bathroom."

"They love it," Greer told him, then excused herself.

She wandered room to room until she reached the game room. Ash and Kyle were in the middle of a game of pool, while Grant Mitchell, Travis and Jason Carpenter, the state trooper who'd been dating her sister, were embroiled in a discussion, no doubt talking shop.

She leaned against the doorjamb and sipped more of her champagne. Ash looked up, gave her a wink, then sank the eight ball, much to Grant's dismay.

Grant set the cue on the table. "Next victim," he said, and reached for a beer.

Ash gave her a grin that had her toes curling in her black pumps. "Care to make it interesting?"

She smiled at him over the rim of her glass. "What did you have in mind?"

His grin turned lecherous and she laughed, something she did a lot more of lately. She still suffered with the occasional nightmare, and even a mild anxiety attack from time to time, but she'd just passed her psyche exam last month and would be starting back at Quantico as an instructor to would-be profilers at the end of the month. She no longer felt the need to save the world from the monsters herself, and agreed with Ash that her talents would be put to better use training the next generation of profilers.

She cleared her throat. "Gentlemen, would you excuse us, please? I have to teach my husband a lesson."

"Uh-oh." Kyle laughed. "I know that kind of look."

"With a baby in the house?" Travis teased. "You mean you *remember* that kind of look."

"Yeah, well," Kyle grumbled good-naturedly as they left the game room.

She picked up the cue stick. "Rack 'em up, baby. I hope you're prepared to lose."

Ash ignored her command and circled the pool table. He slipped behind her and wrapped his arms around her, pulling her close. She tilted her head to the side to give him easier access to the side of her throat, then sighed when his tongue teased just below her ear. "Even if I lose, I win," he reminded her huskily.

Didn't she know it. "There you go," she said. "Showing off again, all arrogant and cocky."

He chuckled, the sound vibrating against her skin and skittering down her spine. "That's not all I've got to show you."

She turned in his arms. "Then let the games begin," she said and kissed him soundly.

Take a look at Kathy Love's
I ONLY HAVE FANGS FOR YOU.
Coming next month from Brava!

"Why are you so scared of me?" Sebastian asked softly.

She shifted away as if she planned to move down a step and then bolt. He couldn't let that happen, not before he understood what had brought on this outburst.

"Wilhelmina, talk to me." He placed a hand on the wall, blocking her escape down the stairs.

She glared at him with more anger and more of that uncomfortable fear.

"You can bully your mortal conquests," she said, her voice low. "But you can't bully me."

Sebastian sighed. "My earlier behavior to the contrary, I don't want to bully you. Or anyone."

'You can't seduce me, either," she informed him.

"I don't . . ." Seduce her? Was that what all this was about?

"Do you want me to seduce you?" he asked with a curious smile. Maybe that was the cause for her crazy outburst. She *was* jealous.

She laughed, the sound abrupt and harsh. "Hardly. I just told you that you *didn't* want to seduce me?"

"No," he said slowly. "You told me *I can't*. That sounds like a challenge."

Irritation flared from her, blotting out some of the fear. "Believe me, I'm *so* not interested."

He raised an eyebrow at her disdain. "Then why do you care about me being with that blonde."

"That blonde?" she said. "Is hair color the way you identify all your women? It's got to be a confusing system, as so many of them have the same names."

He studied her for a minute, noting just a faint flush colored her very pale cheeks

"Are you sure you don't want me to seduce you?" he asked again, because as far as he could tell, there was no other reason for her to care about the identification system for his women.

She growled in irritation, the sound raspy and appealing in a way it shouldn't have been.

Sebastian blinked. He needed to stay focused. This woman thought he was a jerk, that shouldn't be a draw for him.

"Why did you say those things?" he asked. "What have I done to make you think I'm so terrible?"

Her jaw set again, and her midnight eyes locked with his. "Are you going to deny that you're narcissistic?"

He frowned. "Yes. I'm confident maybe, but no, I'm not a narcissist."

She lifted a disbelieving eyebrow at that. "And you are going to deny egocentric, too?"

"Well, since egocentric is pretty much the same as narcissistic, then yes, I'm going to deny it."

Her jaw set even more, and he suspected she was gritting her teeth, which for some reason made him want to smile. He really was driving her nuts. He liked that.

He was hurt that she had such a low opinion of him, but he did like that fact that he seemed to have gotten under her skin.

"I think we can also rule out vain, too," he said, "because again that's pretty darn similar to narcissistic and egocentric." He smiled slightly.

Her eyes narrowed, and she still kept her lips pressed firmly together—their pretty bow shape compressed into a nearly straight line.

"So you see," he continued, "I think this whole awful opinion that you have formulated about me might just be a mixup. What you thought was conceit, which is also another word for narcissism," he couldn't help adding, "was just self-confidence."

His smile broadened, and Wilhelmina fought the urge to scream. He was mocking her. Still the egotistical scoundrel. Even now, after she'd told him exactly what she thought of him. He was worst than what she'd called him. He was . . . unbelievable.

"What about depraved?" she asked. Surely that insult had made him realize what she thought.

"What about it?" he asked, raising an eyebrow, looking every inch the haughty, depraved vampire she'd labeled him.

"Are you going to deny that one, too?" she demanded.

He pretended to consider, then shook his head. "No, I won't deny that one. Although I'd consider myself more debauched, then depraved. In a very nice way, however."

He grinned again, that sinfully sexy twist of his lips, and her gaze dropped to his lips. Full, pouting lips that most women would kill for. But on him, they didn't look the slightest bit feminine.

What was she thinking? Her eyes snapped back to his, but the smug light in his golden eyes stated that he'd already noticed where she'd been staring.

She gritted her teeth and focused on a point over his shoulder, trying not to notice how broad those shoulders were. Or how his closeness made her skin warm.

He shifted so he was even closer, his chest nearly brushing hers. His large body nearly surrounding her in the small stairwell. His closeness, the confines of his large body around hers, should have scared her, but she only felt . . . tingly.

"So, now that we've sorted that out," he said softly. "Why don't we go back to my other question?"

She swallowed, trying to ignore the way his voice felt like a velvety caress on her skin. She didn't allow herself to look at him, scared to see those eyes like perfect topazes.

"Why are you frightened of me, Mina?"

Because she was too weak, she realized. Because, despite what she knew about him, despite the fact that she knew he was dangerous, she liked his smile, his lips, those golden eyes. Because she liked when he called her Mina.

Because she couldn't forget the feeling of his fingers on her skin.

She started as his fingers brushed against her jaw, nudging her chin toward him, so her eyes met his. Golden topazes that glittered as if there was fire locked in their depths.

Once again she was reminded of the ill-fated moth drawn to an enticing flame. She swallowed, but she couldn't break their gaze.

"You don't have to be afraid of me," he assured her quietly.

Yes, she did. God, she did.

Here's a peek at Dianne Castell's
I'LL BE SEEING U.
Available now from Brava!

Quaid answered the door, surprise slipping across his rugged, incredibly handsome face. "Hi," he said with a smile. "I'm glad you're here."

"Well, you won't be." Cynthia folded her arms, trying to add some menace to her words that she didn't feel at all. Hard to be stern with Quaid right in front of her. This was much easier when she practiced in the hall mirror. "I'm here on business, personal business, between-us business."

"Sounds serious." He came outside, closing the screen door quietly behind him, another member of the napping baby club. His familiar unique scent of hot sexy guy filled her head, making her a bit dreamy, until she caught the aroma of . . . "Oh my God." She walked past Quaid and pressed her face to the screen door, not caring that it left little tic-tac-toe marks on her nose. She inhaled deeply. "Fried chicken. Real, honest-to-goodness fried chicken."

"Well, it isn't rubber."

"I know, I had that one over at my house last night." She sniffed in another lungful. "Any leftovers?"

"You came here for Dad's chicken?"

"Not exactly." Maybe a little.

"Kitchen's down the hall to the right. Chicken's in the fridge."

She glanced back at Quaid but the lure of fried chicken dragged her onward and she followed the scent to the fridge in the neat yellow and blue kitchen. She pulled a drumstick from the platter covered with plastic wrap and eyed a thigh that somehow found its way into her other hand. She took a bite, euphoria washing over her and she nearly succumbed to one of Ida's swoons.

"Good?" came Quaid's voice from behind her.

"Terrific," she managed around a mouthful while nudging the fridge door shut with her hip. She took another bite. "I'm starved."

"You're not eating over at your place?"

"Ida and I can't cook. Totally suck at it. Pea soup for dinner, tasted like beebees. Rocks for rolls. Very sad." She licked her thumb.

"Lawrence told you about Dad's chicken, didn't he?"

"He might have mentioned it in passing, right after telling me about steak on the grill, but that's not why I'm here."

With his index finger he swiped a smudge of gravy from her cheek. "Could have fooled me."

He licked the gravy from his finger and for a moment all she could imagine was doing the same thing then maybe tasting him all over. He had a great all over, she was sure, and she didn't get a chance to lick one single part on the dock, but she'd like to do it now. Except she was preoccupied with the chicken and this was business. *Business, business, business.* She wagged the half-eaten drumstick at him. "You sent Preston to Ivy Acres. And you bribed him to stay by offering him free dinners at Slim's. What in the world were you thinking?"

Quaid propped his hip against the counter. "That you run a bed and breakfast and he needed a place to stay and you could do with a little extra cash? And the dinner wasn't a bribe so much as an incentive. Dad hired Preston, and springing for some food seemed like the right thing to do."

"Well, last night Mr. Wright sprang into the shower with Ida, doing the full Monty, and his head ruined a perfectly fine antique vase that was my great-grandmother's."

"Preston did all that?" Quaid stood straight. "Damn. He doesn't seem like that kind of guy. Rory checked him out. He's a retired teacher, impeccable reputation. Oh, he's got this Magnum thing going on but he's harmless. Is Ida okay?"

"She's fine, but I want you to butt out of our lives. The Landons are not a charity case. We just can't cook." She stiffened her spine, suddenly aware that she probably looked beyond charity and more like something the cat dragged in that happened to be hungry. Landons were proud, they were better than this . . . until lately. She hated lately, but she really loved the chicken. "We may not be the high and mighty O'Fallons, but we can still manage on our own. Lawrence does not need your money and neither do Mother and I and—"

"Hey, hold on. I apologize if Preston didn't work out but leave my family and Lawrence out of this. I wanted to help you out, that's all there is to it."

Oh, no, she thought! What if he . . . She jabbed the drumstick in the direction of the docks and lowered her voice. "You didn't . . . I mean *we* didn't . . . because you felt *sorry* for me?"

"Holy hell, Cynthia." He raked his too-long black hair. "Did I act like I was feeling sorry for anyone?"

Well, thank heavens for that.

Here's an advanced peek at Nancy Warren's
"Nights Round Arthur's Table" in
BRITISH BAD BOYS
Available now from Brava!

The night was quiet and still. She liked the dark, though she was intensely aware of the man beside her. Once she stumbled over a rock she hadn't seen and he grabbed her hand to steady her.

He didn't let go. She could have pulled away, but she liked the feel of him, the sturdy, capable hand, the warmth of his skin.

"I bought one of your books today, when I was in town."

"You did? I thought Max was going to lend you one."

"I decided I'd like to have my own."

"Well, thank you. Which book did you choose?"

"*Tying Up Loose Ends*, I think it's called."

The book that first put her on the *Times* list, but she didn't tell him that. "Well, let me know what you think of it."

"I will."

After that, they didn't talk much.

When they reached her cottage, he still didn't talk, merely turned her to him and took her mouth.

Okay, so she'd guessed it was coming, had spent most of the short walk wondering how she felt about it and whether she'd stop him if he tried to kiss her. Now she knew that he wouldn't give her time to stop him and how she felt about it was indescribable. It was even better this time. He was so warm, so strong, his mouth both taking and giving.

Drugging pleasure began to overtake her senses. It had been so long since she'd felt like this. Excited at the possibilities of a man, wanting, with quiet desperation, to be with him. Held by him, taken by him. She began to shiver and he moved closer, so her back was against the stone wall and his warm body pressed against her.

Her hands were in his hair, wonderful, thick, luxurious hair. Her mouth open on his, wanting, giving, taking. She felt him hard against her belly and experienced a purring sense of her own power. And also a stabbing sense of regret.

She couldn't do this, she reminded herself. Her book. Her book was her priority. If and when she finished the novel, then she could think about indulging herself like this. Not until then.

So she tipped her head back out of kissing range and looked up into that dark, intent face. "What was that about?" She'd meant to sound sophisticated and slightly amused. A woman who got hit on all the time on every continent. Instead she sounded husky and, even to her own ears, like a total goner.

"I'm interested. I'm letting you know."

"Telling me with words would be too mundane?"

"Words are your world. I'm more a man of action." Oh, man of action. Oh, aphrodisiac to her senses. She'd always gone for the cerebral types, but there was something about a man who tackled the world in a physical way that appealed to her on the most basic level. His words from dinner came back to her. He'd kill to protect those he loved. Every other man she'd been with had been of the pen is mightier than the sword persuasion, mostly, she suspected, because their swordplay was so minimal.

Arthur was a man who would make her feel safe. When she crawled into bed, terrified of the fruits of her own imagination, she could see herself burrowing against his warm skin, his arms coming round her in comfort.

Then she gave herself a mental slap. What was she doing? Always imagining things. Arthur ran a pub. Was obviously single and probably took a fancy to every unattached woman who rented the cottage. How convenient.

She shook her head, with mingled irritation and regret. "I'm here to work. I really don't have time for . . . anything personal."

"That's a shame." He ran his warm, leathery palm down the side of her neck so she wanted to press against it. Rub at him like a kitten.

"I have to finish this book. I can't afford any distractions."

"I'm glad I distract you," he said, a thread of amusement running through his voice.

"You are?"

"I wouldn't want to think I was the only one feeling . . . distracted."